The One I Hate

Rolling Hills

Book 4

Cover Design: Kari March Designs

Cover model: Ian Brownhill

Cover photographer: Olivia Harvey, Til Death Photo

Editing: Kiezha Smith Ferrell, Librum Artis Editorial Services

Proofreading: Michele Ficht, Amanda Marcello

*If you've ever been called curvy, big, or any other word to
describe your weight, this is for you.
You're beautiful. You're loved.
And if they didn't think so, fuck 'em.*

Prologue
Simon

"Speaking of regrets..."

My words to my friend Wes trail off as a woman barking orders catches my eye. She doesn't just catch my eye; she makes me do a full double-take. I have to blink a few times, because no way can I be seeing who I'm seeing.

We are at a wedding reception for the Rolling Hills wedding of the year for the newly married Jake and Whitley Evans. The object of my attention seems to be the caterer. She's wearing the uniform—a white chef coat that's long on her short stature—and she's pointing to the servers and gesturing wildly. When she waves a hand in dismissal, they all but run to their food stations.

A woman who can command attention. I like it.

Now I'm even more intrigued to see if this woman is who I think she is, or if this is the whiskey playing tricks on me. But just as I shift to get a better angle, she's out of sight.

No. I must've been seeing things. No way that's who I thought it was.

Wes is still talking. What were we talking about? Oh.

1

That's right. How he's fucking things up with the woman who at this point doesn't deserve him because he's acting like an ass.

"Speaking of regrets..." I begin once more. "I don't have many. But I do have one, and it's not telling you what a money-hungry bitch your ex-wife was. We all agreed to keep our mouths shut because at the time you seemed happy. Well, guess what? I'm going to speak now. Only this time you're the one being the little bitch."

"Excuse me?" Wes asks, looking offended.

"I'm saying we didn't do anything to save you from your first wife. But I'm going to try to save you from being miserable for the rest of your life. Betsy is it. You're not going to do better than her. If you fuck this up, her future will be fine. It's your future that's going to suck."

There. I said what I needed to say to Wes. Now I can go back to trying to find the woman who bears a striking resemblance to the girl I once knew as Bug.

When I saw her a minute ago, I would have bet a million dollars it was her. I mean, in theory, it could be. Then again, I haven't seen Charlie Bennett in fifteen years, so what the hell do I know? I don't know where she lives, what she did with her life.

I haven't thought about her in ages. But that was by design. When she vanished without warning, I had to force myself to erase her from my memory. It was the only way I could move on.

But if I'm being honest, my heart never moved on. She broke it that day. No—she fucking shattered it.

I tried to call and text. So many times. Calls went straight to voicemail. But that didn't stop me from leaving message after message. I sent emails. She never told me where she lived, so I couldn't go bang on her door. Which I would've done. I was *that* desperate for answers.

2

Answers I never got.

Over the years I convinced myself that she blocked my number. I don't know the reason why she would've done it, but somehow me being blocked stung less than her hearing and reading every desperate message I sent, only to ignore them.

Frankly, now that I think about it, I don't know what's worse. We were friends. Or so I thought. Yes, we were competitive. Yes, we loved to one-up each other. Yes, we both always wanted to get the last word. We were stubborn and knew how to drive the other crazy. But at the end of the day, we were friends. Before she left, I had actually hoped that we could be more than that. And I thought she felt the same way.

The kiss we shared made me believe so.

The Charlie doppelgänger reappears, and now I know it's her. Well, I'm eighty percent sure. The whiskey I've enjoyed from the open bar is fueling the rest of my confidence. But I'd know Charlie Bennett anywhere.

There's only one problem: Bug was blonde. This woman is a redhead.

Bug...I haven't thought about that name for so long. She hated when I called her that, which only made me want to use it more. I loved riling her up. Seeing her cheeks flush. Making her smile with my antics.

She was beautiful. And if the woman I'm looking at is her, she's just as gorgeous as the last time I saw her. This woman is full figured, just like she was. Curves that drove me fucking crazy. Full breasts and hips that I used to fantasize about digging my fingers into. This woman is filled out even more, and I almost have to bite my fist to keep myself in check.

It wasn't just her body that attracted me to Charlie. She was the total package. Brains, beauty, and boldness. Her confidence was sexy. Her mind was fascinating. And her wit? The woman could verbally spar with me better than anyone. My pants got tight more than once because of that.

Take right now for instance. The woman who might or might not be Charlie is at least four inches shorter than every server she is talking to. Yet, standing there in her chef's coat, pointing her finger in all directions, she's commanding the room. Letting them know who's boss. I can tell she's not taking shit from anyone, and by the look of the workers, they know better than to even say a word.

Hell, even if this woman isn't Charlie, I might have to go introduce myself.

I hear my other best friends, Shane and Oliver, say something to Wes, who is still going on and on about how he might lose the woman he loves, and though Wes is my boy, I couldn't care less right now. Because for the first time since I caught sight of her, the woman I've been staring at turns to face me.

Jesus fucking Christ that's Bug...

She doesn't see me, but I see her. She's like the ghost of memories past. Late nights studying with her random concoction of snacks. The coffee she would make me every day even though I never drank it. Arguing about who should be on the professional wrestling Mount Rushmore. Dance parties in my kitchen because we were slap-happy from pulling all-nighters.

The kiss. The one kiss. The last night I saw her. The kiss I thought was going to change everything.

It did. Just not the way I thought.

Because no one before or since has pushed me the way Charlie did. No one has ever challenged me like her. Or called me on my shit. She was the only one outside my immediate circle who could make me genuinely smile. And no one refused my offers for dinner or a date more than she did.

She was one of a kind. In every way imaginable.

And she never said goodbye.

4

I nearly flip the table over as I start marching toward her. I'm guessing she still hasn't seen me. If she has, she's doing a great job of ignoring me. Which seems fitting considering the way she left all those years ago.

"Charlie!"

I'm pushing through groups of people without apologizing, which I know is a dick move. But I need to stop her before she disappears.

Again.

My pace picks up as I call out for her, but she doesn't turn around.

"Charlie!"

Okay now she has to be ignoring me. It's like the phone calls and text messages all over again. No way she didn't hear me. I just yelled so loud I think the DJ stopped playing music. And judging by the look on everyone's faces, my voice came through just fine. Yet, she's picking up her speed and not even looking back.

I'm just a few feet away from her when she pushes the kitchen door open.

No. Not again. I feel like if she walks through those swinging doors it might be another fifteen years before I see her again.

"Bug!"

This she heard. It stops her on a dime.

I watch with bated breath as she slowly turns around. Now that I'm close, I can truly see the woman Charlie has become. Full curves. Red hair that reminds me of fire, which is exploding wildly on the top of her head in a messy ponytail. Deep blue eyes that I could get lost in so easily. Lips that are currently making a surprised "o" shape.

"Simon?"

We both stand and stare at each other for what feels like

hours. This is the most surreal moment of my life. I honestly thought I'd never see her again. I thought she was a part of my past that was dead and buried. But she's not. She's here. In front of me. As beautiful, and apparently frustrating, as ever.

I want to say so many things. Ask so many things. Yet, only one thing comes out of my mouth.

"What the fuck, Charlie?"

She rears back. Which...fair. Might not have been my best opening line, but it wasn't a lie. Because seriously, what the fuck?

"Nice to see you too, Simon."

Did I mention Charlie was sarcastic? The two of us, when we were both on our game, were a master class in smartass dialogue.

"Were you really not going to stop?"

"Stop?"

"I was yelling for you."

She looks up then back down as she shrugs. "Sorry. I didn't hear you."

Got her.

That's her tell when she's lying. It's subtle. And it hasn't changed in fifteen years.

"Bullshit," I say. And while I'd love to call her out on the lie, I have a more important question. "What are you doing here?"

"Working."

One-word answers. Great.

"Can we talk?"

She shakes her head. "I'm working."

I let out a sigh of frustration. "We already ate dinner. I know the bride and groom, so if you're worried about not getting paid, I'll take care of it. I think you can sneak away for five minutes. Please, Charlie. It's been fifteen years, and, well, I think a talk is the least I'm owed."

I know I'm begging now, but I don't care. This woman owes me an explanation, and I'm not about to have her walk out of my life again without getting one.

She flicks a glance to the kitchen then looks back to me. And for just a second, her hardened demeanor is gone. Her sarcastic shield has been lowered. I only saw this side of Charlie a few times during our years together.

Including the night I thought everything was going to change for the better.

"I'm sorry, Simon. I can't."

She turns to walk away, and out of reaction, I grab her arm and stop her. She looks down at our connection, then back up to me.

Does she feel it, too? Did the jolt of electricity that just shot through me go through her also?

"Bug...please..." My voice is pleading. I'm begging. I didn't know until right now how much I needed this closure.

How much I needed to see her again.

"Please, Simon. Just let me go."

Her words are pained as she pulls her arm from my hold and walks back into the kitchen. And for the second time in my life, Charlie leaves without an explanation.

Only this time I watch her walk away.

I thought for years that her ghosting me was the worst feeling in the world.

I was wrong.

It's this.

Chapter 1
Charlie
~~ 4 months later ~~

There is literally nothing that could make this day worse.

Nothing. Not one damn thing. In fact, I could get hit by a car, and I'd thank the driver for putting me out of my misery.

I barely slept because my niece was up crying most of the night due to an ear infection. When I did wake up from my whopping three hours of restless slumber, I stepped in pee from a dog I barely like. There wasn't any hot water when I took a shower. My hairdryer died one minute into use so I had to come to work with wet hair. Two people called out, and we're booked solid today with prospective client tastings. Oh, and I was out of coffee.

So yeah, how about that hit and run?

"Charlie?" I look up from the onions I'm chopping to realize the shaky voice comes from Bella, one of the apprentices.

"Yeah?"

"We're out of asparagus."

9

I clutch the knife even tighter in my palm. I try to slow my breathing, but I can't. I feel like a volcano about to erupt.

"What do you mean, we're out of asparagus?"

Bella's confused look makes my frustration grow. "I mean we're out. Like we don't have any. Eighty-sixed. I don't think it was ordered."

"How the fuck are we out of asparagus!" My hands, including the one holding the knife, are now flailing as I lose my shit. "It's fucking asparagus! How does a caterer run out of goddamn asparagus? It's not that hard to find. They sell it at fucking Target!"

Bella starts to open her mouth again, but I hold up my free hand, asking her without words to stop speaking. Because if she says one more thing, I can't be held accountable for my actions.

"Okay, here's what we're going to do," I say, exhaling slowly. "I need you to go to the office. Ask for a hundred dollars in petty cash. If anyone says no, tell them I told you. Then, go to the store and buy me every bundle of asparagus you can find."

Bella nods frantically and runs out of the kitchen. I look around to see a dozen sets of eyes staring at me, probably wondering if I'm going to blow again.

Or if I'm going to stab them with the knife I've been waving around.

"What are y'all looking at? Get back to work!"

"Yes Chef!"

They all dive back into whatever dishes they were preparing. My arm is still raised above my shoulder, knife pointed forward, as I feel a grip on my weapon-wielding arm. Yep. They're afraid I'm going to stab them.

"How about we put the knife down, killer? We haven't had a trip to the emergency room in a month. Let's not ruin the streak."

I slowly put the knife down at the request of my work bestie and the best pastry chef I know, Mellie. "Good. That's good, Charlie. How about we take a step outside so we can cool off?"

"I'm fine. I have an appointment in an hour."

"I know, which is why we're going to go outside."

Mellie calls over one of the more capable line cooks on staff and asks them to finish the dishes I was preparing as she guides me to the back alley of the restaurant.

"Sit," she commands, pointing to one of the empty plastic milk crates the line cooks use as stools during their smoke breaks. "Now breathe."

I shoot her a glare, but she returns it right back. She doesn't like to put on her mean face, but she will when she needs to. Which is now, apparently.

"I didn't have you losing your shit over asparagus on my bingo card today," Mellie remarks.

I huff out a laugh. Mellie doesn't swear a lot, and every time she does, it always lightens the mood. Or makes me realize things are serious. "I know I shouldn't have blown up like that. But I couldn't help it. Who the fuck forgets to order asparagus, the vegetable that's in a third of our dishes?"

Mellie raises an eyebrow. "Was that a rhetorical question, or do you really not know?"

I let out a sigh. Yes, I know who forgot.

Billy.

Billy, the boss's son. Billy, who thinks he's God's gift to culinary cuisine. Billy, who thinks the Food Network is going to be knocking on his doorstep any moment. Billy, who burned two steaks last week, tried to pass them off as well done, and refused to believe the customer who lost a tooth biting into it. It wasn't a lie. We saw the tooth.

"Are we surprised?" Mellie asks. "The man wore two different shoes last week. And they weren't the same style."

"I'm not," I say. "But I also know there isn't anything we can do about it."

"Nope. Because Billy's last name is Napoli."

Mario Napoli started his Italian steakhouse in Nashville thirty years ago. Nine years ago, the business branched off and began a catering company that would do events, such as weddings, private parties, and banquets. Five years ago, he brought his son into the business.

Two of those decisions were good.

Billy is the definition of a nepotism hire. He's never had to work for anything, only got into culinary school because of his last name, and thinks his shit doesn't stink—in and out of the kitchen. He's the literal worst.

Oh, and he has a crush on me. And not a cute, shy, doesn't-know-what-to-say crush—he's got the always hits on me, won't-take-no-for-an-answer kind.

"This fucking sucks," I say, throwing my head back. "Everything just fucking sucks."

"I've looked hard for a silver lining, but I can't find it right now," Mellie says, patting my knee in an attempt to comfort me. I appreciate her effort, but the only thing that will work is a restart to this day.

Or maybe this year.

Scratch that. The past fifteen years.

"Want to dream?" she asks, a smile growing on her face.

I nod, knowing exactly what she's doing. And it's exactly what I need. "Yeah."

"Okay," she says as we scooch our crates closer together and join hands. "Close your eyes and tell me all about it."

A tear nearly comes to my eye as I envision the restaurant I want to someday open. Mellie is one of three people who knows my dream. And she only knows it because of a box of wine in a weak moment.

"A diner," I begin. "Breakfast, lunch, dinner, and pastries."

"Best damn pastries in Tennessee, made by yours truly."

This makes me smile. "It's going to be small and intimate. A hundred people, max. Blue booths. Pops of color that liven up the place. White walls. A place where people can go and enjoy a meal that won't break their bank but will leave them satisfied."

"But not so satisfied that people won't want dessert."

"Exactly. In between meals, people will come in for coffee and pastries. Book clubs will bring tables together for their meetings. Writers will use it for their offices. People will say 'let's meet over lunch' and they'll come to my place. And it will be perfect."

To some industry professionals, a restaurant like that might seem lame or easy. I don't care. This restaurant is my dream. Everything over the last fifteen years has been fueled with this goal in mind.

Except it feels so far away that most days I think I should stop trying.

"It's going to be amazing," Mellie says, patting my hand as I open my eyes. "I'm going to make so many cakes. And cupcakes. And cinnamon rolls. My cinnamon rolls are so good."

I laugh. "Well, don't hold your breath. The way things are going, we're going to be working for Billy's children."

"Gross," Mellie says. "That means Billy had—"

Mellie's words trail off as we both shiver. Because that thought is disgusting.

"No," Mellie says, shaking her head. "We can't be here that long. I'm going to manifest this to speed up, because the thought of working for Billy, or Mr. Napoli, for the rest of my life is the actual worst. Are you any closer to finding anything?"

13

I shake my head. "No. I have the money. Or at least, a little. I think. But I can't find the right space. It's either too big, too expensive, or, if it's in my price range, it's a piece of shit."

"Have you tried looking out of town?"

I nod. "Yeah, but nothing has popped up yet. And even if it did, I have Connor and Lila to think about."

She nods her head, knowing my situation isn't normal. Because how many thirty-five-year-old single women do you know that live with their brother and his daughter?

"I wish I could help," Mellie laments.

"No," I say. "I never asked you to do that. Hell, I'm scared asking you to jump ship when you have a steady job."

Mellie shakes her head. "You think I can survive in this place without you? Absolutely not. I go where you go, lady."

I don't know what I did to deserve this woman. We both got hired when Napoli's expanded into the catering business, me to handle the banquet menu and Mellie to handle the pastries. We've been through it all together. I know all of her secrets, and she knows all of mine.

Well, most of them.

"You know what we need? Drinks."

I look over to Mellie to see if she's serious. "Drinks?"

"Yup! Drinks!" She pops up off the crate as if she needs space to present her idea. "We haven't gone out in forever. It's a beautiful night in Nashville, so you know Broadway is going to be so much fun."

"I don't think so."

"Oh, I do. You. Me. Drinks. Rooftop bars. Cowboy boots. Maybe some cowboys."

I shake my head, but can't hold in my laugh as she waggles her eyebrows. "While that sounds great, you know I can't afford a night out."

She shakes her head. "Lucky for you, I can. I might not be able to buy in to a restaurant, but I can get us a few rounds."

"Fine. But only because I know you won't let it go if I say no."

"You know me so well."

We laugh as I hear the door open behind me.

"Chef?"

I look over to the line cook who has popped his head out. "Yeah?"

"Your one o'clock appointment is here."

"Thanks," I say as I push myself off the plastic crate. "Guess it's time to work."

Mellie gives my hand a squeeze. "You got this."

I nod as I make my way inside to find that the cooks did a fine job of putting together the samplings I have prepared for my first client of the day. I was only supposed to have three appointments, but my favorite wedding planner, Whitley Evans, called in asking a favor for her sister-in-law and her fiancé. And since I just catered Whitley's wedding a few months ago, and she's the absolute best, of course I snuck them in.

Well, she's the best. Her wedding? Not so much. You don't care to think back on weddings when you see men from your past you want to stab.

I grab the tray of appetizers I'm going to present, take a deep breath to get into potential client mode, and use my butt to bump open the kitchen door. I walk through the empty part of the restaurant that we use for tastings when I see a man sitting alone at a table.

"You must be Shane. Hi, I'm Charlie." I set down the tray to shake his hand. "I'm one of the sous chefs here, and if you pick us, I'd be the one cooking the food for your wedding."

"Nice to meet you." Shane's words are accompanied with a

forced smile, which I don't think too much of. Most grooms don't like doing wedding things, let alone by themselves.

"Just you today?" I ask, not wanting to assume anything. "Whitley wasn't sure if it was going to be you or your fiancée as well."

This seems to take Shane by surprise. "My fiancée is meeting with the florist today. You know Whitley?"

"I've worked with Whitley on a bunch of weddings, including her own. That's how you guys got in here today with such short notice. Whitley called in a favor."

"Interesting."

I'm not sure what he means by that, but I don't ask. "Okay, let's get started with the appetizers."

Something catches my eye at the entrance of the dining room, and I look up without even thinking.

I feel the color drain from my face, only to be quickly replaced by red-hot anger, as I see Simon Banks leaning against the wide opening. His arms are crossed, his smile is smug, and his eyes are twinkling with mischief.

"Hey, Bug."

I spoke too soon. This day could, and did, just get worse.

Chapter 2
Simon

When my best friend Shane called today to ask if I'd tag along to catering appointments for his fake wedding, I was reluctant. And that's aside from the fact that he and Amelia aren't really engaged. I think. I'm not sure anymore. I'm not sure they know either.

My immediate thought was to make myself scarce. What kind of support can I be when we're just seeing whose chicken sucks the least?

Then I thought about it. I was already in Nashville for some business meetings I have to attend to tomorrow. I had originally planned to spend my day on the golf course or scouting potential houses or buildings I could buy. But that doesn't seem nearly as much fun as going with Shane to the catering company that employs Charlie.

Because yes, I figured out who catered Jake and Whitley's wedding. Yes, I asked Shane if this was one we were going to. I even called to see if she was working.

She is.

And would you look at this? There she is. Looking as flustered and pissed off as ever.

Good. Now she knows how it feels.

"What the hell are you doing here?"

Her voice is clipped, and her face is turning redder by the second. For some reason, that only makes me smile. She was always cute when she was angry.

"Out of all the catering companies in all of Nashville..."

Am I pretending I didn't know this was going to happen? Yes.

Does that make me a prick? Probably.

"What are you doing here?"

I give her a nonchalant shrug as I pat Shane on the back, his face in utter confusion. "I'm the best man at this guy's wedding. I'm here to taste the food. Make sure it doesn't have poison in it."

"He's not my best man," Shane says.

Rude.

"Don't listen to him," I say. "So what do we have here today?"

It's been four months since I've seen Charlie. Four months since I've had to come to grips with the fact that the one who got away is within my reach. At least geographically. Four months of telling myself every day that she wants nothing to do with me.

Which means I should want nothing to do with her.

There's only one problem with that: It sucks, and I don't like it.

I spent fifteen years pushing away the thoughts of Charlie. And I did it. I forgot about the pain she caused when I found out she was gone. I had erased the memory of the last time I saw her. I reluctantly accepted I was never going to know why she left.

Then I saw her, and everything came flooding back. Only this time I haven't been able to push it back.

And frankly, I don't want to.

I slowly pull back my chair and sit down, my eyes fixed on Charlie. I make a show of taking my napkin and giving it a snap before draping it across my lap. Judging by the death glare she is giving me, she doesn't appreciate my show.

Again, rude.

"I don't think it's a good idea for you to be here."

Charlie's voice is shaky, but I push that aside. Because all I'm remembering right now is my begging voice when I saw her in April and how she told me to leave.

"Why not, Bug? Can't concentrate with me around? It's a problem for many."

My cocky response only seems to frustrate her more. Good. That's what I was going for. I always loved riling her up until her cheeks flushed.

"Why are you the way you are?"

"We've been asking that question for years," Shane remarks.

"Oh, stop. You love me," I say to Shane before turning back to Bug. "Now, what are we eating? I just had a mean chicken piccata that it's your job to beat."

The two of us lock eyes in a standoff. If someone were to walk in here and see this, I'm guessing they would be very confused. There's Charlie, taking visible, deep breaths in what I'm assuming is her futile attempts to calm herself. Then there's me, sitting back in my chair, my foot now resting on my knee, my hands relaxed on the chairs next to mine like I don't have a care in the world.

I do, but she's not going to know that. Because I want her angry. I want her mad. I know it's petty and I should be a bigger man, but I'm not. This woman broke my heart without a care in the world, so I don't feel bad for a second.

Charlie turns to Shane, doing her best to keep her voice even. "Shane, I think it would be best if we rescheduled. Maybe when you can come with your fiancée. Or I can have one of our servers bring you out the courses for you to choose from."

Ha! Victory. Simon 1, Charlie 0.

Just as I start relishing in my small win of getting under her skin, I see Shane shoot a look to me.

"Can you just fucking stop it?" he asks.

"What? I'm not doing anything."

"You're existing."

Shane grits out those last two words, and since they were accompanied by a death glare, I'm guessing I've pushed this as far as I can today.

Oh well, it was fun while it lasted.

"Fine." I stand up and toss the napkin back to the table, but make sure to lock eyes with Charlie. "I'll leave. Because I'm a *real* gentleman. I know where I'm not wanted. I don't lie. I don't lead people on. I'm not a douchebag who leaves or lies to you, even though that's how you've decided to treat me. I'm apparently just another asshole who leaves you crying. Isn't that right Bug?"

Charlie's face goes from mad to horrified in a second, and I realize that I did it. I crossed the line.

Because I'm a fucking asshole.

And not my normal lovable brand of asshole. A true one. One that intentionally hurts people I care about. Or did care about. Or still do. Fuck, I don't know. I just know that Charlie is on the verge of tears.

And I put them there.

"Please leave, Simon."

20

The One I Hate

I nod and don't fight her. In fact, if she wouldn't have asked me to leave I would have showed myself the door. Because the moment I said it, I knew I went too far. I give Bug one more look, this time one of apology, though she doesn't see it. She's too busy turning away, trying to fight back tears.

Without another word, I walk out of the dining room. I hear Shane say something to Charlie, but I don't register what it is. I can't hear anything over the voice in my head chastising me for hurting her.

And because that's not good enough, the second I step into the hot August air I let out an actual scream I'm sure anyone in a three-block radius can hear.

It still doesn't make me feel better.

What the fuck is wrong with me? Did I mean to be a prick? Yes. Did I want to get under her skin because every day for the past four months she's been under mine? Also yes. But I don't hurt people. Unless I hate you.

And as much as I want to, I'll never hate Charlie.

I'll hate how she left.

I'll hate how she's made me feel.

I'll hate that I still care about her.

But I'll never hate her.

Even though I'm pretty sure she hates me.

Before today I always wondered why. Because based on my memories of the last time we saw each other, she did the opposite of hate me. Okay, she might not have loved me, but she definitely liked me.

I mean, she kissed me, for fuck's sake.

Now after today I won't have to wonder why she hates me. Because, shockingly, my impulsive actions and words have consequences.

Who knew?

This isn't the first time my big mouth has gotten me in trouble. But that's who I am. I'm impulsive. Sometimes reckless. I say what's on my mind without thinking things through. I set my mind on something and then I'm so blinded by tunnel vision I don't see the possible outcome of my actions.

Take today. All I wanted was for Charlie to feel how I felt at the wedding. Angry and frustrated and helpless.

Instead I brought up a memory I'm sure she'd rather not think about.

"Charlie working tonight?"

I know Bug works Mondays, Wednesdays, and Fridays from ten in the morning until three at Perks, the campus coffee shop on Lane Avenue, but I'm not entirely sure what her schedule is on a Saturday night. At least, I'm not sure what the real schedule is. Every time I ask her out on a Saturday she says she has to work. Though I have a sneaking suspicion that's just an excuse.

"Nope," a worker I don't recognize says. "Won't be back until Monday."

I say thanks as I make my way back to my off-campus house. It's empty tonight; my roommates all decided to go to our fraternity house and Emmett, my only friend who isn't a frat brother, is out of town.

I don't know why I didn't feel like going out. It's a Saturday night in April. Campus is jumping. Everyone has come out of the winter fog and is here for spring.

Except me.

I wasn't feeling it. And I haven't been feeling it for a while.

Nothing excites me. Don't get me wrong, the premise of college life is the best. But I'm also someone who gets bored easily. So the monotony of parties and booze and girls every weekend on repeat is getting boring.

The One I Hate

I need something new. Something different. Something to push me out of my comfort zone.

I need Bug.

She's the only one who can make me think outside my box. She's the only one I don't see what's coming a mile away. Everything that comes out of her mouth is interesting.

I head to the crosswalk and wait for the light to change when I hear the telltale sign of a sob.

I look around to see a woman sitting on the steps to one of the buildings. Her blonde hair is covering her face and her body is jerking. I almost turn to go home, but I take one more glance just as she looks up.

Bug....

It takes me only a few strides to get to her, and yet, I'm not to her in enough time. I can't stand to hear the sound of a woman's tears. It's probably because I grew up in a house with four sisters, but when I hear a woman cry, I immediately want to hurt the person who did it.

And because it's Charlie? I want to fucking murder them.

"Bug?"

She slowly starts looking up at me, and my heart shatters. Her mascara is smeared, her hair is sticking to her forehead, and her lipstick is a mess.

Her red lipstick that always drives me fucking crazy.

"Simon?"

Her sobs start coming again so I quickly move to the step next to her, bringing her into my arms. "Shh...I got you."

She doesn't say anything for a few seconds, though I can tell she's doing her best to make herself quit crying. I want to ask her a million questions. The two biggest ones being, "Who did this to you?" *and* "Where can I find them so I can fucking kill them?"

Or if no one did this to her then the question becomes,

"What can I do to make you stop crying?" Because in this moment, that's all I want to do.

She sits up, using the back of her hand to wipe away the stray tears. "Thank you."

"You never need to thank me," I say. "Are you okay?"

She nods, though I don't know how genuine it is. "I will be."

"Can I ask what happened?"

I can feel her body still against me. At first, I don't think she's going to say anything. Then she slowly moves out of my hold to turn and face me. "I had a date."

My body stills, but I push it down. She needs a friend. She's upset. I remind myself to not get pissy because she agreed to a date with a guy who wasn't me.

Even though I've asked out her once a week since January...

"Did he have bad breath? Nasty cologne? Oh! Wait! He wore an Ed Hardy shirt. All of those would make me cry."

This makes her laugh. "I wish. Turns out he had a girlfriend."

I jump off the step, ready to hunt this guy down. "Who is he?"

Charlie pulls me back to the step. "Easy, tiger."

"Don't easy tiger me, Bug. Who the fuck is he and where can I find him?"

Charlie grabs my hand in hers, and for that brief moment in time, I forget about the fuck face who made her cry. Because this is the first time I've held Charlie's hand. And I know it's not much, but to me right now, it's everything.

"He's a guy I have a few classes with. Seemed nice. Turns out his girlfriend cheated on him, and instead of breaking up, she gave him a free pass."

My eyes double in size. "A free pass?"

"Yup," she says with a shrug. "That's me. I'm the free pass."

24

"How...what...huh?" My words trailing off because what the fuck?

"How did I find out? His drunk friend. We went to meet them at a bar after dinner. I thought it would be fun. Except when he went to get us drinks, his friend—who apparently is pretty loose-lipped after a few Jagerbombs—asked me if I was the 'chubby coffee shop girl.' It only took a few more questions to figure out what he was doing."

Rage. That's all I feel. Pure, crisp, rage. Charlie must see it on my face because she gives my hand a squeeze.

"Easy. Nothing happened. If anything, I need to be thanking Jagerbomb Boy. Who knew being the chubby girl would come in handy?"

I don't laugh at her attempt at a joke. Also I hate it when she calls herself that, because that's not what I see when I look at her.

All I see is my Bug. My beautiful Bug.

"Oh, come on," she says, now laughing. "That part was funny."

I shake my head. "Nothing is funny about this. Five minutes ago you were crying. Now you're trying to put on a brave face and crack jokes. Why? Don't. You don't have to. You shouldn't have to. You're amazing, and that jackass deserves to have his ass kicked."

This makes her laugh again, but I can see the tears forming in her eyes. "It does suck, doesn't it?"

I nod. "Yeah, it does."

She lets her head fall into my shoulder, and we sit there for I don't know how long. I wrap my arms around her as her tears start slowly coming again. I don't pry for any more information, instead just being that shoulder she so clearly needs.

When the air starts to cool down, I move her head just

enough for me to take off my hoodie and give it to her. She looks at it, confused, before back to me.

"You're cold," I say.

"I'm fine."

"Just put it on, Bug," I say, taking it back from her and holding it so she can slip her head into it. She shimmies it on, and it takes all I have to push down the feeling of satisfaction I get from seeing her in an item of my clothing.

"I hate that name."

"No you don't."

She lets out a sigh as she gives in. "Thank you. You didn't have to do this."

"Yes, I did. I'm a gentleman."

She tilts her head and gives me a look. "Really? Since when?"

I smile and put my arm back around her, bringing her head back down to my shoulder. "Since always, Bug. Since always."

The telltale sound of a sob brings me back to the present, and my body goes on high alert. I walk around the side of the building and it's déjà vu—only more than a decade later.

Charlie is sitting on what looks like a crate, hair hanging over her face, sobbing.

I start to walk toward her but stop myself.

She doesn't want my comfort now.

She doesn't want my words.

She doesn't want any part of me.

She hates me.

Which I get, because in this moment, I hate myself.

Chapter 3
Simon

I don't get drunk often.

But when I do, I get fucking sauced.

Which is what I am now. Sauced. Hammered. Shit faced. Four sheets to the rain. Or is it six sheets to the wind?

I don't know the saying. I don't know a lot of things right now. Including how much alcohol I've consumed. Or why the hotel bar kicked me out. It wasn't time to close. I know because I can still kind of see the time on my watch. Wait, I bet it was because I called them liars for saying that they ran out of Johnny Walker. They didn't. They just didn't want me there because I fell off the barstool.

That's why they kicked me out. Victory! I do know one thing.

I'm so smart.

Actually I'm not smart. Because I don't know why I was so mean to Charlie.

Wait! I do. It's because she didn't say goodbye to me after we kissed and I missed her so I did the adult version of pulling on her pigtails.

27

In my defense, her pigtails are *so fun* to pull.

I stumble into the elevator and push the button for every floor because I can't see straight. The only thing keeping me upright is this wall and the sound of my stomach growling for food.

"Did I eat tonight?" I say to no one. I didn't. I forgot. I was too busy drinking because I made Charlie cry. As soon as I left the tasting I parted ways with Shane then went immediately to the hotel bar. I was supposed to have dinner with my buddy Emmett, but I canceled. I had more pressing matters to take care of, like drinking myself stupid to punish myself for how I acted today.

The elevator door opens and closes one by one. It's going to take forever to get to the sixteenth floor. Oh well, gives me time to think about what food I'm going to order.

A burger. No, pizza. No! Tacos.

Wait...I got it...burger-pizza-tacos.

Why has no one invented that? I should.

You know who could invent that? Charlie. She always came up with these delicious and fucking weird food combinations when we studied for tests. I bet that's why she's a chef now.

"What are you doing?"

Bug turns over her shoulder, a smile covering her gorgeous face as she dances in my kitchen to some pop star I know by name only. The song is catchy though.

"Dancing."

"I thought you were making us snacks," I say as I go stand next to her, my back to the counter so I can look at her better. She looks free. Happy. I don't always see that when we study. She

usually looks like she has the weight of the world on her shoulders. Though she'll never admit she does or tell me why.

"You can do two things at once," she says. "Plus, kitchens are made for dancing."

"Really?" I say. "I've never heard that."

"They are," she says as she bops her way to me as she carries some sort of food in her hand.

"What's this?"

"Rice cake pizza."

I blink my eyes a few times. "Excuse me, what?"

"You heard me. Rice cake pizza. Try it."

I shake my head. "Charlie. I'll buy us real pizza."

"Nonsense. Why buy pizza when you can have these?"

"Because real pizza is the best pizza."

"Just try."

She hands me her weird pizza thing and I take a bite. It's good. Really good. Surprisingly light.

But I'm not about to tell her that.

"It's all right," I say, but take another bite to finish it off. Bug sees the smile I'm trying to hide, which brings a blush to her cheeks.

It's fucking adorable.

The song changes, and this one I know. It's a song that actually reminds me of Charlie. Independent. Her own woman. Plus, it's a slower R&B song, which gives me the excuse to do what I'm about to do.

I push myself off the counter and grab her hand, pulling her away from the snack making and into my body.

"What are you doing?" she asks as we start dancing in the middle of my kitchen. My hand is around the small of her back and her hand is perfectly fitted into mine as I hold it against my chest.

"You said kitchens were for dancing. So let's dance, Bug."

. . .

The elevator jerking to a stop snaps me from my memory.

Finally. Because I need to get to my room. And order food. Then eat the food. Then pass out.

Maybe then I'll finally stop thinking about her.

She was so sad today. I made her sad. I don't like that I made her sad.

And she's so pretty. She's always been so pretty. I don't know if she knows how pretty she is, but she's the prettiest.

I somehow get myself into my hotel room and immediately fall to the bed. Before I pass out on accident, I make sure to bring up the food delivery app and order God knows what from who knows where.

Before I put my phone away, I go to the contacts and scroll to a name I don't think I've looked at in years.

Bug.

I never deleted it. I tried. Many times. My fingers were always right there, ready to pull the trigger. But every time something stopped me. Just like something is stopping me right now.

I should delete it. After today, she'll never want to see me again. And I don't blame her. I was a dick. A straight up Richard.

But I miss her. I didn't realize how much I've missed her. Even with her hating me, I still miss her.

Why? Is this because I want what I can't have? The woman has made it clear she wants nothing to do with me. I might be a man who knows what he wants, but I'm also a man who knows when no means no.

Consent, motherfuckers.

But I'm also a man who can't *not* have the last word. It's just not in my DNA. Especially when it comes to Charlie.

And especially when I'm all sorts of fucked up.

So even though I know I'm probably still blocked, and even

though I know she's never going to listen to it even if I'm not, I call her. It rings before going to voicemail. Which I figured.

And that's good. Because now I can say everything I want.

"Bug! It's me. Simon. And I can call you Bug because you aren't here to yell at me so I can call you it all I want. Plus, Bug is cute. Like you.

"Wait. No. You're not cute. Well, you are. You're beautiful. You still are. I know you never believed me when I told you that, but I was telling the truth then and I'm telling it now. You're beautiful.

"But that's not why I'm calling. I need to yell at you. And apologize. But mostly yell. So buckle up buttercup, this is about to be a journey. Also if I say hold on it's because my drunk food is here. I think I ordered tacos.

"Until then, what the fuck, Bug! Why did you leave me? Why didn't you say goodbye? Why did you disappear? Do you know how much that hurt me? I called. And texted. I even went to the coffee shop to see if you were there. No one knew anything. It was just like you vanished into thin air. Poof.

"Why didn't you say goodbye? I know I asked that but you haven't answered. Oh wait, I'm not really talking to you. I'm talking to me. Sorry. I don't know if you could tell, but I'm drunk.

"But the question remains, why didn't you say goodbye? Who does that? Especially after we kissed. I thought it was a good kiss. A *great* kiss. Wasn't it a good kiss? I'm a good kisser, dammit. And so are you. We kissed good. I wanted to kiss you the night of the wedding even though I yelled at you. And today. I wanted to kiss you today. Even though you hurt me. I still wanted to kiss you and hold you and do all the things that we never had a chance to do because you left.

"Do you know I went to the coffee shop every day to see if you came back? You were gone all summer but I tried. Also, I'm

31

not allowed back at Perks. They said I was loitering. Whatever. I don't even like coffee.

"Oh yeah, did you know I don't like coffee? Nope. Never did. I went in every day to that fucking coffee shop and bought coffee I didn't like because I wanted to see you. Yes, you. No other reason.

"So maybe I am a psycho stalker—wait! I'm not. Because I stopped looking. I stopped calling and texting. So I'm not a bad person, thank you very much!

"Until today. What I said was mean and cruel and not very nice. Because I saw you, Bug, and it brought up fifteen years of hurt and pain and sadness, and I fucking miss you. I stopped dancing in the kitchen, even though kitchens were made for dancing. And you want to know the worst thing? I haven't been able to watch wrestling since you left. The Rock is back, and I can't watch it, and it's all your fault! Or so I've been told.

"So, Bug, this is it. This is the end. You clearly don't want to see me, and you know what? I don't want to see you, either.

"That's a lie. I do. I want to see you really bad. I'm in Nashville tonight. The Omni. Room 1614. If you're in Nashville, I want to see you. I want to say I'm sorry for being mean today. And to see your pretty face. But you probably don't want to see me, which I understand. But not really. I miss you, Bug. Okay, I'm going to hang—"

The voice mail cuts me off. Oops. I probably said too much.

Oh well, I said it. My piece. Now I can move on.

Or pass out. Or eat my burger tacos. Whatever happens first.

Chapter 4
Charlie

"More shots!"

"Yes!" Mellie yells back. "Another round, barkeep!"

Should we be ordering more shots? No. Absolutely not.

Are we? Abso-fucking-lutely.

I need to push past this depressing stage of drunk that I'm currently in. I think I'm at shot six. Maybe. I've lost count. Six-drink Charlie is sad.

I bet Seven-drink Charlie is a lot of fun.

"Here," the hot bartender says. "But only if you drink all this water right after."

I force a wink, except I think I do it with both eyes, as the bartender walks away. I was going for sexy. It was not sexy.

"He's hot," I mumble.

"He is," Mellie says as we lick, shoot, then suck the tequila back. "I wonder if he's single."

"Probably," I say, swaying to the background music of Bar 615, the swanky bar off Broadway we like to go to when we're feeling fancy. We tried going to the honkytonks, but there were too many people. And as much as I wanted a fun night on a rooftop bar, I wasn't feeling it. I was in a shitty mood.

Thanks, Simon...

"Are we going to talk about it?"

I look over to Mellie, who is giving me a very sad look. I think. There's two of her right now.

I shake my head, which was a bad idea. "Nope. Not talking about it."

"I think you need to," she says. "When I find my best friend crying in the alley, and all she can ask is if 'he's' gone, I think we need to talk about it."

"We don't. Everything is fine."

Everything is not fine. I thought running into Simon four months ago at the wedding was going to be a one-time thing. So what if it was confirmed we were a few degrees of separation away from each other? That didn't matter. I live in Nashville. I since found out from Whitley that he lives in Rolling Hills. That's a forty-five mile separation. Plenty of space between me and the man who broke my heart and gave me trust issues a mile high.

But when I saw him today, it hit me—Simon Banks is back in my life whether I like it or not. He now knows where I work. It won't take him long to figure out where I live. The man will annoy me and pester me and do whatever it takes to get what he wants—the reason why I left.

Which is hilarious. Like he doesn't know.

"Yoo-hoo!" I wave for the hottie bartender, who comes back toward me, carrying now two glasses of what I hope are tequilas but I'm pretty sure are waters.

"Yes, darlin'?"

Goodness gracious, can I record this man saying "darlin'" and have it as my ringtone? "What's your name, hot bartender man?"

He chuckles. "Max."

"Hi, Max. I'm Charlie. This is Mellie."

"Hi!" she yells with a big wave.

"Can I ask you a question, Max?"

He chuckles. "Sure."

I know I need to talk, but if I could listen to his thick drawl all day, I wouldn't be mad. "Would you ever tell a girl you like them and then go and hook up with another girl hours later?"

"I don't know," he says. "Does she like me?"

I nod as he slides me over another water. "She does."

"Does he know that?"

"Yes. He does."

"Then no," he says, taking a glance down toward the end of the bar then back to me. "If I was into her, and she was into me, then everyone else would disappear."

I point to Max aggressively, which almost makes me fall off my barstool. "This man has it figured out!"

He laughs then points an accusing finger at my untouched glass of water.

He's nice. And hot. I bet he isn't cocky and doesn't call people by stupid nicknames.

"Is that what Simon did?" Mellie asks.

"Huh?"

She nods toward Max. "What you just asked Max. Is that what Simon did?"

Well, shit. I forgot she could hear me.

"He broke my heart," I say, choosing to not go into details. Mellie doesn't know much about Simon, except that I hate him.

"I'm sorry," she says, patting my back. "That sucks."

"He asked me out for months," I begin. "I always said no because I thought he was a sexed-up frat boy who just wanted another notch on his bedpost. Wait, do people actually put notches on bedposts?"

This makes Mellie think for a second. "I bet they did back in the day. I can Google it?" She shakes her head in annoyance. "No. No Goog-ing. Back to the story."

"Yes. Sorry. So we actually became friends. Good friends. Like I think at one point he was my best friend, but I never told him that because his head was already big enough."

"I bet other things were big..."

"Mellie!" I yell. "He's the enemy."

She shrugs. "You have to admit, he's a hot enemy. At least from what I saw today."

"I'm not admitting anything," I say in defiance, even though that's a lie. I'm just a liar-liar- pants-on-fire tonight. Because Simon is hot, and he's only gotten better with age. Which is a shame because he's an asshole. Those crystal blue eyes shouldn't be wasted on Satan.

"I wonder what his beard would feel like?" Mellie says, her eyes staring out, unfocused.

"Stop it!" I say. "We aren't talking about his hotness. Or his beard. Or his body in a suit."

"I didn't say anything about a suit." Mellie wags her eyebrows. "Just admit he's hot."

I groan. "Fine. He's hot. He always has been and apparently always will be."

Mellie smiles. "I'm glad you admit that. Now you can tell me what Hot Satan did to you."

I shake my head. I don't like talking about it. That day began the shitstorm of my life. "Let's just say I thought things were going somewhere, because I, once again, believed the words a man said."

"Men suck."

"Yeah, they do," I say. "Why do they lie?"

"Yeah!" Mellie says. "And why do they say words that aren't true?"

"Yes!" I yell. "They suck."

"Fucking suck bags."

We both raise our glasses of water, because I'm guessing we've been cut off, and cheer to men sucking. Does some spill? Yes. Do we care? Not even a little.

"Wait! Isn't toasting with water bad luck?"

I waive her off. "I've been bad luck most of my life, today included. I didn't need water for that."

And that's no lie. Between having a dad who took off, a single mom who passed away too soon in life, and living paycheck to paycheck, things haven't been a walk in the park. And every time I think something good is about to happen—BAM!—life sends me the equivalent of a bird shitting on my head.

I go to set the glass of water down when I see my cell phone light up with an incoming call. That's not what shocks me. It's the name flashing on the screen.

Speaking of bird shit...

"What the fuck!" I yell, grabbing my phone and holding it closer so I can read it better. Maybe I'm seeing things. How drunk am I that I'm seeing the name "Asshole Banks" flashing on the screen?

"What is it?"

I don't answer Mellie because I'm stabbing the red button and rejecting the call.

"It was him."

Mellie gives me a confused look, clearly not realizing who I'm talking about.

"Him!"

"Who's him?

"Simon!" I scream, waving Max over to get me another shot. I know I shouldn't, but Simon called me, and I don't know how to feel about that.

"Why is he calling?"

"I don't know! It doesn't make sense. I thought I had him blocked. How did he break through my phone fortress?"

I plead with Max to get me a shot, which he agrees to, before I let my head fall into the bar.

How? Why? What? Huh?

Those are the immediate questions that run through my foggy, tequila-soaked brain.

Is he trying to fuck with me? Make me cry even more? Fight again? He has to have better things to do with his time than mess with me. Then again, annoying the hell out of me used to be his favorite hobby.

"Oh!" Mellie chirps, making me raise my head. "He left a voicemail."

I stare at the notification on my phone and don't move. Granted, the room is spinning, but I don't think I'm moving. I'm just staring at the word "Voicemail," which looks like it's in 3-D.

"What did he say?" Mellie tries to grab the phone, but I quickly slap my hand on top of it.

"How would I know?"

"Aren't we going to listen to it?"

"No. We're not."

"What do you mean *no*? Aren't you curious?"

Of course I want to know. I want to know why he's calling. I want to know why he did what he did fifteen years ago. I want to know why that beard looks so good on him.

'Cause it does, and I hate that.

"You're thinking about it," Mellie singsongs.

"Thinking about what?"

"Listening."

I shake my head. "I'm not."

"Liar," she says. "I don't know exactly what he did to you,

38

but I know it hurt you deeply. You need closure. You can't move on because something is still holding you back. If you listen, maybe that will help."

She's right. I hate when I'm not right, but I'll admit this one.

"Okay," I say. "Max! You better hurry with those shots because I'm going to need it after this."

The bar is a little loud, so I doubt I can hear it just on speaker phone. Luckily, I always have my ear buds in my purse.

"I can't do this on my own." I hand Mellie one of the ear buds. She just nods as I hit play.

Here goes nothing...

"Bug! It's me. Simon."

"Aww!" Mellie says. "He calls you Bug? How sweet."

"Shh!" I whisper-scream. I can barely hear him. Though what I am hearing sounds a lot like gibberish. Is he drunk too?

"Wait. No. You're not cute. Well, you are. You're beautiful. You still are. I know you never believed me when I told you that years ago, but I was telling the truth then and I'm telling you it now, you're beautiful."

Well, fuck. No! Stay strong!

"But that's not why I'm calling. I need to yell at you. And apologize. But mostly yell. So buckle up, buttercup, this is about to be a journey. Also if I say hold on it's because my drunk food is here."

"What?" I scream, hitting pause. "He's going to yell at me?"

"Calm down," Mellie says. "Just hear what he has to say. Then appropriately react."

I roll my eyes but do as she says.

Which is hard, because the next part of the voicemail goes on and on about me not saying goodbye and him looking for me and why I went off the grid. Which is hilarious considering his actions are the reason why he's asking all of this. But he's not admitting to any of that.

"But the question remains, why didn't you say goodbye? Who does that? Especially after we kissed. I thought it was a good kiss. A great kiss. Wasn't it a good kiss? I'm a good kisser, dammit. And so are you. We kissed good. I wanted to kiss you the night of the wedding even though I yelled at you. And today. I wanted to kiss you today."

I don't hit pause, hoping Mellie slides over that one. She doesn't.

"He wanted to kiss you today!" she squeals.

I shake my head. "Don't fall for his shit. It's easy to do. But he's a liar."

"Oh, yeah, did you know I don't like coffee?" Simon continues. "Nope. Never did. I went in every day to that fucking coffee shop and bought coffee I didn't like because I wanted to see you. Yes, you. No other reason."

I point to the phone. "See? Liar."

I might say that, but as the next part comes out, I find it hard to remind myself of that.

"What I said was mean and cruel and not very nice. Because I saw you, Bug, and it brought up fifteen years of hurt and pain and sadness, and I fucking miss you. I stopped dancing in the kitchen, even though kitchens were made for dancing. And you want to know the worst thing? I haven't been able to watch wrestling since you left. The Rock is back, and I can't watch it and it's all your fault!"

I can't help but laugh even as I feel the tears starting to form.

"So, Bug, this is it. This is the end. You clearly don't want to see me, and you know what? I don't want to see you, either. Okay, that's a lie. I do. I want to see you really bad. I'm in Nashville tonight. The Omni. Room 1614. If you're in Nash-

40

ville, I want to see you. I want to say I'm sorry for being mean today. And to see your pretty face. But you probably don't want to see me, which I understand. Not really. I miss you, Bug. Okay, I'm going to hang—"

The message abruptly stops and I look up to Mellie, completely speechless.

"Charlie..."

I shake my head. "No. He said some nice things, but he doesn't mean them."

"How do you know that?"

"Because Simon Banks is the same asshole today he was fifteen years ago. He says some nice shit, but in the end, he doesn't mean any of it. You even heard at the beginning of the message. He lied. He said he lied. And he's blaming me for leaving and not admitting to his part at all."

"Then go confront him."

Excuse me, what did she say?

"You want me to what?"

"Go to his hotel. He just said in the message he's in town. And the Omni is only two blocks away. Go and see him. Get your answers. Shut the door on this chapter forever."

I start to protest, but I don't.

Can I? Can I just walk into this man's hotel and demand answers as to why he did what he did? Part of me says I can't. But the tequila says I can. And when has tequila ever caused someone to make a bad decision?

Chapter 5
Simon

Banging on the door jolts me away from sweet oblivion. Or maybe it's the banging in my head. I'm honestly not sure at this point.

How long was I even out?

"Just leave it at the door," I yell. I need the food; I'm just not sure I can walk right now to get it.

There's just one problem: The pounding on the door doesn't stop.

"Fucking stop!"

I don't care who I wake up at this point. I just need it to stop.

I roll out of bed, literally, and fall to the ground. *Fuck*. It doesn't hurt now, but I'm sure I'm going to feel it in the morning.

Or maybe I'll just have a headache from the incessant drubbing on the door that's now getting louder and faster.

"Fuck," I groan as I pick myself up and stumble to the door. When I finally figure out how to turn a doorknob, I open the door to see Charlie holding my food.

Wait, what?

"Bug?"

Charlie storms in my room, leaving me confused as I look out the door, then back to her. "Are you my DoorDasher?"

She drops the food on the table and whips back to me with a look that could kill.

It's fucking hot.

"No, I'm not your DoorDasher. I just took it from him when I realized we were heading to the same room."

"Why?"

She gives me a confused look. I think. She's moving back and forth. Or I am. Maybe both. I might be dizzy, and I might be seeing double, but I can still see how beautiful she is.

Red lips. Full chest. Hips that I want to sink my fingers into. Red hair that I want to wrap around my hand.

Charlie lets out a huff. "Because you called me, dumbass."

"I did?"

"You did."

Shit...I did. In the words of the angelic Canadian songstress, it's all coming back to me now...

Calling her. Apologizing. Demanding answers. Telling her that I wanted to kiss her.

Well, shit...

"Bug..."

"Stop," she says, fixing her stance but stumbling a bit in the process. I think. The room is spinning pretty good right now. "No more of the Bug stuff."

"Ah, man," I say. "But that's my nickname for you. It's only mine. Which means I like it the best. Everyone can call you Charlie. Or Charlene. But only I call you Bug."

Her eyes narrow. "I'm not yours to give a nickname to, Simon. I never was, and I never will be."

I don't know why, but her fiery words and stare of death are

44

only firing me up more. I mean, they always did. The woman could get me going unlike any other. You'd think that would go away after fifteen years, but apparently it hasn't.

I crack my neck, suddenly feeling more sober than I have all night. "Why are you here, Charlie?"

The use of her real name throws her for a second, but she quickly recovers. She lets out a little scream and starts pulling at her hair. "I don't know!"

"You don't know?"

"You!" She points at me, her finger slightly shaking. "Why?"

Maybe I am still drunk, because now I'm confused. "Why what?"

"I was fine!" She starts pacing the room, which is only a few steps each way, before she turns around. "I was living my life. It was a fine life. I had a job. And a friend. And yeah, my job was shit most times, but whose isn't?"

"I like my job."

She snaps back around to me. "I'm talking. You shush."

"Yes, ma'am."

"As I was saying, my life was fine until one night, I was minding my business at work. Doing my thing. Making sure a dear friend had the food she wanted at the wedding of her dreams. And then I hear the one fucking word I hate more than anything in the world."

Damn, I think she's talking about me.

"Wipe that smile off your smug face," she says, her face getting as red as her hair.

"I won't."

"Why are you the way you are?"

"To drive you fucking crazy."

"Well, it's working," she says. "Because I was living a mildly decent life until you came back. Then I thought you were gone again. Cool. Great. Awesome. Then today happens, and what the fuck, Simon? Why are you back in my life?"

"Why am I back in your life?" Is she crazy? How is this on me? "Why are you back in mine?"

Apparently this was the most ridiculous question I could have asked based on how big her eyes get.

"Me? Me! You're the one who showed up at my work. Twice! You're doing this on purpose. It's just like before. It wasn't cute then, and it's not cute now."

"One, yes it is, so don't lie. Two, do you think I want this?" I cut the distance between us to just a few inches apart. "You think I want to be driven mad by you again?"

"What do you mean 'again'?"

Sure, Bug, play dumb. "Do you think I like not being able to think of anyone besides you? I already did that once, Bug. Zero out of ten. Would not recommend."

"Quit calling me Bug."

"Sorry. Can't. Won't. If you won't get out of my head, I'm going to make sure I'm living rent-free in yours."

"You think you have that much power over me?"

"You're here, aren't you?"

My words shut her up for the first time since she's walked into my room. And with the silence, I'm now just realizing how close we are.

I can feel her breath on me. Her perfume is faint but I can smell it—sweet and spicy, just like her. Her chest is heaving, and if I moved just an inch closer I'd feel it against me. Our eyes are locked in a stare so intense I don't know if a bomb exploding could break it.

I give Bug credit; she's not backing down. She's at least half a foot shorter than me, but that's not intimidating her. If anything, it's making her more determined to not break first.

And it's making me want to do something really fucking stupid.

"Why are you here, Bug?"

I watch her eyes heat underneath my gaze. "Why did you call me?"

"I asked first."

"Just answer the question, Simon."

I shake my head and step just a little closer to her. "Why. Are. You. Here."

"Because..."

She's getting flustered. Her breathing is picking up. Good. About time she knows what it feels like to have your heart beating out of your chest.

"Use your words, Bug."

She doesn't use her words. She uses her mouth.

It's on mine out of nowhere. Kissing me. Hard.

But just as fast, she's pushing me away. We're both panting for breath as it clicks to what she just did.

"You have a habit of kissing me."

My smartass comment is met with a snarl from her.

That's it, Bug. Get pissed. Kiss me again.

"I hate you."

I reach out for her hip, taking hold and pulling her into me. Her eyes dilate the second my rock-hard cock presses against her. "No you don't."

"Yes, I do."

I lean in closer, our foreheads only inches apart. "Then don't kiss me again."

Neither of us move. The only sound is the humming of the air conditioner and the panting of our breaths. Her hands are planted firmly at her sides, and it's physically killing me not to let my hand start tracing her soft curves. It's all I've been thinking about since I saw her four months ago.

But I won't. I won't make the first move. This has to be her. Prove to me she doesn't hate me as much as she thinks does.

I mean, she might. But I'll take hate over nothing any day of the week.

"I won't," she says defiantly.

"Prove it."

She shakes her head. "I've kissed you first twice now. I think it's your turn."

Normally I would be able to hold strong. To stand and die on the hill I've created. But not when Charlie's finger is running down the center of my chest, leaving goosebumps in its wake and talking to me in that taunting voice.

Oh, fuck it.

I don't hesitate. I just react. I grab her face and crash my lips to hers. She doesn't fight it. Or me. No. She welcomes me.

There is nothing romantic about this kiss. It's heated and filled with years of hate and want and frustration and lust and every other emotion that gets lumped into those categories.

And it's fucking perfect.

I can taste the faint flavor of tequila on her tongue, as I savor every second of Charlie's mouth on mine. My hands leave her face to grab onto each cheek of her luscious ass, squeezing and kneading. This must flip a switch in her, because her hands go from grabbing my shirt for dear life to ripping it open.

I nearly fucking lose it when I feel her nails clawing down my chest. They aren't long, but hit just enough that I know they're going to leave a mark.

Which is fine. I plan on leaving her ass pink and sore, so tit for tac, in my opinion.

"I hate you," she says as she pushes my shirt off me and starts working on my belt while I rip off my undershirt.

"No, you don't," I say. She whips my belt off me, and I help her by unbuttoning my pants and pushing them down. The short distance between us gives her the chance to look at my body. Suddenly the hours I've spent in the gym with Shane seem worth it.

"Like what you see?"

She looks up then back down as she shrugs.

The tell.

"No."

"Liar."

That flips the switch. "You're such an asshole."

"Tell me something I don't know."

We each step toward each other, the magnetism too powerful to fight.

"I could tell you how to make me come." Charlie's finger is toying up and down my sternum, leaving a trail of heat with every movement. "But I don't want to make this easy for you."

I don't know how I, or my cock, don't physically explode from her words.

"You think I need a cheat sheet?" I lean down closer so my mouth is right on her ear. "The question is going to be how long until you beg for me to stop."

She tilts her head up to me. "Never."

Challenge accepted.

I dive into her mouth without warning. Her hands start clawing at my bare chest, only spurring me to somehow make this kiss deeper. I drop my hands so I can bring her shirt up and quickly unsnap her bra, giving me my first view of Charlie's fucking gorgeous tits.

They're spectacular. Big. Full. More than a handful and then some. Perfect pink nipples. Thoughts of burying my face in them flash through my mind, and it's enough to make me weep.

"Are you just going to stand there and stare?"

I look up at her, fire burning through her eyes, which I'm going to guess matches mine.

"Oh, don't you worry about me," I say, starting to guide her backward to the bed. "I'm just trying to decide what's first."

She falls back to the bed, bouncing slightly as she hits the mattress, which makes her tits bounce in spectacular fashion. Our eyes are locked as I lean down, putting my hands on each side of her as I go in for a quick, but devastating, kiss. I gently push her back so I can rip her leggings and panties off.

Holy fuck... Charlie is laying back on the bed, gloriously naked. Her chest is heaving, and her legs are slightly spread, giving me just a glimpse of a wet pussy that makes me lick my lips. But then there are her tits, and being the breast man that I am, I want to just set up camp there. I feel like a kid at a candy store. I want everything and don't know what to go for first.

"Simon."

My name on her lips breaks my trance. "Yes, Bug?"

Our eyes meet, and I'm shocked she's not telling me to not call her that. Then I see the fire behind her stare, and I know the banter is over.

"Fuck me. Now."

She'll never have to ask me twice. I strip off my boxer briefs and am on her in seconds. Our lips find each other in the hardest and most intense kiss I've ever experienced. Actually, I don't know if you can qualify this as a kiss. It's more like we're trying to devour each other, each of us doing our best to not leave a scrap behind.

I quickly leave her mouth and squeeze the tits that have been taunting me. I suck on one while rolling the other nipple, making her writhe and moan beneath me. I switch sides and internally talk myself down, because I could let go right here, right now.

"Charlie..." Her name trails off as I bury my face between

50

them, feeling her soft flesh around my head. Her nails are on my back, clawing at me to go further. I'm pretty sure she's drawing blood.

Ask me if I care.

I reluctantly leave the place I'd like to live forever, not because I want to, but because if I don't feel Bug's wet pussy on my face in point-five seconds, this is going to be over before it starts.

And since I'm pretty sure this is never going to happen again, I'm making sure I take *everything* I want.

I kiss my way down her soft stomach and push open her legs as I inhale her sweet scent.

"Simon..."

Oh...begging Bug. I like this.

I slide my fingers along her slit and stop just short of her clit.

"What do we say?"

She arches her back, hoping that the movement will cause me to move. She also lets out a frustrating, albeit adorable, scream.

"Simon!"

"While I like the sound of you screaming my name, unfortunately that's not the magic word," I say. "How do we ask nicely when we want our pussy eaten?"

She tosses back and forth, but I'm unwavering at keeping my hand right where it's so close, yet so far away.

"Please, Simon...please..."

I smile. "Good girl. Now was that so hard?"

She shoots a look at me. "Simon!"

"So impatient."

With one slight movement of my fingers, rubbing her clit with just a few strokes, Charlie falls back onto the bed. As her arousal starts coating my hand, I insert two fingers, needing to feel more of her on me as she lets out her first of what I guarantee will be many screams tonight.

"That's it," I say as I position myself in between her legs. "Now, let's see what you taste like."

"What? Oh!"

Charlie doesn't make another audible sound as my tongue licks her from back to front, tasting every single inch of her perfect pussy before I start going to work. My tongue frantically flicks at her swollen clit, my fingers slipping back in so I can work her from the inside as well. I feel her hands latch onto my hair, which has been growing out a bit as of late. When she starts pulling, it only ramps up my efforts, needing more than anything right now to make her come. My cock stiffens even more, knowing in just a few seconds, I'm going to be drowning in her arousal.

"Simon!"

If this was my last minute on Earth, this would be how I'd want to go out, Bug screaming my name as she comes on my face.

I barely let her come down as I sit up and grab each of her legs. "Come here."

She shakes her head. "I don't think I can."

I lean down, our noses nearly touching, her heavy breasts grazing my chest with every breath. "Is that you begging me to stop? Right when I'm about to fuck you?"

My words hit her, and her eyes go from tired to determined in a flash.

"No."

"That's what I thought," I say, lining up my cock against her center. I don't say another word as I press into her tight—*so fucking tight!*—pussy.

I have to take a breath and wait for her to stretch around

me. I gently pump into her as she adjusts to my size, and then the gravity of the situation hits me.

Bug is here. In my bed. Well, a hotel bed. But a bed with me.

And I'm inside her. I've made her come apart, and the scent and taste of her is now forever branded on me.

I realize this is likely a one and done. Tomorrow I'm going to go back to hating her for not telling me where she went, and she's going to hate me for whatever the fuck I apparently did to her.

But for this one night, she's mine.

I feel Charlie's hips start moving, and my blood is now spiking. I collapse down onto her, letting her breasts press against my chest as I take her mouth with mine. I keep pumping into her as she lets her fingers scratch down my back, putting the perfect amount of pressure and pain.

I roll us over, bringing her on top of me. Charlie adjusts so she's now straddling me, her hands gripping onto my chest.

This might have been my best decision of the night, because the sight of Charlie riding me? Her beautiful body on display for me to watch as she uses me for her pleasure? I could die and go to heaven.

Well, I'm going to hell. I already know that. But what a way to go.

"That's it," I encourage, wanting her to fuck me just the way she wants to. "Fuck me how you want to."

And she does. She takes what she wants. A slap on her ass that echoes around the room only makes her go harder.

It's hot as fuck.

She moves her hands back to my thighs, arching back slightly as she continues to ride me like she owns me. And while this is the hottest thing I've ever been on the receiving end of, this isn't how it ends.

It's going to end with her screaming my name one more time.

I grab her hips, guiding her to go harder, wanting her to take what she needs while I also ruin her for anyone else who's going to come after me.

And I'm going to make sure I'm as burned into her brain as she is into mine.

"One more, Bug," I say, my fingers now digging into her soft flesh. "Fucking let go."

"Almost there," she says as her hands fall back to my chest. "Yes! Right there!"

I buck my hips, hitting her exactly how she wants it, and then I see it. I feel my orgasm about to bust through, and I hold it down, because like fucking hell this woman isn't about to come on my cock.

"Yes! Simon!"

Music to my ears...

Charlie falls to my chest as she comes apart on me, my bellow of release echoing hers as I spill into her.

Neither of us move for a second as I wrap my arms around her. Again, I don't know how long this is going to last—pretty sure she's going to realize quickly the position we're in—but until she does, I'm going to bask in the afterglow.

Charlie slowly starts rolling off me and I follow, wrapping my arm around her and bringing her against me.

"Hate me now?"

This makes her laugh softly. "Always."

I chuckle under my breath. "Go to sleep, Bug."

She doesn't answer, and I don't say anything else as I close my eyes and fall asleep with my Bug in my arms.

Chapter 6
Simon

I consider myself the kind of man who knows what he wants. And once that idea is in my head, nothing will stop me.

If I want a house or a piece of property? I buy it.

If I want a woman, I ask her out. Or ask her to come home. Or get stupid drunk, call her on the phone, then have hot drunk sex.

Whatever the occasion demands.

And on this glorious Saturday morning, what is calling to me is french toast from the best diner in all of Tennessee.

> Simon: I want french toast. On my way to Mona's. Who's coming with me?

> Oliver: Did you forget I'm still in London? Though french toast does sound delicious.

> Wes: Wish I could. Football practice this morning.

Simon: Fine. Shane? What about you?

Shane: Can't.

Simon: Why not?

Shane: Just can't.

Simon: If I ask you again, will you come back with a response that's three words?

Shane: Just can't fucker.

Simon: There ya go.

Simon: Wait! That means no one is going to come keep me company?

Wes: I'm sure you can eat a meal alone.

Simon: I can, but I don't want to. french toast alone is depressing.

Oliver: I'm sorry, buddy. Wish I could help.

Simon: I know. That's why you're my number one best friend.

Wes: Fucking stop it with the friend ranking bullshit.

Simon: Says the man who is dying to be in first place.

Shane: Just go get your fucking breakfast and quit texting us.

Simon: Rude. But also I will because I'm hungry. And don't ask me to bring you takeout. Because the answer will be no.

Shane: I'll make sure to cry in my pillow.

The One I Hate

. . .

Okay, apparently I'm going to Mona's alone, so I grab my keys and head out the door to make the short drive into town.

I get it. My friends have lives and responsibilities and other people who rely on them. Oliver is currently putting his heart on the line for the woman he loves. Wes is starting the second chapter of his professional, and personal, life. And Shane...well, things are a little rocky for him right now with Amelia. They've got themselves in a pickle I don't envy. It's why I didn't press him. I know my man is going through it.

Then there's me. Single Simon. No wife. No girlfriend. No kids.

Just the way I like it.

I could call one of my sisters to drive down from Nashville to eat with me, but I don't feel like a lecture. Because that's what always happens. Usually it's about how I'm turning thirty-six years old and have never been in a serious relationship.

No. That does *not* sound like the kind of Saturday I want to have.

Plus, I know where my mind will go: Charlie.

The only one I've ever wanted a serious relationship with.

The one I can still taste and feel, despite it being over a week since we were together.

The one who left before the sun came up. No note. Nothing.

Which makes sense. That's her MO, after all.

Only this time, I expected it. No way did I think I was going to wake up with her warm body next to me. I didn't expect morning cuddles or round two.

Which was disappointing. I love cuddling.

No. Fuck it. I can't let my mind go there again. I need to move on. And you know what helps with that? french toast.

"Mona!"

The gray-haired owner-slash-waitress looks up from the coffee she's pouring. Somehow she doesn't spill. "Simon Banks! How are you, sugar? How's your mom and 'em?"

"She's good. Sisters are good. Dad's good," I say as I sit down at the counter. "Now, the real question is, how's the love of my life?"

She rolls her eyes before turning to grab me a glass of water and an orange juice. "You don't need to butter me up, Simon. You know I'll throw in extra slices of french toast."

I grab her hand and bring it to my mouth for a kiss. "And that is why you're the love of my life."

"Quit pissing on my leg and tellin' me it's raining," Mona says. "Now put that flirt away and let me go get your order in."

I smile and take a sip of my orange juice. The Saturday morning crowd has thinned a bit and the lunch rush hasn't started, but there are still plenty of people here. Mona's is never empty. It's a staple in Rolling Hills. If you've ever stepped foot in this town, you've come here for a meal. And you haven't been disappointed.

Mona's is famous for breakfast, a damn good patty melt, the gossip mill, and prices so cheap they should be illegal. The interior hasn't changed in all the years I've been coming here. Yes, the pictures on the wall have evolved with different little league teams she's sponsored, but some of the originals still remain, including the one of her standing out front under her sign that still hangs today. It was taken the day she opened. You'll always find the same group of men sitting at the front table talking sports and politics. Sewing and book clubs come in and out through the week. When someone thinks of Rolling Hills, they think of Mona's.

The One I Hate

"Excuse me. Can I speak to the owner?"

The question I just overheard makes me sit a little straighter. Because who is asking that question? Mona is the owner. Everyone in town knows Mona is the owner. So who is this outsider? And why is he asking who the owner is?

I turn my head to get a look at this stranger, only to realize it's my college beer pong partner.

"I am," I say as I stand up. "To buy this place you'd need a million dollars cash, Nashville Fury season tickets, and to be able to sing 'Rocky Top' at my beck and call."

I'm greeted with a laugh and a shake of the head. "The million and the season tickets I can do. But no one wants to hear me sing. Ever."

I smile as I reach for Emmett's hand, which he returns before we pull each other into a back-slapping hug.

"What the hell are you doing here?" I sit back down as Emmett takes a seat next to me. "Mona! Get this guy a coffee."

"I was in the neighborhood," he says.

"And you didn't call me?"

"I was going to. Promise. Just had to do a little work first."

Emmett is one of the more standup guys I've met in my life. We were roommates our freshman year of college and remained friends throughout since we were both business majors. We hung out a good amount, but since he wasn't in my fraternity—and in those days I thought Greek life was *the* life— it wasn't a regular thing. But when we did, it was always a damn good time.

We lost touch after graduation—I moved back to Rolling Hills, and he got a job in Nashville. Considering I went on to get my real estate license and he started working for a development company as a property manager, our paths should have crossed more than they did. Despite living an hour apart, we rarely saw each other.

That was until about a month ago, when all my friends were out of town and I was bored. Wes suggested I give him a call, and I'm glad I did. We might not have seen each other in years, but we picked up right where we left off.

"Speaking of not calling," Emmett says. "I thought we were supposed to meet up last week when you were up my way. What happened?"

Flashes of a naked Charlie run through my mind. Because yes, I was supposed to meet Emmett, but I got drunk instead. Considering what that led to, I can't be mad about it. "Got tied up."

He snickers. "I'm sure you did."

"Enough about me. What kind of business brings you down here? There isn't a property available for sale, that I can assure you."

I know this because every time a piece of Rolling Hills real estate hits the market, I'm usually the one who buys it, or finds someone to buy it. Houses, businesses, empty land that one day I'll develop. Hell, I even have a stake in my goddaughter's lemonade stand.

"Technically you're right," he says. "But there's the vacant storefront attached to this building that my boss heard might go up for sale. I was told to come down here and talk to the owner. See if they were really thinking about it, and to see if they were interested in selling to us."

"Ha!" I laugh, shaking my head. "Good luck."

"What's that supposed to mean?"

As if on cue, Mona comes over with a pot of coffee.

"Mona, this is Emmett, my old college roommate. Emmett, meet Mona, the woman who makes the best french toast in all the land and the owner of said building."

"A pleasure."

The two extend their hands. "Pleasure is all mine, ma'am."

Oh shit, he's turning on the Southern charm. I've lived in Tennessee for nearly all of my life and to this day I've never met anyone who has as thick of a drawl as Emmett Collins.

"Well aren't you a cold drink of water on a hot summer's day," Mona says, falling for it hook, line, and sinker.

"Mona! Quit flirting with my friend! I'm sitting right here. And I'd like to point out that I professed my love for you not even ten minutes ago."

"Yeah, yeah," she says as Emmett gives her a wink. "You're old news, buddy."

Rude.

"You think you know a woman," I grumble as Mona walks away, laughing all the way to the kitchen.

"She's something," he says.

"She is. Would give the shirt off her back to anyone in need. Sponsors town events every month. Has fed every resident in this town. And hard-headed as hell."

"Why do you say that?"

"Because despite this building being empty except for this restaurant, the woman refuses to sell."

"How do you know?"

I tilt my head and raise an eyebrow. "Because I've tried. And failed. A lot."

I've lost track how many times I've asked Mona to sell to me. I've even tried to just buy the vacant parts of the building she doesn't use. And every time she has the same answer: "I'm not ready yet."

Which, I get. Fine. Mona is a special person to me, and I'd never force her into selling. It just hurts my real estate agent heart knowing there are buildings that aren't being used. That I could turn them into something that could bring money into Rolling Hills.

And into my pocket. But more for the Rolling Hills part.

"Well, then...that sounds like a challenge."

Emmett makes a show of cracking his knuckles and loosening his neck like he's going into a boxing match.

"Challenge? You think after meeting her for five seconds you can convince her to sell?"

"Hell yeah, I can," Emmett says. "Bet?"

If there is one thing about me that everyone, including Emmet, knows, is that I can't resist a bet. Of any kind. I once bet my nephew on a game of Candyland that I was planning on letting him win. "Hell yeah. Stakes?"

He looks at Mona, takes a sip of his coffee, then looks back to me. "If she says yes, I get your Alabama-Tennessee tickets next season."

I swallow the lump in my throat. He knows how much I look forward to that game every year. Which is why I throw down a doozy of a counter. "Fine. But if you lose, you have to come work for me."

His eyes blink rapidly like he's processing my words. "Excuse me?"

"You heard me." Did this idea just come to me? Yes. But it's perfect. "I have a company separate from my residential real estate that just leases commercial space. I only have a few properties and have been wanting to expand. But to do that I need a competent property manager."

"Have you even looked for a property manager?"

I shake my head. "No. Because I don't hire randoms. I hire people I know. I trust. That, my friend, is you."

I can't believe I'm just thinking of this. I need someone to run the day to day. And though Emmett and I have just reconnected, I know in my gut he's the guy I've been wanting.

I hold my hand out to Emmett as I see Mona walking toward us with our breakfast orders. "Do we have a deal?"

"Deal," he says. "That's how confident I'm feeling."

"Same my friend. Same."

"Here you go boys," Mona says. "Now, why did you tell my new boyfriend here that I was the owner?"

I hold out my hands, signaling for Emmett to shoot his shot. "The floor is yours."

"Well, Mona," Emmett begins, ramping up that charm. "I work for a development and real estate company in Nashville."

"Go on..."

"And I was just curious, knowing that you have some empty space, if you were in the market to talk about selling? The property value is at an all-time—"

"Sure."

Excuse me, what?

I look over to her and Emmett, french toast dangling from the corner of my mouth, in complete shock. I'm dumbfounded. Perplexed. Flabbergasted. Flummoxed.

"Well, great," Emmett begins before I throw my hands up.

"What!?" I yell. "You're interested? You've always told me no!"

Mona shrugs. "You haven't asked in a while. He asked."

Oh, this woman and her delicious french toast...

"Mona!"

"Simon!"

"I..." I don't know what else I was going to say, because I can't think.

No. This can't happen. She can't sell to anyone but me.

"Well, Mona, I'm so glad to hear that," Emmett goes on. "The firm I work for would love to set up a time with you to talk specifics."

Emmett starts to hand his business card over to Mona before I reach over and swat it away.

"Simon!" Mona yells. "Where are your manners? I know your mama raised you better than that."

"You can't sell to him," I say. And this has nothing to do with my tickets. Mostly. Mona's is an institution. Whoever comes in here next I want to make sure is going to spend the next fifty years here as well. It might not be the french toast I know and love—and really, what is—but I want someone in here that will be the next generation's Mona. "Sell to me."

"Simon," Emmett says. "Our firm is ready to make a sizable offer."

"What's the offer?" I say. My tone has lost any hint of joking. I want this property. And I want it today.

"It's valued at eight-hundred-and-seventy-five thousand," he says.

"Well, hot damn," Mona exclaims. "Do you know how many cruises I can go on with that kind of money?"

"I'll give you a million. Cash."

The restaurant goes silent. I'm sure it's a coincidence, but I feel like everyone is staring. I can't even hear the telltale sound of the grill sizzling with bacon.

"Simon. You know it's not worth—"

"Don't 'Simon' me Emmett," I say, turning my focus to Mona. "If you're truly thinking about selling, Mona, sell it to me. Don't sell to some random firm in Nashville that will make it into a freaking chain coffee shop."

She looks over to Emmett, who shrugs his shoulders. "He's right."

"See? Sell to me. I'll make sure the next tenant will keep this as a restaurant. I mean, I'll need my french toast fix from someone. Please Mona, don't sell to them. Keep it in the Rolling Hills family. Please...pretty please...."

I've never in my years as a real estate agent begged for a sale. I've never batted my eyelashes or given a puppy-dog face.

Yet here I am, pouting and pleading like I'm asking my mom for a cookie.

"Fine," Mona says, though it's not enthusiastically. She does realize I'm about to give her a million dollars in actual cash, doesn't she? "I'll sell to you. But under one condition."

"Anything."

"Let me meet whoever decides to lease this," she says. "It has taken me years to realize that it's time for me to step back. This is my baby, Simon. My literal life. I know I can't control or have a say as to who's coming in here, but I want to know my baby is in good hands."

I don't know why, and it definitely wasn't on purpose, but in this moment a thought of Bug flashes in my mind. Fuck...I don't want to think about her. But I couldn't push this image out of my brain if I wanted to.

Her in an apron, her full hips and chest rounding out the image. Her hair up on the top of her head. Her smile lighting up this restaurant as she interacts with customers. Me sitting right here at this very place at the counter, watching her with pride as she makes this place her own.

Maybe sneaking into the back for a quickie...

I nod to Mona, which also brings me out of the fantasy world. "Absolutely, Mona."

"We'll find a good tenant, I promise."

The two of us snap our heads to Emmett, who I'm pretty sure just said that *we'd* find a good tenant. As in plural. As in we.

"You're in?"

Emmett lets out a sigh. "Yeah. I'm in. I couldn't resist the puppy-dog eyes either."

"Well, isn't this beautiful," Mona says, clapping her hands in excitement. "Now you two boys get to finding someone to take this place. I have a cruise to book."

Mona walks away, a million-dollar pep in her step, as Emmett and I clink glasses to a deal sealed.

"Well, isn't this day turning up," I say. "Nothing like making a big sale and starting a new partnership. And winning a bet. Great day."

"Whoa!" Emmett says. "Technically she agreed to sell to me first. I win."

"Fine," I groan. "Double or nothing?"

Emmett shakes his head. "Hell no. Plus, my next bet is for money, and you, my friend, owe that woman a million. And I haven't told you my salary requirements yet."

I laugh as we continue to eat our breakfast. Man, I didn't see this day going like this, but I can't be mad. I got french toast, a business partner, my daily memory of a naked Charlie, and a piece of property I've been eyeing for years.

Not bad for a day's work.

Chapter 7
Charlie

I have never needed a day off more in my life.

Things have been nothing short of chaotic over the past three weeks, both personally and professionally.

Asparagus Gate was the least of the problems I had to deal with on the job front. Two line cooks quit when Billy tried to teach them how to "properly" cook chicken. Billy also forgot to order butter. It made my life quite hard, but I think it broke Mellie. She was so mad she swore.

And I'm not talking a little one. She dropped the big one.

Then there was the icing on the wedding cake when a bridezilla wanted me to guarantee that no one working her big day was an Aries. She made me pinky promise. Which I did. All while internally laughing my ass off with my April thirteenth birthday.

But in one hour and forty-two minutes, all of that is going to be in the rearview. I'm away from the restaurant for the next two days, and I'm already imagining the glorious things I'm going to do in the next forty-eight hours.

Nap. Eat food I didn't cook. Binge watch the newest cult documentary. Nap.

I'm going to nap so damn hard.

Things I'm not going to do: Answer calls from the restaurant. Put on a bra. And the biggest thing on the do-not-do list: Think about Simon Banks.

Or his tongue.

Or his penis.

His perfect fucking penis.

Because of course it was perfect. A man like Simon Banks, who gets everything he wants in life, wasn't going to be randomly cursed with a small, crooked dick. No, he was blessed with a cock that should be sculpted and put in the Louvre for all to admire.

Because life isn't fair.

I hate it. And him. And I hate that if I close my eyes, I can see him doing all the delicious things to my body that I'll deny he did until my dying day.

Ugh...why did I sleep with him? Why did I go to his hotel room? What did I think was actually going to happen? That we were going to talk like rational humans and leave with an agreement to never cross paths again?

Stupid tequila. It's all Jose's fault.

The worst part of all? Is that when I woke up in the middle of the night, my mind delirious and my body sore and sated, I just let myself lay there against him. His arm was draped over me and for a second I let myself bask in his touch.

Because even though I hate Simon, at one point in my life I thought he was it. The one who was different. The one who was going to prove that good men did exist.

Then I remember what he did and why I've cursed his name for years. That's when I wiggled out of his hold, got dressed, and left in the middle of the night.

The One I Hate

This is so damn frustrating. I successfully avoided him for fifteen years. Now he crosses my mind multiple times a day. Which is so Simon. He crawls his way into your life, and then when you're not expecting it, BAM! He fucks your world up.

Oh, and gives you trust issues that you should probably see a therapist about.

"Welcome to Perks. What can I get you?"

The guy standing in front of the counter slowly turns around, and as soon as I see who it is, my blood heats.

Simon Banks. Rich boy. Dean's list. Hot, but he knows it. Dressed head to toe in designer labels. The guy everyone on campus knows. Perfectly styled hair and a smile he thinks works on every woman he encounters. I mean, I get why he thinks it works. I've watched him flirt with girls in our business class, and I roll my eyes every time they fall for his lines.

"Well, hello there, gorgeous. I was going to say a coffee, but maybe my answer should be you."

Barf.

I don't even try to hold my eye roll, which only makes Simon's smug smirk widen.

"I meant drink. What do you want to drink?"

Simon leans down on the counter so his elbows are resting, but it also simultaneously shows off his biceps. Which aren't that impressive.

"What else is on the menu? Maybe your phone number?"

Who does this guy think he is? A cocky asshole, that's who. Because I believe that there are multiple universes and timelines happening at once, and in none of those is the very hot, rich boy asking out the chubby, poor girl from the outskirts of Knoxville.

"I'm not giving you my phone number, Simon. Either order or get out of line."

Shit. I said his name. I could've convinced myself I didn't, until I see his face light up with the recognition.

"You know my name?"

Ugh! Well, no sense in lying. "We're in Business Ethics together."

"Yes!" He slams his fist down on the counter in exclamation. "I knew you looked familiar."

"No, you didn't," I say. "Now, what do you want to order?"

"Your name. Your number. And I guess a coffee."

"I don't even want to give you the coffee."

He flashes that smile I've seen him use one too many times. "Oh, come on. Tell me your name at least. I want to say hi to you in class Friday, and I can't just yell, "Hi, Bug!"

"Bug?"

He points to the headband that I'm wearing, which happens to be red with ladybugs printed on it. "Yes. Bug. Until you tell me your name, that's what you'll be called."

"Please don't."

"Come on, Bug. Don't be like that. I have a feeling this is the start of a beautiful friendship."

"I have a feeling I want to slap you."

He gives me a wink. "That's part of my charm."

"Stop it!" I scold myself, giving my head a shake. No. No more Simon thoughts. I need to keep things in focus: Surviving work and saving for my restaurant.

That's what's important. That needs to remain the focus. Not Simon and his stupid smirk and his stupid mouth and his stupid penis.

I start furiously cleaning my prep station, needing more than ever to get the hell out of here, when my phone rings with a FaceTime call. Normally, we don't answer calls in the kitchen, but I'm the only one here, and frankly, I don't give a fuck. Especially when I see that it's my favorite Nashville event planner.

"Whitley! To what do I owe the honor? Do we have an appointment I forgot about?"

I just saw Whitley a few days ago, and she didn't mention anything about seeing me later in the week, so I don't think I forgot anything. Then again, after the past few weeks, I'm surprised I remembered to put on deodorant today.

Wait, did I? I give my pit a subtle sniff.

"No girl, no appointment. Yet."

"Yet?"

"What are you doing tomorrow morning? Say, eight o'clock?"

Whitley's smile is taking up her entire face, and I think she's bouncing in her seat. The woman is always in a good mood—she once told me it was part of her pageant training—but right now I'm pretty sure a rainbow is coming out of her ass. So this is over the top, even for her.

"Why are you so excited?"

"Girl, I think I found you a restaurant."

I blink a few times, trying to decide whether I heard her right. "You found me a restaurant?"

She nods frantically. "Yup! It's perfect, and you need to come see it. Immediately."

My face drops, because I've been through this before. There's always a "perfect" place, but there's always something that makes it not perfect for me. And I'm not talking about a little makeover or some new plates. I'm talking big things—like affordability. Or walls collapsing in.

"Don't tease me," I say. "That's not nice, and you know it."

She shakes her head. "No. I swear. It's perfect. It's an already established restaurant that's been open for like forty-some years. It's an institution, but the owner is retiring. The company that bought it just wants to lease the space, but wants someone to come in and make it a restaurant of their own."

I don't say anything. I don't breathe as I wait for the other shoe to drop. Because another shoe always drops.

"How do you know this?"

"The owner told me," she says. "She said it was a secret, no one even knows she's sold, but she was wondering if I knew of anyone who would be interested. Of course I thought of you first."

"Thank you," I say. "But I don't know. I haven't even begun to save enough to really be ready."

"No! That's the best part. The restaurant comes fully equipped. She's leaving everything. Yes, you might want to change the interior, but when you don't have to buy the big stuff, everything else is more manageable. And you know the rent in Rolling Hills has to be much cheaper than Nashville. It's perfect. Please come look at it. Pretty please?"

And there's the shoe that fell from the sky straight onto my head.

Rolling Hills.

Where Simon is. Well, it's where I assume he is considering the two times I've seen him it's been with people who live in Rolling Hills.

I knew nothing was perfect.

"Yes Whitley, it does sound great. But I don't think—"

"Charlie, please." Her eyes turn pleading. "Just come look at it. I know how much you hate things at Napoli's, and I think this would be great. Please? Just come and look to say you did."

"I can't."

"And why not?"

"Because—" I stop before I say anymore. She doesn't know about my history with Simon. Yes, it was at her wedding when I

72

saw him for the first time in years. But I wasn't about to stop her in the middle of the happiest day of her life to explain why I had to suddenly leave. After that, I never thought I'd see him again, so why tell her?

And as for our...encounter...last week? No one knows about that. Not even Mellie knows everything that happened.

No. I can't go to Rolling Hills, even to look. I can't imagine having to see Simon every day. Especially now that I know the man has a master's degree in orgasms and a PhD in pussy licking.

"I just can't."

"I don't accept that."

"Excuse me?"

"You heard me," Whitley says, her demeanor now a little tougher. It's the tone she uses when she needs to get vendors in line. "I'm not asking you to sign a lease. Or put down first month's rent. Just come and look. Actually, come down tonight so you don't have to deal with morning Nashville traffic. We can hang out, which we never get to do. I have an impromptu engagement party for my sister-in-law, but the more the merrier."

A party Simon will definitely be at since I've met the fiancé of her sister-in-law, and I know they're friends.

"I'm not going to go to a party of strangers."

"Fine," she groans. "But please come down and look. This place means a lot to this town. I know myself, my husband, and every other resident of Rolling Hills would feel much better knowing that the person who moved into this place wasn't only going to make it theirs, but also make it part of the community. Somewhere people can go for a treat for their kids. An affordable family night out. Breakfast with friends on weekends. A place for kids to study while grabbing a burger. Maybe where a book club comes to meet up."

I start to tear up as Whitley describes my exact vision. I told her that once, and now she's using my own words against me.

How dare she.

"And you think my restaurant fits that bill?"

"You're the only one."

This woman is good. Also, like she said, I don't have to sign anything. And there has to be something wrong with it. That will be my out, and I can put this option, and Rolling Hills, behind me.

"Fine," I groan. "But no promises."

I don't know if Whitley heard that over the squeals she's making on the other end of the call.

"Whitley? Did you hear me? No promises."

"Sure, sure," she says. "Whatever you say."

Chapter 8
Simon

There are some places in the world that just make me feel at peace.

The steam room at the gym.

A golf course in the morning.

A quiet cigar lounge with a good glass of scotch.

And Wes Taylor's backyard.

I don't know what my third-ranking best friend did back here, but it's the perfect place for any occasion. Between the huge swimming pool, two fire pits, a lanai with plenty of seating, and a hot tub, the man has created a backyard oasis. So whether it's a birthday party for his seven-year-old daughter Magnolia, also known as my goddaughter, or tonight when he's hosting an impromptu un-engagement party with our closest friends and family, it works.

If I'm here, that means I'm with my friends, who are like my family. Don't get me wrong, I have a wonderful family. Loving and supportive parents. Sisters who might be a pain in the ass but I love them fiercely. But when it comes to the group of friends who have become my family, I'll lie, steal, and murder for them. No questions asked. They helped me become the man I am today. I'll do anything for them.

Except heavy lifting or yard work. I can; I just don't want to.

Being here tonight, surrounded by my friends and our extended families, is the perfect night and exactly what I need. I've been feeling off the past few weeks. And it doesn't take much to figure out when my funk started.

Charlie fucking Bennett. What power does this woman have over me that she makes it impossible for me to function? Not even buying Mona's has lifted my mood. And buying a piece of property *always* lifts my spirits.

"Hey, man." I feel the pat on my shoulder as Shane comes up next to me, handing me a drink.

"If it isn't the man of the night," I say, tapping my beer to his. "It all worked out."

Shane nods, and I can feel the relief wafting from his body. "It did."

Things with Shane and Amelia had been touch and go for weeks since the taste testing. We thought for a minute they were done for. Nevertheless, with the help of me and the guys, everything worked out. And I say me specifically because it took place at my childhood home, which I had no idea had a significance for the two of them. Turns out I missed a lot of signals about Shane and Amelia over the years.

"So, we're all here," Betsy says as we all take a seat around the fire pit. "And everyone knows everything, right? No other surprises? Things we forgot to mention?"

We all laugh because it's a valid question. Things over the past few months have been actual insanity. And in all that's happened, between Izzy and Oliver, as well as Shane and Amelia, I haven't told anyone that I've bought Mona's.

Not that I meant to hide it from them—and the news of my

recent purchase would absolutely shock them. I just didn't think it was the appropriate time.

Look at me, being considerate and shit.

Plus, Mona and I are keeping this under wraps until we have a new tenant. People don't even know she's selling. Which is shocking considering the Rolling Hills gossip mill could put TMZ out of business. Emmett lined up some showings over the next few days, and Mona agreed to close for "necessary repairs." She told me she was even going to close the curtains so no one could spy.

Smart woman.

So despite me having news that would fit along with Betsy's question, I choose to keep this to myself. I'll tell them when the time is right. Plus, tonight is about Shane and Amelia. Despite what my friends think, I don't steal thunder.

I just borrow it from time to time.

"All good here," Wes says. "Football is good. Kids are good. We're good. Everything is good."

"You know about us," Oliver says, wrapping his arm around Izzy, who got back from London this morning. I'm just about to chime in when Oliver continues, "She's back where she belongs. And, we have an announcement."

"You're already engaged," I say. "And married. You can't keep doing this."

This gets a laugh from the group, even Izzy. I knew I liked her from the second Oliver introduced her to us.

"Shut your face," Oliver says to me. "What I was going to say is that we're going to hold a reception, and a vow renewal, hopefully next month. Of course, I want everyone to be a part of it."

"Hell, yeah!" I say. I might now be the lone single guy in the group, but I love a wedding. "I want to DJ."

Everyone sends me confused looks. Which I get. How

many real estate agents do you know that moonlight as a DJ? And in their defense, I don't. It just seems fun. I have great taste in music, and I'm the best dancer in the group. Obviously, this should be my wedding duty.

"You want to DJ? You can DJ?" Oliver asks.

I shrug. "How hard can it be?"

The only reaction I get from my friends are them shaking their heads and muttering things like "you're ridiculous." Which I'm used to. In this friend group, that's my role.

I'm the outlandish one. Outgoing. I say what's on my mind, and I'm blunt to a fault. I'm the life of the party and the one to likely stir up trouble.

I take a second to look around the fire pit, and you don't need to be a genius, mathematician, or a Keebler elf to realize I'm the only one not in a relationship. And it's not because of the seating arrangements. Take Wes and Betsy. They're sitting across from each other, but no one would doubt that they're together simply based on the looks they share. Izzy is sitting on Oliver's lap, and he refuses to let her go. Amelia has her head on Shane's shoulder, her arms wrapped around his.

For some, this might give them pause or make them wonder if it's time to settle down in their lives. But not me.

I'm Simon Banks. King of the casual relationship.

Love is great and all, but I've never understood why people need it to feel complete. I have everything I need. Friends. Family. A job that I'm excited to go to everyday that also makes me a shit-ton of money. More money than I will ever spend on myself. Which lets me spoil the people I love. But hey, that's my role. The fun uncle. The godfather. The wingman. It's who I am and what I'm good at. So yes, I wake up alone—and most of the time go to sleep alone—but I don't feel like I'm missing out on anything. Life is good.

Plus, the only woman who I've ever even considered dating

seriously has now walked out of my life *twice* after moments that I thought could change everything. So yeah, I'm good on the whole dating thing.

Actually no. I'm not. Well, not the dating thing. But Charlie. Twice now she's ran. I figured she was going to this time—I expected it—but a little part of me hoped she wouldn't. I know we were drunk, so our inhibitions were down, but she'd be a liar if she says she didn't feel the chemistry that ran through us that night.

But, just like I expected, I woke up the next day exhausted, sad, and pissed. It was pretty reminiscent of when she left all those years ago.

Why does she keep running? Why does she hate me? No, I don't like her, but that's because she doesn't like me. And won't tell me what the hell I did. She's driven me fucking mad over the years, and for the life of me I don't know what I did to make her detest me so much.

I just want answers. I don't think that's too much to ask for.

"Actually!" Izzy chimes in. "Amelia or Betsy, I need to talk to Whitley. I'd love to hire her to put the reception together for me."

"Easy enough," Amelia says, taking a quick glance toward the gate. "She should be here any minute now. A friend of hers was coming into town tonight because she was going to look at a piece of property tomorrow. Oh, I remember now! Betsy, it was the caterer from her wedding. You remember her, right? I think her name is Charlie."

What did she say?

I try not to react, but I feel my body stiffen just hearing her name. I think I've quit breathing.

She's coming to look at property? What kind of property? A restaurant maybe? Is it a coincidence that tomorrow is the first day we're showing the restaurant? Is she coming to look at it? She can't be. But she could... Fuck, I don't know. Emmett has been the one to line up the showings, so I have no clue who is coming in. He just told me "a few."

Is Charlie one of the few?

"Simon?" Amelia asks. "Is everything okay?"

"Yup." Apparently I didn't say "yup" right because now I have six sets of eyes staring at me.

"Simon," Shane says, leaning a little closer. He's staring me down, and I know this look. It's the he-knows-I'm-full-of-shit look. Fuck...this man knows me too well. "Anything you want to share with the class?"

"Nope."

"Nothing at all?"

Did I stutter? "I said no."

"So if I say the word 'bug' it isn't going to make you irrationally angry?"

I feel my blood start to boil as he says her nickname. The nickname only I use.

A hush falls over our circle. No one is breathing. No one has blinked as they stare at me, waiting for my response.

What do I say? What can I say? Because I've never told anyone about her. Not even Oliver, who came to Knoxville to visit me on numerous occasions in college. I sure as hell didn't tell them about our night together.

She's my secret. My infatuation. The girl I can't get out of my head. The one who drove, and is driving, me crazy. The one who saw through my bullshit.

The one who left without a word. Twice.

The one who to this day is making me hate that I want her and hate that I can't get her out of my head.

My Bug.

"Simon?" Amelia puts her hand on my knee as her soft tone comes through. "Everything okay?"

80

"Fuck this!"

I don't mean to make a dramatic exit, but I do as I shoot up from my chair and storm across Wes's backyard. I don't say bye to anyone as I race to my car and slam the door shut. Without thinking, I peel out of the driveway.

What the fuck? She's here? In Rolling Hills? I start to turn toward Whitley's house but I stop myself. That's insane behavior. Except I'm feeling a little insane right now. That's how she makes me feel. Crazy and insane and impulsive.

Well, more than normal.

I start driving aimlessly and use the voice command to call Emmett. Because I need answers, and he has at least some of them.

"Hey, man."

"Who are you showing the restaurant to tomorrow?'

"Nice to talk to you too," he says. "My night is going fine, by the way."

"Great. Now answer me."

"I thought you didn't care to know?"

"Well, now I want to."

"Sheesh, chill out," he says. "My first showing is at eight in the morning. A woman named Whitley Evans set up the showing, but she told me she was doing it for a friend who would be the tenant."

"What's that person's name?"

I hold my breath as I wait for the two words I know he's about to say.

"Charlie Bennett."

I almost rip the steering wheel off the column as I turn onto an empty side road. I don't even bother throwing on my flashers. Hell, I barely remember to put the car in park. All I know is that in this moment I can't drive. I can barely think.

She's here.

"I'm going to go out on a limb and say that you know her?"

I try my best to calm down so I can figure out how I want to explain this to Emmett. I know I need to tell him something, but I don't want to tell him everything. Not yet. Not until I know if she's here for good.

No. Not if. When.

Because she's going to be. I'm going to make sure of it.

"She went to college with us."

"Really? I don't remember the name."

"She was in a few of my business classes. And she worked at the coffee shop."

"Don't you hate coffee?"

"I do, but that's beside the point," I say. "I need you to make this happen, Emmett."

"I mean, I figured you wanted it rented quickly," he says. "And I have a lot—"

"No. You don't understand. It needs to be her. It *has* to be her. Only her."

I pictured Charlie the day I was at Mona's and now that picture is even more clear. I can see her smiling and serving the people of Rolling Hills. I can hear her snark and wit come through as she trades barbs with the old men. I can picture it all so clearly.

This is how it's supposed to be. She's meant to be here.

And bonus? I can get my answers. Even if it comes with the punishment of knowing what's underneath her apron.

I'll deal. It's worth it to finally have my answers.

"Can I ask why?" Emmett asks.

"Not yet," I say. The less he knows going into this the better. "Just make her an offer she can't refuse. I don't care if she can only afford a dollar. Then that's her rent."

"Simon, you can't be serious."

"As a heart attack. Make this happen for me, Emmett. It has to be Charlie. Whatever she needs, make it happen."

I know the rent we were going to charge is probably too high. It's fair for the market, but unless things have changed over the years, Charlie was always hard pressed when it came to money. And sensitive about it. She never said it directly, but I could tell that was the case. She worked her ass off every minute she wasn't in class. She didn't talk about her family much, but I never got the impression she could ask for help.

If that's still the case, I know for a fact the four-thousand-dollars-a-month price tag I put on it would be too much. And like hell am I going to let a few bucks get in the way of giving her this.

While also getting something for me in return.

"Fine," he says as I let out a breath. "But under one condition."

"Name it."

"That if, and I'll repeat if, she signs, you need to tell me everything."

"I promise. You'll get your answers when you make it happen. Oh, and one more thing."

"Can't wait."

"Under no circumstance can she know that I'll be the landlord. She can't know anything about me."

"Simon."

"Emmett."

"What the fuck are you getting me into?"

"Don't you worry about it."

"That's all I'm going to do."

"It's nothing illegal, if that makes you feel better."

"Only slightly."

"Just make this happen and call me after it does."

I end the call and sit back, suddenly feeling better than I have in weeks.

Charlie is here. And soon she's going to be here all the time.

Which, I know how that sounds. I hear it in my head. It's insane and stalkerish and downright desperate.

But desperate times call for desperate measures.

And Charlie Bennett has made me a desperate man.

Chapter 9
Charlie

"Are you okay?"

Whitley's words take me by surprise as we walk down the sidewalk of Rolling Hills. Probably because I wasn't paying attention to where I was going and almost ran into a mailbox. And not a small one on a post. A big-ass blue one. That's what happens when you're looking over your shoulder with every step to make sure you don't see the man that makes you want to punch a wall.

I hate that he makes me feel like this. Even without the incident, I think I'd still be reacting this way when it comes to Simon. Fifteen years later and I'm still that emotional girl running from his house on the campus of the University of Tennessee with tears streaming down my face and a broken heart.

I don't want to be her. I want to get over it. It was one kiss, and one subsequent heartbreak, over a decade ago. And an ill-fated drunken sexual encounter. I'm sure that if I could afford therapy, I'd be told to make amends and get over it.

I wish I could. But I can't. He brings out something in me that makes me want to scream. Or run. Or cry. Or kiss him.

Usually all of the above.

"Yeah. I'm fine." I lie.

Why am I even here? If just the thought of seeing Simon makes my body stand on high alert, then I definitely can't run a restaurant, or live, here. I don't think they make stress medication strong enough for that.

This was a bad idea. I should have held my ground and told Whitley no. I should have stayed in Nashville and enjoyed my day off. But no, here I am, bright and early in the morning looking at a restaurant that I'm determined to find inadequate.

Yet, as we get closer to the diner, only one word is popping into my head.

Perfect.

Because of course it is.

A cute brick exterior in the center of a seemingly small town. Windows that let you see inside, but it somehow doesn't feel like it's intrusive. A neighboring parking lot which allows for plenty of patrons. And a sign proudly displayed from the top of the entry that says "Mona's."

Fuck.

I love it.

And that name...the universe couldn't give me a clearer sign. My tears start to well, but I force them back.

Because this is very inconvenient for me. I'm supposed to be finding everything wrong with this place, not falling in love with it.

"This is so exciting!" Whitley squeals as she takes my hand and pulls me toward the door. As we enter, my heart swells.

It's even more perfect. I slowly start walking through the tables set up around the center of the restaurant, booths next to me lining the walls. It's slightly dated, and every single surface is the same buttery yellow, but at the same time that gives it some charm. I'd probably replace the seating fixtures that have seen better days and maybe give the walls a fresh coat of paint that isn't the color of the sun, but otherwise, it works perfectly. It's the size I always imagined having. There's a breakfast counter beside a glass case where Mellie can display her desserts. It's next to a cash register that I'm pretty sure was made in the seventies.

It's annoyingly perfect. Like so perfect that I'm trying to figure out how to design the sign at the front of the building that says "Welcome all. Except for Simon Banks. You know what you did."

"Hello, ladies." My eyes find a giant of a man walking out of the kitchen. "I'm Emmett, the property manager. You must be Whitley and Charlie."

I was expecting to see a restaurant today. I was expecting to have to tell the realtor that I couldn't take it. I wasn't expecting to have to say that to a six-foot-five hunk of a man with perfectly fitting Wranglers and a white T-shirt.

Is this what men in Rolling Hills look like? Because if so, Simon Banks be damned, I'm about to have a new zip code.

"Nice to meet you, Emmett," I say as we shake hands. I know I've never met this man, but for some reason I feel like I've seen him before. "I'm Charlie. Are you the tour guide?"

He shakes his head with a pleasant smile. "I can be if you want. But you seem like a very capable person, so look around all you'd like. Once you've taken the tour, I'll be out here waiting, and we can go over specifics and any questions you have."

"Thanks," I say as Whitley and I go into the kitchen. As soon as the door swings shut, I grab Whitley and turn her to me. "Holy shit! Why didn't you tell me Rolling Hills men were hot?"

Whitley shakes her head. "They are, but he's not one of them."

"Really?"

"Yeah. He must work for whoever bought this place. I know everyone in Rolling Hills. And that guy definitely doesn't live here."

Weird. "So did someone from outside of Rolling Hills buy this place?"

"I honestly don't know," she says as she pulls open the door to the walk-in cooler. "Mona was tight-lipped about the buyer and asked me to keep quiet that she was selling. People don't even know this place is for sale. She gave me Emmett's number and we set up the showing. This has all been weird if you ask me. Usually something like Mona's selling would be all over the Rolling Hills gossip train. But no one knows anything."

Interesting. Not that it matters to me. As long as Emmett is easy to work with and there aren't a million stipulations in the rental agreement, it doesn't matter who owns this place.

Wait, what am I saying? I'm not leasing this. I'm not signing anything. This isn't the beginning of my dream coming true. Because there's no way I can afford this. I guarantee that Emmett is about to pop my fantasy balloon when he tells me what the rent is. Hell, I should stop daydreaming now and ask him how much, so I can return to reality.

The kitchen equipment from first glance is in working order. Maybe a little on the dated side, but would still run without a problem. It has everything I need for my menu, including ovens and a station for Mellie to make all the desserts and pastries she wants. If I close my eyes, I can picture myself cooking back here.

Mellie is across from me, flour all over her, as she bakes. Servers are coming in and out shouting orders. Line cooks are cracking jokes as they bring my creations to life.

Fuck my life...

"Oh my gosh, I can't wait for you to be here!" Whitley gushes as we exit the kitchen, her hands clapping in excitement.

"Don't get your hopes up," I say to her and myself. I need to stay rational and focused. I can't let a cute layout, a name sent from heaven, and a perfect kitchen blind me to the fact that it's probably too expensive for me.

Plus, there's my brother and niece to think about. I can't just ask them to up and move down here with me.

There's also the whole "Simon could walk in at any moment" issue.

Those are all plenty of good reasons to say thanks but no thanks.

"So what do we think?" Emmett asks as we approach his table.

"She'll take it!" Whitley says.

I give Whitley a side-eye as we each take a seat. "I do love it. But that is how I know something is wrong."

"Excuse me?"

"I'm a glass-half-empty kinda gal, Emmett. So let me explain to you what we have here."

This makes him smile as he leans back into his chair. "I'm all ears."

"This is a perfect restaurant in a seemingly perfect town, which means you're going to come back to me with a price I can only afford if I sell pictures of my feet, which, unfortunately, just aren't that pretty. So lay it on me, Emmett. What's the damage so I can politely tell you no. Because unless this place comes in at thirty-five hundred dollars a month, or magically less, then let's both save our breath and end this charade."

Emmett starts laughing, which is one of two responses I planned on getting. My self-deprecating humor usually is met with chuckles or stares. I'm glad Emmett is in the laughing column. He seems like a guy I could have a beer with, or wouldn't mind serving him lunch each day at the counter as we chit-chat about the mundane.

"You're one of a kind, aren't you?"

"I've been told something like that."

We share a friendly smile, but that's all it is. Friendly. Genuine. Nothing flirtatious. Which makes sense and what I've come to expect. This man is in the top five of hottest men I've met in real life. I'm a very curvy, plus-sized woman who puts on makeup once a month and box dyes her hair when she's bored. Men like Emmett don't go for girls like me unless they want one thing. At least, that's been my experience.

Or there are men like Simon, who pretend to be interested when you're really just a conquest.

And sometimes you're drunk enough to let them win.

I shake my head too quickly as I wait for Emmett to respond. Which he hasn't yet. He's just sitting back and smiling.

"Was I so off on the price that you're trying to figure out how to gently let me down? Which I appreciate. Usually I get the 'we'd love to lease to you but...'"

He smiles again and closes the folder. "It's yours."

I open my mouth to tell him that I was right about being out of my financial range when I realize he said it was mine.

It's mine?

"Excuse me, can you repeat that?"

"He says it's yours!" Whitley yells as she starts shaking me in excitement. "I knew this was perfect!"

"Whoa..." I throw my hands up and shake my head. "I feel like I missed about sixteen steps here."

Emmett laughs. "I can see that. Let's talk specifics."

He talks about a two-year lease with my thirty-five-

90

hundred-dollar rent paid monthly. He slides to me the stipulations and legalities in a manila folder, but I'll have to go back and read those later. Right now I can't focus. This is too good to be true.

Which means it likely is. I'm missing something.

"So what do you say?" Emmett asks. "Want to open your restaurant?"

My mind is racing, and I don't know what to say. My gut is telling me to say yes because this has to be a dream and I'm scared I'm going to wake up. Or that Emmett is drunk at eight in the morning and he doesn't know what he's agreeing to.

But the other part of me, the responsible part of me, is telling me to say no. This is crazy. I know what my budget is, and that thirty-five hundred was what I could afford if I only ate Ramen for a year and slept in my office. I still need a place to live, and I won't have Connor to help me with rent. He has a steady job in Nashville, and I can't ask him to give that up.

Plus, can I move to a town where I know one person? Okay, two people, but one of those people I hope falls in a sewer.

No. I can't do this. Even if it feels like I'm throwing away my only chance at making my dreams come true.

"I appreciate this, Emmett. I really do. And you seem like a great guy..."

"Why do I feel like you're breaking up with me?"

I chuckle. That would be a first in the history of my lifetime. "Seriously, I appreciate you saying that. About the price, that is. But I threw that number out almost jokingly. I really can't afford that. I mean, I can, but it's my max budget for a space *and* somewhere to live. It would be straining me to a point where I wouldn't feel comfortable starting a business and a new life. I hope you can understand."

I let out a breath. There. All said out loud. I've officially let

Emmett, and Whitley, down easy. All that's left is for me to now feel horrible about saying no to the perfect place.

"Nope! I refuse to accept this," Whitley says. "You're going to move in with me. I'll pay half the rent here. Whatever you need."

I shoot her a look. "Whitley. I can't move in with you. And you aren't paying any of my rent."

"Why? I have the money. And we have space. And it wouldn't be forever. Just for a few months until the restaurant is up and running and you're a little more liquid with money."

"Thank you, but I can't ask you to do either of those things," I say.

"You didn't ask. I volunteered," she said. "I refuse for that to be the reason you don't open your restaurant."

It's not the only reason...

"I appreciate you." I put my hand on top of hers. "But I don't want a handout. I don't like feeling like I'm accepting charity."

"What if an apartment was included?"

Whitley and I both turn to look at Emmett. "Excuse me?"

"There are vacant apartments upstairs," Emmett says. "The owner doesn't have any immediate plans for them."

"I couldn't—"

"You could," he replies. "The owner gave me a base price on what he would accept. Thirty-five hundred was it. So consider it done."

"I—" I lose my words. Then again, that implies that I had words. Because I don't. This is the perfect restaurant and an apartment for a price I can now afford when they are together? It's a dream come true.

"What's the catch?"

"No catch," he says.

"I don't live in a world where there aren't catches."

"Welcome to Rolling Hills, the land of no catches."

"And you're sure the owner won't mind about the apartment?"

Emmett shakes his head. "I have a feeling the owner will be more than happy to let you stay there."

"I—" I can't form words. I also think I'm about to start crying. "Can I think it over?"

Emmett nods. "Take the day. Hell, take a few days. I'll cancel the other showings."

"You don't have to do that. People might come in with a higher—"

"It's fine," he cuts me off. "This place is meant to be yours. I can tell. And if the price is too high, let me know before saying no. I have my ways with the owner. I bet I can get him to budge. He tries to be a hard ass—but he's a softie."

A tear escapes as I shake Emmett's hand before leaving the restaurant.

As I step into the morning sun, letting the heat hit my face, I realize the town is a little more alive. Cars are driving past. People are strolling the sidewalks in conversation. The late August air of Tennessee is hitting me with a warmth I feel like I don't get in Nashville. I close my eyes and let the undeniable energy fuse through me. And as I stand here, taking it all in, I can't help but feel like this is where I belong.

Even if he's here.

Chapter 10
Charlie

"**B**ug! Wait!"

I hear Simon's voice behind me as I do my best to quickly exit our business ethics class.

It's been a month since we officially met. A month since he started sitting by me. And each day we have class, he asks me my name. And every day I refuse to tell him.

It helps that we have an old school professor who insists on calling us by formal names such as "Miss Bennett" and "Mr. Banks." When he calls on me, it's for an answer. When he calls on Simon it's to get him to quit distracting the class.

Though I must admit that's hard. Simon Banks is a distraction in every sense of the word.

"Why do you run out on me every day?"

"Why do you insist on stalking me every day?"

He gasps and gently grabs onto my arm to stop me. "Me? Stalking? Bug...I would never."

The dramatics in his voice make me simultaneously laugh and roll my eyes.

"Simon, what do you want?"

His smirk that runs on the border of cocky, confident, and cute comes peeking through. I hate that it makes me feel butterflies.

"Let's hang out."

"Me? Hang out with you?"

"Yes." He lets go of my elbow, but doesn't back out of my space. But I don't feel threatened. Or intimidated. It feels...exciting. Which I know sounds silly, but guys like Simon don't flirt— or smile, or talk—to girls like me.

"Why?"

"I need a reason? Can't a guy just want to?"

I shake my head. "In my experience, no."

"Okay." He takes a second before responding. "You want a list of reasons we should hang out?"

"Yes. Detailed."

"All right then. Number one, you fascinate me. I hear your answers in class and I wonder what other ideas and thoughts you have going on in your brain. Second, I think you're beautiful, and if we hang out then we'll get to know each other and maybe one day you'll go on a date with me. And, third, and I think the most important, I'll be one step closer to finding out your name."

I feel my walls breaking down, which is not what I was expecting. Simon is a frat boy player. I feel like this is the beginning of some elaborate prank.

Then again, I get the sense he's being honest. Which I can't believe solely based on what I know about him and my history with men. So I quickly decide to figure out if he's for real or not.

"Okay."

"Okay!?" His eyes light up, and his smile is so big it's kind of adorable.

I hold up a hand. "Yes. But on one condition."

"Name it."

"It's to study."

"To study?"

"Yes," I say. "We have an oral exam in this class on Friday, and it would be best to practice our answers on another person in the class. So if you want to hang out, it's for us to study."

There. If he really wants to hang out, he'll say yes. If he turns it down, then I was right and the man was only after one thing.

"Deal," he says. "Also it should be noted that I didn't make a joke about oral exams. I think that should earn me bonus points."

"Good job, Simon."

"Thanks," he says proudly. "Now, should I come to your place tomorrow?"

I hurry and shake my head. "No. Not my place. I'll come to yours. Or Perks."

He gives me a curious look but doesn't press me on it. "Fine. My place. Tomorrow night. I'll get snacks."

I shake my head. "Let me take care of the snacks."

"But you don't know what I like."

I smile as I start to walk away. "Trust me. I have snacks down to a science. You won't be disappointed."

All I wanted was a lovely nap on my couch that's only comfortable to me. Instead I'm woken up by a memory of Simon and a twenty-pound furball that just cannonballed on my stomach.

"Dammit, Nuggy!" I say as the dog I barely like starts walking up my chest to lick my face. "In what world does it look like I want you to do this?"

The dog doesn't understand me—she rarely does—and continues licking my face despite my attempt to stop her.

"Nuggy! Stop! Quit licking Aunt Charlie!"

To the rescue comes my niece, Lila. Also known as the reason there is a baby cocker spaniel who lives in my house. She's very cute and very persuasive—a deadly combination in a four-year-old.

"Thanks, Sweet Pea," I say, my face suddenly feeling like it needs to go a few rounds with the cleanser. And just as I think the assault is done, Nuggy jumps back onto my stomach.

Super.

"I had her in my room, but she ran fast," she says.

"It's okay," I say. And it really is. I mean, how can I get mad at my adorable niece and the mostly adorable dog? I might be a woman who sees the glass half empty, but I'm not a monster.

"What's going on out here?"

Connor comes slowly walking into the living room from the kitchen, a towel slung over his shoulder.

"Oh nothing," I say. "Apparently Nuggy wanted to make sure I didn't have any crumbs on my face."

"Sounds about right," he says. "Dinner's cooking. My specialty, spaghetti and meatballs. Will be ready in a half hour."

"Thanks," I say with a smile as Connor sits in the recliner as Lila turns on some YouTube Kids thing. I feel old saying this, but what happened to the days of Disney Channel?

"Everything okay?"

It takes me a few seconds to realize that Connor is talking to me. "Yeah. Why?"

He pushes off the recliner and signals me to come toward the kitchen, away from the always-present ears of Lila. I follow him, passing Nuggy over to his proper owner, who has found a juice box and is currently curled up on her oversized bean bag chair.

Such a rough life she lives.

"Okay, now for real, is everything okay?"

My instinct is to lie and say "yes, of course," but then I remember who I'm talking to. My brother might be five years younger than me, but sometimes we share a brain like I've heard twins do. We can read each other with just one look. That's what happens when you've been through everything that we have.

Raised by a single mom who had to work multiple jobs to make sure we never went without.

A dad who couldn't be bothered with, well, anything.

Having to grow up too soon after the only parent you knew was taken too early.

Being there for each other when worlds were flipped upside down.

"I went and saw a restaurant today. And it's perfect."

Connor's eyes light up. "That's amazing!"

I shake my head. "No, it's not."

"Okay...I'm confused," he says. "Let's start over. Did you go see a restaurant?"

"Yes."

"And you liked it?"

"Yes."

"And you can afford it?"

I laugh, because somehow that part still doesn't seem real. "Yes."

"Then help me out, because I'm failing to see the problem."

I tilt my head and give him a look that I'm hoping he picks up on, because I don't want to be the one to say it.

"Are you kidding me? You're going to turn this down because of me and Lila?"

"Of course I am. It's an hour away from here in Rolling Hills and...well...there are other reasons. But having to move away from you and Lila is the main reason I can't take it."

"The fuck you can't."

"Daddy! Bad word!"

"Sorry, Beanie!" he yells to Lila before turning back to me, his voice a little lower. "Listen here. You will not—I repeat, will not—put your life on hold again for me and Lila. I won't let you. You've done too much for us already."

I knew he was going to say that. Which makes me want to stay here even more.

Since Lila was an infant, it's been the three of us. An unexpected Three Musketeers of sorts. One day Connor was a carefree bachelor in Knoxville, and the next he was opening his front door to a baby in a dilapidated stroller, a baby bag that had one diaper and a single set of pajamas in it, and a note apologizing for leaving her, but that she couldn't do it anymore. It was shit out of a movie.

When he showed up at my Nashville apartment, scared shitless and holding his crying baby, I knew everything was about to change. And it did, but in the best way possible. So I did what I always do—I stepped up.

I watched Lila for the night so he could go back to Knoxville and get his stuff. I found us a bigger place. I even tried—though unsuccessfully—to contact the mother.

Since then it's been us. And I don't regret a thing. I got to see her first steps. I've watched her learn new things every day and become a smart as hell little girl. I've watched her become a tiny human. Plus, she's my buddy. Despite getting a dog that likes to terrorize me, which she named after her favorite food, I wouldn't trade these years for anything. And I can't imagine not being here for her. Or for Connor.

I just can't. I'm tearing up just thinking about it.

"Charlie," Connor says, taking my hands into his. "I will never, and I mean never, be able to repay you for everything you've done for us."

"And I'll never ask you to."

100

He nods. "I know. But this is how I can do it. I can tell you to go. Quit holding yourself back for me and Lila. It's not fair to you."

"I'm not worried about me."

"But I am," he says. "You have wanted this our entire lives. You used to make me play restaurant when we were kids. And let's not forget the promise you made Mom."

I throw him an evil eye. "You really had to bring Mom into this?"

He shrugs. "Yes. I did. Because if she were here, she'd kick your ass and make you go."

I push back the wave of tears that threaten at just thinking about my mom. Besides the fact that she left us way too early—cancer can suck a small flaccid dick—she was always the one who knew what to say. Who knew what to do. She's the reason I want to have a restaurant like Mona's. She's the reason for everything.

Hell, I think she's the reason for this. It's not lost on me that the restaurant is called Mona's and my mom's name was Ramona. The woman who made me promise her before she passed away that no matter what, however long it took me, I'd find a way to live my dream.

And here it is.

Yet I can't make myself pull the trigger.

"There's one more problem," I admit, hating that I have to bring this up.

"What's that?"

"It's in Rolling Hills."

"Yes, you've already said that."

"There's a problem with Rolling Hills."

"And that is?"

I take a breath, realizing this is the first time I'm saying these words out loud. "Simon lives there."

It takes Connor a second to put it together, but once he does, I see it immediately on his face. His face is as red as the tomato sauce simmering on the stove.

"Simon? That fucking douchebag who fucking broke your heart?"

And did other things...

I nod. "Yeah. Small world, huh?"

Connor stands up and starts pacing our tiny kitchen. I figured he was going to have this reaction. Because if Connor ever sees Simon in person, he might kill him.

I might hate Simon for what he did to me all those years ago, but Connor loathes him. And that's without him knowing about our recent tryst.

I get it. Connor's my protector. He might be my little brother, but he's been my person for our entire lives. He saw me cry for weeks over Simon. No brother ever reacts well when he finds out his sister has had her heart shattered. And that was on top of the tears I was crying knowing that we had just days left with my mom. It was the lowest and darkest point of my life.

"You know what?" he says as he turns back to face me. "You're going to go."

That wasn't the answer I was expecting. "Excuse me?"

"You're going to go to Rolling Hills, head held high, and you're going to open the best damn restaurant that town has ever seen. You're going to make him look at you every day, knowing what he did, and watching you fucking thrive. So yeah, you're going to go to Rolling Hills, and you're going to fucking *kill it*."

Wow. I never thought about it like that. I was so blinded by my hatred—and a little frightened if I'm being honest—that I never thought the best revenge might be success.

I like that. I like that a lot.

"Okay," I say, letting my mind settle on this. "But what about you and Lila? I really can't stand the thought of leaving you two."

"We'll be fine," he says, sitting back down at the table. "Has splitting rent helped? Yes. But I can manage. Plus, maybe if you like it down there, Lila and I will move down. The thought of her going to school in a small town rather than metro Nashville has some appeal."

I smile, the tears now flowing. "I'd love that."

At that moment, I hear Nuggy running on the kitchen tile, jumping on my lap.

"I might even miss you," I say to her, nuzzling her nose as she tries to lick me.

"You can do this, you know that, right?"

I nod. "I know. It's just scary as fuck."

"I know. But all good things are."

At that moment, Lila comes into the kitchen and climbs on Connor's lap. She snuggles into him, and I watch my gruff brother become a puddle as he loves on his baby girl.

He's right. The good things are hard but worth it. Look at the two of them. Nothing has been harder for him than suddenly becoming a dad. And not only has he stepped up, but he's the best damn dad I know.

He's overcome scarier things. Hell, so have I.

So I am going to take that restaurant. And it's going to be better than anything I've ever imagined.

And if it comes with getting some revenge on Simon? That will make success all the more sweeter.

Chapter 11
Simon

Simon: Any news?

Emmett: She just texted me. She's in. Needs the apartment upstairs though. I told her it was included.

Simon: Good. Get it ready. Spare no expense. And while you're at it, upgrade all of the kitchen appliances. State of the art.

Emmett: You don't think she'll notice brand-new ovens and coolers?

Simon: I don't care if she notices. Make up an excuse.

Emmett: I'm on my way over. You owe me answers.

Simon: Front door is unlocked. Let yourself in. And bring lunch.

Emmett: Anything else, Your Majesty?

I lean back into my desk chair and tilt my head to the ceiling. I let out a long, relieved breath as I realize my plan worked. Charlie is going to be here.

Now, what's next?

Despite what Emmett might be thinking, I don't have a grand plan. Hell, I didn't even know I had *this* plan until I found out she was interested in Mona's. I guess it's time to come up with one.

Though in my defense, I didn't have a plan with her all those years ago either. Yes, I thought she was smart. And pretty. And I wanted to get to know her. But there was no grand plan to courting her. There was no method to my madness. I was just an idiot kid who thought his shit didn't stink, trying to get a date with the girl he couldn't stop thinking about.

"What are you doing this weekend?"

Bug doesn't even look up from her textbook. "Not going out with you."

I dramatically throw my hand over my heart, which makes her look up from the textbook she's studying from. "One, how dare you think that's how I would ask you out. And two, how do you know that's what I was asking?"

She slams her highlighter down and gives me a scathing look. "Because every time we study you ask me out. Sometimes it's subtle. Sometimes it's direct. Sometimes it's vague, like today. But every time I say no, that does not change."

The One I Hate

"I'm hurt," I say sarcastically. Though I kind of am, which of course I'll never admit to anyone. "Why do you say no?"

She cocks an eyebrow. "Really?"

"Yes, really. I think we'd have fun. I like you. I think you tolerate me, which means you actually love me."

"I do NOT love you."

"So you say." I close her textbook and push it to the other side of the table we're at in the library. "Come on, Bug. What would you like to do? Whatever you want. Nothing too big or small."

This makes her pause, and I watch as her eyes light up in what I can only describe as mischief. "Whatever I want?"

Her smile makes me excited. And also slightly nervous. "Whatever you want."

"Okay." She inches a little closer. "Sunday night is WrestleMania."

"WrestleMania?" I mean, I knew that, but I didn't expect Bug to know.

"You heard me. My brother and I go watch it every year at a local sports bar. He's on a class trip so he can't make it. I don't want to miss it, and if you really want to take me out, that's what we're doing. But it's not a date. It's two mutual acquaintances hanging out and one of them is paying. That's you."

I can't help but smile as I realize this is actually going to happen. I never expected it to take months to get Bug to say yes, and honestly, after a while, asking her out just became part of our interactions. We study together at least once a week, and every day she's working I go visit her at Perks.

Like her nickname, that girl has crawled under my skin. Except I like it, and I don't want her to leave.

Which is strange on so many levels. I haven't dated anyone seriously since I came to college, and I didn't think I wanted to. Playing the field and doing my own thing suits me.

Then I met Bug and...I don't know...something about her intrigued me. And the more I get to know her, the more intrigued I become.

Take today. I shouldn't be shocked she is proposing something out of left field. In every way, shape, or form, she's not like the other girls on campus I've gone out with. Those girls are the stereotypical sorority girls—decked from head to toe in designer clothing, worried that a salad will make them gain five pounds. Blonde hair so white it makes your eyes hurt.

Then there's Bug. Her blonde hair is on the darker side, and I don't think I've ever seen it down. It's always thrown on top of her head in an adorable, messy heap. I don't think she owns a piece of clothing that's name brand, but I know the T-shirts she wears hug her full chest and drive me insane. If I had told any other girl they could pick whatever and wherever for a date, they'd suggest a high-end restaurant that would make my dad give me a lecture when he saw the credit card bill. But Bug? No. She wants wings, beer, and grown men wrestling.

I think I love this woman, and I still don't even know her name.

"It's settled," I say. "Sunday night. Date night."

"Not a date."

"Fine, I won't call it a date under one condition."

She sighs. "I've backed myself into a corner, haven't I?"

I flash her a smile and lean down on my elbows. "Yes, you have."

"Fine. What is it?"

"I won't call this a date. And in exchange, you finally tell me your name."

She throws back her head in defeat as I snicker in my chair.

"Come on, Bug. Tell me. It's only fair."

"Fine," she groans, tilting her head back up. "Charlie."

I don't know what name I was expecting, but it wasn't that. But I love it. It's perfect for her in so many ways.

"Charlie..."

"Yeah," she says, almost as if she's a little embarrassed. "It's short for Charlene."

"Well, it's beautiful." I say. "Unique. Just like you."

She shakes her head. "You don't have to lie, Simon."

"Nope," I say, taking her hand. As soon as I have my fingers wrapped around hers, I feel a heat between us that takes me off guard. But I push that down, because she needs to get one thing clear. "I'm not lying. I don't lie. If I say it, then I mean it. Especially about people I care about."

This seems to take her aback, and frankly, it does the same thing to me. I didn't mean to lay all that out there. It's not like I planned any of this. Yes, I'm impulsive and rarely have plans, but with Charlie, I'm completely winging it. She's the treasure I'm searching for without a map.

"Well, thank you," she says. A blush comes over her cheeks, and I have to hold myself back from leaning over the table and kissing her just to see what her warm skin would feel like.

"You're welcome." I reluctantly let go of her as we fall back into our studies. "You know I'm still going to call you Bug, right?"

She looks up, then back down again, and shrugs.

"I figured as much. Even though I hate that name."

She doesn't hate it. She doesn't hate it at all.

"Here you go," Emmett says, placing down two takeout bags of what smells like burgers and fries. "And in case you wondered, I put them on your credit card."

I reach for the bag and pull out the foam container, but Emmett swipes it away from me. "Hey! What's that for?"

"No food until you tell me why you had me do everything you just had me do."

"That's not fair."

"Simon, I spent my drive over here calling in favors to fix up an apartment for a woman I barely know who is about to not pay rent on said apartment, which she doesn't know. I need answers more than you need this burger."

So he says. Little does he know I only had a smoothie for breakfast.

"Fine, what do you want to know?"

"How about everything?"

"Everything? That will take forever, and I'm really hungry."

"Then quit stalling and start fucking talking."

"Fine..."

I start at the beginning, all the way back to the days at UT. That yes, I was interested in her, and that it might have started with me asking her out incessantly, that we developed a genuine friendship.

"How did I never meet her?" Emmett asks as he slides me my burger. Thank God. My stomach was starting to growl.

"I don't know," I say. "I mean, junior year we didn't hang out a ton. And if you never went to the coffee shop, that could be why."

"I guess," he says. "And I don't blame you for hanging out with her. She's cool as hell. Cute too. And her sense of humor? Holy shit, I was cracking up."

I try to hold it down, but I can feel jealousy creeping over my body as Emmett sings Charlie's many virtues.

"Oh...I see," Emmett drawls, abandoning his burger to send me a knowing look. "It finally became more than friends, didn't it?"

My face doesn't budge. If anything, I only get more angry.

"Goddamn it, Simon! When did you sleep with her?"

I drop my tasty burger. "About a month ago."

"A month ago?" he squawks.

"That's not the important part of this story," I say.

"I think it is."

I shake my head. "I'll go back to it. But I need to finish the first part."

Emmett sits up a little straighter. "Consider me intrigued."

"Anyway. We hung out for months. For most of it, we were just friends, which I was okay with. I really was. Like you said, she's cool as hell. And funny. And, I don't know, I liked being with her."

I swallow the frog in my throat as I transport myself back to that moment fifteen years ago. "It was the last night before move-out day. We were having a party at the house."

"I remember that party," he says. "Hell of a send-off. Cops showed up, didn't they?"

"Yup," I say. "I asked Charlie to come to our parties all semester, and she finally came. I was so excited. We laughed. We drank. It was probably the best night of my whole college experience. And then we kissed."

I can still see everything so clearly. Us sneaking up to my roof to get away from the noise. Talking like I only could with her. Then the kiss. The one that is forever seared into my memory.

"What happened next?" Emmett asks.

"I was going back to Rolling Hills for the summer. But I wanted to see her before I left," I say. "Except when I tried to call her the next day, she never answered. I texted. I called. I even drove back to Knoxville to the coffee shop to see if she was working. They said she'd quit. It's like she had just vanished."

"Like vanished as in gone?"

"Poof. Like a ghost."

"Wow," he says. "She never told you what happened?"

"Nope. I never saw her again. Until I went to a wedding last spring. And then a month ago."

I fill Emmett in on the gaps between April and now. And the bare minimum details of our night together. Motherfucker doesn't need to know that Charlie's naked body still keeps me up at night and has been the vision of multiple individual sessions.

"Okay, let me see if I can get this all straight," Emmett says. "A girl you had a thing for fifteen years ago, who ghosted you after one kiss—"

"One *epic* kiss."

"Apologies. A girl who ghosted you after one *epic* kiss—"

"Thank you."

"Quit interrupting. She's back in your life. And you've had sex with her. Yet, after all of that, you still don't know the answer to the biggest unknown of your life: why she left. So instead of trying to have a nice and normal conversation with her, you go and pull strings like a puppet master to make sure she gets a restaurant in your town so you can have her close, therefore allowing to you to get the answer to a question that's been digging in your craw for more than a decade."

"Yes." I say with a firm nod. "But in my defense, she won't talk to me. The first time she ran away. The second I made her cry. The next time we had sex."

"You're an idiot."

"I've been called worse."

Emmett shakes his head in clear frustration. "Do you have a plan? What happens when she finds out you're the landlord? What happens when she finds out about any of this?"

"She won't," I say with mock confidence. "You're now sworn to secrecy. No one in town knows that I bought Mona's. And when they find out which company bought it, they are going to see Magnolia Properties. The only people who know I own that are my best friends. This is going to be fine. I've got this under control."

"But do you?" Emmett says with a head tilt. "Because I don't think you do."

I shrug. "I'm really just winging it. But it will be fine. It always is."

"Simon," Emmett says, shaking his head as he bows it and clasps his hands together. Why do I feel like I'm about to get a lecture? "What is your intention in all this? What's the end game?"

That's the easiest question I've been asked all day. "To get my answer."

"That's it?"

"Yeah, that's it," I say. "Yes, I know sleeping with her complicates things, but that was a one and done. She wants nothing to do with me, and after I know my answer, I likely won't want anything to do with her."

"I don't really believe that, but okay..."

"Emmett. It's fine. I know what I'm doing. Mostly. If she sees me every day, I'm going to wear her down. It worked before; it will work again. And then, once I get my answer, I'll tell her I own the place. She'll probably be mad at me, but she's been mad at me for years, so I don't see it being a big deal. And at that point I'll have my answer. That's all I need, and we can move on with our lives."

Emmett leans back in the chair and starts rubbing his fingers against his temples. "This is going to blow up in your face. And I'm going to be caught in the damn middle. All because you can't have a damn conversation without you or your dick getting in the way."

"Have a little faith."

"That's the thing I have the least of." Emmett sits back up and locks eyes with me. "Just promise me one thing."

"Yes, I'll give you a raise after this is over."

"Not that, but I am going to hold you to it," Emmett says. "Charlie's a good girl. She wants this restaurant. I can tell. She's exactly the kind of person Mona wants to take over. Do not, and I repeat, do not sabotage this for her. Don't fuck with her in any way. If I get the feeling for one second you are, I don't care that you're my boss and my friend, I will blow your shit up on the spot, no questions asked."

I hold my hand up in an oath. "I promise I won't. I don't want her to fail. Not in the littlest bit. I just want answers. I swear."

Emmett stares me down, assessing if I'm telling the truth. But I am. Yes, I might be a little devious with this plan, but I don't want Charlie to fail. I want her to thrive. I'll give her whatever she wants.

And all I want in return are my answers.

"Promise?"

"Cross my heart," I say. "Once we finally talk, I'll drop everything and move on. She'll just be a tenant, and I'll just be her landlord."

Emmett gives me a skeptical look. "Will you, though?"

I shrug and take a big bite of my burger. "Debatable."

Chapter 12
Charlie

Charlie: Are you sure I'm supposed to be here? I feel like I'm spying.

Emmett: Yes. You wanted to see a normal morning at Mona's, and she wants to meet you. Just go in and introduce yourself.

Charlie: You're sure she wants to meet me? Like she said those words?

Emmett: Just go in, Charlie. Sit at the counter. Get the pancakes. They're delicious.

Charlie: I'm more of a french toast kinda gal, but thanks for the rec.

Emmett: Of course you are...

Charlie: Why do you say that?

Emmett: Never mind. Just go in. I promise you'll be fine.

Easy for him to say. He's not the one about to go meet the woman who you're trying to take the place of after she's fed a town for a few generations.

Though french toast does sound good. Like really good. Because I'm really freaking hungry.

I take a few deep breaths as I walk into the hustle and bustle of a Friday morning at Mona's.

Holy shit, it's packed.

Every booth and table is full. A few waitresses are zipping around, carrying more plates than I think is actually possible. Conversations are on top of each other, drowning out the faint music that's playing in the background, and the smell of bacon, coffee, and maple syrup is overtaking my senses.

It's perfect.

And at this moment it really hits me that this place is soon going to be mine.

"Charlie! Over here! I saved you a spot at the counter."

It takes me a second to realize that someone is calling my name, not another guy named Charlie. When I look to the counter there's an older woman standing in front of an empty stool, coffee pot in one hand and a smile on her face that immediately puts me at ease.

"You must be Mona," I say as I take a seat.

"The one and only."

I laugh as she pours me a cup of coffee. "How did you know it was me?"

"Emmett told me to look out for a redhead who looked nervous."

"Sounds about right." I feel the slight heat come over my cheeks in embarrassment. "I hope it's okay I came in today."

"I'm glad you did," she says. "The breakfast rush is coming to a close. Let me get you some food, then maybe we can chat?"

"Perfect," I say. "French toast and an orange juice?"

"Coming right up, sweetie."

Mona walks back to the kitchen, and I let out a slight sigh of relief. I pick up the steaming cup of coffee, but when I bring it to my mouth, the smell suddenly makes my stomach twist. Weird. Who knows...my stomach has been hating me lately.

But it wants french toast immediately.

I take another look around the diner and now I'm wondering what I was scared about. Mona seems lovely. This place is exactly what I expected, and I can't wait to make it my own, while also keeping the vibe Mona has created.

AKA no more yellow walls.

"I can do this," I say to myself. "I really can do this."

I reach for my phone so I can make a few notes and observations that I don't want to forget when I see the door to the restaurant open out of the corner of my eye. I turn to look out of habit, and the second I do I hate myself for doing it.

I also forget to keep breathing.

Because walking in, in all his arrogant glory, is Simon Banks.

Breathe, Charlie...you knew this was going to happen. You knew this could happen today. This is fine. Get it over with. Then the next time won't be so bad.

And don't think about his tongue or dick.

I know I should look away, but I can't make myself do it. He has his own gravitational pull, I swear.

Unless I run. That's always an option.

But I can't do that now. I mean, I could. But I won't do that to Mona. Or myself. Like Connor said, the best revenge on Simon is making him watch me succeed. And that starts here and now.

"Is that Charlie Bennett I see?" Simon smirks as he takes

the conveniently empty seat next to me at the counter. "I must say, this is a pleasant surprise."

"Speak for yourself," I say, tearing my eyes away from him and focusing back on my phone. I hate how hard that is. Because as much as I might hate him, I'll never be able to deny how stupid hot he is. Especially now that I know what he looks like naked.

The asshole is one of those guys that has gotten better looking with age—and he wasn't hurting in the looks department in college. His brown hair looks like he just got out of the shower and has a slight curl to it, yet still perfectly styled. He smells of light body soap and cologne that is hitting my senses in the best way. I don't know what the scent it is, but it smells expensive and sexy. His beard is neatly trimmed, but still leaves plenty of hair that I can somehow feel between my thighs as I sit here.

Fuck my life...why did I sleep with him? That was single-handedly the stupidest decision I've ever made.

But I did, and now I'm here, sitting next to this infuriatingly hot man who's wearing a polo shirt that showcases his toned biceps in a way that makes you want to stare.

And hold on to them while he does delicious things to your body.

No. I'm not going to. That's what he wants. At the end of the day, that's who Simon Banks is. The guy who wants the spotlight. Center of attention. And I'm not going to give him the satisfaction.

Why am I here?

Despite me putting up walls that could have separated communist countries once upon a time, Simon has somehow infiltrated my life with his adorable smirk and annoying persis-

tence. That's the only thing I can think of as to why I agreed to come to his party tonight.

At his house. With his roommates. And friends. And probably half of the University of Tennessee campus. Where he is currently dancing on a table with girls all around him.

I've been on campus for three years, and I've never once gone to a party. I was invited to a few freshman year, but I always declined. They just never felt like my scene, so I usually picked up extra shifts at Perks. These are all kids who are living the full college experience. Partying on weekends. Living off their trust funds or scholarships. Then there's me. The commuter who lives fifteen miles away and the only reason I can even afford to come here is because my mom works in one of the dining halls.

I suddenly feel self-conscious as a group of girls bops past me, holding up their drinks as they slink through the crowd. I don't know if it's their designer clothes or their size-two waists, but any confidence I had coming in here is out the window.

Again, why am I here? Oh, that's right. Because Simon flashed me his smile, batted his beautiful blue eyes at me, and begged me to come to their last party of the year. Finals finished today, and everyone will be clearing campus tomorrow for the summer. I originally said no—like I do most times with Simon—but somehow those nos are becoming less and less.

I don't know what it is about him. At first I was convinced he was bored and that's why he was hanging out at the coffee shop every day. Then when he started asking me out all the time, I was convinced it had to be a bet. Because that's the only way Simon Banks is seen with a girl like me. That's not self-deprecating—it's just true. My attempt at a date last month proved that.

As I've gotten to know Simon, I feel like his cocky demeanor is just an act. Well, not all of it. At his core he's a handsome, arrogant man who loves to have the spotlight. But what I've learned is that he's a good friend. Smart. Hilarious. A hell of a dancer. And he went toe-to-toe with me in trivia during our WrestleMania not-a-date date.

And then there was the night he held me as I cried because of a douchebag guy.

He's more than what he shows to the world. He's a good guy.

And I have a fucking crush on him. Which is really bad.

Because I know he doesn't like me like that. He might show some signs here and there that would make me think he does, but I know how this ends. In heartbreak. It's how the stories of kids from the opposite sides of the track always end. The handsome prince never ends up with the common girl from the village.

I should leave. Yes. I need to. This is Simon's element. I don't belong here.

And just as I turn, I hear the one syllable that will stop me in my tracks until the day I die.

"Bug!"

The damn nickname. The nickname that I used to hate and now don't hate at all.

"Hey," I say as I turn around. Sweat is dripping from his forehead. His breathing is heavy, and I can't help but let my eyes travel to his toned abs as he brings his shirt up to wipe off his forehead.

I've only imagined what Simon looks like without a shirt. And apparently my imagination was NOT active enough.

"Did you just get here?"

I nod. "I did, but I think I'm going to go."

His face goes from excited to sad in a heartbeat. "Go? Why?"

"This isn't my thing," I say. "Plus, it looks like you have plenty of company..."

I didn't mean to say it as insulting or insinuating that he had a harem of girls on him, even though that's how it came out.

It doesn't help his case that two of the girls have slithered their way next to him.

"Simon? We were just getting started."

He gently steps away from being the filling in the sorority sister sandwich. "Thanks. I'm good. You two go have fun."

They both give an overexaggerated pout, but walk away. As soon as they are gone, I feel Simon take my hand in his. It shocks me a little, even though this isn't the first time he's done this. Or we've touched. That's why I'm still wondering why I feel like I've been shocked every time our skin makes contact.

"Come on," he says, pulling my hand out of the living room where everyone is congregated.

"Where are we going?"

He turns back to me, his smile stealing my breath away. "You'll see."

"So whatcha doin'?"

I fight back an eye roll and do what I know will piss him off more than anything—I don't react at all.

I see him inch closer to me so he's now looking over my shoulder. But I stay strong and keep my gaze forward.

"Well, since that's your notes app, I'm going to guess making notes. Or maybe a list. You always loved making lists."

I don't say anything, which only makes him come closer.

"Hmm, let's see. Finalize menus. Ask about utility costs. Bug? Why are you making those notes?"

I grind my teeth as he uses his nickname for me. "None of your business."

"She speaks," he says. Out of the corner of my eye I see his cocky grin.

I hate that grin.

I hate it so much.

"Here we go, my dear. French toast and an orange juice." Mona puts my plate in front of me before noticing the unwanted guest next to me. "Simon! What are you doing here?"

"Hey, Mona," he says. "I was hoping to get the same thing the lady has here. It looks delicious. But make mine to go."

"Add poison to it," I say under my breath.

"What was that, Charlie?"

I shake my head as Simon snickers. "Nothing."

She gives me a questioning look, but doesn't press. "Okay. I'm going to put in his order and then we can go talk. Enjoy."

Mona walks away as I feel Simon turn to face me.

"What are you talking to Mona about? How do you know Mona? What are you doing in Rolling Hills? Did you miss me? What is the list for? Why aren't you blonde anymore? Where did you go fifteen years ago? And why did you leave in the middle of the night last month? How many orgasms did I give you? Gosh...I just have so many questions..."

I love french toast more than life itself. Yet right now I'm willing to waste it so I can slam this dish into Simon's smug face.

"I'm not answering any of those questions," I say as I take a bite. Holy shit, this is good. I make good french toast, but I might need to see if I can get Mona's secret and keep these on the menu.

"Can you answer one? I'd really like to know the orgasm one. Or the where you went one. But I'm not picky."

I look over to Simon, and I'm angry at myself the second I turn my head.

Besides the grin, which has never been more pompous, I lock eyes with him, and that's my downfall.

Those fucking eyes. They are the clearest blue I've ever seen. I don't even know how to describe them. I just know that's his secret weapon. They get me every fucking time. Whether it was fifteen years ago, a month ago, or right now, I'm a goner when I look into sparkling blues.

"Fine," I groan, hoping then he'll leave me alone. "I'll answer one."

He celebrates with a fist pump, but I quickly cut him off. "But I get to pick the question. And it's not about orgasms."

He sighs like a toddler. "Fine."

"You'll find this out soon enough—" I lower my voice to make sure that stray ears don't pick up on this. "But I'm opening a restaurant here. Mona is retiring, and this space is going to be mine."

"What!" Simon yells, drawing a few eyeballs our way. Though they leave just as quickly, which I'm guessing means this town is used to Simon's antics. "You're taking over Mona's? This is great! Can this be my permanent seat? I want to come in every day. Be a regular. Have my name yelled and cheered when I walk through the door. I'll be your Norm!"

"Absolutely not," I say. "Actually, if you could never come in here, I'd appreciate that."

"You can't do that," he says, indignant. "I have rights."

"Not here you don't. No shirt. No shoes. No Simon."

He furrows his brow. "I don't think that's how it goes."

"That's how it goes here."

"I can't believe you'd do that, Bug," he says, pretending to be hurt. "After all we've been through. And it's been so much..."

"Exactly," I say, my eyes narrowing. "After *all* we've been through."

We stare at each other for more than a few seconds, anger radiating off the both of us. Mine is more visceral, though. I can feel my face turning the color of my fading red-dyed hair.

How dare he think that he can be so casual about how

things ended. And how dare he be the one to ask me where I went fifteen years ago. If there's anyone who has to come up with answers for how things ended, it's him.

As for the walking out part, I'll take that. But the other stuff is what I'm more concerned about.

"Here you go, Simon," Mona says, breaking our stares. "Everything okay here?"

Neither of us say anything as we slowly lean away from each other. We might not be trying to shoot lasers into each other, but that doesn't mean the tension isn't still thick. I don't know if there's a knife in this restaurant that can cut through it.

"Thanks, Mona," he says, giving her a wink. "I'll let you two talk."

"Take care, Simon," Mona says as he slides what looks like way too much money toward her.

"See you around, Bug. Every day. Maybe sometimes twice a day. You know I can come multiple times."

Asshole.

"Fuck you, Simon."

"Again? Here? Bug, what do you take me for?"

I shake my head in frustration. "I hate you."

He smiles and leans in closer. "This is going to be great. Just like old times. Can't wait."

"I hope you choke on your french toast."

"Oh. Ouch." He steps away, holding his heart as if I hurt him, but the smile on his face says otherwise. "This is going to be so much fun."

"Just leave me alone, Simon. I'm going to be here and living here and working here. I'd like to just run my restaurant without having to worry about you."

He shrugs and leans back in. "Can't do that, Bug. Sorry. Welcome to Rolling Hills."

And with that Simon strolls out of the diner like he doesn't have a care in the world.

Asshole.

"Oh, this is good," Mona says with a laugh.

"What is good?"

She nods to the door. "You and Simon. I didn't know you two knew each other. I also didn't know for a second there if y'all were going to fuck or fight."

My eyes go wide, a little taken aback by Mona's phrasing. Also wondering if somehow she knows. "Fight, Mona. Definitely fight."

"Whatever you need to tell yourself to sleep at night."

"You have it all wrong," I say as Mona comes around and takes a seat next to me. "He's my mortal enemy."

"You keep telling yourself that," she says with a laugh. "I know I need to retire and take a vacation, but this makes me want to stick around. I'd love to see how that plays out."

Chapter 13
Simon

"Holy shit, it's packed in here."

I look over to Oliver and Izzy, who are trying to push their way next to me and the rest of the crew who have gathered at Mona's for her final day of operation.

"Why are you late?" I ask. The festivities started ten minutes ago with a speech from the mayor—which is still going on.

"We got...busy," Oliver says.

"Oh, the honeymoon stage," Wes says, slapping his back. "Nothing like it."

"How many honeymoon stages does he get?" Shane asks. "The oops wedding? The upcoming, kind-of real wedding? The engagement that's not really an engagement?"

"As many as we want," Oliver says, pulling Izzy to him for a quick kiss. He doesn't let her go as she stands in front of him, his arms wrapped around her waist. He's probably doing it because the man would touch his wife twenty-four-seven if he could. But in reality, it's necessary for how many people are packed in here.

I think every person who is living in Rolling Hills is in attendance. It's likely a fire hazard, but considering the fire chief is now shaking the mayor's hand to begin his speech about how many years Mona has served him and his crew, I doubt he's kicking anyone out. We're in the back, which is good. I wanted to blend in today, which is not normally my mode of operation. But today is about Mona.

And about Bug, who's officially being introduced to the town of Rolling Hills.

"Which one is she?" Oliver whispers.

"The one next to the counter," Shane answers.

"Cute," Oliver says. "Different from the normal girls he goes for. But also seems completely like someone he'd pursue."

"Right? That's what I thought," Shane says in an excited tone I've never heard from him in all our years of friendship. "When we met her at the taste testing, I was confused, knowing the women we've seen him with. But then when they started talking, I knew something was between them. There were sparks. I saw them with my own eyes."

"Shut the fuck up." I slap Shane on the arm, which makes the entire crew laugh.

"What's the matter, Simon?" Wes asks. "Not so much fun when you're on the receiving end of the jabs?"

"Will you three shut your traps?" I whisper-yell, not wanting to draw attention to us. Though I can't help but glance at Charlie for likely the fiftieth time today. She's only caught me twice though. Which I think is a pretty good success rate.

My instinct is to get under her skin. Make her unable to forget that I'm here. But I won't. Not today. This is a big day for her, and I don't want to ruin that.

The One I Hate

I can do that any other day and all the days going forward.

However, that doesn't mean I can't sit here and cast glances at her that she doesn't see.

Her hair is down, which is a change from the last two times I saw her. The red is fading and the blonde is starting to show through, which makes me smile. I miss my blonde Bug. She has on black leggings and a flowy blue top that's cut just low enough in the front to be modest, but also drive me insane. Especially since I know what those magnificent breasts feel and taste like. Her makeup is done, and she's wearing a red lipstick that is making me hope for round two, only so I can see a ring around my cock.

"We'll shut our traps if you shut your jaw," Wes says, giving my apparently—and unknowing—hanging jaw a tap up to close my mouth. "As my Pops says, no one likes a man who drools."

I wipe my mouth and ignore my asshole friends laughing at me. Of course there's no drool, but I needed to make sure.

"Just fucking listen to the speeches and be polite," I say.

"Oh, this is so good."

Shane's comment blends into the crowd as everyone starts applauding for Mona to come up on the makeshift stage, which is really a few wooden boxes pushed together.

"I didn't know this many people could fit in this place," Mona says, getting a small laugh from the crowd. "I started this diner more than forty years ago. And frankly, I had no idea what I was doing. I just knew that I could cook a few decent meals and I wanted a place to call my own. I never knew it would give me the years it has with you fine folks."

A round of applause hits as Mona continues to talk about her favorite memories. Which makes me think of my favorite memories here. Dinners after football practice when my mom didn't want to cook. Me and the guys coming here after school, thinking we were hot shit while also thinking this was our version of "The Maxx" from *Saved by the Bell*. My first date was here. And this is where I survived my first heartbreak.

"Simon! 'Bout time you came in to see me."

I look up to Mona, and I must not do a good enough job of hiding my sullen expression.

"What's the matter? Why do you look like someone ran over your dog?"

I look down at my phone again before back up to Mona. It's the text I wrote for Bug, begging and pleading for her to just call me back. Send any sort of message that she's okay. But like all the others, it won't go through.

I'm blocked.

What did I do? Was it the kiss? It couldn't have been, right? It was an amazing kiss. The best kiss. A kiss I didn't want to end. And I thought she felt the same.

When she first didn't answer me, I thought maybe she was just busy. And then I called. And called. And left message after message. I started to get worried.

So when I went back to campus this past weekend for my roommate's birthday, I made a beeline for Perks. I needed to see her. Make sure she was okay. That's when I found out she quit.

I might not be the smartest guy, but I know when to take a hint.

She's gone.

"It's nothing," I say quickly. I can tell she knows I'm full of shit, but she doesn't press me.

"How about some pancakes?" she asks. "Those always cheer you up."

I start to nod my head but stop. "No. Can I get french toast?"

Mona cocks her head. "Since when do you eat french toast?"
I shrug. "It sounds good."
Mona taps my hands before walking away as I let Bug's voice and smile infiltrate my memory for the hundredth time today.

Because when I think of french toast, I will forever think of my Bug.

We had gone to get breakfast after a final—I got my usual pancakes while she ordered french toast. I didn't realize my breakfast order was going to lead to a twenty-minute dissertation on how and why french toast was the superior breakfast food and that pancakes were trash. I, of course, egged her on by insisting pancakes were better.

It riled her up. I loved it. I just sat back and watched as she got so passionate over breakfast food. She was so cute. Determined. Fiery.

My Bug.

And as Mona slides the plate in front of me, I wonder if I'm ever going to get to see her again...

"Now, I couldn't let y'all go hungry," Mona says as I come back to the present. "I know for a fact some of you don't know how to boil an egg, let alone cook yourself a proper meal."

The crowd chuckles as Mona waves for Charlie to go up on stage. "Well, don't worry, I'm not leaving you hanging. This here is Charlie Bennett, and from now on, she's the one going to be cooking for you."

The crowd applauds as Charlie gives a small wave. Her cheeks are flushed and her motions are small. She mouths "hello" to a few people, but other than that, she's yet to say a word.

Or look at me.

"So that's Bug, huh?"

I give a side-eye to Oliver. "Yes, that's Bug. But you don't call her that."

"Oh...I get it now."

"Get what?"

He nods to the stage. "She's the one who got away."

I look over to Oliver like he's an idiot. Because he is. Mostly. "You don't know what you're talking about."

"I remember that summer. Wes and Shane weren't here, but I was. You were a shell of yourself. You tried to put on a brave face and be your normal cocky self, but I knew you were hurting. I remember asking if you were okay and you brushed me off. Many times. But I knew you were broken. I just didn't know who it was that shattered your heart."

I nod and swallow the lump in my throat as Charlie clears hers to begin speaking.

"Physically, she's like no one you've ever gone after. Shorter and curvy. Not your normal wanna-be-runway-model types. And I'm betting once I talk to her she's probably going to blow me away with a wit and tongue that no other woman you've ever chased has possessed."

I hate how well he knows me.

"Everything now makes sense."

I look over to Oliver. "How do you know that?"

He nods toward her. "Because I always knew the woman who finally broke Simon Banks wouldn't be anyone ordinary."

I look over at Charlie as she begins to give everyone a warm welcome. I can't help but smile and feel a sense of pride as I look at her.

Oliver's right. My Bug is nothing short of extraordinary.

"I want to start off by saying thank you to Mona, who has

132

been nothing but gracious since I signed the lease to take over this spot."

The two of them hug, and I hope it doesn't show, but I get a bit choked up by the action.

"I was raised by a single mom," she begins. I feel myself leaning closer to where she's standing, like the inch I move forward will help me hear better. I barely knew anything about her family. I knew she had a brother, but that's it. "We didn't have a lot of extra money, but every once in a while, she took me and my brother to a diner in our town just outside of Knoxville. And yes, go Vols!"

"Go Vols!" The crowd chants back to her, and I feel the smile growing on my face as I watch her talk to my friends and neighbors.

"That diner is where some of my best memories were made. I fell in love with cooking as a child, and it was my dream to one day open a restaurant exactly like that. Exactly like this."

She pauses for a second, and I wait for her next words with bated breath.

"There isn't a lot that's happened in my life to make me believe that dreams come true." She stops for a second and takes a deep breath. Her eyes are closed, like she's begging a higher power for strength to continue. When she opens them back up, she scans the crowd, her eyes stopping the second they lock with mine. "And I still believe that. Dreams don't come true. White knights don't ride into town to save the day. So I learned a long time ago I had to make my own dreams come true. I worked hard. Put in my time as a sous chef. All for the goal of one day having my own place. But in that time, I realized that I might not need a white knight, but I did need a little help."

She pauses and releases her stare from me. When she does, I finally exhale.

"So there are people I want to thank. First, the town of Rolling Hills for welcoming me with open arms. Thank you to Emmett and Magnolia Properties for helping me through every step of this process and making this dream come true. Mona, for your guidance. I hope I make you proud. And to my mom, who oddly enough was named Ramona, for being my guardian angel. So in honor of the two women who have guided me to where I am today, this restaurant will continue being called Mona's. This is just Charlie's version."

Applause erupts, but I am jerked to standing and dragged out the side door of the diner before she can continue.

"Did we just hear what we thought we heard?"

I look back to the diner then back to my three best friends, who are all staring at me like they are about to kick my ass.

"What did you hear?"

Shane's eyes turn violent. "She just thanked Magnolia Properties. You own Magnolia Properties."

"Oh. Yeah. My bad. I forgot to tell you guys. I bought Mona's."

"What?" Oliver yells. "How could you not tell us?"

"I wanted to," I begin. "I swear. Unlike some people *who keep secrets*, I wanted to tell everyone."

We all shoot our sights to Shane, who is holding his hands up in defense. "That was Amelia's idea. And since she's working and can't be here to defend herself, let's move on and remember that Simon has bought Mona's."

They all turn their sights back to me. "Technically, it's not Mona's. Well, I guess it is. It's Charlie's Mona's."

The three of them look at each other before turning back to me.

"Simon." Wes steps closer, his voice low like he's about to reprimand one of his kids. "The woman in there who just gave an emotional and heartfelt speech is a woman from your past."

"A woman who hates you," Shane says.

"Hate's a strong word…"

"Simon," Wes continues. "Please, swear to me on a stack of Bibles and your season UT tickets that you didn't buy this restaurant simply to fuck with the woman who hurt you fifteen years ago?"

I let out a breath, loving that I get to technically tell the truth.

"Wes, I solemnly swear I did not buy the restaurant to fuck with Charlie."

There. Easy peasy. And the truth. I've got this.

That's all of the things I'm thinking until I catch Shane's eye.

"What?" I ask him.

"Spill."

"Spill what?"

"The actual truth."

"I just told you the truth."

"Yes. But not all of it. I can tell."

"How? Please. Elaborate."

Shane works his jaw back and forth. Fuck. He means business. "Because she said Magnolia Properties. That woman hates you. I saw it in her eyes that day. She would have cut off your dick and sold it to the highest bidder if she could have. Yet, she just thanked your company, and Emmett, for making her dream come true. So either you two made up—which I doubt— or she doesn't know. Which is it?"

Damn Shane and his police skills.

"Fine. Yes. I bought it. No, she doesn't know. But I have a good reason. I promise."

"And that is?" Wes asks.

"She won't talk to me."

The three of them look at each other like they're missing something. Oliver is the first to speak up. "That's it?"

I shrug. "I mean, that's the Cliffs Notes. If you want to hear the whole story, which also now has an updated chapter from recently, that's going to require a lot of beer. And privacy. Wes. Back to your place. I hope you're stocked up."

Chapter 14
Simon

S he's here.
  She actually came.
  She almost ran. But she didn't.
She came to my party.
The one she doesn't know I threw for her.

Well, not just for her. My roommates wondered what we were going to do with all the leftover booze from the year before we had to move out of the house. I suggested we have one final bash. A true going away party. They were down and invited the entire campus.

I invited one person. And now she's here. Sitting on the roof outside my bedroom, away from the craziness of the party, because if I have Charlie here, I'm not about to spend it surrounded by anyone else. Not my friends. Not my sister and her college friends, who randomly showed up today.

No, this night and this moment is for me and Bug.

"It's beautiful up here," she says as she takes a sip of the water she asked for.

"It is," I say back, though I'm not looking at the view of

campus. How can I when she's sitting inches away from me, smelling like flowers and wearing red lipstick that is driving me fucking insane? She never wears makeup, yet, she is tonight. She was already gorgeous. But now? She's stunning.

She looks over to me and starts laughing. "What are you staring at, weirdo?"

"You."

"Well, stop."

"Nope," I say, inching a little closer to her. "It's a free country, and I'm choosing to exercise my freedom by looking at the most beautiful girl in the world."

She turns toward me, and she's giving me the "quit being an idiot" look. It's one I know well from her. And usually I am being an idiot. But not tonight. I'm dead serious. She's the most beautiful woman in the world to me.

"Simon?"

"Yeah, Bug?"

"Don't call me that."

"Can't. It's your name."

She lets out a groan. "Why am I here?"

Her question takes me off guard. I was expecting her to ask why I'm calling her beautiful, because she's asked that before. She usually asks me why I am the way that I am. And that is usually answered with another smartass remark.

But I wasn't ready for this.

Now I need to quickly decide how to say what I need to. Because how do you say "well, I made my roommates have an entire party so I had an excuse to see you one more time before I left for the summer because I need you to know that I'm crazy about you, and you think I'm joking when I ask you out, but I'm not. You're really pretty, and I want to kiss you and cuddle you and, if you'd let me, touch your butt. And boobs. I'd like that. But not because I'm a horn ball who just wants to get laid.

Because you're so pretty and smart and funny and you fascinate me. But you don't think I'm serious, and I don't know how to make you know I'm serious without coming across as stalker or a creep," without sounding creepy?

How do I trim that down? Or make it sound normal? How do I not sound like a potential serial killer?

I don't know. I know I need to try, though. Summer is about to begin, and I don't want to leave without telling her how I feel.

"Because I wanted you here."

Okay. Good start. Not creepy.

"Why?"

"Do I need a reason?"

"Yes," she says. "Simon, despite the fact that you are one of the most infuriating people on the planet, I enjoy spending time with you."

"It's my sick dance moves, isn't it?"

She laughs under her breath. "They definitely don't hurt. But, despite the fact that you're arrogant and insufferable, you're actually a good friend."

Fuck. Friend. Worst word a guy can hear.

"But, we're not the type of friends who hang out at parties together. We're school friends. And that is very different from after-school friends."

Okay, now I'm confused. "What's that supposed to mean?"

Her shoulders slump. "Are you going to make me say it?"

"Yes. Because I don't know why there has to be that designation."

We both turn so we're fully facing each other. "Simon. I'm not like those girls downstairs."

"I know. That's what I like about you."

"But do you? I'm not the girl a guy like you should be on a roof with. Or that he should be calling beautiful."

"Don't tell me who I can be friends with. Or who I can call beautiful."

"I'm not. It's just..." she trails off for a second. "Simon? What am I doing here?"

I see the slightest hint of a tear forming in the corner of her eye, and that's my signal to shut down the smartass. Crying women are my weakness. I can't handle it. Especially Bug. And I'm not about to be the reason the woman I'm mildly obsessed with is crying.

"You're here because"—I take a breath because, holy shit, I'm about to admit this—"You're here because I want you here. So much so that I threw this party for you."

She narrows her eyes at me. She clearly doesn't believe me.

Okay, here we go. Stalker mode activated.

"It's true," I say. "My roommates invited the entire school, but I only invited you. Because I didn't give a flying fuck who else came. You were the only one who mattered."

She shakes her head, clearly not believing me. "Let's just say for a moment that's true. Then why did I walk in to see you putting on the Simon Banks Show next to your troop of backup dancers?"

I think back to what she saw. Oh. Yes.

"Listen, I can't be held responsible for my actions when Flo Rida comes on."

"Be serious for once, Simon." She stops for a second, but just to take in a breath. "You were on a makeshift stage with a flock of girls, who likely have modeling contracts, dancing. Clearly you cared a lot about if I was here or not."

"Did you see my hands on them?"

My question is sharp and to the point. She wants serious? I'll give her serious.

"No. Not then," she says, her words not as sure as before.

"Exactly."

"But I don't know what happened before I got here."

So this is how she wants to play it? "Charlie. I promise you that I didn't touch them. Yes, they were dancing next to me, and I didn't want to be a dick in front of a hundred people by pushing them away."

"Really, Simon? Hot girls were grinding on you and you didn't touch them?"

"No. I didn't. And do you want to know why?"

"I'd love to."

"Because they weren't you."

My words echo in the empty sky. She doesn't say anything at first, and I wonder for a second if I actually said that or if I was making this up in my head.

Then I hear the faint sound of her whisper.

"You wanted them to be me?"

I laugh, because I don't know how much more serious I can be. I tilt up her chin, holding it so she has no choice but to look in my eyes. "Charlie. Since the day I turned around and saw you in that coffee shop, you've had me under your spell."

"A spell?"

"Yes. A spell. Now, I know sometimes I come across as the asshole or the jokester."

"Sometimes?"

"Fair. But I want you to know who I'm not. I'm not the guy who's going to lie to you about thinking you're the most beautiful girl I've ever met. I'm not going to be the fucking dickhead who tricks you into going out with him because I'm bored like that douchebag did. I'm not the guy who's going to take advantage of you. I'm not the guy who's going to talk some game just to hook up and then bolt before you wake up the next day. No matter how bad I actually want to have sex with you."

Her eyes double in size. "You want to...have sex...with me?"

"More than I want my next breath," I say, pushing down the

thought of Charlie and I together. No. Not the time. "If you told me that I could kiss you right now but never do anything else, I'd take it. Because you, Bug...you're fucking everything, and I don't know how to say it so you believe me. Hell, all of this has probably freaked—"

I know I started rambling, and I think I blacked out. Yes, that has to be what's happening.

Otherwise it's real life that Charlie has grabbed my face and is kissing me.

Holy shit, Charlie is kissing me!

It's...I don't have words. I could talk for hours about nothing, and right now I can't think of a single one.

So I don't.

I just kiss her back.

Holy shit, this feels amazing. She tastes like cherries, and from here on out, that will be my favorite flavor.

But before I can settle in she quickly pulls away. Her eyes are wide, and I think it's her turn to black out.

"I'm sorry," she says.

"Why?"

"Because I kissed you."

Oh, this girl...she doesn't realize that since she's now kissed me, she's stuck with me forever.

And I don't share.

"Bug..." I take her hand and pull her to me. She doesn't resist as I pull her up, signaling for her to sit across my lap. "Did you like it?"

She nods. "I did."

"Do you want to do it again?"

"Yes."

"Good. Because I'm about to."

And I do. I lean in and take her lips in mine, and it's even better than it was just a moment ago. She opens her mouth for me, and I take advantage, letting my tongue enter and explore her mouth. Her hands become a little more sure of themselves, traveling up and down my back as I hold her close to me.

Fuck...we're both completely dressed and my body is already on fire for hers. Her curves are soft in my hands and against me. I let my lips travel a little, kissing down the column of her neck, and with every new piece of skin I touch, she somehow gets sweeter.

Exactly how I always thought my Bug would taste.

Just as I'm about to head back to her lips, the telltale sound of a college student's worst nightmare comes blaring up to my house.

Campus police.

"Shit," I groan, pulling away as I watch the red and blue lights swirling as they drive up to the house.

"Oh God," she says, trying to move herself from my lap. I don't move. No, I just pull her in tighter. "Simon, you have to go deal with that. There are cops at your house."

"I know," I say, kissing her forehead. "And yes, I have to deal with this. My name is the first on the lease, and my dad technically owns the house."

"Simon! Get down there."

"Not yet," I say. "Because I need to know this isn't it. I don't know how long this is going to take, and I don't want you anywhere near this because who knows why they are here, but I need to see you again before I leave for the summer. No way in hell I'm not going to kiss you again."

A blush comes over her cheeks that is the cutest, and sexiest, thing I've ever seen.

"Okay," she says.

"Promise. I'll call you tomorrow. I want to see you before I go. I need to see you."

She smiles. "I promise."

. . .

I sit back and take a sip of my beer. "And that's the whole story."

"That was beautiful," Oliver says, and while most might think he's dabbing his eyes to be dramatic, he's not. He's in actual tears.

"You promise?" Wes asks, ignoring Oliver. "Nothing else happened?"

"Well...."

"Simon," Shane snarls. "What did you do?"

"Nothing then," I begin. "She never returned a message or call. She never came back to campus. I didn't see her again until Jake and Whitley's wedding."

"But?"

I look over to Wes and shrug, because either I lie to them or I rip the bandage off and tell them everything.

Fuck it. Let's go.

"Maybe...kind of, sort of...after I went with Shane to the taste testing, I stayed in Nashville, got super drunk, called her, somehow it got through even though I thought I was blocked because I had been for years, and she might have come to my hotel to yell at me but instead we had sex."

"Simon!" Wes yells. "And here I was ready to praise you for not doing anything stupid."

"It wasn't stupid. It was fucking amazing."

All three simultaneously roll their eyes.

"What can I say? I am who I am."

"That's the problem," Shane groans. "So you then, what—bought a diner to somehow lure her to you?"

I shake my head. "No. I swear that was coincidence. I bought the diner not knowing she was even looking for a place

144

of her own. Sometimes things just work out. That's what happens when you're one of God's favorites."

"Yeah, you're his favorite pain in the ass."

I balk at Shane. "That was rude."

"No. Rude is not telling her you're her landlord. Rude is sleeping with her. Rude is—"

I cut Shane off. "Is it the best plan? No. I know that. But for years this woman ignored me. Left me wondering. I need answers that only she can give me. You have to understand that, right? Wondering for years what could have been?"

Did I just tap into Shane's many years pining for Amelia? Yup. Am I ashamed? Not in the least.

"That was fucking low," Shane says.

"I never said I played fair."

"So what happens after she finds out?" Shane pushes back. "Let's say in two months you get your answer. What then?"

"That's future Simon's problem," I say.

"That's smart," Wes quips. "This is going to bite you in the ass so hard..."

"Probably," I say, though realizing they're all right. "Am I stupid? Seriously. Am I being an idiot?"

Oliver raises a curious eye brow. "Are we being serious or telling you what you want to hear?"

I shake my head. "Serious."

"Yeah, you are," Wes says. "But at the same time, I get it."

"Same," Shane says. "Which I hate saying, because this is stupid. But I get what it's like to be pushed to the brink, when sometimes the stupid decision is somehow your only one."

I nod a thanks. "Oliver? Thoughts?"

Oliver looks over to me, a kind smile on his face. "Was she the one who got away?"

I should have known a question like this was going to come from him. "Yeah. She was."

"Then get your closure. Do it so you can move on. Just be careful."

I nod, appreciating his advice. Though I don't know if he's telling me to be careful with her, or to be careful with myself.

Honestly, it's probably both.

Yes, I need my closure. Yes, I need answers. But at the end of the day, I need to make sure she doesn't break my heart.

Again.

Chapter 15
Charlie

I pull my car to the curb in front of the building that is about to become my whole life.

I'm here. I'm doing this. I'm a resident, and about to be business owner, in Rolling Hills.

Holy shit. What the fuck am I doing?

I let out a yawn and just sit for a second before mustering up the energy to start taking some of my things upstairs to the apartment. There's still plenty of sunlight, despite it being after six o'clock at night. The warm rays are going to put me to sleep if I sit here any longer.

Which would be nice. This week has been a lot.

On top of starting to get things ready for the new restaurant, I officially put in my notice at Napoli's. Mellie squealed in excitement, then also put in her notice. Mr. Napoli begged me to stay and even offered me a raise. Billy thought he could charm me into staying by offering "private cooking classes" where he'd be on the menu. But, I told everyone thank you for years of employment and that opening my own restaurant had always been a dream of mine.

Inside I was telling everyone where to go and how to get there.

Because I'm leaving soon, Mr. Napoli didn't think it was wise of me to meet with prospective clients, so my workload is pretty light. The only event I have is Oliver and Izzy's reception, which takes place in one week, then my time at Napoli's is officially done. And while I wish I could use the time to rest and recharge, there frankly isn't enough time. I need every spare second to pack, move, and get the diner ready. Which is why I'm here after work, moving clothes, instead of taking a nap.

I love naps so much.

"Come on, Charlie," I say to myself as I give my head a shake to wake me up. "The totes aren't going to move themselves upstairs."

With a heave, I push the door open to my 2012 Honda Civic and pop the trunk. My tiny car is filled to the brim with bags, totes, and anything else I could stuff in for the drive down tonight. Even with one week left at Napoli's, I'll actually be here more than there, so I figured it was time to bite the bullet and officially make my move to Rolling Hills.

Which...shit...I promised Connor I'd text him when I got here.

Connor: Did you make it?

Oops...

Charlie: Sorry. Just pulled up. Shut my eyes for a bit. Long day.

Connor: You sure you're okay? You've been running yourself ragged. I can still come down and help you move.

The One I Hate

> Charlie: I'm fine. It will only take me a few trips to carry everything up.

> Connor: I hate I didn't come to help.

> Charlie: There was no reason. It's just totes. No big furniture. And you would have had to find a sitter for Lila.

> Connor: Stubborn as always, I see.

> Charlie: You're gonna miss me and you know it.

> Connor: We already do.

My brother follows that last message up with a picture of him and Lila blowing me a kiss. Damn him...now I'm about to cry.

Correction. I *am* crying.

Last night was more emotional than I thought it was going to be. Every time I looked at Lila and Connor, I broke into a crying fit. I was so emotional I even cried when Nuggy licked my face. I knew it was going to be hard to leave them, but I didn't expect that. I haven't cried like that in years. Probably since the day of Mom's funeral.

"You got this," I say to myself. "One step at a time."

With one more deep breath, I get out of my car and look at the building that's about to become my world. A sense of calm runs through me as I take everything in.

This is right. It's what I'm supposed to be doing.

But just as quick as the calm comes, it's replaced by an uneasiness I feel from head to toe.

"Bug! You're here!"

Oh, now it makes sense.

"Hello, Simon," I say without making eye contact. I see him

approaching, but I don't give him the satisfaction of looking at him.

"Are you just getting into town? Where are you living, by the way? Are we neighbors? That would be fun. Also, do you plan on ghosting me again? It's happened twice now, so I'd just like to be prepared if you think it's going to become a regular thing."

Breathe. This is what he does. Don't let him get under your skin on day one.

I turn and square my shoulders. I need to remember that my goal here is to make him watch my success. That's not going to happen if I cower to him out of the gate.

"To answer your questions in order: Yes. None of your business. God, I hope not. And no, I'm not. But that's more because I don't plan on ever, and I mean ever, touching you again."

Boom. Yes. That felt good. Strong. Not the wimpy girl crushing on the hot guy. Or the drunk girl who was...well, just drunk.

Except that feeling of confidence starts to dim as Simon's cocky smile forms on his stupidly handsome face.

"You know I'm going to find out where you live, right?"

"I don't care." I say as confidently as I can. "It's a small town. It'll happen when it does."

Simon looks into my open trunk, then toward the restaurant, then back to me. "Are you living in the kitchen? I don't think it would be very comfortable, though you could probably get a cot to fit in there. Do you have a cot? Do you want me to call my cot guy?"

I raise an eyebrow. "You have a cot guy?"

"You don't?"

I just shake my head and turn to start grabbing totes out of the trunk when I feel Simon slide up next to me.

"What are you doing?"

"Helping."

"Who asked you to help?"

"I thought I'd be a gentle—I thought I'd be a nice guy."

I slam the car door shut, nearly taking off Simon's hands as he hurries and lifts a tote. "Please leave me alone. Stop whatever this is that you're doing. You think this is cute. It's not."

"Sorry, Bug, can't do that. You live in my town. We're going to see each other. Like I said, I'm your Norm, so you should get used to this."

"Why do you insist on making my life miserable?"

He shakes his head. "I don't wanna make your life miserable. I want us to be friends. Best friends, maybe with benefits. You have to admit, the benefits were pretty good..."

"What's your point, Simon?"

"Sorry. Answers."

"Answers?"

"Yes. Answers. You have the answers I want, and until I get them, you're going to have to put up with me every day."

I drop the tote I'm holding and throw my hands on my hips. This man is unbelievable.

"The fact that you don't know the answer is laughable."

"I surely don't know what you mean."

"You want answers? Well, guess what, buddy, so do I. Because you think I started this, but it was you."

Wow. That stopped him in his tracks.

"Me?"

"Yes, you. So until you fess up to what you did, then I have nothing to say."

I grab the tote and start marching toward the entrance to the diner. I hear him yell something, but I don't pay attention.

I know he has to have the last word, which is fine. Let him

have this one. Because I know at the end of the day, I'm going to get the one that counts.

* * *

Groceries. I need groceries.

Yes, I realized that last night after my sixth trip to the car, but I was too tired to do anything about it. I didn't even eat dinner. Nothing sounded good, and frankly, I was too tired to even think about leaving. For one, I would have had to move. And second, I would risk running into Simon again. One dose of him for the day was more than enough. That and the bed that was provided in the fully furnished apartment was the most comfortable thing I've ever laid on. You couldn't have paid me to leave that thing.

But today is a new day. I feel a bit more refreshed, have the whole day off, and I plan on making this day my bitch, starting with groceries.

I love that Rolling Hills doesn't have a mega supercenter in town. No, the only grocery store in town is family-owned, and according to the signage has been in town and owned by the same family since 1945. I absolutely love it. The aisles are small and the selection is limited, but there is a meat department with a butcher on staff and a bakery taking custom cake orders. While I'd love to go sample the sweets, those aren't on the shopping list today. No, I need fruits, vegetables, and anything else that will power me through these next few weeks.

What I don't need is Simon Banks, staring at me while holding a peach in his hands.

Oh for fuck's sake...

"Well isn't this a coincidence," Simon says, tossing the peach up slightly and catching it. "Are we synced up on our grocery days? We should be shopping buddies. We could go get coffee, do some shopping, maybe some lunch where you can answer the question of why you never returned a phone call and blocked me. Or! You can tell me which position was your favorite. Mine was when you—"

I hold a finger to his mouth, shutting him up. Except the act makes him smile, which was not my intention.

"Are you stalking me?"

His smile turns to a face of fake shock as I lower my finger. "Bug! I would never."

"Yes you would, and you know it."

"I'm just a man doing my grocery shopping." He takes the peach and takes a huge bite out of it, our eyes locking. "And I had a hankering for peaches. I just, I don't know, wanted something I could really sink my teeth and fingers into, you know?"

I hate, hate, hate, hate, that my pussy clenches when he says that. I can feel his fingers digging into my hips and ass. The nibbles he bit into my thighs.

Fuck, this is so bad.

"You're the worst," I say, doing my best to regain my composure. Though guessing by the smirk on his face, he knows he's won this round.

"Actually, I think I'm the best. At many, many things."

"Yes. Best at being an asshole."

"Aw, is that your nickname for me? Bug and Asshole. I think it has a ring to it."

"You're insufferable," I say as I start grabbing every piece of produce I can find and throwing them haphazardly into my buggy.

"You love me," he says, handing me a plastic bag.

I snatch it from him. "Just leave me alone."

"I could do that. All you have to do is tell me what I want to know."

I stuff three tomatoes into the bag and swing them around,

nearly hitting him. "And I told you, you have to confess what you did before you get an answer."

"And I told you I don't know what the fuck I did."

I realize at this point that people are staring. Great. Way to make a good first impression on the new town. He pulls me to the corner, a little out of the way, which I appreciate. What I don't appreciate is my body growing hot just by his simple touch.

"Whether you believe me or not, I don't know what you think I did."

I shake my head. "Denial doesn't look good on you, Simon."

He pulls at his hair, and I'm pretty sure if we weren't in public, he'd be letting out a scream of frustration. "Charlie. I don't know what you want me to say. Because if I did, I'd say it."

"Admit what you did."

I must give him credit; he's earning an Academy Award for this performance of "Confused Asshole in a Comedy."

"I can't admit something I didn't do. Or even know what it is."

I take a step closer, somehow feeling empowered by his lies and denial. "You know what you did. So when you're ready to take your share of the blame, then you come and see me. Until then, don't speak to me."

I march back to my buggy, leaving Simon staring and seething.

Whew. Things got a bit dicey there for a second, but I think we can confidently call this round another win for me.

* * *

I did not want to get out of bed today.

My stomach hates me. I'm tired from pulling double duty

at the restaurant and Napoli's. Mellie's helping at the diner, but she's also still working so she's doing what she can. I just want to curl up on the couch with some Funyuns and the cult documentary I still haven't had time to watch. But no...I have to be a responsible adult and shit.

It's the worst.

But since it's a beautiful day, and I'm hopeful some sunshine will serve as the medicine to wake me up, I choose to do the task I've been putting off all week—washing the windows and touching up the exterior.

There are people walking along the streets who stop to tell me hello and to introduce themselves. While I hate meeting everyone wearing raggedy denim shorts, a tank top, and my hair in a bandanna like I'm Rosie the Riveter, it's nice to feel like I'm officially being welcomed into Rolling Hills. I'm also glad that no one seems to be bringing up my altercation with Simon at the grocery store the other day. Then again, another blow-up could happen at any moment if he keeps running past my diner like he has been for the last twenty minutes.

And not just running. Running shirtless.

Asshole.

And even worse than him running shirtless, sweating and tanned, is that he's doing exactly what I asked him to do. He's not talking. Not acknowledging me. Not even waving hello.

What an asshole.

I catch him out of the corner of my eye, which to my count would be his sixth time past in I don't know how many minutes. Is he doing laps around my building on purpose? He must be. Not that I mean to be counting. It's just hard not to notice when a ripped, tanned, sweating man, who has given you the best orgasms of your life, runs past you.

Don't think about orgasms.

Or how those abs felt when you trailed your fingers down them.

Or how his arms felt holding you. Or when you grabbed onto them when you were about to fall apart.

Ironically, the sight of him coming past for lap seven is what breaks me from my trip down orgasm memory lane.

"Enough!" I yell, throwing the sponge into the bucket, which of course means it splashes water and soap all over me. "What are you doing?"

He stops in front of me, his breathing heavy as he hits a few buttons on his smartwatch. I wait for him to say something, anything, but he doesn't. He just stands there, breathing. Sweating. Looking annoyingly hot.

"Simon! What the hell are you doing?"

He leans in to me so he can whisper. "Am I allowed to talk? I didn't know if I had permission."

I take a step back and throw my hands in the air. "Oh my God. Yes. Just speak."

"Phew. I didn't know what the rules were anymore. In fact, I don't know a lot of things right now."

I ignore his comment. "What are you doing?"

He looks down at himself then back to me. "Isn't it obvious? I'm getting in my cardiovascular workout."

"Are you ever not a smart ass?"

"I think you know the answer to that question, Bug."

I bend over to grab my sponge, which I am now just realizing gives him a clear view down my shirt. Part of me wants to hit myself for doing that, but the other part of me, the one who is now noticing him swallowing a huge lump in his throat, is glad she put on the free show.

Good. Glad I'm not the only one suffering right now.

I start to turn back to continue my window washing when Simon starts walking toward me, paralyzing me in place.

His eyes are heated. Burning. They remind me of the night —from what I remember—in the hotel. I remember my body being on fire from just his gaze.

It's my turn to swallow the lump in my throat. "What are you doing?"

He uses a finger to gently brush away some of the soap bubbles that are on my face.

"You just had a little something on you."

It takes everything in my power to not lean into his touch. Because it would be too easy to do it. To ask for a repeat of that night. He's already half naked. Hell, I'm not far behind him. It would be so easy...

Then the sound of a loud and irritating alarm goes off, breaking me from my trance.

"Oops! Time for another lap!" Simon says, moving back from me, completely unfazed. "See you in a few minutes, Bug!"

And just like that, he's off and running, leaving me more hot and bothered than I'd like to admit.

So I do what every other rational woman would do in this situation—I throw my sponge at him.

Chapter 16
Simon

There are things about me that always seem to surprise people, no matter how long they know me.

Everyone thought because I was the pretty boy who didn't like to get dirty that I'd be horrible at football. Wrong. I was the best running back in the county my junior and senior years. I also had the best game day fits.

People think because I'm not hurting in the money department that I'm an entitled asshole. Little do they know I've been working since I was fourteen and give half of my money to charity. Or spend it on family and friends.

People also think because I'm the perpetual single man who has never had a serious relationship, that I must hate weddings. And those people couldn't be more wrong. I love weddings. Open bar? Good music? A dance floor that I can take over? Now that's my kind of night.

And tonight's wedding is no exception. Well, wedding reception. Wedding bash? I don't know what Oliver and Izzy are calling it, I just know it's a damn good time.

I mean, it should be, I'm playing the music. My pre-dinner

music has had people on and off the dance floor since they came in. And no one is ready for my "After the wedding cake" playlist.

"Uncle Simon! Uncle Simon!"

I look down to see my seven-year-old goddaughter, Magnolia, jumping and waving her arms for me.

"Easy there," I say, taking a step toward her before kneeling down to her eye level. "Have I told you how pretty you look tonight?"

She shakes her head, but smiles as she does a little twirl in her pink flower girl dress. "Thank you. Do you like my dress? It has pockets!"

"I love it!" I say as I stand up. "What do you think about my suit?"

She giggles as I show off the bright pink suit I'm wearing. To match her. Because she asked me to.

I might be ruthless in real estate, but I'm a goner when it comes to this kid.

"You look silly."

"Silly!" I pretend to overreact as I pull off some modeling moves perfected in *Zoolander*. "You told me to wear this!"

"I didn't think you'd wear *all* pink. I love pink. But that's a lot Uncle Simon."

"Nonsense," I say, kneeling back down. "There is no such thing as too much pink. I personally love pink."

She wrinkles her nose. "Boys don't like pink."

I gasp. "Who said?"

She shrugs. "Boys at school."

"Well, they just haven't learned yet." I lean in to whisper to her. "You tell them next time that real men not only like, but wear, pink. And don't you ever forget that."

She nods her head firmly. "Got it."

"Hey," I hurry and grab my phone. "Selfie time!"

This isn't the first selfie I've taken with this child, and I hope like hell it's not going to be the last. We have a whole album. She assumes her position, always on my right side, as we take our standard three selfies—one smiling, one silly, and one with duck faces.

I do an awesome duck face.

"Perfect," I say, kissing her head. "Now you go and have fun while you wait for dinner to come out."

"Okay!" She says, planting a kiss on my cheek. "Can you play my favorite song?"

"Of course. But only if you promise to save me a dance later."

"Deal," she says before skipping back to the dance floor. I can't help but smile as I watch the little girl who has had me wrapped around her finger since the day I met her take over the dance floor without an ounce of fear or self-consciousness. Since dinner hasn't been served, no one is on it right now. She doesn't care. She's out there shaking it off just like the song I'm playing for her says to.

She might not be my kid by blood, but she sure as hell takes after her Uncle Simon.

I make sure I have the dinner music cued and ready when out of the corner of my eye, I see someone staring at me. I don't even have to turn my head to know it's Charlie. I'd know that curvy body anywhere.

You'd think now that I see her every day I'd start becoming immune to it. Quite the opposite. The more I see her, the more I want to find a hidden spot so we can do all the things we didn't get to do during our night together.

Then I remember I currently hate her. Which is really inconvenient. Because we could be having phenomenal sex.

But wait, what is she doing here? I knew that Oliver and Izzy went with her former restaurant for the food tonight, but I didn't think she was working there anymore. She's been in Rolling Hills every day for the past two weeks. I should know. I make sure to see her—and hound her—every day. And by the little that I can see without turning my head, she's in her full chef gear.

"Take a picture, Bug. It will last longer."

I see her jump a little, which of course puts a smile on my face. I pull the lapels of my pink jacket and adjust my black tie as I slowly turn toward her. Before I can approach, she's already trying to walk away.

"Were you staring, Bug?" I say before she can get too far. "I heard that the sight of a man with a child is sexy. Do you think I'm sexy? You think I'm sexy!"

I see her let out a huff before turning back to me. "I wasn't staring. And you're not as sexy as you think."

I wiggle my eyebrows. "But you think I'm a little sexy?"

Her face is angry and beautiful, and I have to make myself not grab her and kiss it. The conflicting feelings that go through my head every time I'm around this woman are maddening.

"Goodbye, Simon."

She turns to walk away, but I hurry and jump in front of her. "What are you doing here? Are you working? Why are you working? I thought you were in Rolling Hills full time now? Also you never answered if you think I'm a little sexy."

"Why do you always ask me so many questions?"

"I'm a curious person."

"You're a frustrating person."

I shrug. "Two things can be true at the same time."

"I—" Charlie starts to speak when a man in his early thirties starts marching toward her, shouting her name at the top of his lungs. He's short, skinny, and I can smell his Axe body spray from twenty yards.

I don't know who this guy is, but I want to punch him.

"Charlie!" He yells, stopping beside us. "Where have you been?"

She turns to him as frustration paints her beautiful face. "I was taking a break. Is something wrong, Billy?"

Billy tries to puff out his chest, which is a futile attempt. He looks like a toddler trying to buff out.

"Everything is wrong, Charlie," he says, a hint of arrogance in his voice. "For starters, your staff is putting out the wrong course."

She looks over his shoulder as servers are walking around, delivering salads to each table.

"It's the first course. Salads are the first course. What exactly is wrong?"

Billy huffs, hems, and haws as he scrambles for an answer. Who the fuck is this guy, and can I punch him yet?

"Just—just come back to the kitchen. This might be your last night, but you still work for me and I don't appreciate you slacking. Plus, there are things we need to take care of before you leave. We can't afford to get behind tonight."

Yup. I'm probably going to punch him.

"Fine. I'll be right there."

"Yes. She'll be right there."

Billy apparently doesn't appreciate my chiming in. "Who are you?"

"Simon Banks. DJ tonight. Best friend of the groom. And longtime friend of Charlie here." I extend my hand. "And you are?"

He doesn't say anything, instead just staring at me. He's jealous of the suit. I can tell.

"Why are you wearing a suit you stole from Barbie?"

Oh, now he's gone and done it. "First of all, I'd be proud to be a Ken. Two, it's not Barbie Pink, it's Bright Pink, you fuck.

And three, you never answered my question: Who the hell are you and why are you ordering around Bug?"

"Who's Bug?"

"Oh, I'm sorry," I say, my sarcasm rapidly ramping up. "That's what I call Charlie. It's my pet name for her. She loves it."

His face reddens. Oh. I see. He likes Bug.

Cute he thinks he has a chance. Adorable, really.

Billy ignores me and turns his attention back to Charlie. "If you want paid for your last night, you'll be back in the kitchen in two minutes."

He glares at me before turns sharply and storms away.

"Bye! Nice meeting you!"

Charlie slaps me on the chest. "Stop it. Ignore him and let me go back to work."

"Sorry, Bug. Can't do. You know I don't like to ignore things."

She rolls her eyes and starts walking away.

"Why are you still working?"

She turns back her head to me as she continues to power walk to the kitchen. "What?"

I grab her arm, pulling her toward a corner where we are a little more out of sight. "Why are you still working? I thought you were in Rolling Hills full time?"

She shakes her arm free. "Why do you care? Is my second job putting a damper on you harassing me every day?"

"I—" I stop myself, remembering that I need to choose my words wisely here. I can't let the emotion of the situation make me say stupid shit.

Wow. Is this what it's like thinking before speaking? I don't think I've ever done this before.

"I just thought since you were living in Rolling Hills that

you would be concentrating all your energy into the new place. That's all."

Her face is getting more red by the second. "Not that it's any of your business, but some of us aren't made of money. I couldn't afford to not work. So I've been pulling double duty. And if you don't let go of me, I won't receive a much-needed final paycheck."

"Fuck that. How much? I'll give you the money."

She shakes her head. "I'm not taking your money, Simon."

"Why not? You'll take his but not mine?"

She rolls her eyes. "It's different, and you know it."

I do, but I don't care to be rational right now. My blood is starting to boil thinking about her working all those hours. Fixing up the restaurant by herself. Why didn't she ask for help? I mean, I know she wouldn't have asked me. But she could have asked Emmett. He knows he can give her whatever she wants.

Note to self: Tell Emmett to offer her whatever she needs under a bullshit reason.

"Fine," I say as I take a step back. "But you know he wants to fuck you, right? Like he's probably going to try something before you leave."

She rolls her eyes. "He's not. And even if he was, it's none of your concern."

I open my mouth to tell her it's without a doubt my concern, but I don't. Because it's not. Even though I think it is. It's not. And I know that.

She's not mine. She never was. We were fleeting moments and one unforgettable night.

But she never was, and likely never will be, mine.

"Just promise me you'll be careful."

"Fine," she groans. "Now will you take your pink tuxedo ass back to your makeshift DJ booth?"

I laugh. "You love the pink, don't you?"

"You look ridiculous."

"You're pronouncing sexy wrong."

She shakes her head, but a little laugh sneaks out as she walks back into the kitchen.

But not before turning back and giving me one more glance.

And that, my friends, is what I call a win.

* * *

I'm an amazing fucking DJ.

The dance floor hasn't been empty all night. I hate weddings when the DJ plays a great song, only to follow it with something that's a drag.

Not me. This has been banger after banger. Even the older guests have been busting a move to what can only be classified as peak millennial hip-hop and dance music. People are going to be talking about this reception for ages.

"I hate to admit it, but you're pretty good at this."

I look over to Wes, who is shaking his head in disbelief. "Did you think I was going to suck? This is Izzy and Oliver's wedding. I wasn't going to let my best friend down."

"Of course you weren't," he says. "Do you need a break? You've been back here all night."

I switch the song to a ballad, because it's been a minute since I've slowed it down, and I guess it is a wedding. Plus, I haven't seen Bug since before dinner. Yes, I want to annoy her. But something also isn't sitting right with me about Billy.

"Yeah, if you don't mind," I say. "The next few songs are cued up. If I'm not back in time, play anything that isn't your emo rock bullshit. Actually, you know what? Don't pretend to know what to play. Ask your kids. They'll know."

"I take offense to that," he says as I move past him. "But you're right."

I pat him on the back and don't even pretend to go anywhere other than straight toward the kitchen. I know I'm not allowed to go in there to check on her, but is anyone really going to stop me?

I walk through the doors only to see a quiet kitchen. A few cooks are cleaning, and some of the servers are milling around, but no sign of Bug or Billy.

I keep walking through, no one saying anything to me, when I hear a noise coming from the back office.

"What the fuck, Billy? Get away from me!"

I don't wait. I don't hesitate. I definitely don't think. I just blow through the closed office door to find the slimeball trapping Charlie against the wall as she tries to push him away.

Yup. I'm going to punch him.

No. I'm going to fucking kill him.

"Get the fuck off her!" I yell, pulling him away and throwing him against a wall. My fist is cocked back when I feel Charlie's hands on my arm.

"Simon! Don't!"

I turn to look at her, her eyes pleading as she digs her fingers into my arm.

"Did he hurt you?"

My voice is clipped and my arm is pulsing, wanting more than anything to knock him out cold. Charlie shakes her head as she slowly lets go of me. "No. I'm fine."

I give her one more check before turning my attention back to the weasel. I take a step toward him, which only allows me to tower over him more than I already do. "You do not, ever, and I mean ever, come near her again. Do you understand?"

"Or what? You going to do something in your pink fucking suit?"

I have to give him credit. He might be small, but his confidence is through the roof. I mean, it's about to get him his ass kicked. But I appreciate the confidence. Kind of.

I take another step, pinning him against the wall. I watch as the confidence he had a minute ago evaporates into thin air. "Don't fucking touch her. Never to speak to her again. Don't contact her. Don't think about her. Oh, and you're going to pay her double on her last check."

"Why would I do that?"

I tighten my hold on him, making his eyes start to bulge. "Because I'm letting you live."

I see him gulp, and any amount of confidence he had is now gone. As it should be.

"Do you understand?"

Billy frantically nods his head as I jerk him forward by his shirt before throwing him into the wall for good measure. He slides to the ground, moaning in pain. I turn my attention back to Charlie. I don't say anything, and neither does she, as I grab her hand and take her outside.

The crisp September air hits us as soon as we step through the door. I grab her face, assessing her for injuries, when I feel her shiver in my hold.

"Here," I say, quickly taking off my jacket and putting it around her shoulders. "Did he hurt you?"

I know I already asked that, but for my sanity I need to hear the words again.

"I'm fine," she says. "A little freaked out. But he didn't touch me."

"Thank fuck," I say, bringing her into my embrace. I expect her to fight me. To push me away. But she doesn't. She actually does the last thing I expect her to do—she relaxes into my hold.

Fuck, she feels good; but those thoughts need pushed to the side. She's clearly shook up. I need to forget about our past and anything that's happened between us recently. Right now, she needs a friend.

She needs the guy she knew all those years ago.

"Here," I say, walking us over to a bench I see against the building. We sit down, and I don't let her go.

I might never.

"I lied," she says, her voice just above a whisper.

"About?"

"Billy," she says. I think she feels me tensing up, because she quickly catches up her words. "I knew he had a crush on me."

"Oh," I say. "So that's your way of saying I was right."

She laughs under her breath, her head on my shoulder. "Yes. You were right."

"I think those might be the four sexiest words you've ever said to me."

This makes her fully laugh as she sits up, playfully smacking my chest for good measure. Which I'll take. I might still need to know what happened all those years ago, but I need her touch more than that.

Fuck. I need her. I need her in whatever way I can have her. Having her back in my life these past few weeks has been...I don't know how to explain it. I feel whole again. Like I'm not just going through the motions of the day.

So whether it's as a friend, something more, or just the woman who serves me french toast every weekend, I'm going to take it. Because having any form of Charlie in my life is better than no Charlie at all.

"Thank you," she says. "I think I could have taken him, but I'm glad I didn't have to."

"You absolutely could have," I say. "What happened?"

"I'm not quite sure," she begins. "I wasn't feeling well

today. I think it's just exhaustion from working so much. I actually almost passed out."

"What!"

"I'm fine," she quickly says. "But I was lightheaded, and I felt like I was going to pass out, so I went back to the office. He followed me. At first I thought he was just helping me get my balance. Next thing I know he was pressing me against the wall."

"That fucker," I say, trying to stand up, but Charlie grabs my arm in time to pull me back down.

"He's not worth it. Plus, you'll get blood on your suit."

I know she's trying to make a joke, but it's not the time. "He tried to take advantage of you while you were sick. My fist through his face should be the least of his problems."

She shakes her head. "He's not worth it. And I'm never going to see him again."

"Damn right you aren't."

"Instead I get a different pain in the ass in Rolling Hills."

I smile as she starts to put me at ease. "Damn right you do. And he's much better looking. And can reach the top shelf."

She can't hold in her laughter.

"You're the actual worst." Charlie slaps my chest again, but this time I catch her hand before she can pull it away.

Our eyes lock as I take hold of it, moving it up over my racing heart. She can feel it. I can tell just by looking into her beautiful blue eyes. So many emotions are racing through them.

Confusion. Want. Need. A little hate. A lot of want.

I recognize them because I know that's what's going through mine.

The energy between us right now is charged in a way I've never felt before. It's almost like I can feel the current pulling us together. It's the attraction I feel every time I'm with her, only...more.

170

Again, I don't think. Apparently that's my MO tonight as I squeeze her hand against my chest and slowly start to lean in. She surprises me again by not pulling away—in fact, leaning forward as well. I can almost taste her cherry lips when the loudest noise I've ever heard in my life breaks the moment.

What the actual fuck...

"I'm sorry, Chef," a teenage guy says as he hauls three garbage bags toward the dumpster. "I thought you had gone home. Billy said you left. I didn't mean to slam the door open."

"It's okay," she says, quickly standing up and taking off my jacket she's been wearing. "I should go."

She turns to walk away, but I grab her elbow. "Let me take you home."

Charlie shakes her head. "I'm fine. Plus, you have a wedding to finish DJing."

"I don't give a shit about that."

She shakes her head. "I'm fine. Go back. Have fun. I'll see you around."

I watch as Charlie heads back inside, only this time, she doesn't turn back around for one more look.

Chapter 17
Charlie

Yellow.

So much yellow.

Yellow walls. Lemons. Sunshines. Sunflowers.

There isn't a part of this restaurant that isn't in yellow.

And if there is one color I hate, it's yellow.

"Okay," I say to myself. "Let's do this."

I crank up the '00s hip-hop and R&B playlist on my Bluetooth speaker before bringing over the ladder and paint supplies to begin "Operation White Walls."

I can never repay Mona for leaving everything here and keeping this restaurant in perfect working order. And not just in working order; some of this stuff is brand new. I don't know how I missed that on my walkthrough, but I'm not going to say no to state-of-the-art ovens.

Everything else is updating or cosmetic. New plates, cutlery, and mugs. Actually getting POS systems that take credit cards. Maybe new upholstery on the booths, but that's only if there's time and money.

And most importantly: painting. Though that's easier said

than done, considering I'm about to go through roughly ninety-two gallons of white paint to transform this place from the yellow submarine to my dream restaurant.

This is by far the biggest project, and I've been putting it off for weeks. But we're a little more than week away from opening, and I can't procrastinate any longer. And yes, I could have asked Mellie to help me, but the poor girl spent ten hours deep cleaning the kitchen, pantry, and coolers. I felt bad asking her to say.

So it's just me. Time to paint until I pass out from exhaustion or the fumes—whichever one happens first.

Though judging by my last few weeks, the exhaustion is going to win. I never realized how tired I'd be opening this place up. Like, I need a nap every day to function. It doesn't help that my stomach has been hating me so much I can barely eat.

Oh well. I don't have time to think about any of that now. I have walls to de-yellow.

"Knock, knock. We heard there was a paint party happening tonight?"

The voice startles me, and I turn to see three women walking in carrying pizza, paint brushes, and drinks.

"Izzy? What are you doing here?"

"What does it look like?" She holds up the drinks she's carrying. "You've met Betsy and Amelia, right?"

I wave at the two women who I've met in passing a few times. "Hi. Yes. But you didn't answer my question. What are you doing here?"

"Um..." They all look at each other, none of them seemingly able to say anything. Which is very, very, suspicious. "We were in the neighborhood."

"In the neighborhood? On a Friday night? With the exact things I need to paint?"

"Exactly," Betsy says as she grabs a paint brush. "Now where do you want us?"

They quickly disperse, not making eye contact with me as they find a wall to start painting.

"Hold it!" I yell. They all turn, guilty looks in their eyes. "Everyone sit."

I see their shoulders slump as they do as I ask.

"I don't know y'all very well. However, I'm going to go out on a limb and say that I doubt you all had a sudden urge to paint a restaurant tonight."

"That's not true," Betsy says. "I love a good sip and paint."

"But you're right," Amelia says. "Simon suggested we come down."

I throw my hands in the air. "Of course he did."

That asshole is playing dirty. Every day over the past week since the wedding he's been stopping in and asking what he could help with. Each day I've told him no. Each day he's refused to listen.

Mellie thinks it's hilarious. I think it's infuriating.

But he hasn't helped by actually getting his hands dirty. No. That's not how Simon Banks does things.

One day landscapers showed up asking what I needed help with for the front of the building. The next day a guy from a print shop magically appeared asking me how he could help with my menu and signage needs. And yesterday I was woken up to the sound of an asphalt truck paving the parking lot. Now that one I think was Magnolia Properties, but I could also see Simon doing it.

When he came in earlier today and saw the cans of paint, he tried to convince me to let him hire people. I immediately kicked him out.

"Y'all, I appreciate the sentiment, but you don't have to do this," I say. "It's Friday night, and I'm sure you have much better things to do than help a stranger paint."

Betsy shakes her head. "We don't. All the kids are hanging out at Amelia's house while the guys play poker at mine. I wanted an excuse to leave."

"Plus, it's about time we get to know you," Izzy says. "I mean, besides the fact that you're a damn good cook and you have our Simon *smitten*, it felt like time we got to know the newest Rolling Hills resident."

"What?" My voice comes out in a weird high-pitched tone I barely recognize. "Simon is not smitten."

The three of them clearly don't buy my bullshit. Probably doesn't help that my attempt at a poker face is being ruined by the thought of the near kiss from the other night.

"Your words say one thing, but your face says another," Izzy says with a smirk as she grabs a paint brush. "I should know. Been there, done that."

"It's not like that," I protest. "Simon and I...well, it's complicated."

Amelia laughs as she stands up. "Most love stories are."

I shake my head and wave my arms. "Oh, no. That's where you're wrong. Simon and I are no love story."

That's one emotion I know I'm not confused about. I don't love Simon. Yes, I might have felt something that wasn't hate when he pulled Billy away from me. And when he held me in his arms and calmed me down. And when we nearly kissed. But that's not love. Appreciation. That's what it was.

You can't love someone you hate, can you? Because I do hate him. At least, I think I still do. It's becoming more confusing by the day. Because that's what Simon does—he burrows his way into your life and makes you forget things like how he hurt you.

But then he flashes that damn smirk, and I have to remind myself to not melt.

"You tell yourself what you need to," Amelia says. "I just know he's been different since you came into town. And I don't believe that's a coincidence. I've known the man for nearly thirty years, and he's never been like this before."

"Like what?" I ask, curiosity getting the best of me.

Apparently that was the wrong question to ask.

"Enamored."

"Charmed."

"Slightly obsessed."

"And he calls you Bug!" Betsy exclaims with hearts in her eyes. "I heard the guys say he calls you Bug, and I think that's freaking adorable."

"Yes, he does. But it's not adorable."

"It kind of is," Betsy says. "I know you hate him, or something, but it's...I just never pegged Simon as a nickname guy. That's very big Book Boyfriend Energy right there."

I laugh, because he's the farthest thing from a book boyfriend. Or any kind of boyfriend.

Though if he put half the energy he does into annoying me into being a boyfriend, he'd be a pretty damn good one. Attentive. Gorgeous. Never boring. And the sex? My cheeks flush just thinking about that one night...

"Uh-oh!" Izzy yells, pointing at me. "I think she just realized it."

"What?" I ask. "What did I just realize?"

"That Simon isn't as bad as you think."

"That's—" I stop mid sentence, because fuck...she's right.

Dammit to hell, Simon Banks...you've done it again.

* * *

The girls left about an hour ago—we got very little done—but I still had some juice in me. Which means I need all of the '00s hip-hop to get me through this one wall.

By the power of T-Pain let me finish this tonight!

My hips start swaying as I roll the white paint up and down. With every brush and elimination of the yellow, my soul becomes a little more filled.

The company tonight has a lot to do with that. Those women are amazing. We laughed. We ate. We drank. Well, they did. The thought of a hard seltzer made my stomach flip. Yes, they might have brought up uncomfortable feelings I'm not ready to talk about yet when it comes to Simon, but they did it out of a good place. They want him to be happy. And even though we just met, I think they want the same for me. Spending time with those women made me feel a little more at ease about moving here.

Besides Mellie, I've never had a lot of girlfriends. A few in high school and college. But never a tribe like that. And it didn't feel overwhelming or like I didn't fit in. I felt like I was supposed to be with them. And even more so, that this is where I'm supposed to be.

"You were always so cute when you danced like no one was watching."

The sound of Simon's voice scares me so much I not only jump out of my skin, I throw the wet paint roller, which somehow hits my face and chest before falling to the floor.

"Shit! Simon! What the fuck?"

He snickers as I do my best to wipe away any paint on my face. "I heard music and peeked in to see some familiar dance moves. Though I thought you only danced in your kitchen."

His fingers come up to my face, and for some reason, I slap it away. "What are you doing?"

"You missed a spot."

The One I Hate

I stare at him as his fingers come across my cheek, wiping away the paint. His touch is comforting. The way he's looking at me is heated. And my mind? It's confused and rattled.

At any point he could lean in and his lips would be on mine, and I don't think I'd push him away.

I should. But I won't.

Dammit, this has to stop. I can't keep going on like this. The push and pull and the confusion and want and hate and lust is too much, and I feel like I'm going to explode.

"No!" I yell, quickly walking away—and immediately missing his touch. "Simon this has to stop."

"Agree, I think it's about time we get everything on the table. The weather is about to cool down so I don't have many shirtless running days left."

I'm simultaneously disappointed and relieved.

The two of us sit down at a table across from each other, stares barreling into each other as to who's going to go first.

"Ladies first," he says.

"Fine," I say. "Who was she?"

He tilts his head, acting confused. "Who was who?"

My eyes roll as I take a seat across from him. "You know who I'm talking about."

"I promise you I don't."

I laugh. "You're going to sit here, when we're actually airing this dirty laundry out, and you're going to continue to play dumb about what started this whole chain of events."

"Charlie, I swear to you, I have no idea who, or what, you're talking about."

The use of my real name takes me off guard.

"You're being serious?"

"As a heart attack."

"Can I refresh your memory?"

"Please do," he says. "I'm all ears."

. . .

My heart is racing as I approach Simon's house. I look up to the roof where we sat last night, and it's like I can feel him kissing me all over again. Who knew a kiss could linger for hours after it happened?

But it has. I could barely sleep last night after I left. I've only had a few kisses in my life, and none were anything like that. It was...I don't know if I can describe it. I've never felt so cherished, or wanted, in my life.

And I want more of it. And I want it with Simon.

Which sounds ridiculous. This is Simon Banks, and part of me still can't believe he's interested in a girl like me. But he is. I truly believe that now.

I know he said we'd see each other before he left, and I know I should have waited for him to text me, but I couldn't wait anymore.

Apparently this is what it's like to be head over heels.

I'm all smiles as I walk up his front steps, avoiding a few beer cans and other trash that's still lingering from last night. The door is wide open, and just as I'm about to take a step inside, I'm nearly run over by one of his roommates carrying a huge box.

"Is Simon here?" I ask.

"Upstairs."

The house is chaos as I walk through the entryway. Boxes are everywhere. People are in and out as they carry things to cars and trucks. No one is even looking at me as I make my way up the staircase toward what I now know is Simon's room. His is the only door shut, which I don't find odd, but I also don't feel comfortable just walking in.

I raise my hand to knock, but before I can, it opens. Only Simon isn't the one standing across from me.

It's one of the girls that was dancing on the makeshift stage last night.

And she's wearing one of his shirts.

And that's all.

"Hi!" she says, her bubbly voice sounding like nails on a chalkboard. "Are you looking for someone?"

I swallow and force back tears. "I'm looking for Simon."

"Oh. He's in the shower. Can I tell him you came by?"

I shake my head and start backing away. I don't say another word as I race down the stairs and sprint out of the house to my car. I peel away, but only make it down the street before I pull into a parking lot and just cry.

And cry. And cry some more.

He made me believe I was different.

He made me think I was special. He told me I was. He made me feel like I was.

I wasn't just the poor, chubby girl who no one gave a second look to. I was someone. Someone special.

Then he kissed me. He kissed me like no one had ever kissed me before.

And it was all just a lie.

Because once again I'm not the girl guys like him go for. I'm just the one they have a good time with and get their rocks off by fucking with.

Once again, I'm not enough.

I'm crying so hard I barely hear the sound of my phone ringing. I do my best to stop crying when I realize it's Connor calling.

"Hello?"

"Hey. You need to come home."

This gets my attention. Something in Connor's voice is freaking me out. "Why? What's the matter?"

"It's Mom. It's not good, Charlie. Just get home. Now."

"My mom died a week later. My brother was sixteen, and I was suddenly his legal guardian. I had to drop out of school and start working full time to support him."

The tears are pouring from my eyes, but I keep on going. "So thanks. In the blink of an eye I lost my two best friends in the entire world. One because of an illness that fucking sucks and the other because of a man who couldn't keep it in his pants."

Simon doesn't react to my choice of words, or my retelling of one of the worst moments of my life, instead just moving next to me and taking my hands in his. And because I'm too much of an emotional basket case right now, I don't fight it.

"I'm so sorry about your mom," he says. "I didn't know."

"I never told you," I say. "I didn't want anyone to know."

"You should have," he said. "I would have been there. I would have come to you. Been there with you. You shouldn't have had to go through that alone."

I laugh through the tears. "And bring your blonde, thin, perfect girlfriend? Or did you miss that part?"

He shakes his head, and I can tell he's trying to suppress a laugh.

"Are you laughing?"

He shakes his head. "No. Yes. But not in the funny way."

I pull my hands away from his hold. "Please. Elaborate."

"I don't think you want to know."

"Yes,

I fucking do!"

"Are you sure? Because you're not going to like what I have to say."

"Try me."

"Okay," he says, pulling out his phone.

"What are you doing?"

"Finding evidence to prove my innocence," he says. After a few more scrolls, he holds up a picture to me. "Is this her?"

It's a blast from the past as I stare into the eyes of the woman who sent me into the lowest point of my life. But there she is. Older in this picture, but still just as beautiful. She's standing next to Simon, but they aren't alone. It's her, Simon, two people who are old enough to be Simon's parents, and three other women.

Oh shit...

"Was that the girl you saw?"

There's a coldness to his voice. His gaze is hard. Then there's the dread, shame, and growing embarrassment that's running through me.

"Yes."

"Then you've met my sister Maeve."

My jaw drops a little as I do my best to remember that night. "Your sister?"

I watch as his jaw clenches and his face starts to flush.

"Yes," he says, but not before letting out a frustrated breath. "She and her friends randomly came into town the day of the party."

His words are clipped. My mind is racing, replaying everything from that day.

"She was wearing your shirt."

"Because she forgot to pack something to sleep in."

"She was dancing by you when I came in. I saw her."

"Yes. On the end. Not by me. Now her friends? They were a different story. One had a big crush on me." Simon's voice is as loud as I've ever heard it. "If you remember that night, I didn't touch any of them. I told you that. Point blank. Because there was only one girl I was interested in. And I thought after I *kissed her* and told her as much, she'd have believed me. Apparently I was wrong."

The crack in his voice at the end cuts through me.

"I—" I don't have words as shame courses through me. "I'm sorry, Simon."

He stands up, and for the first time in his life, he doesn't say anything. He just hangs his head as he starts slowly walking to the door.

"Simon!" I follow him to the door. "Please say something."

He stops, but doesn't make eye contact with me. "No."

"No?"

He turns around and when he finally looks up, I see a tear well in his eye.

The tear I put there.

"If I stay here another minute, I'm going to say something I can't take back." His voice is low, and I can tell he's doing his best to keep it steady. "I'm going to leave before I do or say something I'll regret."

"Simon...please..."

He doesn't answer my plea. He doesn't say another word as he walks out of the diner.

The day I cried over Simon was the most tears I've ever shed—even over the day my mom died. Simon broke me that day, and I didn't think I'd ever put myself back together.

Now here I am, crying over him yet again.

And I only have myself to blame.

Chapter 18
Simon

> Oliver: Earth to Simon. You alive?

I look at my phone and toss it back on my couch, not wanting to deal with Oliver's antics today. That is, until the incessant buzzing of text messages coming through leaves me no choice but to read whatever the hell my friends are saying.

> Shane: We saw him last night. He's fine.

> Wes: But is he? I called his bluff, and he didn't even flip a table.

> Shane: True. And he left strangely early. I bet he was going to see a certain person...

> Oliver: Oh! Did you? Did you go see Charlie? Did something happen? I only ask because you are strangely silent, and I don't know how to handle this version of Simon Banks.

> Wes: Guys, this is huge. Simon's in his feelings about a woman.

185

> Shane: Now, let's not jump to conclusions. We don't know if this about Bug. He could have just scuffed his new shoes.

I furiously start typing.

> Simon: Quit calling her Bug. I'm the only one who calls her that. You hear me?

> Shane: There it is. Thought that would get your attention...

Fucker. I played right into his hands.

> Oliver: We're coming over.

> Simon: No, you aren't.

> Wes: Yes, we are. You've done this for us, now it's time to return the favor.

> Simon: The doors are locked, and I'm not letting you in.

> Shane: The man who has keys to all our houses thinks we don't have one for his? Put on pants. We'll be over in twenty.

Like clockwork, twenty minutes later my three best friends are standing in front of me, staring at me in a way they never have before.

Disbelief.

Curiosity.

Pity.

That one's the worst.

"Fuck," Shane says. "Have you slept?"

"Are those the clothes you had on last night?"

I nod as everyone takes a seat around me in my living room. "No and yes."

"Fuck," Shane says. "It's worse than we thought."

"I'll call for food to be delivered," Wes says.

"I'll go make sure he has booze," Shane adds with a heavy sigh.

Oliver pulls out his phone. "I'll text the girls and tell them we'll be a while."

Even in my exhaustion, I can't help but feel grateful at my three best friends dropping everything to come here. They're right that I've done it for them. We all have. I guess I never realized it would one day be my turn.

Though in my defense, this is only happening because Charlie is back in my life. Women don't get under my skin. I've never met one who made me want more. I could never see myself with anyone past one night. No one held my interest long enough, or made me give a fuck.

But I do with Charlie. Or I did. Fuck I don't know. After last night, I don't know anything anymore.

For years I thought it was me. That I did something wrong. She made me wonder and question everything about myself, only to find out it was because of a misunderstanding I never knew happened.

If only I would've showered ten minutes later. Or my sister would've remembered a fucking sleep shirt. Or that the cops wouldn't have been called the night before. There are so many little things that could've changed the course of history.

But no. They happened. And here we are. Fifteen years lost and a mix of emotions that I don't know how to fucking process.

"Okay," Oliver says, sitting by me on the couch as Wes and Shane take their seats in the two chairs I have in my living room. "What happened?"

I sit back, my head to the ceiling as I try to decide where to start. "You know the saying about being careful what you wish for?"

"Oh shit," Wes says. "I take it that you finally got your answer?"

I nod. "Yup. And it's made me question everything."

My friends intently listen as I tell them about last night. I leave out the part where I thought we were going to kiss again and go straight for the reason I look and smell like a dirty sock. When I get to the bomb—the one that still has me rattled—I watch each of their reactions almost in slow motion. Dropped jaws, wide eyes, open mouths that aren't making any sounds.

At least I know what I likely looked like last night when Charlie was recounting this fateful night.

"So that's it," I say. "She saw Maeve, and it scared her off. Charlie didn't know she was in town—I don't even think she knew I had a sister—saw her in my shirt, and that was that. Add that on top of the shit with her mom, and poof, Charlie was mist in the wind."

"Wow," Oliver says. "I can't imagine what she was going through. Mom dying and becoming a guardian to your sibling? That has to be tough."

I snap a look at him. "You're taking her side?"

He holds his hands up in surrender. "I didn't say that. I meant I could see that she was going through a lot, and, shockingly, she has a point in this story."

"You have to admit, it didn't look good," Wes says. "Maeve is a beautiful woman."

"Don't fucking talk about my sister," I snap.

"You know that's not what I meant. I'm just saying, just on looks, I can see where the confusion happened. Imagine if you went to her place and saw a shirtless, good-looking guy."

I grind my teeth, not wanting to agree with his point.

"Fine. Let's go with that for a second. The question still remains, why didn't she ask me? Confront me? Why did she just run?"

"Her Mom was dying, you fuckhead!" Shane yells. "You expect to be on the top of her mind when she was losing her only fucking parent!"

"I know," I say, and I do. And I know my words aren't coming out right, but I have so many feelings and emotions that things are getting twisted. "I could have been there. I should have been there. This all could have been fucking solved if she just would have—"

"What?" Shane stands up, which is how I know he's about to tough-love me. "She was hurt, Simon. She thought you hurt her. Whether you did or not, that was what she was feeling. And you can't take that away from her."

"Fuck!" I yell, because he's right. "But she had to know that I wouldn't have done that to her! Why did she just assume that I would kiss her and then turn around and hook up with someone else?"

"Because sometimes it has nothing to do with you. Shockingly, not everything is about Simon Banks."

Shane's words hit me like a semi.

He's right.

Back then, when Charlie would turn me down, I wondered what she didn't like about me. She would never give me the time of day, but would date other guys.

After she ghosted me, I thought the same thing. What did *I* do that made her run?

Maybe if I would've taken five seconds to think about someone other than myself, I would've realized this wasn't about me. It was about her. About her insecurities. About how she thought she was so different from me. Or other girls.

Girls like my sister and her friends.

She tried to tell me so many times how she felt. Even that night on the roof. And I heard her. I did.

But maybe I didn't...

"Dammit," I say, sitting back down and holding my head between my hands. "This is so fucking jacked up."

"It is," Oliver says. "Imagine after all these years learning that, in a minute, your entire life changed."

"That's what I can't stop thinking about. The what-ifs. What if the cops hadn't come? What if we could've stayed on that roof all night? What if Maeve and her friends hadn't come to town? What if her mom hadn't been sick?"

Oliver clears his throat. "Or... What if this is how it was supposed to happen?"

Oh, please. "I'm not in the mood for your glass-half-full bullshit."

"Just hear me out," he says. "You can't change the past. So there's no point in dwelling. You could what-if yourself to death, and it looks like you're already halfway there."

"Make your point, Oliver."

"What I'm saying is, maybe you two weren't ready for each other back then. You have no idea what would've happened if you were together when her mom passed away. A death like that takes a toll on people in ways you can't fathom. Add in the fact that she had to become her brother's guardian? Come on, Simon. You two wouldn't have survived that."

"Yes, we would have."

"You don't know that and don't pretend to," Wes chimes in. "What Oliver is trying to say is that you both were young and in situations that neither of you could have handled with skill. And rightfully so. You were young and dumb and president of your frat. She was suddenly responsible for a household. Tell me those are good odds?"

The One I Hate

Why are all my friends being right today? It's fucking bullshit.

"This just...ah!" I yell as I pull at my hair. "I'm just so mad."

"That's valid," Shane says. "No one's telling you not to be mad. But, let's go a layer deeper. What specifically are you mad about?"

I look over to him. "When did you become a shrink?"

"Humor me."

"I'm..." I trail off because I suddenly realize I need to think about this. "I'm mad that she assumed."

"Fair. What else?"

"I'm mad that I couldn't help her. I'm mad that I couldn't make her see how much I cared about her. I'm mad that she didn't see herself like I did. And I'm mad that she had a really hard fucking life and I wasn't there for her. I'm mad that she was forced to become so damn independent when I could have made it easier on her. I'm mad that I spent years wondering what was wrong with me. And I'm mad we've wasted years because of one fucking dumbass moment that changed the course of history."

I look up from my monologue to see three sets of eyes looking at me like I'm the only one who doesn't know the answer.

"What?"

"Go to her," Wes says. "Tell her everything you just told us."

"Really?"

Oliver pats my leg. "Yes, really. You said once you got your answer, you could move on. Now you have your answer. Now you can move on, with each other. Or at least you can give it an honest try."

I think about that for a second. I don't know why that never occurred to me. I figured once I knew what happened, I'd want nothing to do with her. That anything I felt would be washed away.

I was wrong. So wrong.

"You like her, that much is clear," Shane says.

"How do you know?"

"I knew that day when Mona introduced her to the town. Because Simon Banks doesn't stare. He doesn't step out of the spotlight for a person. Not unless he cares for them."

Damn, he's right...

"You wondered what happened all those years ago. Don't spend the next fifteen wondering what could have been."

Chapter 19
Charlie

"Charlie? Sweetie? You okay?"

I slowly blink open my eyes to see Mellie staring down at me, brushing my hair off my forehead.

"Mellie? What are you doing here? Why are you in my apartment?"

"Well, you asked me to the diner today so we could start organizing the kitchen, but the doors were locked and you weren't answering your phone. Luckily, the property manager happened to be here and let me in. He's a really nice guy. Cute, too. And when he called me 'darlin'' I about lost it. Do you think—"

I don't hear another word as a wave of nausea overtakes me. I throw the covers off me, possibly slapping Mellie in the process, race down the hall, barely making it to my bathroom.

And then, I throw up.

I throw up so much.

This is the worst. The actual worst.

I've been sick at least once a day for weeks now. I've lost

track of how many times I've thrown up. And no matter what I do, eat, or take, it isn't going away.

"Girl, did you get drunk last night without me?" Mellie asks as I rest my head on my arm, which is currently draped across the toilet—also known as my new best friend.

"I wish. At least this would have a reason," I say. "I haven't drank in months. Too much going on."

I hear the sound of water running before feeling a cool compress on the back of my neck. "Did you eat something weird?"

"No. Hell, I can barely eat anything these days."

"Wait. How long have you been sick?"

I sit up, keeping the wash cloth on my neck. "I don't know? Few weeks?"

"And haven't you told me you've been overly tired?"

"Yeah, but that's because of the long hours and the double duty. And the manual labor is more than what I'm used to."

"And you haven't seen a doctor?"

I shake my head. "I don't need to see a doctor because I've been a little nauseous. That's what Pepto is for. You know. The pink stuff."

"Well, you're going to need a doctor, since you're pregnant."

I snap my gaze to hers, which makes me want to be sick all over again. "What did you just say?"

"I think, possibly, maybe, you might be pregnant."

I laugh. I actually laugh so much I throw up again, that's how funny it is.

When that round's done, I take the washcloth off my neck and quickly wipe my mouth with it. "Listen, I know we haven't seen each other as much as we were used to, but I can assure you, I'm not pregnant."

"Really? Morning sickness. Constant exhaustion. Steady

nausea. And while I promise I wasn't staring, your boobs are looking rather...generous."

I take a second to think about it, and shit, they are sore. So sore.

Which I noticed over the last few days, but I just thought that was a sign of my period coming.

The period that hasn't come.

That I haven't had since I moved here.

"Oh my God! I haven't had my period. Since...I don't know!" Fuck, fuck, fuck, fuck!. "Oh my God, Mellie, I can't be pregnant. I can't be."

I mean it. I can't be. There's never a good time to be accidentally pregnant, but this is for sure the worst time for me. I'm days away from the restaurant opening. Supplies are starting to be delivered, and we're in the final stages of getting everything ready. I was supposed to meet with the line cooks who wanted to stay on from Mona's this week. I have a whole restaurant to set up. I don't have time to be pregnant.

And then there's the whole fact that if I am, this is Simon's baby.

The man who most likely hates me now.

The man who, as it turns out, I don't hate at all.

I curl up in a ball against my bathtub as my friend comes over and puts her arms around me. "Hey, we don't know anything yet. I'm sorry I freaked you out. It's probably not the case. You know I like to assume the worst."

"You are a literal ray of fucking sunshine, and the glass is always overflowing. Quit trying to make me feel better."

"I'm sorry," she says as she pulls me in tighter. "Okay. Apparently my observation might have some possibilities, which means there's only one thing to do."

"Crawl in a hole, hope this was a false alarm, and hide from the world until it passes?"

She laughs. "Unfortunately, no. It's time you pee on the stick."

* * *

I couldn't go and buy it. One, I was embarrassed, and two, another round of sickness hit, making me physically unable to leave my bathroom. And bless Mellie's heart, she drove a half hour out of town to buy six different kinds of tests.

And all six are telling me that I'm pregnant.

"Holy shit! You're going to be a mama!" Mellie is squeezing me while jumping up and down as I stand still, and in shock, in my bathroom.

I don't say anything. I don't think I even blink. I just stare down at the six tests and the ten pink lines staring back at me. It's not twelve because one of the tests just says "pregnant."

Thanks, test. Really drove the point home when I saw it in writing.

"I'm going to be a mom."

I might have whispered the words, but I might as well have shouted them from the rooftops. And the second the last word comes out, the reality hits.

I'm going to be a mom.

A single mom.

A broke, single mom who just took the biggest leap of faith in her life and now is questioning every decision I've made over the last month.

A broke, single mom who is carrying a baby by a man who probably hates her.

An about-to-be mom who really misses her mom right now.

Because I don't know what to do. And my mom would. She'd know exactly what to do.

And all I can think to do right now is cry.

"Hey," Mellie says, joining me on the cool tile that I just slid down to. "I know you're scared."

"That's one way to put it."

"And you don't have to make any decisions today."

I nod, though I already know that I'm keeping it. I always wanted to be a mom. I just thought since I was thirty-six and had no prospects and couldn't afford to do it on my own, that it wasn't in the cards for me.

But here it is. Just not exactly as planned.

"There's no decision to make. I'm keeping it."

"Okay, then," she says. "Can I ask?"

"It's Simon's."

"Oh. When you..."

I nod. "Yup. This baby was literally conceived because of hate and tequila."

"It will be quite a story when it makes its way to the world. And I was there to make it happen. Oh! Aunt Mellie. I love it. Can I buy the first baby apron? I already know the Etsy store."

I laugh and sit back, letting my head rest against the wall. "Mellie? What am I going to do?"

She takes my hand in hers and gives it a squeeze. "What you always do. Survive. Make shit happen. Be the badass you are. And know that this little person is going to have the best mama in the world."

And now I'm crying again. "I don't know about that. I didn't even realize I was pregnant."

"But you do now. And you're already making the plan in your head. Which is how I know this baby is going to be the best surprise of your life."

That's one way to look at it. The other part is, holy shit, what am I doing, can I do this? I mean, I have to. I want to. And I will. Even if I have to do this alone.

Oh God, what am I going to tell Simon? How am I going to

tell Simon? How is he going to react? The man is a bachelor to his core. Always has been, and I'm guessing since I haven't seen him with anyone since I've moved here, always will be. All of his friends have settled down. I'm guessing if he wanted that in his life, he would've already done it by now.

Then I stop and think about when I saw him at the wedding with the little girl who I've since found out is his goddaughter. The way he interacted with her made me look at Simon in a whole new light.

Is that the kind of dad he'd be? I know he can be frustrating and aggravating, but I know that's just part of him. I might have hated him for the better part of two decades, but I remember the man I got to know. The man I've started to see more recently. The man who pulled Billy off me. The man who sent workers to the restaurant every day.

The man who's about to be my baby's father.

"I have to tell Simon," I say. "I can't let this wait."

"Agreed," Mellie says. "You can do it on his daily drop-in. Is he still doing those?"

I shake my head. "I doubt it. We... had a fight on Saturday. He didn't come by at all yesterday."

"Oh," she says. "I'm sure it was a coincidence."

"It wasn't. And I don't know when, or if, he'll come back."

I go on to explain our fall-out two days ago; as I repeat it the sordid tale, I'm even more embarrassed than I was then.

His sister. All these years and all my rage, and it was because of his sister. And worse, I shut him out. I disappeared from the world and left him hanging.

I don't need an internet forum to tell me what I now know: I *am* the asshole.

"I want to apologize, but what do I say? I've held a grudge for years because of my own insecurities and past pretenses. How do you apologize for something like that?"

"I don't know," Mellie says. "Cook for him?"

I appreciate Mellie's attempt to lighten the mood, but it's not working. "Thanks. I don't know if there's enough french toast in the world to make up for this."

A banging on the door, followed by Simon's voice startles me. "Bug! Charlie! Open the door!"

How loud is he yelling? I'm in the back of the apartment, and I can hear him clear as day.

"Shit! What is he doing here?"

"Coming for french toast?"

"You're not helping!" I say, doing my best to stand up, despite being a little lightheaded. "He can't see me like this!"

"Charlie! If you don't open the door in thirty seconds, I'm breaking it down."

"You splash some water on your face. I'll go let him in." Mellie gives me a quick hug before exiting the bathroom, leaving me to gather myself.

I stare at my reflection and debate if this is the time to tell him. The short answer is yes. I have to. For one, I don't know why he's here, but if it's to tell me he never wants to see me again—which I'd understand—I need him to know. After what Lila's mom did to Connor, I will not keep the other parent of this child in the dark.

"We got this." I put my hand over my stomach, which somehow gives me the little bit of strength I need to turn and leave the bathroom. But before I can even take a step out of the door, Simon comes barreling in, almost running me over as he barges into my bathroom.

"What the hell?"

"Are you okay?"

His eyes are wild and his breathing is heavy. His hands are holding my face like he's checking to make sure I'm not hurt.

"I'm fine." Relatively speaking. "I should be asking if you're okay. Why are you rushing in here? And what's in the bag?"

"Me. I'm fine. In the bag?" He opens it up looks down at the inventory. "Four different kinds of medicines. A bottle of orange juice. Ginger ale. And an essential oil that a girl with a nose ring at the counter slipped in for free. But enough about that. Are you okay? I was worried."

"How did you know I was sick?"

Simon's breathing finally slows. "Emmett said you weren't picking up your phone and Mellie couldn't get in—lovely girl, by the way—so he let her in. Then he noticed that she left but came back an hour later with a bag from a drug store. So I took a shot."

I'm too confused to be grateful. "Wait a second. You got all of this from Emmett? Why are you talking to my building manager?"

He opens his mouth to say something, but nothing comes out for a few seconds. "I stopped by. Saw him here. Never mind that. Are you okay?"

"Let's go talk in the living room," I say, guiding him out of the bathroom before he spies the pregnancy tests lining my sink. Thank goodness my hips are big enough to block views sometimes. Really comes in handy.

"Sit." I sit next to him as he puts his bag of drug store remedies on the coffee table. "Before you say anything else, I need to say I'm sorry."

He shakes his head. "I don't care."

Excuse me? "You don't care?"

"Well, I do care. Thank you. I really do. That's not what I meant to say. And you can say you're sorry later. But I need to say what I practiced or I'm going to forget it."

"You practiced what you wanted to say? Like in front of a mirror?"

"In fact it was. I don't think before I speak most times, and I didn't want to say anything stupid." Simon pauses to breathe and takes my hands in his. "Bug, I understand why you reacted the way you did back then. Hell, if the shoe was on the other foot, I can honestly say I probably would have done the same thing. Or I would have gone to jail for killing a guy. Either way, I would have acted first and thought later. I know who I am as a person. And what you went through with your mom, I can't even imagine."

I nod. "Thank you. That means a lot."

"I'm not done."

"Apologies. Continue."

"Thank you." He takes another deep breath, and I feel my smile forming at how cute and nervous he looks. It reminds me of the night of our first kiss. Funny how just a few days ago, thinking of that night brought me nothing but sadness. Now all I feel are butterflies. "We can't change the past. And while I know I was living in it, begging for answers, I don't want to be that man anymore. I just want to think about the future. And, I want that future to be with you."

I think my jaw just dropped. "You what?"

He smiles that beautiful smile. "Charlie, I'm not one to believe in signs or the grand scheme of a universe, but it has to mean something that after all these years, you're back in my life. And in this town. In this building. And, well, if you're here, I want to be here with you. I don't want to waste another day, Bug. I want to be with you. That is, if you'll have me."

I feel the tears welling in my eyes. He sounds so sure. So convicted.

And I'm about to drop the other shoe square on his head.

"Simon..."

"No. Don't say anything else."

"What?"

"Before you reject me, might I remind you that I brought you medicine? And I practiced. I thought before I spoke. You know how hard that was for me." He looks downright reproachful.

I laugh. "It's not that. And I'm not rejecting you. There's just something else you need to know. Something that might change your mind."

He shakes his head. "Nope. Don't care. Whatever it is, I'm not changing my mind about us."

"You say that now..."

"Whatever you say, Bug, I promise I won't change my mind. Lay it on me."

Welp, here goes nothing.

"I'm pregnant."

Chapter 20
Simon

"Y" ou're pregnant?"

"Yes."

"I'm the dad?"

"Also yes."

"You're the mom."

"Obviously."

"We're going to be parents."

"All those things."

"Okay, then." I sit back on Charlie's couch, utterly speechless.

I'm rarely speechless. I've been talking in full sentences since before I was potty trained. Teachers had to give me time limits in class of how long I could talk when they called on me.

But here I am. Without words.

Charlie's pregnant.

With my baby.

I'm going to be a dad.

I should be freaking out. Like full-blown, breathing-into-a-bag panic.

But I'm not.

Not at all.

Why am I not freaking out? Me? A dad? I'm the fun uncle. The happy-go-lucky godfather. Never once in Magnolia's lifetime has Wes asked me to babysit, and with good reason. I don't know how to take care of a kid. Every fiber in my body should be on high alert panic mode right now.

But it's not. And I have a feeling why.

It has everything to do with the woman in front of me. She's the one who has always been different. Made me want different things. Made me think in different ways. The only one I could ever picture a future with.

The mother of my child.

So this might not be happening in the order it should be. Or maybe the order I ever imagined. But I was honest when I said that I wanted a future with Charlie. And if it's going to include a little mini us, then let's fucking go.

Oh my God...I'm going to be a dad!

"Simon?" Charlie says, worry in her voice. "Please say something. When you don't talk that worries me more than anything. It's unnatural. Please—"

I don't let her finish that sentence. She can't, when I'm kissing the words out of her mouth.

I'll speak eventually, when I come up with the appropriate words, but until then, she needs to know I'm in. I'm all in. And if I can let her know through my lips, or my touch, then dammit, that's what I'm going to do.

I cup her face with my hands, brushing away a stray tear that's coming down her cheek. Our lips are finding a rhythm, and I know there are a lot more pressing issues to deal with, but I just realized that kissing Charlie is about to become a regular thing for me, and that makes me very, very excited.

"Oh my God, we're having a baby!" My mouth travels

down to her stomach, where I start peppering her with kisses. "Hey, little baby. I'm your daddy."

"Please don't say daddy. That's weird."

"Fine," I groan. "I'm your dad. Ugh. Boring. Don't worry, I'll work on your mama, and she'll come around to me saying daddy. Or you can come up with a nickname for me. Because you already have one, Baby Bug."

"Baby Bug?"

"Yup. She's my Baby Bug. Our Baby Bug. It's perfect."

"She? Simon, you found out I was pregnant fifty seconds ago. I found out twenty minutes before that. Let's cool it on the gender and nicknames and figure out what the hell we're going to do."

"We can see who the fun parent is going to be," I whisper to Baby Bug, leaving one more kiss on Charlie's stomach, only to be greeted by a dark look that sends a shiver down my spine.

"What I meant to say is that you're fun, too."

"That's what I thought," Charlie says. "Now, let's have an actual conversation, please. Because while you're planning the gender reveal, I'm mildly freaking out. And I was expecting you to be mad or upset, so the whole belly kissing thing is really throwing me for a loop."

Shit...chill out, Simon.

"Of course. What do you need? What can I get? What do you want me to do?"

She shakes her head, but the small smile on her face is comforting. "Can we just talk? Make sure we're on the same page?"

"Yes. Perfect. Talking. I'm great at talking. First, obviously, you're moving in with me."

Her eyes go wide. "Whoa! Wait a hot second. Who said anything about moving in together?"

"Me. Just now. When you asked me to talk."

"Simon..." I'm trying to read her right now, but it's hard. She's taking deep breaths. Her eyes are closed. It reminds me of when I was little and my mom was trying to reason with me but I was being...well, me. That's probably not a good sign.

"Let's take eighteen steps back. You came over here today to ask me to date you. Which I haven't even agreed to yet."

"Wait! Does having a baby together not automatically mean we're together?"

She shakes her head. "Can we put a pause on the whole us dating thing? I haven't properly freaked out about the whole I'm having a baby thing, and I'd really like to do that first."

Oh. Shit. What an asshole I am. Here I go, yet again, only thinking about myself, when it's her feelings and her emotions that I need to be taking cues from.

"I'm sorry," I say, opening my arms, which she comes into. "How about this? Let's freak out together."

"You're freaked? What happened to Baby Bug and stomach kisses?"

"I'm a multitasker," I say, squeezing her tighter. "I might be excited. And I'm all in. But now that you're making me sit here and think, the freak-out is coming."

She laughs, though I can tell the dam has broken. She's crying again. She grabs onto my shirt, clinging to me, as we both let our emotions even out. At this point, though, I hope she's holding onto me for comfort and not because she thinks I'm going to run.

I'm not.

"We're going to have a baby," she whispers.

I kiss the top of her head and brush the hair off her forehead. "We're going to have a baby."

"Do you still hate me?"

Her question kind of takes me by surprise, but I'm glad she asked it. "No. I never hated you. Not really. Was I angry for years? Yes. Was I angry the other night when you told me? Yes."

"I don't blame you," she says. "I'm so sorry. I need to say that again. I should have confronted you. I shouldn't have assumed."

"Thank you for the apology, but I meant what I said. It was the past. And who knows what would have happened. We can woulda, coulda, shoulda ourselves until we're blue in the face. But that's not going to do either of us any good."

"You're right," she says, turning herself so she's lying against my chest. "Why live in the past when our present just got a little more interesting?"

I laugh and let my hand travel down to her stomach. Obviously she's not showing yet, but the thought of us being in this same position, her back against my front, as we sit on the couch together, my hands on her swollen, pregnant belly, makes me overly excited in many, many ways.

"One stupid night," she mumbles.

"One drunk night."

"One unsafe night."

"One *epic* night."

This makes her laugh. "What are we going to do, Simon?"

I kiss her head again. "We're going to have a baby. We're going to figure us out as we go along, and in the meantime, we're going to get ready for the blessing we didn't know we needed."

She sits up and turns to me. "But are we ready? You're... well..."

"A grown-ass manchild who you're questioning if he's ready for the responsibility of fatherhood?"

She shrugs. "I was trying to say that nicely."

"No need. I know who I am as a person."

"So yeah, you're...you. And I'm me. We don't even know

what we're like together, let alone as parents. I just moved here. I'm a week away from the soft opening of the restaurant. I took this huge leap of faith, while barely being able to afford it, and now I have to add on doctor's visits and baby things. And who is going to watch the baby when it's born? Can Mellie run the restaurant when I'm on maternity leave? Oh my God, I'm not ready, and I'm freaking the hell out."

Charlie's shaking now, overwhelmed in every possible way.

"Hey," I say, taking her hands and kissing each of them. This seems to calm her a little, but I can still see the fear on her face. "For starters, if you think for a fucking second I'm going to let you pay for anything in regard to our child, then you've apparently never met me."

"Simon, I can't ask—"

"No. Stop." My tone of voice is as serious as it's ever been. "I can't carry this baby for you. Or take away your morning sickness or do any of those things. But you know what I can do? Spend money. You know what I have? More money than I know what to do with. This is how I'm helping. This is how I'm taking some stress from you. Let me do this for you. For us. For Baby Bug."

I see the tears starting to well again. "I want to say yes."

"It's cute to think you have a choice."

This makes her laugh a little. "Are you sure? I feel bad."

"If you apologize again you'll have a new car by morning."

"Okay," she yelps, eyes wide. "Thank you."

"You never need to thank me. This is how I know to help. How to show I care. Please let me do this."

"All right," she says, a little more sure this time. "There's still a lot more to figure out."

"That's okay," I say, bringing her back against my chest. "We have plenty of time."

"I don't know. The baby will be here before we know it."

"When is it due?"

She shrugs. "I don't know. I guess we should go to the doctor. Shit, I don't have insurance yet. Or know any doctors."

"Don't worry. I have an insurance guy."

"Of course you do."

"Okay. Then that's first. You get insurance, even though I'll be paying all of your bills. We can find a doctor. I wonder if Amelia knows any? I can ask her."

"No!" she yells, popping up. "We can't tell anyone yet. It's too early."

"Really? I want to tell everyone. Like, I want to go to the roof right now and yell it out with a bullhorn."

"Simon, please," she begs. "At least wait until we go to the doctor and confirm everything. I can Google doctors. Though I'm sure you already know a guy."

I shake my head. "I have a lot of guys for a lot of things. But shockingly, I've never needed one for babies."

This makes her laugh. The first real one of the day. "Let's just take a breather. Keep it to ourselves for a bit. Get the restaurant open. Then after, we can tell everyone. Deal?"

"Fine. But I want one thing in return."

She sighs. "What?"

"Since I can't tell anyone, and I am *very* excited about this, permission to freak out here, in front of you?"

The smile she gives me lights up the room. "Permission granted."

"Yes!" I jump off the couch and get some serious air. "I'm going to be a daddy!"

"Please quit saying daddy."

"Nope! Because that's what I am! Daddy Simon, coming soon!"

"This is going to be the longest eight months of my life..."

Chapter 21
Charlie

"There they are! The mama and daddy to be!"

"See?" Simon says, gesturing to Mellie as we walk into the kitchen of the diner. "She calls me daddy."

"Quit saying daddy," I snap as I plop down on the stool I now keep permanently in the kitchen. It's easier than going to get it every time I feel nauseous or tired. Which is ninety percent of the time. "The word gives me the ick, and enough things are giving me the actual ick that make me throw up, so can we limit the use of the word daddy? And I swear, Mellie, if you say that even *one* of your cakes is moist, you're fired."

She firmly nods. "Got it, boss."

"Don't let her get to you," Simon says as he puts down the loads of takeout he insisted on picking up from The Joint, the neighborhood bar and grill. "Today has been a rough day. Which is why I'm making it better with lunch for not only my beautiful Bug, but for everyone. A well- fed crew is a productive crew."

"You bought lunch for everyone?" Mellie asks.

He smiles proudly, which makes my annoyed demeanor crack just a little. "He did. Which was very nice. Except he insisted on ordering in person and making us wait for it instead of calling ahead like a normal person."

"Well, I think it's all very sweet," Mellie says as she brings her own stool over to the counter as I start to unload the takeout boxes.

"It's just who I am," Simon says, picking up a few of the bags. "You two dig in. I'll take these to the guys."

Simon gives me a kiss on the temple before taking lunch to the men working on my dining room—the ones he hired to come and finish painting because he nearly had a heart attack when he realized I'd been breathing paint fumes.

"Okay, I'm sorry, but he's adorable," Mellie says as she digs into the fresh-cut fries.

"My stomach, nor my mood swings, can handle your brand of chipper today."

She laughs as she flicks a fry at me. "Oh, come on. Even in your grumpy state you have to admit that the man is really freaking cute. And doting. And protective. And hot. Basically the best baby daddy ever."

I shoot her a glare.

"Oops. Sorry."

I sigh as I dunk a chicken tender into my honey mustard. "I'm sorry. He's been great. And I'm not ungrateful. I'm just extra irritable today."

"Oh no, I'm sorry," she says. "Has the morning sickness died down?"

"Nope. And whoever named it morning sickness needs to be shot. Because it's most-of-the-day sickness."

"I'm sorry," she says. "But tell me about your appointment. How did it go?"

I feel the smile creeping on my face as I take a big bite of the chicken finger. Damn this is good. Mark this on the safe list of foods. "Well, in case we didn't know, I'm pregnant. Nine weeks along. The baby is the size of a grape. And I'm pretty sure my doctor hates us because of the roughly six hundred questions Simon asked."

Mellie laughs as she hands me the ginger ale she knows I'm going to need since I mainline the stuff most days. "That's fantastic."

"Embarrassing. The word you were looking for is embarrassing."

"It couldn't have been that bad."

"He asked how much sex we could have."

"Oh...Wait, are you two having sex?"

"We're not. He's hopeful."

"He told the doctor that?"

"Those were his exact words."

Mellie starts cracking up as my cheeks heat in secondhand embarrassment all over again. The questions started minor, like how much sleep should I be getting and what was on the banned list of foods. They morphed into him wondering if he needed to be measuring my stomach for progress and if we were to have sex, were any positions banned.

I didn't have find a new doctor on my to do list today, but that's obviously happening because I can never show my face there again.

"Okay, so he's a little eager," Mellie says. "But that's better than the alternative."

"What's the alternative? Because I'd like that as an option."

"That he not be here at all."

Well, shit. Leave it to Little Miss Sunshine to bring down the mood.

"You're right," I say, throwing down my french fry. "He's here. And very present. Sometimes too much, but you're right.

It's better than him not being here at all. Especially in this insane week."

"Exactly," she says. "And hey, give yourself some grace. You found out you're pregnant on the week of your dream coming true. It's okay to be all over the place."

"Thanks," I say. "I just feel like everything is out of control. Like we aren't ready. I'm not ready. This has to go perfectly, and I just feel like it's going to be a disaster because I've been distracted."

She shakes her head. "We're ready. The staff is hired and coming in tomorrow for training, which they barely need since most of them worked for Mona. Menus were delivered yesterday. Painting is set to be done today. The first wave of food gets here tomorrow morning. All of the plates, glasses, mugs, and cutlery came in today. We are ready for the soft opening, my friend."

"How did this all happen?" I ask myself, though I say it out loud. "I don't feel like I've done any of that, yet somehow it's done."

"You did. But you had some help." Mellie jumps off her stool and comes around to give me a side hug. "Get used to it, girl. You have a team here who wants to see you succeed. And we're going to make sure this place is nothing but the best."

Emotion runs through me as Mellie walks back toward the office. She's right. I've had help, whether I wanted it, or thought I needed it. She's driven in from Nashville each day to help oversee things while I was running around like a mad woman, doing things like opening bank and vendor accounts. Emmett came in with the health inspector to make sure everything was up to code and in proper order. Mona even reached out to the suppliers for me, including a mushroom guy she uses that she says is stoned most of the time but has good product.

Works for me.

The One I Hate

And then there's Simon. The father of my child has been in overdrive to make sure he's taking things off my plate where he can. Also known as what he can throw money at to fix for me. I objected at first—I hate taking charity in any form, but especially monetarily—before I quickly realized it was an act of futility. The man is more stubborn than I am, which is saying a lot.

It's also how he shows he cares. I never understood gift giving as a love language, but I'm starting to. Because that's Simon Banks to his core.

He's also really sexy when he takes charge. A feeling I'm allowed to feel since we're now...together? I don't know exactly what we are. But I do know that what we are includes things like small kisses and touches. And me ogling him from across the room.

I look around the kitchen, making mental notes of the things I can do to get ready for the food delivery tomorrow, before going to check on the painters' progress in the dining room. I've been so busy the last few days I don't even know the last time I've stepped foot out here.

And when I walk out, I have no idea what I'm looking at.

Because this isn't my restaurant.

No, it's better.

Fresh white walls. Not a drop of yellow anywhere. Pops of fun art perfectly placed on the walls in a way I could have never thought to do.

Then there are the brand-new booths and tables. I wanted to reupholster them, but I ran out of time and knew it wasn't the best way to spend my money. But these? They're perfect. Shiny silver tables and chairs that are modern, but not snobby. Booths in the perfect shade of blue I always imagined.

It's perfect.

If that didn't send me over the emotional cliff, I turn to the breakfast bar. That's when the waterworks hit. White and gray shiplap line the front of the counter, which you can see even with the brand-new stools neatly lining the row. New white exposed shelves are behind it, and the dishes I ordered are stacked in a decorative, yet functional, way.

"Oh my..."

"Aw, Bug! You ruined the surprise!"

I turn to Simon, who is coming in from the front door as I watch a literal moving truck drive away. "What is all this?"

"This, my Bug, is your new restaurant. Surprise!"

I'm suddenly lightheaded and go take a seat at the counter, but for the first time in a while, I don't think it's because of the baby.

"What do you think?"

"It's perfect..." I continue to look around in awe. I couldn't have imagined this looking any better than it does. "How? When? How did you know exactly what I wanted?"

Simon smiles and takes my hands in his. "Mellie was a big help with that, though we still guessed in a few areas. Getting guys to paint was easy. Even finding a decorator was easy."

"You're telling me you know a decorator?"

"I do." His smile is a little nervous, and I don't know if he's nervous to tell me something or worried how I'll react. "You remember my sister Maeve?"

It was the latter.

"The sister I thought fucked you?"

"That's the one. She's an interior designer. She can't wait to meet you, by the way."

How many times in a day can one be embarrassed?

"Anyway," he continues. "The painting and the decorating were easy. But the booths and the tables, those were a bit harder. I looked into fixing and patching what was at O.G. Mona's—that's what I've decided to call old Mona's—but when

216

Mellie described what you had always pictured, and the colors you wanted weren't what O.G. Mona's had, I figured it was just easier to get you new stuff. So I made a few calls."

"Simon! This had to cost a fortune."

"Don't worry about that."

"I absolutely will," I say looking around trying to do mental math of how much he had to have spent to get this done in two days. "It's one thing to hire painters. I could come to terms with that. But Simon, these are really nice! I can't afford these."

"But I can." He pulls me in, wrapping his arms around my waist. "Plus, I've never got to say I overnighted an entire restaurant from New York. I feel like I can add that to my resume. And now I have a table and booth guy. This was just as much for me as for you, Bug."

I want to laugh, but I'm also very confused.

"You have a résumé? Wait. What do you even do? Oh my God, I'm having a baby with a man who has a shit-ton of money, and for all I know he's in the mob. Is that how you knew guys in New York? And why do you always have guys for things? That's what mob guys say."

He laughs, and instead of immediately answering me, he kisses my nose for longer than I think is necessary. "I'm in real estate."

"Oh. Well, that makes sense, how you would know painters and people who could help."

"Exactly. Anyway, I wanted to surprise you."

"Wait! Is this why you stalled today and refused to call in the takeout order?"

"Guilty as charged."

I slap his chest, though he makes sure to catch and hold my hand to his heart. "Bug, this is your dream. Which means that it's now my dream. And this is where our child is going to grow up. She—"

"Or he."

"Fine. Baby Bug is going to grow up in these booths. Have a permanent high chair. Pictures of our kid are going to go up on these walls. Depending on the time of day and who is here, they will probably watch it for a few minutes because the people in this town have no boundaries. This is where it could maybe take its first steps. If you don't think I'm going to do everything in my power and means to make this place absolutely perfect for you and my baby? Well then, Bug, you don't know me at all."

I can't let him speak anymore. If he does, I'll cry. And I'm tired of crying. So I pull him in for a kiss that I hope says everything I want to say when I can't form the words.

He answers my kiss, cupping my face as I pull him in by his shirt.

This man...how did he do it? And not just the restaurant. For the second time in our lives, he makes me change everything I think about him for the better. One second I hate him. The next I only kind of do. Then I was pretty sure he hated me. Snap to now, and we're having a baby together and he's actively making my dreams come true.

What did I do to deserve this? Do I deserve this? He should have never talked to me again, considering everything. But not only did he forgive me, he's giving us the chance we never had.

And so am I. Because I've had a life without Simon. It was just okay. But Simon Banks in my life? Well, there's nothing quite like it.

"Simon?"

"Yeah?"

"Remember when you said you'd do anything you could for me?"

"Of course." I giggle as his mouth continues to nibble on my neck.

"How about we go upstairs?"

He quickly stops kissing me. "Why? Are you sick? Feeling okay? Do you need to lay down?"

I stand up as sexy as I can, considering I feel like a bloated blob. I take his hand and pull him with me, leading him toward the stairs to my apartment. "I do need to lay down. With you on top of me."

Chapter 22
Charlie

Simon blinks a few times. I'm guessing not sure if he heard me right.

Hell, I don't even know if I heard me right. Because I'm pretty sure I just said the cheesiest thing in the history of ever to ask my boy...baby dad...whatever he is...to have sex with me.

God, I'm pathetic. It's been so long since I've had sober sex, and I don't even know how to indicate it properly.

Except the way Simon's eyes have flipped a switch from concerned and attentive to downright ravenous, I'm guessing my line worked.

"Upstairs. Now."

Yup. It worked.

I turn to start walking back toward the kitchen, which leads to the stairs to my apartment, when I feel a smack on my ass.

"What the!" I jump and turn around, only to see Simon with the most devilish look I've ever seen before. "Excuse you!"

He tugs me back into him by the elastic band of my leggings, my back colliding with his hard body.

221

"If you don't want me to do that again, you better move faster."

A zing of excitement runs down my spine as I power walk through the kitchen, past the office, where I zoom right past Mellie, and up the stairs. I hear Simon's footsteps behind me, and while part of me wants to go quicker, part of me also wouldn't mind feeling his hand against my ass again.

What are these pregnancy hormones doing to me?

At least, that's what this has to be. My whopping four sexual partners before Simon would never describe me as adventurous. I'm pretty sure me being on top is the kinkiest thing I had ever done. And that caused me nothing but stress because normally I was heavier than them.

Then came my tequila-fueled night with Simon. I don't remember it all, but I remember most. I remember how I felt sexual and wanted and desired and passionate. I didn't worry about my weight. I was in the drunken moment. The feelings were foreign. A little exciting.

And I want to do them again.

And then some.

"Not fast enough, Bug." Simon is pressing me against my apartment door as I do my best to unlock it. I'm fumbling the keys, unable to concentrate with his hard cock pressing against me and his mouth sucking on my neck.

I hear the click of the lock, and I almost lose my footing as Simon and I stumble over each other into my apartment. I don't even have my bearings before he spins me around and smashes his lips into mine. If his arms weren't around me, holding me tighter than I've ever been held before, I'm sure I would have fallen.

Yet somehow I don't think Simon would have let that happen.

His intensity doesn't settle once we get inside. Our hands

and mouths are all over each other as we clumsily walk down the hall into my bedroom. He starts to pull my shirt up as my knees hit the bed, making me fall and bringing Simon with me.

Which is when I notice that my room is full of the afternoon sunlight.

Normally I love the natural light of this room when I push my black out curtains to the side. Right now? Not so much.

"Bug?"

Shit. I hoped the inside thoughts would stay inside.

"Yeah?"

"What's going on in that head of yours?"

"Nothing."

"Nope. We're not going to lie. Talk to me."

I throw my head back, hating that I gave this away with my body language and now I have to say it out loud. "Let's just say that I had more confidence ten minutes ago than I do now."

I hate sounding like the whiny big girl. And most days I can fight off the negative thoughts. I wouldn't say I love my body all the time, but I've come to accept it. I am who I am, extra pounds and all. Some days I'm more confident than others.

Today is apparently not one of those days.

He rests his head on one hand, his free hand beginning to trace circles on my stomach—also known as the part I wish he'd ignore.

"Am I still fighting away the little boys?" Simon repositions himself on his knees, my legs now under him and encased by his muscular thighs. "Did I not show you enough the night we made Little Bug how much I wanted you? Because if I didn't, I apologize. That's on me."

"It's not that. It's just...I was too drunk to think about it."

"Ah, the liquid courage." His hands slowly start moving up the sides of my torso, bringing my shirt over my head. As soon as my stomach is exposed, my hands reflexively cover myself, feebly trying to hide it.

"Nope. Not going to work." He takes my hands and pins them over my head while dropping a kiss on my nose. "I know you don't think words mean much. So I could sit here all day and tell you how beautiful I think you are. How utterly perfect every inch of you is. How you walk into a room and you take my breath away. But I know words are shit."

This makes me smile through the threatening tears. "Something like that."

"Would you believe me if I showed you?"

What is this man saying? "And how would you do that?"

There's a wicked smile on my face that hits me in my gut. "You just lay back and relax. Leave all the work to me."

His fingers gently brush down the sides of my arms before wrapping under my back so he can bring me up to him. He begins kissing me with a sensual passion I don't think I've ever felt as he unhooks my bra and tosses it to the side. His mouth starts moving across my cheek, down my neck and shoulder, before placing gentle kisses all the way down my arm. When he gets to my fingers, he brings them to his mouth, kissing each tip before a lingering one on the top of my hand.

"So beautiful." His mouth is moving back up my arm as he slowly lowers me back down. I do my best to relax and focus on Simon's expert mouth, which is easier than I thought it would be. Then again, Simon is making sure every centimeter of my skin is touched right now. I feel him everywhere, in the best way.

Just as I'm relaxing into his touch, my body jerks as his tongue laps one of my peaked nipples. Wow...wasn't expecting that.

I almost forgot how much I enjoyed the feeling of his mouth on my breasts. Yes, I remember what it felt like from our night together. But with a clear head? And pregnant? Somehow it's better.

So much better...

I've never had my brain and body fight control like this. My head is telling me to think every negative thought about my body I've ever had. My body—fueled pregnancy hormones and Simon's wicked tongue—want him to just fuck me already.

Talk about an angel and the devil on each shoulder...

"I can hear your thoughts, and they're interrupting me during my favorite part," he says, though he never fully takes his mouth off my breast.

I can't help but smile as Simon's words somehow relax me. The man is a conundrum. In some ways he's intense and put together. Always dressed for the party, normally in a suit, and commanding authority. Seeing him this week around the restaurant, bossing people around, I quickly learned that when it comes to business, this man doesn't play.

Then there's his goofy side. The one that makes perfectly timed jokes to ease the mood. Or like right now, when he somehow knew I needed a sliver of levity.

And last but not least, his smartass side. Most days it drives me crazy. But Simon wouldn't be Simon without it.

It's part of who he is.

And I like who he is. I like him a whole lot.

I also like whatever he is doing right now with his tongue and fingers on my nipples.

"Oh! Oh, Simon... right there."

He doesn't let up, my words of encouragement only spurring him on as he gently twists one nipple while flicking my other with his tongue. His beard is lightly scratching against my skin, which only stokes the flames I'm feeling.

I run my fingers through Simon's hair, my nails scratching his head before I pull slightly at his short curls. I feel him purr into my skin, and it might be the sexiest sound I've ever heard. It also makes him latch on more, sucking on me like if he doesn't he might die.

Funny, I might die if I don't have an orgasm in the next minute.

"Simon...please..."

My fingers are now digging into his scalp, begging him for more. "Ah!" I yell, throwing my hands back above my head as Simon's mouth releases my nipple with a pop before he moves down my chest. I suck in a breath and tighten my eyes shut as he reaches my stomach. It's soft and flabby, and we're not going to start on the fupa. And that's all before the baby belly.

Yet somehow, despite the intrusive thoughts and demeaning comments my brain is wrestling with, all I can feel is Simon's gentle, yet heated mouth on my skin. It's like he's somehow kissing away each insecurity. Each negative word I've told myself over the years. I don't know how he's doing it, but I feel myself truly begin to relax.

"That's it, Bug," he says as he starts pulling down my leggings and panties, his mouth never leaving a piece of my skin. "Just feel."

And I do. Somehow I do. I feel his expert tongue tracing circles on my stomach. I feel his fingers slowly sliding against my wet pussy. I feel my hands touching my own breasts, wanting any and all sensations I can have. I open my eyes to watch Simon, and just with a look, my body is an inferno.

I don't know this feeling. It's foreign and strange and exciting and amazing.

And I never want it to go away.

"Simon, please. I need you."

I don't have to wait long. With one last searing kiss to my stomach, Simon quickly stands, but only to strip off his pants and boxer briefs. His eyes stay glued to me as he crawls back into bed. It's intense and powerful and...it's because of me. Simon is looking at me like this. This isn't something you can fake. This isn't a few well-placed words with some empty promises.

This is hunger.

And Simon is starving.

For me.

He wants me. Not anyone else. After all these years, after our lives changing in the blink of an eye, the man wants me.

And I want him.

All of him.

I reach out, bringing him down on top of me in a heated kiss, only to roll him over on his back. His hands hold my face as I begin stroking his already hard cock. The groan he lets out only makes me go faster. Harder. Never in my life have I had this kind of effect on a man. And I must say, it's addicting. Hearing the noises Simon is making, watching how his body reacts, it's something I could get used to.

And it's the only reason I do what I'm about to do.

Blowjobs have never been my thing. I've done them when needed to, but never have I felt the urge to give one just because. Or because I wanted to.

I guess you should never say never.

"Charlie..."

I peek up to see Simon now looking at me, his eyes wide and in wonder.

"Yes?"

"You don't have to."

"I know." I give his dick one more stroke. "I want to."

Words I never thought I'd say, but I fully mean at this moment. Especially when I slowly lick his cock from root to tip and hear the guttural moan come from his mouth.

I slowly take him in, opening as wide as I can to accommodate his thickness. I slowly start going up and down, letting my tongue trail as my mouth works him the best I know how.

"That's my fucking girl," he says, gathering my hair in his hands. "You can take it."

Why did those few words suddenly make me want to give the best blowjob in the history of blow jobs?

It was also at this moment I realized I have a praise kink.

I double down my efforts, wanting nothing more than to drive this man wild and to give him every ounce of pleasure I can. I'm a woman on a mission—licking, sucking, and stroking, all in the name of bringing this man to his knees.

Just when I'm getting in a groove, though, Simon pulls me away and has me on my back in a matter of seconds.

"What's the matter? Did I—"

Simon kisses the words out of my mouth. "Oh, nothing is the matter. In fact, that was good. Too good."

"Then why did you stop?"

Simon lifts one leg up, giving him all the access he wants to line his cock to my entrance.

"Because, Bug. You come first. Always."

My only reply is the yelp I let out as Simon pushes into me. Holy shit, he's fucking huge. It's like I can feel him everywhere.

I remember this from last time, but I also thought that I was imagining how full it felt. I mean, I was drunk, and the adrenaline of the night was making me do crazy things.

Except now I know I wasn't imagining. If anything, I wasn't remembering enough. Because of the feel of him dragging out of me, only to push back in, is hitting every nerve.

Every. Single. Nerve.

"More, Simon. I need more."

He doesn't make me ask twice. Instead, he brings my other leg under his arm before lifting both of them to his shoulders.

Holy shit, I didn't know my legs went that high. Or straight. Or...Oh...Oh!

Simon's pace is picking up, and I don't know what spot he is hitting, but it's one that I didn't know existed until right now.

"Yes!" I yell, seeing the release in the distance, but not knowing how to get there. "So close."

"Touch yourself." I look up to Simon, wondering if I heard what I think I just heard. His face is serious, and his gaze is burning into me again.

He said it. And he was serious.

"Touch yourself. Don't be shy. Do it for me."

I bite my lip, suddenly nervous. Yet, something in me knows that I want to touch my clit.

So I do. I rub circles around the swollen bud, and holy shit...he was right. It feels good. So good. The tandem of me and him is something I never knew could be felt.

"Good girl. Now come for me."

I didn't know I could orgasm on command, but apparently I can. Either that or Simon knows the secret switch, because in a matter of seconds, I'm losing it. I let out a scream that I'm pretty sure the whole town can hear. Simon isn't far behind, dropping my legs and holding me tight as he spills into me.

We lay there for more than a few minutes as we come down from the highs. He rolls off me, only to immediately bring me into his chest.

Feeling his naked body against mine, still and unmoving, it's then I realize he did exactly what he set out to do.

He made me forget.

About the light of day.

About my insecurities.

About all the boys from before.

And I can't wait to do it again.

Chapter 23
Simon

I could stay in this bed all day. The blackout curtains in Charlie's apartment are doing their job. The bed is warm, and the woman who is currently serving as my big spoon is soft and perfect.

Don't get me wrong, I love being the big spoon. But if a man is telling you he doesn't like being little spoon he's a fucking liar.

This is the life. I don't know what time it is, and I frankly don't care. I've found heaven, and you don't want to leave heaven after you realized you've been in hell for years.

Because that's what life before Bug was. Hell.

Yesterday, and last night, were...I can't describe it. Which is happening more and more these days. Beautiful. Perfect. Amazing. Those are all true, but they somehow don't really grasp the totality of the night.

Watching Charlie become more confident in herself and her sexuality. Watching her come apart. Feeling her all over me. It's what I want for the rest of my life.

Because she's it for me. Always was, has been, and will be.

"Mmmm."

Charlie's hand falls off me, but I'll forgive her because that moan was downright erotic. I roll over to face her, and be a creep and watch her sleep, when I'm greeted by the most beautiful thing I've ever seen.

Boob. Popped out of her tank top. A crease of the morning light that got past the curtains is shining right on it. Like a beam from the heavens sent by angels.

It's glorious.

And because my Bug has the most spectacular tits I've ever seen, and I'm just a man, I give into the temptation of her perfect, round, pink nipple. I begin to lick and suckle as she starts gently moving.

"What are you doing?"

The sound of Charlie's raspy morning voice, combined with her breast in my mouth, makes me hard in two seconds flat. Then again, I think anything Charlie does, or will do, will have that effect on me.

"Snacking."

Her laughter fills the room as I continue to enjoy the start to my morning. I know Charlie has to get up soon, it's a busy day at the restaurant with the opening in a few days, but I also want her to relax as long as she can. It's been a hectic week, and I know she is running herself ragged. The least I can do is maybe start her day with an orgasm.

Actually, I think it's my job as the baby daddy and her partner to make sure she does.

I don't know at what point last night she got up and put on shorts and a tank top, but they are getting in the way of me having open access to my beautiful girl. I keep my mouth latched on as my fingers travel down, underneath her shorts and panties, to her waiting pussy. I tease it a little before inserting a finger, knowing she must be sore from last night.

232

Not that I'm patting myself on the back—though I am—but we went until we both passed out. I actually think when we did tap out it was with my dick inside her.

Again, glorious.

"Simon, your phone's buzzing," Charlie mumbles as her body starts responding to my mouth and fingers.

"Don't care," I say as I let go of her breast so I can go down and eat what I really want. "Still snacking."

I didn't hear my phone vibrating before, but I do now. Thankfully, it stops just as I pull Charlie's shorts and panties down. Good. I don't need any distractions right now.

Except just as I'm about to slowly lick her from bottom to top, tasting her sweetness, it starts buzzing again. Only this time it's not stopping.

"I swear, someone better be dying." I jump up from the end of the bed and reach for my phone on Charlie's nightstand. "What the fuck do you want?"

"Simon Alan Banks, is that any way to talk to your mother?"

I fall to the bed, my dick instantly limp at the sound of Demetria Banks's voice on the other end of the call. "Sorry, Mom. Didn't see it was you. What do I owe the pleasure?"

Charlie does all she can to hold in her laughter, but fails as a few snickers sneak out. She rolls out of bed, and I have to sit in suffering silence as my mom yells at me about my profane language. I have no idea what she's saying because I'm distracted by the view of Charlie stripping as she walks to the en suite bathroom.

Oh, that vixen knows what she's doing...and I never want her to stop.

"...so, Simon, are you going to tell me who you got pregnant?"

Well, that got my attention.

"Huh?'

"Jesus, I'm going to need you to take all the wheels right now." Mom lets out a sigh, which gives me time to recoup. Because how in the hell does my mom know Charlie's pregnant? "Simon, please explain why Loretta Perkins was walking her cat yesterday, minding her business, when she looked over to the obstetrician's office to see you walking out, hand in hand, with a woman she didn't know?"

"Why is Loretta walking her cat? I think we need to be talking about that."

"Dammit, Simon. Focus." And I would, but now I'm thinking about her hairless cat on a leash. "Why did Loretta see that and tell me last night at bingo? Why am I the last to know?"

Charlie comes back into her room, wrapped in a towel from her quick rinse. Shit. Because of fucking Loretta and her fucking cat, I not only I have to tell my mother about Charlie, but I also missed out on shower sex.

"Does it make you feel better that you're the first to know?"

"I don't need your sass right now, Simon Banks."

My choice of words gets Charlie's attention as she comes to sit next to me on the bed. We have a quick, yet silent conversation, ending with both of us slowly nodding.

"Well, Mom..." I put the phone on speaker so Charlie can be part of this. "The reason Loretta saw me at the doctor's is because yes, I'm going to be a dad."

Silence. That's it. A pin drop would set off a noise indicator.

Charlie and I join hands, waiting for any reaction from my mom.

"You're going to be a daddy?"

I snicker as Charlie rolls her eyes. "Yes. I'm going to be a daddy."

234

"Who is she?"

Her voice is worried, and I get it. My mom knows my track record. She knows I've never had a serious relationship. If she didn't ask this question I would've been worried.

"You know the woman who is moving into Mona's?"

"Charlie? Oh, we've heard all about her. Mona hasn't shut up about how great she is."

Charlie and I share a smile. "Yeah. I think she's pretty great, too."

"Oh my goodness, Simon. This is so exciting!"

"I think so, too." I don't know if my mom heard that over her cheers and squeals.

"When can we meet her?"

"Oh, well, I'm not sure about that."

"And why not?"

"Mom, her restaurant is opening in two days. Things are crazy. Plus, we weren't ready to tell people yet. Give us until next week when things calm down."

"How about dinner tonight?"

Did she not listen to a thing I just said? I check out Charlie's reaction, and judging by the fact that she hasn't blinked in a few seconds, she doesn't know what to say either.

"Tonight? Mom, I'm sorry, but it's too hard. Charlie has a busy day ahead, and I'm here helping her. Can't this wait? We promise we'll come over as soon as we can."

"Are you two planning on eating dinner tonight? You can't be working *all* day."

I know Demetria Banks doesn't take no for an answer. I just have never been on the receiving end of it.

"Well, yeah. At some point we'll probably grab something to eat."

"Then you can grab it over here. Is there anything that's making her sick right now?"

Charlie and I share a knowing look, realizing arguing with my mother is a lost cause at this point.

"Fish," I say confidently. The reassuring smile Charlie sends my way fills me with pride. "And nothing too heavy on dairy."

"Pork chops it is. See you at seven."

"Mom. It really would—" I don't get a chance to finish that sentence. "I guess you're meeting my parents tonight."

"Is there any way we can get out of this?"

I shake my head. "Nope. Hurricane Demetria is at a category four. There's no stopping it at this point."

* * *

Want to know something you never have to do when you only do casual relationships? Bring a woman home to meet your parents. The last girl Mom and Dad met was my senior prom date, and that was only because everyone came to our house for pictures before the dance.

"Are you okay?" Charlie asks as we pull onto the street of my childhood home. "Because you aren't allowed to be nervous when I'm terrified."

I look over to Charlie, and yup, nothing but fear in her eyes.

"We can't both be afraid," I say.

"Agree. So I win."

"Wait—how does that work?"

"I'm meeting your family for the first time. I'm the Jezebel that seduced their precious baby boy and wound up pregnant."

"You'll see very shortly that they have never called me their precious baby boy."

"That's not the point. I'm the outsider. The new person. And I'm meeting them for the first time with heartburn and after puking three times today."

236

She's right. She wins.

"What can I say to ease your mind?"

"Nothing," she groans. "I just want to make a good first impression. But here I am, a swollen face, my hair a mess because I didn't have time to do it after we left the restaurant, and, did I put on deodorant today?"

"Yes, you did. And I think you look beautiful." I reach across the console and rest my hand on her thigh. I have to remember to keep my eyes on the road because all I want to do right now is stare at her. Light makeup. Rosy cheeks. The red lipstick she only wears when it's a special occasion. And then there's the dress she's wearing. It's modest, but somehow, also fucking sexy. "You're going to make a great first impression just by being yourself. Charm them the way you charmed me."

"Be mean and snarky to them?"

"Might work on my dad." This makes her laugh, and I give her leg one more squeeze before taking her hand. "You're going to be fine. My parents are going to love you. I guarantee you'll be picking out baby names with my mom by the end of the night."

Charlie quickly turns to face me, and from the quick glimpse I take, my words have not reassured her. "Simon. What are we going to say when they ask us how this happened? We can't tell them that we were both drunk and hate-fucked."

"Hate-fucked is a little drastic. I prefer to say angry-banged."

"This is not the time for jokes, Simon! This is serious."

I turn my car into the driveway and put it in park. "We're going to say the truth. That we knew each other in college. We recently reconnected. The rest is history."

I lean in and place a soft kiss to her forehead. "Ready to meet the parents?"

She lets out a deep breath. "Can I say no?"

"Nope." I hurry and exit the car, running to the other side to help her out. She yelled at me yesterday when I did this, saying she could do it on her own just fine. Today nothing.

Damn, she really is nervous.

"This place is huge," she says, staring slack jawed at my parent's six-bedroom house on the outskirts of Rolling Hills.

"It's just a house." I do my best to calm her nerves, remembering that our difference in tax brackets has always worried her. The only problem with me calming her is that no one is calming me. Especially when I realize that there are extra cars here.

"Fuck..."

"What?"

I squeeze her hand. "I'm so sorry for what's about to happen."

As soon as we walk into the front door, I hear voices down the hall in the living room. As we walk closer, my suspicions are confirmed.

The whole damn fam is here.

Chants of "Oh my God!" and "She's real!" fill the air as three of my four sisters rush over to us.

"Hi. I'm Ainsley." As this sister does, she wraps Charlie into a hug that she didn't get a choice about. She's a hugger. "Oh my gosh, you are absolutely stunning. I'm going to need the shade of that lipstick immediately."

"Um...it's red?" Charlie replies as she tries to get her bearings once Ainsley lets her go.

"Sorry, she's a little overeager." This comes from the baby of the family, Stella. "But for real, that lipstick is great."

"Y'all, back off. Give the poor girl some room."

I look to Charlie and watch every ounce of color drain from her face as she sees Maeve for the first time. Yes, we've all grown and changed over the past fifteen years, but Maeve has

238

perfected how to get older yet still look exactly how she did in her twenties. And that's even with having a kid.

"Hey, Charlie," Maeve says.

"Hi, Maeve."

The two stare at each other for a beat before Maeve leans in and whispers something in Charlie's ear. I can't hear what it is, but it visibly relaxes Charlie, judging by her loosening the death grip on my hand.

Maeve makes her way to me and brings me in for a hug.

"Did you all drive in from Nashville?" I whisper.

"Of course. Did you think we were going to miss this? Not a chance."

"Now now, we can all get to know each other over dinner. Which is ready." Mom comes over and snags Charlie away from me, looping their arms together as she leads her to the dining room. "Girls, go pull everything out of the warmers. Charlie, I'm Demetria, but you can call me Demi. Oh! Maybe the baby can call me DiDi!"

Mom leads Charlie toward the dining room, leaving me standing alone and a little overwhelmed by the last five minutes.

"Dad?" I ask as my pops comes to stand next to me. "What just happened?"

He gives me a firm slap on the back. "Don't try and understand. Just go with it. That's what I've been doing for forty years."

* * *

So far, so good.

Dinner has come and gone. We're now sitting in the living room, everyone having their version of a night cap as Charlie is peppered with questions. All have been pretty basic, and mostly about Charlie moving to Rolling Hills, her family, and of course, the diner. Her face lit up when she started talking about all the things she was adding to the menu, while keeping some of the staples that Mona's was known for. Including french toast.

That was my request.

"So how long have you been seeing each other?"

Shit, we didn't practice this answer.

"Um..."

I don't know how to answer Ainsley's question. Probably because I don't know the actual answer and when our clock officially began. Was it in college or the wedding or when we drunk fucked or when she told me about the baby?

"Are we finally getting to the good part? I promised I'd FaceTime Quinn."

"What?" I ask. "Why are you doing that?"

"She has FOMO. It's not every day our big brother, who claimed he only had fun uncle energy, tells us about how he is now an expectant daddy."

I might be annoyed that they are calling my sister who lives in Arizona, but I can't hide my smile. "See, Bug, everyone is calling me daddy."

She shakes her head in disapproval. "Just stop."

"Oh my God, is that what he calls you?" Ainsley gushes. "That's so romantic."

Maeve shoots our third sister a look. "You think a stranger looking at you in a grocery store is romantic."

"Enough!" Quinn's voice comes barking through the living room. Which is impressive because she's only a face in a telephone. I didn't know she could yell like that. Then again she's an elementary school teacher, so that makes sense. "Apologies. I hate having to raise my voice like that, but Simon, you're avoiding the question. How long have you been together, and when am I booking a ticket home to see my niece or nephew?"

"Well," I stutter again. Shit. I need an answer.

"We reconnected a few months ago," Charlie chimes in, saving the day. "And the baby is due in May."

Phew. At least Charlie remembered the "keep it simple, stupid" plan.

I glance over to Maeve, whose eyebrows are raised and questions are written all over her face. Out of all my sisters, Maeve knows me the best. She's the closest to me in age and the oldest of the girls. If there's anyone who knows when I'm throwing out a line of bullshit, it's her.

"Simon?"

"Yeah, Sis?"

"I came in and decorated this lovely woman's restaurant just a few days ago. And I understand about you not mentioning the baby. However, I find it odd that when you asked me to come decorate a restaurant, you didn't mention it was for your girlfriend."

Every set of eyes turns on me and I instinctively swallow the lump in my throat. "Well...she...I..."

"Simon?" This comes from Mom with her patented disapproving tone. "Are you two not dating? I thought you were together?"

"We are, Mom."

Charlie lets out a small gasp. "We are? When did this happen?"

My jaw drops a little at her reaction. I mean, we didn't have the talk, but I thought we were on the same page. Especially after last night.

Then I see the small, yet devilish, smirk on her face. Oh... she's going to pay for this later.

"Simon Banks! Did you not properly ask this woman to be your girlfriend?"

"Mom...it's not like that."

"Jesus Christ, son." My dad's tone is laced in disapproval, and this whole situation is getting very out of hand.

"Listen!" Raising my voice only makes my sisters and Charlie snicker more. It only deepens the disappointment on my parents' faces. "We're together. No I didn't ask her because I'm not sixteen. But also, this woman knows for a damn fact that I'm nuts about her, and I'm pretty much whipped already and we've been officially together for less than a week."

Charlie takes my hand and gives it a reassuring squeeze. "He's right. Plus, he's like a stray cat. I've fed him once. I know he's just going to keep coming back."

This makes everyone laugh. "Exactly. She's stuck with me."

"I am." Charlie leans into me as I put my arm around her shoulder. "I tried to resist. I really did."

"We get it," Maeve says. "The man has wormed his way into everything in his life. Why would this be different?"

"But we also know that he can be a bit much," Stella says. "So when you need a break, just come up to Nashville. We'll take you out for the day. Oh! Please come up so we can go baby shopping! I never need an excuse to shop, but I'll take one when I can."

"And if it's a boy, you can have whatever you want that I still have," Maeve says.

"It's not a boy," I say confidently.

"Isn't it too early to know?"

"It is," Charlie says with a side-eye my way. "He's 'got a feeling.'"

Maeve rolls her eyes. "Of course he does."

The girls begin talking and start planning a trip to Nashville after the restaurant opens. I sit back and watch as Charlie blends seamlessly with my family.

Just like I knew she would.

I happen to share a look with my dad, who just gives me a nod and his version of a smile. And for the first time in my life, I get it.

I get the meaning of this.

Family.

I take after my dad in a lot of ways. I didn't go into law like him, but his drive to be the best was ingrained in me from an early age. He retired last year from his firm, where he had been partner for more than twenty years. The man was ruthless in the courtroom. He was the best. And that's what I wanted to be: the best.

What I never wanted was the family. I didn't get the appeal. I mean, look at my family. We're loud, messy, and constantly in each other's business. There was not one moment of peace growing up. Who in their right minds would want that?

But I get it now. Because I do. I want a flock of kids and the loud and the messy.

And I want them with Charlie.

Chapter 24
Charlie

"I 'm going to need another batch of sausage gravy. Also, Mellie, people keep asking for the cinnamon rolls, so don't stop now."

"Woo hoo!"

I smile over at Mellie, who is doing a happy dance at her bakery station. "Enough dancing. More baking."

She smiles at me, her hips still moving to the non-existent song. "In this kitchen, we dance. Especially when I'm told to make more cinnamon rolls."

We do dance here. And we've been doing happy dances all morning. Because it's been nonstop since we opened the doors for the first official day of Mona's: Charlie's version.

I mean, that's not the official name, but it's what I jokingly like to call it. Because while there is still her patty melt, french toast, and triple stack BLT on the menu, there are new things, like my sausage gravy that has been a huge hit, Mellie's to die for cinnamon rolls, and, based on the orders, a crowd favorite: The Breakfast Burger, which is a cheeseburger in between two halves of Mellie's freshly baked glazed donuts with a fried egg and bacon.

Don't knock it till you try it. At least that's what I told the servers to say when people were skeptical about ordering it.

"I knew these were going to be a hit." I snag a cinnamon roll from Mellie's tray. Consider it the boss tax.

"No. This is a hit. The whole thing. You did it, girl."

"*We* did it."

We hug each other so tight one of us might pop. But it's needed. From working in the hellscape that was Napoli's to landing in this dream situation, this hug is long overdue and needed.

"Hey, we have this covered back here," she says. "How about you go out there and see your fans?"

I look over to the line cooks, who are all doing everything they are supposed to be doing. "You sure?"

She points to the door. "Go. If it gets crazy, I'll come get you. Bask in this day, girl. You've earned it."

"Thanks." I grab my tumbler of water, because me and this little one are thirsty, as I head to the dining room. I try and sneak out, wanting to take in as much as I can unnoticed, but the second I'm out the door, my shadow is right next to me.

"You okay? Do you need to sit? You should probably sit."

I sigh loud enough for the whole restaurant to hear. "I'm fine, Simon. Things are evening out in the back, and I was told it would be good for me to make an appearance in the dining room. I just wanted to see what's going on."

Simon puts one hand on my not-showing stomach and kisses my temple. "Good. I'm glad you did. It's been amazing."

He steps away, but switches his hand to the small of my back, as I take in the sight of my first day. Every table is full. Families and friends are eating and laughing. Servers are zooming around with plates and drinks. The jukebox that had been at Mona's for years is currently playing one of my mom's favorite country songs.

And that's when I lose it.

"Hey? You okay?"

I nod as Simon wraps his arms around me. "I wish my mom were here."

Simon kisses my temple and holds me a little tighter. "I know you do. And while I never knew her, I bet good money she'd be so proud of you."

I cry into his shoulder for a second, not wanting to show my new patrons that I'm an emotional basket case, when I hear two of the best words being shouted by the sweetest little voice.

"Aunt Charlie!"

I quickly wipe my tears and turn around as Lila sprints toward me. "Sweet Pea!"

Lila jumps into my arms, and I don't know if I've ever hugged her so hard. I swing her back and forth, my hold only getting stronger, as I sprinkle kisses on her cheek. "I've missed you."

"I miss you," she says between giggles. "Daddy said I can have as much as I want!"

"I did not say that," Connor says as he steps up to us, giving me a kiss on the cheek. "I said you can pick anything you want. But you aren't going to eat the whole menu."

"Yes, you can," I whisper. "You just tell me what you want, and I'll get it for you."

The sound of Lila's sweet giggles helps me relax for the first time in weeks. I forgot how much this kid can change my mood just from her toothy grin.

"Who are you?"

I follow Lila's eyes to Simon, who took a step back, but I knew likely wasn't too far away.

"I'm Simon. What's your name?"

Connor all but rips Lila out of my arms, which takes her by surprise. "None of your concern."

Oh...shit...

Shit, shit, shit...

"Hey Lila, remember my friend Mellie?"

"The cake lady!"

"Yup. The very one. How about we go visit her in the kitchen, and maybe she'll let you help with the cinnamon rolls. While I'm doing that, how about your Dad and Simon go outside so we can have a nice, *calm,* chat when I get out there?"

I signal both of them to go outside as I take Lila from Connor. I ignore the death glare Connor shoots Simon, as well as the signature Simon Banks "fuck you" smugness he returns as the two walk out my front door.

Shit...this is going to be bad.

As soon as Lila's feet hit the ground she's in a full sprint to the kitchen, nearly knocking over one of the servers when she throws open the door. Normally I'd tell her not to run, but today the kid is moving at the exact pace I need. Because I need to get outside quickly. Otherwise, my restaurant opening might also be accompanied by at least a fight, not to mention probable homicide.

I'm beating myself up as I race out the back door and around the building. How did I forget to tell Connor about Simon? I mean, I know why. I've barely remembered my name over the past few months. And between my insanity, his work schedule, and now taking care of Lila on his own, we haven't talked more than a few texts a day. Which means he doesn't know a lot of things.

Like that I don't hate Simon anymore.

And that he's about to be an uncle.

And that Simon is the father of why he's about to be an uncle.

As soon as I turn the corner, my body instinctively bends over as a gulp for breath. Though I quickly realize I don't have time for that.

"I saw you in there." Connor points his finger into Simon's chest. "Who the fuck do you think you are touching my sister?"

"First, don't fucking touch me. Second, who the fuck are you to tell me what I can and can't do?"

"I'm her brother, you asshole."

"Oh! Well, nice to officially meet you. Simon Banks."

Simon's sarcastic enthusiasm doesn't go over well with Connor, who's just staring at the hand Simon extended to him.

No, not staring. Scowling.

"I know who you are, asshole. Which is why I've been waiting years to do this."

Connor cocks back his arm and I run over just in time to stop him.

"Stop! Both of you!"

Connor's arm tenses in my hands, but luckily he doesn't budge. Then there's Simon, who's standing there with a conceited smirk.

"Okay, let's cool down," I say, putting myself between the two men. "Connor, there are things you need to know."

"Please, Charlie, because I feel like I'm missing a whole hell of a lot."

I happen to turn toward the restaurant, where I can see every set of eyes glued to the window. I want to die of embarrassment, especially when I see someone literally holding their plate so they can continue eating while they watch.

I wanted a memorable first day. I just should have been more specific in my wish.

"Connor, I know you hate Simon. And for what we thought was a good reason."

"It *is* a good reason, Charlie. He hurt you."

"That's what I thought too. But I was wrong. It was a huge misunderstanding."

Connor looks at me, then Simon, then back to me, clearly not believing any of this. "Misunderstanding? Is that what he's telling you?"

I shake my head. "Yes, he told me, but it's true. The woman I saw was his sister."

"Sister?" Connor huffs a laugh and shakes his head in disbelief. "He's going with the sister line? Come on, Charlie, you're smarter than this."

"It's true."

I turn my head to see Maeve walking toward us, along with Simon's entire family. Talk about timing...

"Who are you?"

"I'm Maeve. The sister who didn't fuck her brother."

Connor looks to Maeve, then back to Simon and me. "What the hell is going on?"

"This is how I know he's telling the truth. Maeve had no idea who I was, and I didn't know her." I turn back to Connor, begging him with my eyes and words to see and believe I was in the wrong. "I was sad and angry. And then you called me about Mom. I was mad at the world. I cut everyone off, including Simon. I never gave him a chance to explain and for years let myself believe what I wanted to."

"So what does this mean?" Connor says. "Don't tell me..."

I take a step back and slip my hand into Simon's. "Yes. We're together."

"Oh! Did you make it official? I know you said you didn't need to, but with the baby and all..."

Everyone shoots a look over to Mrs. Banks, whose eyes double in size when she realizes what she just said.

"Baby?" Connor's eyes are darting from person to person. "Did she say baby?"

"Yes. I'm pregnant."

There's silence on the street. No one knows what to say.

Everyone except Simon.

"I'm sorry, but we're all acting like this is a sad announcement, when it's the greatest thing in the world. Charlie and I are having a baby!"

"Jesus fucking Christ..."

I mutter the Lord's name in vain into my hands as I smack my forehead. What in the literal fuck is happening right now?

"Charlie Bennett and I are having a baby! Baby Bug is due in May. I'm going to be a daddy!"

"Wait, what? Did you just say Baby Bug?"

We turn to the new voice—how many people are on this sidewalk right now?—which belongs to Wes. He's accompanied by Betsy, the rest of the friend crew, and all of their kids.

"Yup! You're about to be Uncle Wes."

"Damn," Oliver says shaking his head. "I did *not* have that on my bingo card."

* * *

Despite the shit show that happened outside, followed immediately by Simon coming into the diner and announcing to everyone that not only were we expecting, but that he was buying everyone's meal, things have settled down.

And I can now say, it was a success. Even with the shit show.

We were only open through lunch today, figuring we didn't need to jump into the fire feet first. A few customers are still finishing their meals, including a group of women who told me that this was going to be their new Friday lunch spot. Everyone was complimentary of the menu—especially the breakfast burger. A few of Mona's older customers told me that the coffee tasted different, but they wouldn't hold it against me.

It was the same coffee.

The best part? Everything in the back of the house was smooth sailing. Mellie had her groove going. The line cooks are damn good, and I have no worries about leaving them on their own. My servers are angels, and even the two high school kids I hired to wash dishes and bus were on their game.

It's almost too good to be true...

"Well, Sis, you did it."

I smile as Connor takes a seat across from me at the table I sat down at five minutes ago, just meaning to take a rest. I'm now wondering how I'm going to get back up. "Something like that."

"Don't downplay this," he says. "I want you to say it out loud. 'I crushed it.'"

"Well, it wasn't just me."

He shakes his head. "We all know that. But you need to take your credit for this. Say it."

"I crushed it," I whisper.

"Louder."

"I crushed it."

"One more time."

"I crushed it!"

I didn't mean to yell that loud, but I must say it felt good. Until I realize that my exclamation has stirred a napping Lila in the neighboring booth.

"Oh shit," I whisper. "Sorry."

"She's fine." Connor looks over to his daughter, a softness in his eyes he only has for her. "It's the sugar crash."

I laugh, knowing that Lila ate her weight in sweets today. Mellie said she wasn't the best helper when it came to icing, but was masterful in taste testing. I feel a rush of emotion watching her, her thumb in her mouth as she does sometimes still, and wondering what it's going to look like when my child inevitably takes a nap here.

Is it a boy? Or is Simon right with the girl? Is it going to have fair, blonde hair like Lila and I had as a baby, or dark like Simon? I've thought about these things from time to time since I found out I was pregnant, but I think this is the first time it has occupied my thoughts.

"I wish you'd have told me."

I turn back to Connor, though I can't bring myself to look at him. "I know. And I'm sorry. I didn't want you finding out like this."

"Which part?"

I finally look up. "Both?"

We both softly laugh as Lila stirs a little more.

"Simon, huh?"

"Believe me, I wasn't expecting it either."

I look out the window to see the father of my child talking to people walking past, shaking their hands and pointing to the restaurant. I don't know what he's saying, but I can clearly tell he's talking about Mona's and the pride on his face is unmistakable.

"And he's in? He's ready to be a father?"

I smile as I think about his antics earlier today. "Did you not hear the announcement in front of the whole town or witness the baby pool he started?"

"Yeah, but it's easy to put on an act."

"You're right, it is, but he isn't. He's..." I look out the window again, only this time Simon and I make eye contact. He shoots me a wink that somehow travels through the space and foundation of the restaurant to warm my entire body. "This is how it was meant to be."

Chapter 25
Simon

"So guys, what do we want to talk about?"

Zero laughter from my three best friends.

Rude.

"Oh, come on," I say as I walk back to the fire pit at Wes's. It might be October, but it's not too cold that we can't enjoy a night outside. "You have to admit, that was funny."

"Is this a time for jokes?" Wes asks, signaling to the seat they left open for me. "That wasn't sarcastic. I'm genuinely curious. I don't know how to act right now."

"It is," I say, grabbing the beer from Shane's hand. "Jokes. Or congratulations. Anything that can be classified in the happy or joyful department."

I twist open the bottle as my friends remain silent. I know *what* they want to talk to me about, which makes sense. If I found out one of them, after years of saying they'd never settle down, is not only in a committed relationship, but also expecting a child, I'd be acting the same way.

I sit back and observe as they have a silent conversation,

which we are damn good at doing. We perfected it freshman year in English class when we were separated into the four corners of the classroom because we couldn't stop talking. Well, Oliver and I couldn't. Wes and Shane were guilty by association.

They give a nod and turn their sights back to me. And if I had to take a guess, I'm going to assume that Shane kicks this off with his brand of stoic interrogation.

"Simon, we need you to repeat what you said earlier today, just to make sure we're not living in an alternate reality."

Nailed it.

"I say a lot of things, Shane."

"Don't fuck around Simon. Did you or did you not say that you—the man who doesn't like getting dirty—is about to be elbows deep in diapers for the next few years because he's about to become a father?"

I couldn't contain my smile if I tried. "Yes, Shane. In fact, I did say, in front of you, our friends and family, and the entire town, that I, along with my beautiful girlfriend Charlie, are expecting a child this spring."

It's Wes's turn to take over the questioning.

"You and Charlie are together?"

"We are."

"And you're having a *human* child?"

"Indeed. Right now it's the size of a kumquat."

"And you know that you can't hype it up on sugar then give it away? Like, it's yours. Forever."

"I do. And I prefer to call *it* Baby Bug, so please address my unborn child properly."

"Jesus fucking Christ..." Shane mumbles, apparently not liking the tone of my responses. "Simon. This is for real. This is not you wanting to be a DJ for a day because it seems like fun."

"He knows that," Oliver says in my defense. "Right? You *do* know that?"

I hold up my beer to Oliver. "I do. But thank you for giving me the benefit of the doubt. Back up to number one best friend."

That makes him smile. "Good. Feels right to be back at the top."

"Can we focus?" Wes yells before turning his attention back to me. "Simon, please, tell us how we got here. And I swear to Christ, if you give me a smart ass remark about how babies are made, I'm going to punch you."

"Well I wouldn't need to tell it to you. You have three kids. Now Shane, maybe..."

"Simon..."

Shane's near growl, along with a head shake from Wes and a concerned look on Oliver's face, means the sarcastic portion of tonight's talk has come to a close. Which is sad. I had a few jokes in the chamber about Wes having to now share the daddy spotlight with me.

"Okay," I say, evening my tone. "Ask away."

"How are you?"

Oliver's question is sincere, and I appreciate that he's the one kicking things off.

"I'm good."

"That's good. But you know, if you are feeling other things, it's okay. Finding out you're going to be a dad is a big deal."

"I am." Though now that he mentions it, there are a few things I've ignored that I figured would go away if I ignored them long enough. "I mean, I'm happy. I was immediately all in. And I still am."

"Is there a 'but' coming?"

I shake my head at Wes's question. "Not necessarily a but...

it's just...I think the shock and adrenaline is wearing off, so other feelings are starting to creep in."

"Are you scared?"

I nod and let out a low laugh. "Fucking terrified."

"Good," Wes says. "Then you're feeling the most appropriate response."

"Thank fuck."

"The scared comes and goes," Wes adds. "Sometimes you'll think you've got it and things are smooth sailing. Then something will happen and you'll go back to terrified."

"When does it go away?"

Wes shakes his head. "I'll let you know when it happens."

"Fuck..." I take another sip of beer. "Okay. How about this? Is it normal to never want to leave Charlie? Like, I want to be around her all the time. I haven't talked to her for two hours and it's driving me batty."

"That one I can't answer to. You knew my ex," Wes says. "I think that's a Simon thing."

"Really?"

"Why do you never want to leave her?" Oliver asks.

"It's everything," I say. "Obviously the baby. I want to make sure they're okay. Make sure she's not going too hard or pushing herself too much. Or maybe she'll need a hand at the restaurant. Or she needs me to get something for her off the top shelf because she's short. Or...I mean, there's so many things I want to help with but I know I can't but I want to be there in case I can. And I want to make sure she's eating. And staying hydrated."

"That makes sense."

"But it's more than that. We didn't stay with each other last night—"

"Wow, now we know it's serious. Simon Banks is having overnight stays."

I shoot a look to Shane. "If I'm done with the smart ass, so are you."

He laughs and holds his hands up. "Sorry. It was there. I had to take it."

"As I was saying...We didn't stay together because of the restaurant opening. And...I don't know how to explain it..."

"You missed her?"

"Your bed felt empty?"

"You woke up in the middle of the night panicking she wasn't next to you?"

"All of those! Why is that?"

My three friends smile at each other.

"What? Someone say something."

"You're in love," Oliver says.

Now that's hilarious. "No, I'm not. We haven't even been together two weeks. Officially. Or unofficially. Hell at this time last month she hated me and I hated that she hated me."

"What's the old saying? There's a thin line between love and hate?"

I shake my head at Wes. "That's not it. Do I care about her? Yes. Do I want to spend every day with her? Also yes. Do I want to kiss and hold her all the time? Of course. If she left right now do I feel like I'd die? Yes. But..."

Oliver slowly smiles. "I think he's getting there guys..."

Wait. Am I? Is this?

"Holy shit, I'm in love."

Wes claps his hands together. "There it is."

Wow. Love? I wasn't expecting that.

"No," I say. "It's too soon. Way too soon."

Shane huffs out a laugh. "Simon Banks, the man who has made his entire personality acting before thinking, all of a sudden is worried that he might be jumping into something, or declaring something, too soon? You once bought a house to sell that hadn't even been built yet."

"That's just money. It's just...I don't know...I thought you had to know someone for years before you fell in love?"

"I knew I loved Izzy the moment I saw her."

I shake my head at Oliver. "You don't count thirty-four proposals."

"I didn't know what I felt toward Amelia was love at first," Shane says.

"What made you realize it?"

"The second she walked toward me in her prom dress."

I roll my eyes. "I don't need puppy love bullshit. Wes, please, help me."

Wes sets his beer down and rests his elbows on his knees. "I've been in love twice. And I can say with certainty and proof that no two loves are the same. No two timelines are the same. Simon, love is different for everyone. People show it differently. It has its own tempo, and it's never the same for anyone else. You just have to ask yourself a few questions."

"What are those?"

"Is your life better with Charlie in it?"

"Yes. Without question."

"Does the thought of her not in your life physically pain you?"

"So much I don't want to think about it."

"And finally, can you see a future with her? And don't say yes just because it's what you think you should say. Close your eyes and think about it."

I do as he says, because I was about to say yes. As soon as I shut my eyes, I see Charlie holding our daughter—because yes, we're going to have a daughter—rocking her in the room I already designated as the nursery. I walk over to her, watching in awe as she nurses Baby Bug, and place a kiss on her forehead. I catch the glimpse of a ring I've apparently put on her finger. Which sends me into another vision as Charlie walks down the aisle to me. The guys are standing next to me as we pledge our love for each other.

Holy shit, I'm in love...

"Aw guys...our little boy is all grown up."

I don't even come back with a witty comment. Because Oliver's right.

I'm in love. "So this is what it feels like to be you guys, huh?"

Wes laughs. "Welcome to the club. Oliver made jackets."

"I hate to be the downer of the group," Shane says. "But I need to rain on the parade for a second."

I look over to Shane. "I don't think it would be right if you didn't."

"You love her."

"Yes."

"She tolerates you."

"So far."

"She's willing to have a child with you."

"All things we've discussed."

"Here's one. Does she know you own her restaurant?"

Did you hear that? That was the sound of Shane Cunningham bursting my bubble.

"By his dumbfounded expression and look of sheer panic, I'm thinking no."

"I said no more smart ass, Wes!" I stand up and start pacing. "She doesn't. I think I forgot."

"Well, you should probably change that."

I shoot a look to Shane. "I know...I just don't know how."

"Easy. You say, 'Charlie, before we were together, when you hated me, I bought this building.'"

"Sure, Shane. Easy peasy. Then I can just throw in the part

about me making sure Emmett didn't tell her I owned it, that giving her the apartment was a desperation move for her to take it, that I fixed all of the issues with Mona's so she wouldn't have to, including buying all new equipment, and that I haven't cashed a rent check yet."

Oliver's eyes double in size. "Simon!"

"I know," I hang my head. "It's just...she hates charity. She hates feeling like she owes anyone. The only reason I got away with the new tables and booths is because I did it behind her back so when they showed up she had no choice but to go with it. Helps that she liked them."

"Simon, you can't start your relationship like this," Wes says. "Believe me when I say, clear communication is a must."

He's right. They all are. I need to tell her.

"I know. And I will."

"Promise?"

I shake Shane's hand. "Promise."

At that moment, I feel a text coming through and before I look I somehow know it's from Charlie.

> Charlie: I hate to ask this...

> Simon: Ask away.

> Charlie: Can you bring me ice cream? Strawberry. Oh! And fries from The Joint? I know there are some downstairs but I don't want to cook another thing today.

> Simon: Daddy's got it *wink emoji*

> Charlie: I'll let you have that one because you're bringing me food.

> Simon: I'll call it in now. Be over in 30 minutes?

The One I Hate

Charlie: Thanks....Daddy...(Nope, still weird.)

A genuine smile crosses my face as I slip my phone back in my pocket.

Soon. I'll tell her soon.

Just not tonight.

Chapter 26
Charlie

Why am I nervous?

Oh, I know why, I'm going on a date.

With Simon.

My boyfriend.

All of that is still baffling to think about.

Is that why I'm nervous? Everything about Simon compared to the men I've dated in the past is different.

Different in the best way.

When I sit and think about it, this doesn't feel real. For so many years I hated this man. The slightest thought of him would make my blood boil. Now my body heats for a different reason when he's around.

Which is a lot. We see each other every day. He has a permanent spot at the breakfast counter that is essentially his office. We take turns spending evenings at his house or my apartment. We've even become an official couple with our first television binge.

And we've had sex. A lot of sex.

So much sex.

Not that I'm complaining. Between the fact that we're in the honeymoon stage of the relationship and I'm firmly into my second trimester, the sex is welcomed with open arms.

Or is it open legs?

But in all those nights and days spent together, we haven't done one thing—go on a date. Which Simon is bound and determined to rectify today with what he's calling "Last First Date Palooza."

On the outside I rolled my eyes.

On the inside I swooned so damn hard.

> Simon: Leaving my house now. You ready?

> Charlie: You mean for the date where I don't know where we're going or what we're doing?

> Simon: The very one.

> Charlie: Yes, I'm ready.

> Simon: Good. See you soon. This is about to be the best date ever!

I laugh and toss my phone back on my bed as I grab my ballet flats to slip on. The only thing Simon told me was to wear something appropriate for "fancy and for fun." When I asked him what that meant, he refused to elaborate. So I did the best I could and found a red dress that I felt comfortable in, considering my leggings and pants are starting to become a little snug, and paired it with ballet flats. I could pretend I'm wearing flats because of the baby, but let's be real here—heels were invented by Lucifer himself and they can burn in hell.

I do one last check in the mirror, and give one more swipe of my lipstick, before grabbing my purse and heading out the door. But as soon as I open it, I see Simon standing in front of me, a dozen red roses in his hands.

"Aw, Bug...I had a whole reveal planned."

"You know you don't need to impress me anymore." I lean in and kiss his cheek, taking the roses from him.

"Not true. I need to continue woo-ing you. Just because you're my girlfriend and baby mama doesn't mean the romance stops."

"I think I might hate baby mama worse than daddy."

"Well, we can discuss alternate names on our way to date stop number one."

"Number one? There are more than one?"

A cheeky grin comes across his face.

"Mind out of the gutter, Banks."

"Sorry. Anyway..." Simon opens the door a little wider so I can step out. "The theme of this date is past, present, and future."

"Why do I feel like I'm in that Christmas movie with the Muppets?"

He laughs and places his hand on the small of my back as he leads me down the stairs. "Oh, Bug, this is going to be so much better."

* * *

"Simon Banks, we are not spending two thousand dollars on a crib!"

Simon turns to me with a perplexed look. "Why not?"

"Because it's too much."

He shakes his head. "There will never be too much when it comes to Baby Bug."

I don't even know why I'm trying to argue with him. He's been like this since we walked into the high-end baby boutique he found in Franklin—also known as the "future" part of our date.

Which I thought was adorable. I mean, what man plans part of a date as picking out baby stuff? Then I saw the price tags, and I wanted to vomit.

"Which one do you like better?" Simon is standing back, examining two nearly identical—in both price and looks—cribs. I'm talking fingers under his chin, eyes narrowed and brows pinched. "The white one is a four-in-one convertible. The gray is only a three-in-one, but it has drawers built in, which are handy."

"I'm sure we can find perfectly good ones for half the price. Especially since we'll need two."

Simon snaps his head to me. "What do you mean two?"

"For your place and mine."

He starts blinking rapidly, like he's trying to figure out what I'm saying. "Why do you still have a place?"

"Because that's where I live?"

"Why?"

"Um...I'm not sure how I'm supposed to answer this question."

Simon takes my arm and leads me to a corner of the store and his tone lowers. "You aren't moving in with me?"

"I mean, we haven't talked about that." Why am I explaining this? Either Simon had a conversation with me I wasn't aware of or the man is assuming a lot. "This is our first date, which is completely ass backwards if you think about the order we did things. But that doesn't change that we haven't *actually* talked about it."

"I've mentioned it."

I quickly scan my brain. "Are you talking about the time you blurted it out five seconds after I told you I was pregnant?"

"Yes."

"Oh, Simon." Bless his eager beaver heart. "I know you like

to jump first and figure out the landing on the way down, but I don't work like that."

He nods and lets out a breath. "You're right. I get that. It's just...I figured that once the baby was born, we'd be moved in together. I'd hoped you were on that page too."

"I am," I say, rising on my toes to kiss his cheek. "But I don't like to assume. If things go in that direction—"

"When they go in that direction."

"*When* they go in that direction, we'll revisit. But for now, can we be a normal couple and take things at a normal pace?"

Simon pouts, but in a playful way. "Fine. On one condition."

"Deal."

"You don't argue with me on the price of the crib."

Now it's my turn to groan. "Deal. But we're going to buy a reasonably priced stroller."

"Sorry, Bug, no can do," Simon says, putting his arm around my shoulders and leading us back to the cribs. "I've got my eye on a gold-rimmed one with all terrain wheels and front-wheel suspension."

"Of course you do..."

* * *

"So tell me about yourself."

I stare blankly at Simon with my bite of lasagna an inch from my mouth. "Excuse me?"

He shrugs as he cuts a piece of his steak. "That's a first-date question. This is the present. In the present, we're on our first date, so I figured I'd ask you first-date questions."

Somehow this makes sense. But is ridiculous at the same time.

Much like me and Simon.

"Okay." I dab the corners of my mouth with my cloth napkin. "Though I don't know what you don't know about me."

"Well let's figure it out. We're together now. We're on a date. This is what you do when you date. At least that's what Oliver said."

"You needed Oliver to tell you about dates?"

Simon takes a sip of his whiskey and leans back slightly in his chair. "Contrary to popular belief, I haven't dated much."

I find that hard to believe. "What's your definition of haven't dated much?"

He leans forward, resting his forearms on the table. I don't know why, but at this moment I can't help but marvel at how his arms fill out his black dress shirt. "Dating to me was more..."

"Short term?"

"Kind of."

"Temporary."

"Isn't that the same thing?"

"Hit it and quit it?"

"That's more accurate."

I nod and let out a chuckle, because that doesn't surprise me.

"Why are you laughing? Aren't you jealous?"

"Are you jealous of my past boyfriends?"

"Yes," he says firmly. "How many are we talking?"

"Simon..." I reach across the table and take each of his hands. "There was a fifteen-year gap of time when neither of us wanted to think about each other. In fact, once you accidentally came up in conversation with Mellie, and I broke a plate."

"Did you drop it because you remembered me as the hot guy you let get away?"

"No. I threw it against the wall and got suspended because I swore so loud customers heard me."

"You still thought of me. I'll take that as a win."

Simon adds a wink that only makes me laugh.

"As I was saying, there were a lot of years where neither of us would have ever thought that this would happen. Especially the happenstance of seeing each other, and then the diner, and the baby."

Simon tenses slightly before relaxing again. "What I'm saying is that we have histories separate from each other. That's what happens when you're adults in relationships."

"You're right."

"Of course I am," I say as I put my attention back toward my lasagna. I don't know what the secret is in this tomato sauce, but I'm half tempted to ask the chef. "So back to the original question...what don't you know about me?"

He thinks about it for a second. "What's your biggest fear?"

"Easy. Failure."

"In the general sense or anything specific?"

"Both? In general, I don't want to let down the people in my life. The diner is a big part of that."

"Understandable."

"But it's more than just if the diner does well or not. I left Connor and Lila in Nashville to pursue this. I promised my mom on her death bed that I'd take this leap. Mona trusted me with her space. Mellie left her job. If this doesn't work, and I fail, I'll be letting so many people down."

Now it's Simon's turn to take my hand. "It sounds like you're more scared of failing others than failing yourself."

Interesting. I never thought of it like that. "I guess I am. And there are so many more to consider. You for one."

"Me?"

"Yes, you. You're invested in this."

This makes Simon go still. "How am I invested?"

"I mean, there's the fact that you overnighted basically a whole new restaurant to me. Which I'm going to pay you back for. And how supportive you've been. I feel like you're in this with me."

He lets out a breath like he's relieved. "Yes, I do feel like I'm in this with you, but you have to know, there is no way I'd ever think you failed. No matter what happens. And you're never paying me back for those booths or tables. Those were a gift."

"Of course you'd say that."

"And I mean every word."

He brings up my hand and places a kiss below my knuckles.

"Okay enough about me. What about you? Biggest fear?"

"Again, easy. Snakes."

"Snakes?

"Snakes."

"Out of all the things in the world, that's what you want to go with?"

"Absolutely. Those fuckers are terrifying. Oh, and I'm scared of clowns, so none of those ever at our child's birthday parties."

"Agree. No clowns...but now I need the serious answer."

His gaze travels down, and he takes the moment to give my hands another squeeze. "Losing you."

That takes me by surprise. "Are you serious?"

He looks up at me, his eyes sad. "I know you think I speak and act without thinking. And most of the time that's true. But there is something I haven't said..."

Why is he scaring me? "Simon?"

"I love you Bug. I love you so much it hurts. You're my reason for everything. And I want you to know...even if Baby Bug weren't on her way..."

"It's way."

"Her way...I'd still be in love with you. And if I lost you...if

272

I ever did anything in my stupid ways that would make it where you weren't in my life...I don't know how I'd survive. And that's fucking scary."

"Hey..." I get up and move to the empty seat next to him, taking his face in my hands to bring him in for a reassuring kiss. "Thank you."

"For what?"

"Sharing that with me."

He nods. "I meant every word."

"I know."

I bring him in for another kiss—one that is probably not fancy Italian steakhouse restaurant appropriate—and the weight of his words hits me. I also realize in this moment that I love him too. I thought I did, but I also thought it was too soon.

Then again, Simon and I have never been on a normal clock, why start now?

We break the kiss, but I don't let go of him. "I love you too."

My heart melts with the smile that adorns his handsome face. "You do?"

I nod. "I do...Daddy..."

If there's ever the look described as "got a puppy for Christmas" it's the one on Simon's face. "Will you say that again, but so I can record it and make it my ringtone?"

"Absolutely not. That was a one and done."

"Fine," he mumbles before perking back up. "How about this? I'll make you a bet."

"A bet? What are the terms?"

"If I beat you at the past part of the date, which is scheduled to begin in thirty minutes, you record yourself saying Daddy. And if you win, I'll drop it and even make sure Baby Bug sticks to Dada."

I reach out my hand. "Deal."

∗ ∗ ∗

"Putt-Putt? You're taking me to Putt-Putt?"

Simon shakes his head. "Technically this is indoor mini golf. Putt-Putt is actually a trademarked term and has very specific course specifications. Anything with a windmill, like this one, is mini golf."

"How in the hell do you know that?"

"I'm basically a pro..."

Simon pays the attendant, grabs two balls and two putters, and leads me to the first hole.

"Welcome to the past."

"How is this the past?"

"Because this was going to be our first date."

I nearly drop the ball he just handed me. "You had it planned out?"

"I did." He sneaks a kiss on my cheek before guiding me to the first hole. "Since you insisted that WrestleMania was not our first date, I always thought about what we would do if you ever said yes to a real date. And, because I was a cocky guy who wanted to impress you—"

"*Was* a cocky guy?"

He smiles and pulls me into him. "Touché."

"Please tell me you were going to do the whole 'let me show you how it's done' move?"

I think I just made him blush. "It was a much better idea when I was twenty-one."

"It's still a good idea." I lean up and kiss his cheek. "Why don't you show me?"

A small fire lights in his eyes. "Turn around. Put your ball on the ground and stand with your feet part, the ball in the middle."

I do as he says. "Like this?"

274

"Like that." Simon positions himself behind me and wraps his arms so they are on top of mine. He takes my hands and helps me place them on the putter, which of course puts his cock right into my ass. I can't help but wiggle against it.

"You're playing dirty," he whispers in my ear, giving it a gentle nibble.

"I play to win."

The groan he lets out vibrates through my body, which only makes me press into him more.

"Bug..."

"Simon..."

"Anyway..." I giggle as he takes a second to collect himself. "Hold your hands like this, then slowly bring it back and push it forward."

I follow his motion, not hitting the ball yet. "Like this?"

"Just like that."

Simon steps away and I reline up the shot. The first one is easy, only one hill in the back.

I swing the putter back and push it forward, giving it the perfect speed to ring around the cup once before falling in.

I turn to him with all smiles. "Like that?"

Simon's mouth is hanging open. He looks like a cartoon character. "How..."

"You're not the only one who is, what was it...basically a pro."

He laughs and throws his head back. "I'm going to lose, aren't I?"

"Damn right you are, Dada. You're up."

* * *

"You *hustled* me."

I laugh as I lean over the console and kiss Simon on the

cheek as he drives us back to Rolling Hills. "In my defense, I didn't hustle you. You assumed."

"Still..." His pout makes me simultaneously laugh and feel bad. "Now I'm going to have to be Dada. Or worse...Dad. How boring is that?"

"Maybe you can come up with your own name?"

"Maybe..."

"Is there anything I can do to ease the pain?"

I say that as I start to kiss and nibble along his neck, right under his ear. He shivers as my warm breath graces his skin.

"Bug..."

"What?" I say as I undo my seatbelt. "I'm just trying to make you feel better."

My hand starts rubbing across his growing cock, which is getting harder with every kiss I leave behind.

"I know you are...and it feels too good, and we have twenty minutes before we get home so I'm going to need you to..."

"What?" I ask, undoing his belt and pulling down his zipper.

"Charlie..."

"I think this will make you forget all about it..."

I don't know what's coming over me right now, but between this night, my raging hormones, and wanting Simon to not be sad, the only thing I want to do right now is give this man a blow job.

And not just any blow job: road head.

A thing I didn't realize was on my sexual bucket list.

"Fuck, Charlie..." he pushes back his seat slightly as I reposition myself, careful not to let everyone driving on Route 65 see my ass in the air.

I lick around his thick cock before I take him all, moving up and down as my hand works in tandem.

"Dammit, Bug, you feel too good..."

I don't reply; I just double down my efforts. I can feel the air hitting the top of my thighs and ass. I know if anyone were to drive by right now they'd be getting a show.

Ask me if I care.

My jaw is starting to ache, but I push through, not wanting to stop for one second. I lick around his tip before slowly taking him all in, my lips hitting his base. It makes him buck into me, and I swear he's hitting the back of my throat.

And holy shit is that a turn on I was not expecting.

"That's my girl...you can take it..."

I feel Simon veering to the side of the highway and slowing down before eventually stopping so he can pump into me. I don't stop. I keep going. Harder. Faster. Needing more than anything right now to have this man finish in my mouth.

And he does. With a guttural scream as he wraps my hair in his fist, the man comes in my mouth to the point where I don't know if it's ever going to stop.

And I take it all.

Bucket list item: check.

Chapter 27
Simon

"Quit pacing."

I look over to Charlie, who is lying in a gown at the OB/GYN's office, ready for her twenty-one week appointment.

Also known as the day we'll find out that Baby Bug's a girl.

"I'm sorry." I sit down in the chair next to her, though my leg is still bouncing a mile a minute. "I'm just so excited."

Charlie reaches for my hand, which I obviously give her, cupping it in both of mine. "I know you are. And so am I. But we're not finding out today, *remember?*"

She narrows her eyes at me, which I've started fondly calling the "it's your fault" look. "I know...But won't it be that much more fun finding out at the gender reveal party?"

"The gender reveal party that I thought was going to be small but you're going overboard with?"

"The very one."

"So you're excited that you want to know the gender right now. But you don't want to know the gender because you want to be surprised at the party?"

279

"Exactly. It's the baby father version of having your cake and eating it too."

I kiss Charlie's hand as our laughter fills the exam room. I love this woman for many different reasons, but this week's main reason is because she's letting me "go full Simon" with the gender reveal party. Her words, not mine. It's on New Year's Eve, and we are ringing in the year with a reveal. I'm talking live band, cake, cupcakes and every pastry Mellie can whip up, and of course, activities for all ages, including games and an indoor bounce house for the kids and betting tables for the adults on every single thing we can bet on when it comes to the baby.

This isn't your normal gender reveal party—it's a Simon gender reveal.

Go big or go home.

"Hello, Charlie. Simon. How are we doing?"

"I'm a little tired," I say. "Busy, you know. Work. Baby coming."

Charlie, along with Dr. Monty, give me the same baffled look.

"Oh, you weren't talking to me. Got it."

"Ignore him," Charlie says. "I try to most of the time."

This makes Dr. Monty laugh as she prepares Charlie for the ultrasound. I've been to every appointment with Charlie, but I don't know if I'll ever get over the awe and admiration I have during this process. Seeing it on the monitor. Hearing the heartbeat. Listening to Dr. Monty as she tells us about the growth, it's...I have no words. It's like the love I have for Charlie and the baby triple each time I see it. I can only imagine what I'm going to feel like the day Baby Bug is born.

"There it is," Dr. Monty says. "Baby is looking good. Strong heartbeat. Have you felt it kicking yet?"

Charlie nods. "Yes. I'm already planning on karate classes in my future."

"Sounds about right. And you want me to put the gender into an envelope without y'all knowing?"

"Yes—"

"No—"

Charlie's confused look says it all. "No?"

I smile and kiss her hand again. "Put it in the envelope, but can you make two? One for the party, and one for us."

Dr. Monty smiles. "Absolutely. They'll be ready for you at the desk."

I stand up to get Charlie's clothes for her, but she just stays sitting on the table, a little dumbfounded as to what I just did.

"You really want to know?"

I nod. "I do. I want us to sit together in the future nursery. I want you to be in my arms when we open the envelope together. I want us to share the reaction when we see girl or boy. Just us. Nothing flashy. Nothing big. Just you and me and Baby Bug."

Charlie's in tears as she holds out her arms for me. "I love that."

"I love you." I wrap my arms around her, holding her tighter than necessary. "But we're still having the party because I had to call in a favor with my bounce house guy, and I can't get that deposit back."

This makes her laugh as she comes up, wiping the tears away. "You have a bounce house guy?"

"Cute you think I didn't. What kind of fun uncle would I be if I didn't have a bounce house guy?"

She pops off the table and grabs her clothes. "One of these days I'm going to quit being surprised by you."

I lean down and kiss the top of her head. "I hope you never do."

* * *

"What's all this?"

Charlie looks up from where she is on the floor of the nursery—which right now is just an empty room. "Dinner."

I smile and sit down on the blanket that Charlie has laid out. Sandwiches. Fruits and veggies. A few slices of Mellie's cheesecake. A bottle of sparkling grape juice.

And the envelope.

"If we're going to make this a night to remember, let's do it right."

I dive in for a kiss, but make sure I'm careful to not let it get out of hand. We have important things to do tonight. "When did you do all this?"

A coy smile crosses her face. "You're not the only one who has a guy."

I laugh and swoop in for one more kiss. My hand goes to her stomach, which I do multiple times a day. Like Baby Bug knows what's going to happen, I feel a kick.

"She's really going," I say.

"Yes, it is..."

"Any final guesses?"

She shakes her head. "Healthy. And prone to sleeping through the night."

I laugh. "You know I want that too, right?"

"I know."

Our foreheads touch as we take in the moment. "You ready?"

She nods. "Let's do it."

We take the envelope together and Charlie gently tears it open, but doesn't take it out. "Together?"

"Together."

Each of us takes a corner of the picture of the ultrasound

282

from today that's in the envelope. We turn it over, and there, in bright pink letters, are the words I always knew to be true.

"It's a girl..." My voice is a whisper. "We're having a baby girl."

Charlie is smiling through the happy tears as we kiss and embrace and hold each other on the floor of the nursery where our daughter is going to grow up.

Daughter... Holy shit, we're having a daughter.

"A dancer. Our little girl is a dancer..."

"Makes sense, seeing as you're her father."

I readjust so I'm now lying across Charlie's lap, my head resting against where Baby Bug is doing her first performance. "Stella grew up dancing. I was dragged to more competitions than I'd care to admit, but I can see it now. We're going to be dance parents, and I'm going to carry props on the stage and wear shirts that say 'Prop Security' and get into Dad Dance-offs. And win."

"Obviously."

"Or maybe she'll want to be a soccer player. Or play basketball."

"She can do whatever she wants."

"Fuck yes, she can. Or maybe we have a musical prodigy on our hands. Or the first woman president. Or maybe she'll want to go to space."

Charlie's laughter fills the room as I rattle off every single thing our daughter could be.

"You hear that Baby Bug?" I roll over to Charlie's stomach. "I'm your daddy—wait, I can't say that—"

"Yes, you can," Charlie says, running her fingers through my hair. "I lift the ban."

I pop up for a quick kiss. "See Baby Bug? Your mama is the best ever. Anyway, as I was saying, I'm your daddy, and I love you so much already. And you can be whatever you want.

Except an Alabama fan. In this house we cheer for Tennessee."

"Really? That's what you're putting the boundary on?"

"Yes. And boys. Or girls. No dating until you're thirty."

"Don't listen to him, baby," Charlie interrupts. "I doubt he'll be able to say no to the two of us when we team up against him."

Shit. She's right. I already know I'm going to be a pushover if it's them against me.

"We'll figure it out." I move to my knees so I can lean down better to place a long kiss to her stomach.

To our daughter.

"I love you, Baby Bug." I give her one more kiss before sitting up. "And I love you Bug."

It's funny that just a few months ago I didn't know what love was. Not love like this. And now it consumes me so much I wonder how I went so long without it.

Though I know that answer. It's because it's Charlie. Bug. My Bug. There was going to be no love without her.

Because I'm nothing without her and this life we're creating together.

Which means I need to tell her. Soon. Before it's too late.

"Simon?"

"Yeah?"

"Does your offer still stand?"

I have to think for a second, because I'm trying to remember what offer I made her recently. "I'm not sure which one you are referring to, but the answer is yes."

She giggles. "The one about me moving in."

Did I just hear her right? Did she say she wants to move in?

"Bug...you're going to need to be very clear with your words here to make sure I'm not hallucinating."

"Simon." Her smile is big and beautiful and I think I might

284

remember this moment for the rest of my life. "Does the offer still stand for me to move in here? Because I thought it would be nice to live together for our first Christmas together, and the New Year. I talked to my property manager and he said—"

"Yes!" I yell, hugging her so hard that we end up laying on the ground. Our laughter fills the room as I pepper kisses all over her face. I'm so excited it barely registers that she talked to Emmett about this and he didn't tell me. I'll have to give him shit about that later.

But not now. Now is for being in this moment with Bug.

I roll to my side so I can look at her.

The mother of my daughter.

The love of my life.

My Bug.

"I love you," I say, leaning down to give her another kiss. "Thank you for loving me."

"Thank you for bugging me until I did."

I laugh and then it hits me. "Holy shit! I bugged Bug until she loved me! And because I bugged her, we have Baby Bug!"

I laugh as she rolls her eyes. "I knew I always hated that nickname."

"No, you don't."

She runs her hand along my face. "I hate that you're right."

"Is that all you hate about me?"

Charlie shrugs and wraps her hands around my neck, bringing me down to her. "I hate that you're not inside me."

"Well, that's funny..." I reposition myself on top of her, bringing her shirt up from her body as I do. "Because I hate that too."

Chapter 28
Charlie

"**B**ug? You here?"

I groan and fall without a touch of grace onto my bed. "Yes. But also go away!"

I know Simon isn't going to listen, even though I'd like him to. And it's not that I don't want to see him. I do. But not like this.

I knew this day was coming. The day my clothes stopped fitting and I just felt pregnant.

That day came today, at twenty-two weeks pregnant.

There is now no doubt I'm with child. My boobs, which have never been small, are too much to handle. The morning sickness has slowed down, but only for the heartburn to ramp up.

Then came the day I knew was coming: Not one piece of my clothing fits.

Welcome to the halfway point, Charlie. Just wait until you're as big as a beach ball...

For a while, I had some old, and very stretched out leggings that worked. Sweatpants have been my best friend.

They are now my enemy.

"Well, what do we have here?"

I turn my head to look at Simon, making sure he can fully see the daggers I'm shooting him.

"I'm fat and tired and everything hurts."

I feel the bed move as I bury my head back into my pillow. I don't know where Simon is finding a place to sit, considering my bed is currently covered in every piece of clothing I own. Hell, I don't know how he made it into the room considering it's filled with boxes and bags that I've packed to officially move to his place.

"We know my thoughts on this subject, but why are you saying this right now?"

"Why are you like this?"

"Like what?"

I turn again so I can see him. "Nice. And supportive. And wanting to say the polite thing instead of agreeing with me?"

Simon starts gently massaging my back. "Because I'm always going to support you. And tell you how beautiful you are. And contrary to popular belief, I am a nice guy."

"I think me and four other people in this world know that."

"The correct number is six. Eleven if you count their kids."

I laugh and sit up, realizing at this point, I'm only in my bra and underwear. "You're ridiculous, you know that?"

"Part of my charm."

For some reason, this makes me start to cry. In my defense, everything makes me cry these days.

"Hey," he says, gently taking a finger to wipe away the stray tears. "Reason for tears?"

This is something Simon has started asking me since we now see each other every day. And it's smart. One time he came into the restaurant and I was crying, and he panicked because I was sitting down. It was really just the onions. Once I started crying after announcing that I got a text from Connor. He thought it was bad news, but it was just a super cute video of Lila and Nuggy. I'm all over the place, and he's been nothing but wonderful. But asking for a reason is a safeguard for him to know how to navigate.

"Work was horrible today. The construction next door is loud as hell. My pregnancy brain led to multiple orders of burned bacon, and the cherry on top is that my mushroom guy just quit making deliveries."

"I'm sorry. Anything I can do to help?"

"No. Thank you. I have it handled. I think. Well, I was going to handle it with the mushroom guy, so I came upstairs to change to drive out and see what the hell was up. That was my first mistake because I put on leggings."

"Am I dumb to ask why that was a mistake?"

My shoulders slump. "Because they didn't fit. Then I put on my trusty, go-to, ratty sweatpants. And they didn't fit. Next thing I knew I tried on every piece of clothing I owned and nothing fit. Which is why I'm sitting here nearly naked and I don't have maternity clothes. And I know my body is changing and this day was going to happen, but I didn't know it would be today..."

"I'm sorry," Simon says, brushing a loose strand of hair behind my ear. "Do you need to go shopping?"

"Yes? No. Probably. I don't have the extra cash right now for new clothes."

Simon narrows his eyes at me.

"Let's not get into a money spat," I say, knowing that this conversation has the possibility of turning into that. I'm getting better with accepting Simon paying for stuff—even after the stupid expensive crib—but I'm not completely comfortable yet. "It's not just the pain in the ass of needing new clothes."

"What is it?"

I take in a breath, wanting to think about how I phrase this next part. "You know how I feel, and have felt, about my body."

He nods but doesn't say anything.

"Over the past few years, I had finally come to terms with the fact that I'm a bigger woman. And I didn't hate my body anymore. I didn't love it, but I was comfortable. Mostly. Sometimes even confident. Never sex with lights on, as you know, but I was mostly okay."

Simon's eyes narrow even further. "Can you say what you need to say without talking about other men?"

His jealousy is funny to me. Even when I hated him, somewhere in the back of my mind I knew no other man compared. "Sorry."

"Apology accepted." He tops off the apology with a kiss on my forehead, which eases me in a way I don't know he realizes.

"Anyway...I was finally at a place in my life when I was okay with my body. And it was good. I felt pretty good. And being with you has...well I've never felt better. Then today... and I know it's because of the baby...it's just...with one ill-fitting pair of pants and my boobs popping out of my bra...I feel like all that mental work I did is gone."

"Well, I'd like to first say, I'm not mad *one bit* about the boobs."

I shake my head with a laugh. "Of course you aren't."

"Second of all, you need to know that I think you are fucking beautiful. And you are only getting more beautiful every day."

"And you have to say that."

"Charlene Marie Bennett," Simon turns me a little so I'm looking right into his crystal blue eyes. "After all these years, do you *still* not believe how fucking gorgeous you are?"

I shrug. "You know I've never seen me the way you do. Even at my best..."

Simon stands up and holds his hand out for me.

"What are you doing?"

"If you don't want to believe how beautiful I think you are, I have no other option but to show you."

I give him my hand as a devious, and sexy, smiles cross over his handsome face. He pulls me from the bed, positioning me in front of him—and turning us to face my full-length mirror.

I immediately avert my eyes from the mirror. This is maybe the most uncomfortable thing ever. I might be more confident in my body, but that doesn't mean I like looking at it. Especially today.

But Simon doesn't let me. His one hand holds me around my soft stomach as his other lifts my chin up, making me look at our reflections.

"Look at me."

I reluctantly do as he says.

"Now, I could ask you what you see, but I have a feeling you aren't going to say the right answer. So I'm going to tell you what *I* see."

Simon's hand leaves my chin and slides down until he finds the front clasp of my bra. I can't even be impressed by his one-handed unlatching. I'm too mesmerized by the fire in his eyes right now. I always described his eyes as nearly crystal blue. But now? It reminds me of the subtle blue that you see in a flame.

He's on fire. For me.

"I don't think it's a lie that I'm pretty obsessed with these," he says, massaging both of my breasts in his strong hands. The mixture of pressure and pleasure is intoxicating. "But now, knowing that soon they are going to give our child nourishment? Because you're growing our baby? It's a feeling I can't describe."

He pulls me in even closer, and I feel his cock hardening against me.

"And this?" His hands travel down to my stomach, placing them securely on the baby bump. "The fantasies I have about you and your body changing through every stage should be illegal."

I stare as his hand continues traveling down, separating my legs slightly so he can slide a finger along my pussy.

"Do you know how fucking sexy it is when you're wet and waiting for me? How beautiful you are, knowing this pussy is mine and only mine?"

I let my head tip back, reveling in the feeling of his fingers teasing my entrance. "Eyes on me, Bug. And don't you dare look away."

I do as he says, though I don't know if I'm ready for the next part of his show.

His mouth starts kissing down my neck and across my shoulder as he steps in front of me. His mouth continues to leave a trail across my body, making sure to make a stop at my breasts as he sucks on each one of them, giving each ample attention.

He doesn't stay there too long, continuing his journey down as he lowers himself to his knees.

"Simon?"

"Are you watching?"

"Yes..."

And I am. I couldn't take my eyes off him if I wanted to. He separates my legs just enough so he has access to my pussy, licking it from back to front as I watch in awe.

He's not relenting. My legs are about to give out, but he's holding onto me with such steadfastness I know I won't fall.

And then there's his tongue, which is taking whatever it wants, however it wants. My hands are pulling at his hair so hard it might come out. Yet it only seems to make him go harder. Faster. Further.

"Simon…"

My moan is only answered with him inserting a finger, now working in tandem with his tongue. I let go of his hair with one of my hands, needing more touch. I take my nipple between my fingers, rolling it around to get that perfect twinge of pain to accompany Simon's pleasure.

It's at that moment I take my eyes off him and look at myself. I'm naked. Flushed. My breathing is heavy, and my legs are weak.

But for maybe the first time in my life I look past that. I see a sensual woman who is taking in every ounce of pleasure from a man who is making it his life's mission to satisfy me. I see a woman who wants to watch in the mirror as she takes his cock and screams his name.

That woman is me. I'm her.

And for the first time in maybe my life, I finally see what Simon does.

"Fuck me, Simon." I say through heavy breaths. "Fuck me now."

With one more lick, Simon comes up and leads me to the bed.

"No," I say as he lays me back.

"I thought…"

I shake my head, rising up so I can kiss him, loving the taste of myself on his lips. "I want to watch."

His eyes go back to that fire blue as he yanks off his pants. While I'm waiting, I position myself on all fours on my bed so I'm facing the mirror. I watch intently as he comes behind me, stroking himself before he leans down, his stomach to my back as he gently kisses my shoulder.

"Do you know how fucking hot you are right now?"

I nod. "I do."

He smiles. "Good girl."

With one kiss to my back Simon lines himself up and thrusts into me, making me close my eyes just from the sheer impact of his thick cock filling me to the brim.

"Eyes on me, Charlie." I do as he says, locking eyes with the man who owns every inch of me right now. "Now watch."

And I do. I watch as he drives in and out of me, passion, lust, and desire fueling every minute. I watch as his hand comes from holding my hips to grabbing onto each of my dangling tits. He's squeezing hard, but I'm savoring the feeling.

He pinches one of my nipples, and it nearly sends me over the edge. I don't want it to be over, but considering I can feel his eyes just as deep as I can feel his cock, I don't know how much longer I can hold out.

"I love you, Charlie," he says, his eyes locked with mine. "I love you so fucking much."

"I love you," I repeat, and not just because we're in the throes of passion. Or because he said it. Because I do. I love this man. I love him so fucking much it hurts.

"Bug..." he cries out as his hands go back to my hips and gives them a squeeze. The slap on my ass is an added bonus.

"Yes, Simon! Yes!"

With a few more thrusts I come apart, and he's not far behind. Our gazes finally unlock as he collapses onto me, both of us coming down from an orgasm that I felt in every cell of my body.

Eventually he rolls off me, but only to bring me into his arms, holding me like I might run away.

Which I get. I used to be a flight risk. Hell, there's receipts of me doing that exact thing.

But that was then. This is now.

There's not a chance in hell I'm going anywhere.

Chapter 29
Charlie

I get why everyone loves Christmas.

And so do I, don't get me wrong.

But to me, there's something more special about Christmas Eve.

There's the excitement and anticipation. The wonder if you were in fact good all year, and if Santa was going to visit.

But for me, it's more than that. This is the day I remember the most from my childhood. Every Christmas Eve, Mom would take Connor and I to our version of Mona's. She'd let us order whatever we wanted before we'd go home and make cookies until we were out of icing and sprinkles.

It was the best day of the year.

Which is why I insisted on being open today, even if it was just for breakfast.

"You're serving today?"

I turn to see my favorite property manager, Emmett, walking through the doors. And I know I'm with Simon. And I love that man more than I thought possible, but you'd have to be blind to not appreciate the hunk of a man Emmett Collins is.

"Skeleton crew for the holiday. Plus, I like to be on this side every once in a while." I grab a mug and pour him his coffee. "And what are you doing here? I figured this would be the Tuesday you'd take off."

He shakes his head. "Today is the last day for the crew before we close down until the New Year. So this is going to be the last time I head this way for a while. And you know I can't go that long without your waffles."

I shake my head at Emmett's compliment, taking his ticket to the window. I never had to deal with a property manager before, but I'd have to assume that Emmett is one of the more hands-on ones in the business. He comes in every Tuesday, like clockwork, to check on me. He's also checking in on the construction next door, which has been going since I took over this space. I have no clue what's going in there; I just know they've been gutting it to the studs.

But hey, they come in for lunch every day, so I'm not complaining.

"So anything special going on for the holiday?" I ask.

He shakes his head. "I'll go home to Kentucky for Christmas. I have the rest of the year off, so I'll probably relax there before I come back. Though I'll want to avoid Nashville for New Year's. It's a shit show."

An idea comes to me, and it might be the best idea I've had in a while. "If you want to do something for New Year's, why don't you come to our gender reveal?"

Emmett nearly chokes on his coffee at the sound of my suggestion. "Oh...um...I don't think that's a good idea..."

"Don't be silly." Why is he acting weird about this? "Simon insisted on having a blow out, and New Year's was the perfect time to have it. There will be plenty of food and an open bar. Plus, you can meet some Rolling Hills people and we can maybe convince you to move here. Who knows, maybe you'll find someone to kiss at midnight."

"Thanks, but no thanks."

His quick tone takes me aback. "Okay then...just thought I'd offer."

I watch as his shoulders slump. "I'm sorry, Charlie. That was rude of me. I'm just not a big New Years guy."

"Oh, well that makes sense." And because my pregnancy brain is all over the place, the talk of the new year reminds me of something. "Oh! Wait here, I need to get my rent check for next month."

I head back to my office and hurriedly write my monthly rent check. Yes I know it's old school. Yes, I know, I could just transfer my rent through my bank. But I like it this way. It works for me and that's all that matters.

When I come back out to the dining room, with Emmett's food in hand, I notice he's furiously typing something on his phone.

"Here we go, one rent check and one plate of waffles. Oh, and can you see why my October check wasn't cashed?"

His head snaps up. "What was that?"

"My October rent check. I was doing my books the other day and I noticed it wasn't cashed, which I thought was weird. I meant to text you about it, but preggo brain got in the way. Can you make sure everything is okay?"

"Oh, I will." I don't know why I find his tone weird, but it is. It's like he's pissed about it.

This man is just confusing the hell out of me today.

His phone vibrates on the counter, and I watch as he mumbles a few choice words before taking a huge bite of his waffles.

"Charlie? Can I get my bill? I have to go."

"Oh, okay." I don't know why the sudden need for Emmett to leave takes me off guard. "Want me to box this up for you?"

"No, thanks. Maybe a to-go cup?"

"You got it."

Sensing Emmett is in a hurry, I quickly pour his complimentary cup of coffee. He still insists on paying for his food, but he's started to accept the free cup of Joe each time he comes in.

He barely says goodbye as he throws too much money on the counter and hurries out the door. I normally wouldn't watch Emmett leave, but I can't help but notice that he goes from a near sprint to a dead stop as soon as the door swings open.

In his defense, everyone stops and stares as Santa comes strutting through the door.

Wait, why is Santa here? I didn't order a Santa.

"Ho! Ho! Ho! Merry Christmas!"

Oh, that makes much more sense.

The packed diner turns to watch as the Santa I'm stuck with for the rest of my life struts in. "I heard this is where all the good boys and girls eat. And Santa needs to fuel up before his big night!"

I don't know whether to laugh, roll my eyes, or hide in the back as Santa—a.k.a. the father of my child—walks through the diner, saying hello to every customer.

And is he passing out presents?

"Order up!"

I turn away from Santa Simon, who is being tackled by the few kids that are in here this morning, as I go and deliver three plates to my three favorite customers.

"Is that Simon, dear?"

The question comes from Penny, the ringleader of the trio who comes in every Tuesday. Each week they sit at the same table, order the same three dishes, and split them between themselves so they can have a little of everything. Then they sit here for hours and play a weird dice game I've yet to figure out.

And I tried. I spent an entire day trying to learn.

So even though it's Christmas Eve, it's still Tuesday, and my Dice Gals are here and waiting for their breakfast.

"It is. But please don't ask me where he got the Santa suit. I did *not* see that in the closet this morning."

The three laugh as they start divvying up their breakfast.

"Doesn't surprise me," Penny says. "I've known him since he was a boy. I remember when his family first moved to Rolling Hills. Stole the show every chance he got."

I look over to Simon, who is now letting the children sit on his lap as he asks them what they want for Christmas. I take a step back and put my hands on my stomach out of habit, as I watch Simon take such care and interest into what each child says. I don't know what he's saying now, but the little girl on his lap is giggling so hard she might fall off his lap.

He's going to be the best father. I just know it. He's made mention on numerous occasions that he never thought he had it in him. I now see that wasn't even close to being true.

This man was made to be a father. A girl dad if I ever saw one.

I slowly make my way to the impromptu Santa station as a little boy hops off his lap.

"Oh, boys and girls! Santa has a very important visitor!"

I smile and wave. "Did you all get to see Santa?"

The host of children eagerly nod their heads.

"Well, if you want him to come to your houses tonight and bring you all those presents he promised, then what do we need to make sure we have?"

They all yell in unison. "Cookies!"

"That's right. Now, how about I go back in the kitchen and

see if we have any that you all can take home? Santa? Want to help me?"

"I'd love to! Ho, ho ho!"

I laugh under my breath as Simon waves to the kids before following me back into the kitchen. "Mellie, do we have some extra cookies I can send home with kids for Santa?"

"Of course! Oh! I should make some fresh sugar cookies. They can be in the shape of Santa."

"That sounds delicious," Simon says.

I look over to him with a raised brow. "You know you're actually not going to be the one eating these cookies, right?"

He looks disappointed.

I shake my head at the ridiculousness of Simon. "Can you take them to the kids?"

"Of course." Mellie claps her hands as she gets back to baking. "This is my favorite holiday."

I heard through the grapevine that a famous actress known for holiday movies lives in Rolling Hills. Maybe she can come into the diner and base a character off Mellie, who I swear would be the perfect Mrs. Clause if she was thirty-three, bubbly, and lived for baking Christmas cookies.

I signal for Simon to follow me back to the office, where I shut the door and double check that the blinds are closed.

"Oh my," he says in his Santa voice. "Does someone have a present for Santa?"

Simon's eyebrows start waggling but I shake my head. "Not that kind of present."

"Dammit."

I laugh as I take the small gift I got for him out of my desk drawer. I didn't plan on giving this to him here, but it feels right.

"What's this?"

"A present."

"We said no gifts."

"I know," I shrug. "But I knew you weren't going to stick to that rule, so I didn't either."

He pulls me in by my waist and gives me a firm kiss. "You know me so well."

Shopping for Simon Banks might be the hardest thing to do on Earth. The man has everything. Or if he doesn't, he has the money to buy it.

And I think I nailed it. But that doesn't mean I'm not nervous for him to open it.

I expected Simon to be a rip the paper open with his teeth kind of guy. But surprisingly, he's not. He's taking his time, making sure not to rip the paper. Almost as if it's part of the present.

The man is a conundrum, to say the least...

I watch his face as he opens the present. It goes from curiosity, to shock, to awe, back to a look of utter surprise. Who knew that my present would be getting to watch him unwrap his?

"Bug...When? Was this—"

I smile as he looks deeper into the picture frame that has a spot for two pictures—one is from the night we found out Bug was a girl. The second was from our one "not date" in college.

"I didn't think there was a picture of us," he says, his voice filled with wonder and curiosity.

"This is the only one," I say. "From the crappy disposable camera I had on WrestleMania night."

He thinks about it for a second before I see the lightbulb come on. "Holy shit! I made you take it!"

There we were, sitting at the local sports bar on the date that wasn't a date. I was looking for something in my purse when I took the camera out. I don't even remember why I had it. Either way, Simon got a hold of it and took a few of himself, before making a stranger take one of him and me.

"I didn't even get it developed until that summer," I say. "And I almost threw it away."

"But you didn't," he says, his genuine smile from earlier now replaced with the cocky one.

"I didn't."

Simon reaches for me, his hand behind my head, as he pulls me in for a passionate, yet too short for my liking, kiss. "Thank you. It's perfect."

Perfect. I didn't think that word was possible for anything. Nothing could be perfect.

I was wrong. So wrong.

"So how long do you have that Santa suit?" I ask.

A flicker of confusion runs through his eyes before his whole face lights up. "It's Oliver's. I'll buy it from him if necessary."

"Good," I say. "Merry Christmas to me..."

Chapter 30
Simon

Emmett: Hey, slight problem I forgot to tell you about.

Simon: What's that?

Emmett: Charlie invited me tonight.

Simon: What do you mean Charlie invited you? When?

Emmett: I don't know how I could be any more clear. I came by the restaurant last week to check in, you know, the day you were playing Santa. She asked me before you randomly showed up.

Simon: What did you say?

> Emmett: I told her thanks but no thanks. Some bullshit excuse about not liking to be around people on New Year's. But she just texted me again asking if I changed my mind because there's still time to get there before midnight. So if she says anything, don't act weird.

> Simon: I mean, that wasn't a lie. You really don't like people.

> Emmett: At least one of us is telling the truth...

I hate that he's right. Fuck. How have I not told her yet? I told myself a hundred times that I wasn't starting the new year with her not knowing everything. Yet here we are, New Year's Eve, and she still doesn't know that the rent she pays every month goes to me.

Well, it goes to a bank account that I don't touch. Well, now it does. I didn't cash the first few months.

Fuck. I need to tell her. But I can't now. We're an hour away from the New Year's Gender Reveal Blowout Bash. She's spent the day making sure the caterers she reluctantly hired are doing everything the way she wants. I'm making sure the betting stations are set and the band has everything they need.

And if being busy wasn't a good enough reason, no one should have drama on a big event day. We're celebrating Baby Bug with our friends and loved ones, and I'm not going to ruin it because of the dumbass decision I made months ago.

What's a few more days going to hurt?

> Simon: I know. I'll tell her. Soon.

> Emmett: You better, because I'm tired of lying for your ass.

Simon: I will.

Emmett: I'll believe it when I see it.

"You okay?"

I hurry and put the phone into the pocket of my bright pink suit—yes, the suit from Oliver and Izzy's reception—as I turn to Charlie. She, as to not give it away that we know the gender, is wearing a baby blue dress that hugs her curves, and baby bump, perfectly. The color matches her eyes, and along with her now strawberry blonde hair, I don't know how she could look more beautiful.

"Yeah." I pull her into me, taking the opportunity to steal a kiss. "Just putting out a fire."

She gives me another concerned look, but I take that away with another kiss. The only problem is, this kiss doesn't stop. I didn't mean for it to keep going. But what started as an innocent peck to deflect is quickly turning into a heated one that is two seconds away from us needing to sneak into a broom closet.

"Watch it. Children are here. They don't need to see how the baby was made."

We pull away, guilty looks covering our faces, as we turn to Connor and Lila.

"Sorry," Charlie says, quickly trying to fix her red lipstick that I'm sure I smeared. "Are you both having a good time?"

"Yes!" Lila claps. "I was playing with Jayce."

"That's fun," I say, kneeling down to her level. "You know, that's my nephew. His mommy is my sister."

"Wow, really? He's my boyfriend!"

I nearly choke on my own spit. Charlie can't hold in her holler. And as I sneak a peek at Connor, his eyes are about to bulge out of his head.

Charlie steps forward and takes Lila's hand, still stifling her laugh. "How fun is that? Can you introduce me to him?"

Lila doesn't think twice as she leads Charlie away. I stand up next to Connor and give him a pat on the back. "Welcome to the family."

"I never thought you'd be in my family, let alone my daughter furthering the ties."

We chuckle and go take a seat, which gives me a view of the entire banquet hall. The band I hired has kept everyone on the dance floor all night. The betting tables have been busy as people have been placing their wagers on the gender, the date of birth, and the other prop bets we've put in place, like whether or not I'm going to pass out in the delivery room and how long Charlie will be in labor.

But the best part of all? Everyone in my and Charlie's life who means anything to us is here. My entire crew of friends and their children; my whole family, including Maeve and Jayce, Stella and her fiancé Duncan, Ainsley, and even my sister Quinn came in from Arizona; and of course, the people in town who are like family. Mona took a break from her retirement travels to be here. Regulars from the diner are here. The icing on the cake for Charlie was that Connor and Lila made it down from Nashville.

"Thanks for being here," I say to him. "I know how much it means to Charlie."

"We wouldn't have missed it."

There's a pause in his words, and I feel like he wants to say more.

"Let me have it," I say, helping him along.

"Have what?"

"You paused, which usually means there was a 'but' coming. Or in this case, whatever it is you've been dying to say to me for months now."

Connor chuckles as he sits back and crosses his foot over his knee. "There were days back then that Charlie never stopped crying. If you didn't know, one would have guessed it was because Mom was dying. But I knew it wasn't just because of that. And sometimes it wasn't because of that at all."

"I wish I knew," I say. "Believe me, I tried to reach out. I wanted to talk to her. I hated how things were left."

"I know. Well, I know that now. But that doesn't change the fact that for years I thought you were the asshole who broke my sister's heart."

"I get it," I say, nodding to where my sisters are all out on the dance floor, dancing to a cover of a popular song from our youth that they used to drive me insane with. "If I knew any man fucked with my sisters, hating them would be the bare minimum of my feelings toward them."

"Exactly," Connor says. "Charlie gave up her life for me when our Mom died. She was twenty-one years old and took on guardianship of a sixteen-year-old kid who was mad at the world because his mother was just taken from him and his dad never gave a shit. She took me and Lila in without missing a beat, when I was scared to even hold the baby I didn't know I had."

"She's a good woman."

"No, she's a *great* woman," Connor emphasizes.

"You're right," I say. "She's the best person I know. She makes me a better person."

"That's what she does. And for that, she deserves the world."

"I couldn't agree more," I say. "And I want to give her that. Whether it's with us, or the diner, or our family, I want to give her everything she wants and needs."

"I know you do," Connor says, but he pauses. I follow his line of sight to Charlie dancing with Lila and Jayce. Her smile is lighting up the room as she happens to look over at the two of us. "She comes off as strong. She wants to do everything for herself. Take care of everything herself. Never ask for help."

"I'm well aware," I say, the ping of guilt stabbing me in the gut as Connor talks. It's like he knows.

"What I'm saying is, for years I thought you were the enemy. But now you're an ally. Help her where you can. Be strong for her so she doesn't have to do it all the time. Be her partner. Just...be there for her."

I nod and extend my hand. "You have my word."

We stand and shake hands. I'm a little shocked when Connor pulls me in for a bro hug.

"Oh, and Simon?"

"Yeah?"

"Hurt her and I'll kill you."

I laugh, but nod as we step away. "I figured you felt that way."

"Don't all brothers?"

I take a glance at the dance floor to see not only my sisters, but all of the women in my life who I love like family, are all gathering. My heart doubles in size as I take them all in, knowing that I'd do anything to make sure these women were taken care of.

"Yeah. Yeah, we do."

The DJ announces that there's five minutes left until the ball drops.

AKA—five minutes until this place is covered in pink.

Connor and I walk to the dance floor as he scoops up Lila and I take Charlie by the hand.

"You ready?"

Her smile and radiating happiness nearly knocks me on my ass. "Let's go, Daddy."

I kiss her hand as we make our way to the microphone. Because of course I have to give a speech.

"Friends, family, I want to thank you all for spending your New Year's Eve with us."

"And we'd like to thank you for paying for the open bar!"

Everyone laughs at Wes's joke as I hold up the glass of champagne I was just handed. "This is a night of celebration. For everyone, this is the start of a New Year. For Charlie and I, this year is going to be one we're never going to forget."

A round of "awes" echo as I kiss the top of her head. "Now, I hope that you have all placed your bets, because in thirty seconds, the ball is going to drop in Rolling Hills. If you'd like, grab your confetti cannons, which are packed full of either pink or blue confetti. But remember, don't set them off until the clock strikes midnight!"

A round of applause is quieted by the traditional countdown to New Year's. I take Bug and lead her to the floor so we can take in the moment with those we love.

"I love you, Simon Banks," Charlie says, her hands resting on my shoulders.

I pull her in tighter as the countdown hits five. "You have no idea how much I love you."

"Three! Two! One! Happy New Year!"

The band starts playing the traditional New Year's song as people kiss their loved ones and the kids go crazy with the noisemakers and confetti cannons. Before we know it, a mass of pink balloons float down from the ceiling, causing an uproar of cheers.

"Hell, yes!" Wes says as he's the first one to congratulate me. "Welcome to the world of being a girl dad."

"Glad to be here," I say before accepting hugs from Oliver and Shane. Izzy, Betsy, and Amelia have Charlie wrapped in a group hug.

I think this is the first time I've seen Charlie with them. I wasn't expecting for this sight to hit me like this. But it is. Because Charlie's part of this group. This family we've made for ourselves. She's one of them. One of the girls.

The ones who made us whole.

Betsy brought Wes back to life after his divorce, and she's the mom his kids deserved after growing up with the Wicked Witch. Izzy showed Oliver what love was after years of searching. And Amelia? She might have been our sister growing up, but now I know the real reason she was with us. It was because she was meant for Shane.

Then there's Charlie. She was truly the missing piece to my puzzle. She makes me want more. She makes me want to be a man who thinks about more than himself and what building or house he's buying next.

This is it. Our family. Our foundation. Charlie not only completed me, but our group.

This is it. This is us. Forever.

"Hey," Charlie whispers in my ear. "Follow me."

I can't object before she takes my hand to lead me off the dance floor. We're stopped by congratulations with every step, but that doesn't stop her. If anything, it makes her speed up more.

"Bug? Are you okay?"

She doesn't answer; she only picks up speed. Before I know it, she's opening the door to what I believe is the coat closet. "Pants off, Banks."

I know she can't see how big my eyes are. "Excuse me?"

"You heard me." I hear the click of Charlie locking the door as my eyes start to adjust to the darkness. Before I know it, Charlie is in front of me, her hands working to loosen my belt. "Sex. Now."

I've heard about second trimester pregnancy hormones.

I've read about them, Wes warned me, and the Facebook group I'm in for expectant fathers has had numerous posts about this. But I didn't know if it was real.

"Charlie, while I love you, and will never turn down sex, you know we're in a closet where people are probably going to need coats sooner rather than later?"

Her hand is down my pants and beginning to stroke me. "Well, then, we better hurry up."

Any protest I had dies on my tongue as Charlie pushes my pants down and falls to her knees. The only sound that comes from my mouth is a muffled f-bomb as Charlie begins sucking me like her life depends on it.

If I ever get bored with the feeling of this woman's mouth on me, then someone needs to take me out back and end it all.

I want this. Her. For the rest of my life. I want sneak-away trysts in closets. I want to make love to her in our bed. I want to have six more kids. I want her to walk down the aisle to me.

I want everything. And I want it with Charlie.

"Up," I command, pulling her off me and if I could see, I'd bet I could see her spit still coating my cock. "I need inside you."

Charlie doesn't hesitate, she stands up and I turn her around, leading her to a wall as I suck on her neck. My hands pull at her dress and bra, bringing them down so her fantastic tits spill over.

"Hold on." I push the coats aside, giving her a base to hold onto. "This is going to be quick."

"Please..."

I let go of her only long enough to push her dress up and slide her panties down. I slide a finger along her pussy to find it already wet for me.

Like she always is.

I slam into her, and her scream is so loud I'm sure anyone standing outside could have heard her.

Let them hear. Ask me if I care.

I don't. Let them hear her scream for me. Let them hear the sounds I make because this woman's cunt is holding onto me so tight it might never let me go. Let them know we want each other so much that we're fucking in a coat closet because we can't *not* do this.

"So good," I say as I reach around, holding each of her dangling tits into my hands. "Do you know how much I fucking love you?"

"Yes..."

"How much I need you..."

"Yes..."

"That I can't breathe without you..."

"Yes, Simon. I love you..."

"You're mine, Bug." I pick up the pace of my thrusts, and I feel my balls tightening with every push. "Do you hear that? Mine."

"Yours...Forever."

Those words coming off her tongue is my undoing. I feel her also coming apart around me, and I hold her tighter as our orgasms chase through us.

That might have been the most intense thing I've ever felt in my life. Which makes sense.

It's Charlie. My Bug.

Intense is the only word that even comes close to describing what I feel for her.

The sound of our breaths is interrupted by a banging on the door—and a very pissed off Shane yelling at us.

"Simon! For the love of God! I know you're in there, and we need to get our coats. Get the fuck out."

"Hold your fucking horses!"

The One I Hate

Charlie starts giggling as I slide out of her. She adjusts herself as I pull my pants back up, but I don't walk to the door yet.

"Come here," I say, pulling her into my chest. "Happy New Year, Bug."

She places a gentle kiss to the corner of my mouth, and somehow that hits me just as hard as what we just finished doing. "Happy New Year, Daddy."

Maybe the four best words I've ever heard...

Chapter 31
Charlie

"What's this?" I kick off my shoes as I enter Simon's house—which I guess is now my house —to see that multiple pans are on the stove and steam is coming out of them. "Are you cooking?"

Simon turns to me as he pulls a sheet pan out of the oven. I don't know what's on it, but it's burned. And he's wearing a "Kiss the Chef" apron I didn't know he owned.

"I was. I'm not anymore."

I laugh as I make my way to one of the stools at his kitchen island. This kitchen is a dream. Double ovens. Plenty of prep space. The handy water spout at the stove. Storage that never ends. And in the now month I've lived here, I've never seen him use it until right now.

"Where did you get that apron? And why are you cooking?"

"Well," he pauses to come over and give me a kiss. "I originally bought it for you since you are the chef in the house. And I'm a fan of kissing you. But since I decided today I was cooking, I figured I'd try it on to see how it feels. Turns out, just wearing an apron that says you're a chef doesn't make you one. So dinner is being ordered from The Joint and will be delivered in an hour."

I laugh, which is the wrong choice.

"Shit!"

"What? Are you okay?"

I shake my head. "I peed a little."

I drop my head into my hands in embarrassment, though Simon's slight chuckles make me want to laugh again. I feel him wrap his arms around me as he stands behind me, resting his cheek on my back.

"Can I take a nap right here?" I mumble, suddenly realizing how tired I am.

"You could, but then I'll have to give you a massage later to get the kink out of your neck. Which will lead to sex. So that, my darling, is up to you."

I groan as I sit up, Simon moving next to me. "Honestly I'm so tired I don't know if I even have the energy to spread my legs."

"I'd like it to be noted for the record that I could have made a joke about not needing you to move for sex, but I didn't."

"Thank you," I groan, falling into his arms. "This might have been the hardest day yet."

He brushes my hair back and kisses the top of my head. "Want to talk about it?"

"Today was a shit show," I say. "My back has been killing me all week, so I was trying to take it easy at the diner. Which didn't happen, because the ice machine stopped working, there was a leak in the ceiling, and both servers got sick and had to call off. Oh, and the fucking mushroom guy is still just delivering my orders whenever he wants to."

"Why didn't you call me?"

"What were you going to do? Fix an ice machine? Go pick up my order from the mushroom guy?"

"No. I have guys."

"I know you do. But it's not your responsibility to fix my problems. Or get my mushrooms," I say. "Plus, I called Emmett, and he came in to help with the leak."

I feel Simon tense against me, which is weird. Then again, everything feels weird these days so I don't think much of it.

"Anyway. All of that happened on top of the baby deciding today would be a great day to make her audition tape for America's Next Karate Kid. I can't stop peeing, and I just want this day to be over."

I hate complaining, especially because I know that even on this bad day, I'm blessed to have help and support and love.

But also fuck this day.

"Okay, here's what we're going to do." Simon gently moves me up so he can stand, guiding me up with him and leading us away from the kitchen to our bedroom. "You're going to go take off those greasy smelling work clothes and go take a shower. After that, put on that fluffy robe you love so much. And then, come back here for a delicious meal of burgers, fries, and the mozzarella sticks you love so much."

I stand up, but not before giving him a deserving kiss. "It's days like this where I really love you."

"Who knew all I needed to win your heart was to order you fried cheese?"

I smile for the first time today as I walk down the hall to the master bedroom. I'm still in awe of how big this space is. I'm pretty sure just this room is bigger than my first apartment. Hell, just the walk-in closet rivals it.

Then there's this bathroom. White tiles. Gold fixtures. A bathtub with jets and a heat setting I can't wait to use the second this kid is out. But for now, the shower will have to do.

However many minutes of scrubbing and soaking later, I pop out, wrap my hair in a towel and pat myself dry before grabbing the robe that is calling my name. I slip it over my shoulders, but don't close it right away, instead taking a second to look at my bump in the full-length bathroom mirror.

I don't do this often—take in my bump that is. I know it's there. I peek at it every day. Simon makes sure to rub it multiple times a day, including when he applies the belly butter that he insists is his job. But I rarely stand in front of the mirror and really just look at the baby I'm making.

I'm making a baby.

That's still baffling, even as I enter my third trimester. In just a few months I'm going to be holding her in my arms. She's going to be nursing from me. She's going to be smiling and giggling and crying and all the things babies do.

I'm going to be a mom.

I push back the tears that threaten every time I have this thought, because it always makes me think of my mom. I wish she was here. I wish I could share this with her. There have been so many times I've wanted to call her to ask her about random things I'm feeling, or ask her what I liked as a baby in case Baby Bug likes or dislikes the same things.

When she passed away, I thought of all the things she'd miss, and this was one of them. But I didn't realize then how much it would hurt when those things happened.

But they do. They hurt like a bitch.

"Hey, you okay?"

I turn to see Simon leaning against the door.

"Yeah. Just a little caught up in the moment."

He nods but doesn't say anything. I wipe away my loose tears and tie the robe before he walks with me back to the living room. And when I see the takeout boxes covering every inch of the coffee table, I'm crying for a whole new reason.

"I loved you before, but I love you even more now," I say as I take a seat. I grab the box labeled "mozzarella sticks" and open it to be greeted by six perfectly fried pieces of cheese, and extra marinara sauce.

The man knows me too well.

"ERMYGERD." I know it's not a word, but that's the appropriate response for a foodgasm. My nonsensical word turns into a moan when I feel Simon taking my feet and swinging them so they are now on his lap. "What are you doing?"

"You said you were on your feet all day."

Between the fried cheese and Simon's thumbs working into my arches, there's a very good chance I'm going to have an orgasm in three seconds. "Remember when I said I loved you more like five seconds ago?"

"Yeah."

"It's even more now."

He laughs. "Eat. Let me work my magic."

And he does. I can't even finish my mozzarella sticks because I'm basking in the feeling of Simon's hands working my feet and legs. I know I said I wasn't in the mood for sex earlier, but that was then, and this is now, and if he keeps this up we're about to check the couch off as another spot in this house we've christened.

"So I was thinking," he says as he switches feet.

"Should I be scared?"

"Ha. Ha. Keep that up and I'll stop."

"Never mind what I said. You were thinking, and I'm sure it was the most profound notion ever."

"That's what I thought." He sends me a wink. "No, I was thinking about baby names."

"Oh," I say, not expecting that. "Yeah, I guess we should start talking about it."

"Exactly. I was thinking, and I'm not saying I nailed it on the first try, but I'm pretty sure I nailed it on the first try."

Okay, now I am scared. "Care to share with the class?"

My favorite shit-eating grin grows on his face. "Simone."

Of course he would...

"Really? Simone?"

"Yeah. I think it's great."

"I think you're an idiot."

"Well, at least I have a name. What suggestion are you offering?"

I return the smug smile. "I think Charlotte sounds lovely."

"Oh so that's how it's going to be." Simon takes my foot and pulls me closer to him, giving him free access to lean down to kiss me. "For the record I think Charlotte Simone sounds like a lovely name."

"It does. But people will think we're the most conceited people in Tennessee if we name our kid after ourselves."

"Well, they already think that about me."

"I always knew you'd give me a bad rap."

Simon steals one more kiss before I lie back down on the couch. Only now I'm snuggling into Simon, our food long forgotten. "I always liked the name Emily."

Simon furiously shakes his head. "Hard pass. Veto. Absolutely not."

I tilt my head as I study his reaction. "Let me guess, ex girlfriend?"

"I wouldn't call it a girlfriend. Let's just say the name Emily around this town doesn't have the best reputation."

"Fair enough."

"How about Annie?"

"Like the orphan?"

"Exactly. And for Halloween she can go as the iconic character, and I can dress up as Daddy War-Banks. Get it. Instead of War—"

I put up my hand. "I get it. We'll put it in the maybe column."

"Thank you."

Names seem to elude us as we go back to eating our now-cold dinner. Doesn't matter to me though, this burger is still amazing. And maybe with some protein in me I'll be able to think of any name, because right now, my mind is drawing a blank.

"Lainey..."

I look over to Simon, a little confused.

"Lainey?"

"Yeah." His voice is quiet as we both set our food down. "I think it should be something that means something to both of us."

"I love that idea."

"So I was thinking right now, what is something that's meaningful for who we are? And every time I think of that, I remember the first time we met at Perks."

I let that sit for a second when it hits me. "Perks on Lane Avenue."

"Lane Avenue."

"Lainey." The happy tears are working their way up. "It's perfect."

"Really?"

I take his hands in mine. "Really. Lainey Banks."

Now it's his turn to cry. "Lainey Banks."

I move across the couch as much as my pregnant self can to sit on his lap. It's the best way for me to kiss him how I desperately want to right now.

"I love you, you know that, right?"

He pushes a piece of hair behind my ear. "Not nearly as much as I love you."

His hand drifts to my stomach, and right on cue, Baby Bug kicks.

No...Lainey kicks.

"Hey, Lainey, it's daddy," he says, putting his face next to my stomach. "Your mommy and I can't wait to meet you. But please hold off for a few more months, because I haven't called my paint guy yet and I need to make your nursery the best nursery there's ever been."

I laugh, and cry a little, as Simon kisses my stomach. My hands brush through his hair as we just sit and bask in the moment. If this was six months ago, I'd be telling myself that the other shoe is about to drop. I'd be looking up for the rain clouds or for the anvil to come crashing down on my head.

But not anymore. Because right now at this moment, I don't know how anything could ruin what we have.

Chapter 32
Simon

I don't think a day can go bad when it starts with french toast.

And sex.

Sex and french toast. Better than any coffee on the planet.

"Quit smiling," Charlie says as she pours me a cup of coffee. "Customers are going to suspect something."

"Can't a guy smile?"

"Not like that unless he's auditioning for the role of a Disney villain."

"Very funny." I lean over the counter to give her a quick kiss. "What do I owe the pleasure of you being here to serve me my coffee?"

"I'm just in a good mood," she says. "Things are running smoothly. The baby is cooperating so far today. My mushroom order appeared last night, which means my stern talking-to with my weed loving mushroom distributor finally worked. And I get to see to my...boyfriend...baby dad...you."

I laugh. "Not liking any of my official titles?"

She shrugs as she takes off her apron and puts on her coat.

"Boyfriend feels high school. You know how I feel about baby daddy. Partner is the best, but still sounds like we work at a law firm together. Just nothing feels right."

"I agree," I say as I lean a little closer. "I think husband would sound much better."

I'm greeted by her patented "you're ridiculous" eye roll and a smile.

It's her love language for me.

"How about one major life event at a time?" Charlie comes around the counter and gives me a kiss on the cheek. "I have to run to the bank. Your french toast is being made now and one of the girls will bring it to you."

"You're the best."

"I know."

She gives me a wink before heading out the door. I watch as she crosses the street, choosing to walk the block and a half toward the bank instead of driving. I don't blame her. It's a beautiful February day. A little chilly, but the sun is a welcome change from the days of dreary winter we've had.

Once she's out of sight I turn back to the counter, where I'm greeted by my plate of french toast.

"The perfect start to the morning."

"Don't mind if I do."

Before I realize what's happening, Emmett is grabbing my plate of syrupy deliciousness and sliding it in front of him.

"What the fuck are you doing here?"

"Getting breakfast."

I look around to quickly see if anyone is noticing us. Or if Charlie has made the quickest trip to the bank in recorded history. "You know what I mean."

My whisper-yell is shortened when the waitress comes over and pours Emmett a cup of coffee. "Thank you, darlin'.'"

I watch the blush cross her cheeks as she slowly walks

away. Any other day I'd love to play wingman for my friend and business partner, but right now I need to know what the fuck he's doing here.

"Done flirting yet?"

"Never."

"You're an asshole." I signal for him to follow me through the kitchen and into the office. I know this isn't the best place for this conversation, but in here we can close the door and shut the blinds. I ignore the greeting from Mellie as I storm through the kitchen, which I'm sure is going to raise a few red flags but I can't focus on that right now.

"What the fuck are you doing here?"

"No matter how many times you ask me that question, the answer is going to be the same. Getting breakfast."

"Why? Don't they have breakfast places in Nashville?"

Emmett goes to sit on the corner of Charlie's desk. "They do. But every Tuesday is Rolling Hills day. You would know this if you read your emails."

"I read them. Mostly..."

Emmett shakes his head. "To catch you up, each Tuesday I come into town and start my day off with breakfast from this amazing place. The Breakfast Burger is something to rave about."

"I can send you one so you don't have to make an appearance."

"Not the same. Anyway, I come in for breakfast, grab a coffee to go and then head next door to the construction zone we're currently in to make sure things are on track for that project. You know, the construction you're paying for? Anyway, today I'm also doing a walkthrough of the apartment that Charlie has moved out of so we can potentially rent it. You know, so you'll *actually* make some money on this place since I know you aren't cashing Charlie's rent checks."

"I'm cashing them. Now," I defend. "I'm just not taking the money."

"Same thing," he says.

"It's not."

"In her mind it's going to be," Emmett says before letting out a frustrated breath. "And when she finds out that the apartment she thought was too good to be true actually was? How do you think that will make her feel?"

"She'll understand." I say.

The growl Emmett lets out is almost feral. "Simon, I need you to hear this. I've gotten to know Charlie pretty well these last few months. What do you think her reaction is going to be when she realizes that you're behind every single part of the restaurant without her knowledge? That her hard work is going to seem for nothing."

"It's not for nothing," I say. "She's still paying rent. She's managing this place. This is all her. She's making money off her customers and her food."

"What about when the ice machine shit the bed? You think a new one would have magically appeared in twenty-four hours if it were anyone else?"

"Well..."

"Or when the ceiling leaked? How should that be explained when it was fixed in a matter of hours?"

"But that's the owner's responsibility. That one I'm good on."

"While that might be true, you got it done when she didn't have to close for a day. Not many people would have done that."

"We can just say that we provide top-tier service for our tenants."

"Does that include driving twenty miles outside of town to

get the mushrooms? Because I know that guy just didn't suddenly start delivering again."

I start to reply, but don't say anything. That one I thought I was getting away with. "The asshole needed to realize he wasn't going to fuck with her."

"And did he?"

I shake my head. "He was pretty stoned. It's just easier if I pick them up and have them delivered each week."

"Does that kind of customer service go to all your tenants?"

Okay, now I'm getting angry. "I'm not a slum lord, Emmett."

"I'm not saying you are." Emmett takes a deep breath. "I'm just saying, if this were one of your Nashville properties, or any of the other Rolling Hills buildings you own, you wouldn't have called in the favors you did. You sure as hell wouldn't have driven to a fucking shroom farm on a weekly basis."

He's right. That farm was dirty as hell. "Okay. You're right. You happy?"

"No! I'm not happy." Emmett starts pacing around the small office. "You have to tell her. Today. Right now."

"I can't today."

"Why not?"

I scramble for an answer. Because there is no answer. I'm just scared to do it, but like hell I'm going to admit that to Emmett. "Because I can't. But I will."

"When Simon? Because you saying that you'll do it soon doesn't hold a lot of weight these days."

"I will."

"No you won't," he says. "You made me believe it would have happened by now. So when? Tonight? Tomorrow? During the delivery of your daughter? Or maybe if you two get married it can be part of your vows. Maybe then you can tell Charlie everything."

"Tell me what?"

Emmett and I turn to see Charlie, who's standing at the door of her office. She looks confused, and a little scared.

Fuck my life.

"Simon? What's going on?"

* * *

"Simon, you have three seconds to explain everything, or I'm going to fucking lose it."

"Bug, please sit—"

"Don't you Bug me. Start talking. Now."

Okay, she means business. Not that I didn't think she meant business. Hell, her face is redder than any shade her hair has been and her nostrils are actually flaring.

I fucked up. So bad.

Now I can only hope that somehow I can dig my way out of this.

"I don't know where to start." I admit.

"Convenient." She's marching around the living room, her stomps getting heavier with each one. I wish she'd sit, her blood pressure is rising, and this can't be good for her or the baby. I also know better than to suggest that right now. "Well, then, let me help you. How about you tell me why you were in my office having an argument with my property manager?"

This is it. This is where I come clean. The things I should have told her months ago when I could've controlled this.

But I didn't. Because I'm an idiot.

"Because he's *my* property manager."

"What?" She blinks a few times, not seeming to understand my words. "You use him too?"

I shake my head. "No. He only works for me."

Charlie doesn't say anything for a second, letting my words sink in. "You're Magnolia Properties?"

"I am."

"Which means you're my landlord."

"Yes."

This makes her take a seat.

"How? When? Why didn't you..."

Were those questions rhetorical? "I don't know which one you want me to answer..."

She snaps a look of murder to me. "This isn't time for your smartass remarks. Just fucking start talking."

Noted.

"If you want the true beginning, Emmett and I were roommates our freshman year of college."

"What? Oh my God...that first day I met him, I knew he looked familiar."

I nod. "We stayed friends. Had some classes together. We reconnected last year."

"Great story, but what does that have to do with this?"

"A lot, I promise." I take a breath, knowing that it's only going to get worse from here. "Emmett actually came to Mona's months ago and made her an offer. She was going to sell to him when I convinced her to sell to me. In the course of that conversation, I also persuaded Emmett to come work for me and be my manager for Magnolia Properties."

"I thought you were a real estate agent? Like, sold houses?"

"I am. I do. But I also have commercial properties. It was just a few, but I wanted to expand. And to do that I needed a property manager."

"And you got them both that day."

"I want to go on the record, before I say anything else, I bought Mona's before I knew you were looking for a restaurant. I swear on everything I have."

"When did you find out I was looking for a space?"

I say the next part quickly so I can brace for the blow back. "The night before you were scheduled to look at it."

I watch the realization come over her beautiful, yet pissed off, face. "So from the beginning. Oh my God! We had slept together by then! What the fuck, Simon!"

She's back up and pacing. "How did you find out?"

"By accident." My tone is creeping into the pleading side, and if I had to take a guess, I'll be full out begging by the end of this. "Emmett told me he had a showing and who you were. He didn't recognize your name from college, so he had no idea. He also didn't know why I told him what to do next."

She stops and glares at me. "Which was?"

Here it goes..."Make sure you take the restaurant, no matter what."

I expect screaming. Profanities. Maybe her throwing one of her knives at me.

What I don't expect is calm.

Eerie calm.

Which I'm now realizing is more terrifying than Charlie yelling at me.

"No matter what?" She sits back down across from me. Our eyes are locked, and a chill runs through me when I see how much anger and hurt are in her eyes. "So my dream restaurant that I thought no way could be as cheap as it was, that happened to come with an apartment for no extra rent, that was you?"

"Yes. It was me."

"And the up-to-date kitchen equipment that I was curious as to why Mona would upgrade when she was selling?"

"I replaced them before you got here."

"Oh my God!" She yells, now popping back up. "You got me the ice machine. And fixed the ceiling! Didn't you?"

"Well, Emmett did those things…"

"Quit with the fucking technicalities, Simon. Oh my God! The mushroom guy! Are you why I suddenly have mushrooms again?"

I nod, but hang my head in the process in shame. "It was just easier if I went and picked them up for you."

"Fucking Christ!" She falls back on the couch, almost in a defeated way. "So here's me, thinking I walked into my dream. That my hard work and blood and sweat and tears and slaving away with grunt work for God knows how long, that this was me being rewarded. But the whole time, it wasn't my hard work or luck or good fortune, it was you playing the fucking puppet master."

"No!"

"Quit lying Simon! It was you! Everything was you!"

"Fine!" I yell, finally snapping. "Yes, it was me. I made sure you got your restaurant. I told Emmett to cancel every other showing and to rent it to you for a penny if he wanted to."

"Why would you do that? Do you hear how insane that sounds?"

"Yes, I do, and it was insane, but that's what you were making me!"

This seems to take her aback.

"Me? Making you insane? I'd love to hear this…"

I know she's pissed at me, and she has every reason. But I had, and still have, my reasons for what I did. And she needs to know them.

"I did it because I needed you here. I needed to make sure you wouldn't run again."

She stops whatever it was she was about to say. "Keep me here?"

"Yes," I try to even my tone, but I don't know if it's working. "After fifteen years you were back in my life. And I needed answers. I needed you to talk to me, but you wouldn't. I was going crazy, and I didn't know how else to make that happen."

"So you bought me a fucking restaurant?"

"Technically I rented it to you."

Charlie's eyes are daggers right now. "You're the reason why I thought there was a problem with my checks? Did you not cash them?"

I nod. "Not at first. But then I did. But I haven't spent a dime of it. I promise."

She huffs out a laugh. "That's even worse! Making me think I was doing this all on my own. Especially when you know how much I hate handouts."

I take a few steps closer to her. "Charlie, I know you're pissed, and rightfully so, but you have to listen to me. You were back in my life. Not once, but twice. And both times you ran. You left before I could get the answers I needed. The answers that had been driving me crazy for more than a decade. I was manic. I didn't know what else to do."

"How about a conversation?" She says. "How about, 'Hey Charlie. Let's talk.'"

"Would you have?" I ask. "Because I seem to remember me doing that, and you slamming a door in my face. Or leaving before the sun came up."

She doesn't respond. She knows I'm right. At least about that. The anger in her eyes says as much.

"I'm sorry I didn't tell you," I begin, grabbing her hand and bringing her to sit next to me on the couch. "I know I should've told you when we first got together. And I'm sorry if you feel like this is charity, because I didn't mean it to come off like that. That I am sorry for. But I'm not sorry for what I did."

She rips her hand from mine. "Excuse me?"

"I helped you get your dream," I say. "Yes, it wasn't the best way to do it. But I helped make that happen for you. Seeing you happy and thriving and getting everything you deserve, that's all I want for you. Even when you hated me, I wanted you to succeed. And you know what? I'd do it again. Because you getting everything you want in life is all that matters to me."

There, the cards are on the table.

And Charlie isn't saying a thing.

This isn't like the eerie silence from a few minutes ago. No...this feels like the part of the storm where you think it's over, only to get slammed by one more flood.

Charlie stands up, and I follow, but she quickly holds her hands up to stop me. "No. I need some space."

"Space?"

She nods. "For months now I felt like absolute shit for not letting you explain yourself to me. That for fifteen years we wasted time because of a miscommunication. And here this whole time you were straight up lying to me. A lie you don't even feel bad about."

"Charlie, I didn't mean it like that..."

I see the tear fall from her eye and that is my undoing. "Simon Banks never says anything he doesn't mean. Isn't that right?"

I hang my head.

"Exactly. You finally told the truth. That you lied to me. For months. I...I just need some time."

Charlie starts walking out of the living room toward our bedroom. "Where are you going?"

I feel my own tears welling as I watch her crying, standing in the hallway and looking so broken.

I did that. I broke her.

The thing I would have done anything to prevent, I did.

"I'm going to go to the apartment."

"Whatever you want." I quickly say before realizing that she shouldn't be leaving. "No. I'll go there. You stay here."

"No, Simon. I need to be away. I just...I just can't be here right now."

"For how long?"

She shrugs. "I don't know, Simon...I don't know."

Charlie turns without another word and walks back to the bedroom. Twenty minutes later, with a bag in her hand, she leaves without saying another word.

I thought my heart hurt earlier. But that was nothing compared to now.

Because this is what it feels like when your heart is shattered.

And you only have yourself to blame.

Chapter 33
Charlie

"**B**oss Lady. We need to eighty-six eggs for about an hour while I run to the store and grab a few dozen."

I turn to Mike, my head line cook. "What do you mean we're out of eggs?"

"It means we're out of eggs?"

That can't be right. I march into the walk-in cooler, knowing that I'm going to see dozens of eggs on the shelf where they are normally stored. Except when I walk in, it's empty.

Actually, the entire cooler is nearly empty.

What the fuck?

"Where is all the food?" I yell as I march out of the cooler. "We're out of eggs. Half the produce. I think we have one case of chicken left. What the hell is going on?"

No one in the kitchen makes eye contact with me. Not one of my cooks. Not the servers. Everyone right now seems to be very concerned with their shoes.

"You didn't do the order."

The voice comes from Mellie, who is the only one daring to make eye contact with me right now.

"I didn't forget to do the order."

"You did," she says gently. "Normally you do it on Tuesday. Tuesday you..."

She doesn't finish that sentence, which is smart for her.

"Everyone back to work," Mellie announces, which everyone follows. She might be a ray of sunshine, but in the kitchen, everyone knows she means business. "You. Follow me."

I don't have a chance to protest as my best friend grabs me by the hand and pulls me toward the office before slamming the door.

"Sit."

"I'm sorry I forgot to do the order," I say as she leans back on my chair. "Pregnancy brain."

She shakes her head. "This isn't about the eggs or the food. Or your pregnancy brain. Which I know is a real thing, and if it were just you being a little spacy, we wouldn't be having this conversation. But you yelling at everyone? Acting like an asshole boss? That's why you're here."

I brush her off. "I'm not acting like an asshole."

"You know what look I just saw out there? The one we used to have when Mr. Napoli would come in and scream at everyone for shit he did. Or when Billy got on his high horse and decided he was going to make everyone feel dumb. You remember how we felt when that happened, right?"

I do. It was days like that that made me want to quit. To open a restaurant where no employees ever felt like that.

Fuck...

"I'm sorry," I say. "I'll go apologize."

"Not yet you aren't." Mellie pulls over the other chair and sits in front of me. "Because this wasn't just today or the food order. You were like this yesterday and the day before too. So spill. Because they aren't normal mood swings. This is just you acting like a b-i-t-c-h."

I audibly gasp. "You just called me a bitch."

"I know. And I don't like it. So start talking."

I knew I was on edge for the last two days, since I left Simon's, but I didn't realize I'd gone so far as to make Mellie use, or spell, curse words.

"Simon and I had a fight," I begin.

"I figured as much when I saw you were sleeping at the apartment."

"You knew? I thought I'd done a good job of hiding it."

The look she's giving me says otherwise. "I get here at four in the morning every day. You don't think I've noticed your car is here? Or that Simon hasn't been in here in two days, which is very strange. Add in your outbursts, bigger than normal preggo brain, and the bloodshot eyes, and it didn't take the cast of *Law and Order* to figure it out."

Well, when she puts it like that...

"It was bad Mellie. So bad."

She leans forward and puts a gentle hand on my knee. "Do you want to talk about it?"

I nod, not realizing until right now how much I need to. "He owns the diner."

"He what? Did I just hear you right?"

"Simon owns the diner. He *is* Magnolia Properties."

"Wow," Mellie says as she sits back into the chair. "I didn't see that coming."

"Exactly how I felt."

I start from the beginning, telling her about how I heard him and Emmett arguing in the office. How I made him come clean to me about what I heard, and all the things I didn't know.

How he rigged it so I got Mona's.

How he bought things and helped me get the restaurant ready right under my nose.

How he was fixing things behind the scenes.

How he lied to me for months when I thought we were starting our lives together.

"Wow," Mellie says.

"Yeah. Wow is an understatement."

"I feel like an idiot," I admit. "How could I have missed all the signs?"

"Were there signs? Not that I'm saying there weren't. I'm just genuinely wondering how there were signs. Because if there were, I missed them too."

"I don't know. Little things. A few times he tensed up when Emmett came up in conversation. There was Christmas Eve, when Emmett was acting very strange. And how every time there was a problem here, it was magically fixed somehow. Then there's the biggest one."

"Which was?"

"The restaurant in the first place."

"Charlie..."

"I'm serious. I should have known something was up. It was too good to be true that not only was this place perfect, already named after my mother, and that the rent was so cheap it should have been criminal. And the apartment? I should have trusted my gut more that something was up. Nothing that good happens without something falling from the sky. Especially to me."

Mellie doesn't say anything, and suddenly, she looks... sheepish. Yeah. Sheepish.

"Say it."

"What?"

"Whatever it is you're thinking that you know I'm going to hate."

"It's kind of romantic..."

I throw my hands in the air. "Romantic? How about manipulative? Or conniving. Or so conceited that you think you can rig the world so you can get your way?"

"Or...and hear me out—" She pauses for dramatic effect. "That he wanted you so much, and wanted you to have this restaurant, that he'd do anything and everything in his power to make it happen."

"Speaking of *Law and Order* plots..."

"I mean, he didn't kill anyone. Or stalk you."

I quirk an eyebrow. "Do you not remember the weeks of him showing up everywhere when I got to town? Or running past the restaurant shirtless each morning?"

Now it's her turn to give me the questioning eye. "You can say all you want how you hated it, but I remember the stares you gave him. And they were not ones of the mean variety."

I don't comment because she's right. "It's more than that. He's always been like this. He's the rich boy who doesn't like it when things don't go his way, so he rigs the system."

"What did he rig?" Mellie asks.

"Me getting this place," I say. "When he found out I was interested, he turned everyone else away. Told Emmett to basically let me have it for whatever I could afford."

Mellie sighs. Romantically.

"Don't make that sound. It's not sweet or romantic."

"It kind of is," she says.

"He told Emmett to offer me whatever I could afford so I'd sign the lease."

"And why did he do that? Why did he want to make sure you were here."

"He said it was because he wanted answers and he was afraid I was going to run."

Her look goes from romantic to pointed. "Was he wrong?"

"Excuse me?"

"You would've run," she says. "If you knew he owned it before you saw it, you would have never even looked. Hell, you could barely convince yourself to do it when he just lived here. So yes, you would have run if you knew the truth."

"But—"

"No. Let me finish." She might be the nice one, but right now she's giving off scary librarian vibes. "He's right. You ran when you first saw him. You ran after you slept together. He deserved answers, and you ran. So, maybe not be so hard on him for that?"

Some best friend Mellie is. I thought best friends were supposed to support the delusion.

"Quit taking his side!"

"I'm not," she says, her voice is back to gentle, like what I imagine Disney princesses having. "I'm just trying to make you see it from a different perspective."

"And what perspective would that be? That I can't be mad that the man I love and the father of my child has been lying to me for months?"

"I didn't say that," Mellie says gently. "You can be mad. That's a valid feeling, and no one is telling you that you can't feel that way. I'm just saying, let's look at his side of things."

I pout and cross my arms. "Fine."

"You have to admit, the running thing is valid. That's kind of your default with him."

"Yes." I say sulkily. "We've established that."

"Second, did he mean any harm?"

"What do you mean?"

"You said he bought the restaurant before he knew you were looking for a space, correct?"

"Yes."

"So he didn't sabotage you. He could have. If anything, he

did the opposite. He essentially helped you accomplish your dream."

"You say helped. I say manipulated."

"Okay, let's think about it like this," she says. "Those new booths and tables. And the paint. Things you knew about. Did you consider that helping? Or manipulative?"

"That's different. Those were gifts."

She tilts her head at me, clearly knowing my answer was bullshit.

"Fine. We settled on it being a gift because it was the only way I could live with taking that kind of help from him."

"And there lies the true problem in all of this."

"What?"

"You're so stubborn and hate asking for help so much that you're going to let it ruin the true love of your life."

"I..." my words trail off.

Shit...she's right.

For years I've been the one hung up over the money. Not him. I've made it an issue at every point I could. Not him.

And they're both right. I would've run.

I would've run so fucking fast.

"Dammit!" I moan, throwing my head back. "Okay. Fine. But...I'm still mad."

"As you should be."

"And I love him."

"I figured you did."

"So where does that leave me?"

"Only you know that answer," she says. "Should he have told you? Absolutely. And for the methods he used, you should make him grovel and beg for forgiveness and accept nothing less than him changing every three a.m. diaper. But maybe give him a pass on the outcome. Because at the end of the day, the man helped you achieve your dream. The key word there is helped. Yes, he might have thrown in a few bucks that you wouldn't have been able to afford, but this place is still your vision. Your food. Your vision. Simon had nothing to do with that. This is all you. Simon just was your Fairy God Daddy behind the scenes."

I laugh as I feel a few tears bubbling up. "He'll love that."

"I figured he would." Mellie stands up and gives me a hug as I let this whole conversation start running through my mind. "You've in love, Charlie. The kind of love people like me dream about. You're about to have a baby and start a family. So you have to ask yourself, is this one mistake worth losing a lifetime of happiness?"

She leaves the office, leaving me to sit with my own thoughts.

She's right. I can be mad and am mad. That doesn't change.

She's also right that I'm living my dream, and I don't know if I would be if it weren't for Simon.

Chapter 34
Simon

Simon: Everyone. My house. One hour.

Wes: Can I ask why or am I going to regret it?

Simon: Just come. I have beer, and I need help.

Shane: Simon Banks is asking for help? What did you do?

Oliver: Who's the new number? Why isn't this in the regular group chat?

Emmett: Simon, I have strong feelings about group texts. Actually, just one. I hate them. Why did you add me to this?

Simon: Everyone, Emmett is now in the chat. Because he's in this.

Wes: In what?

Oliver: I'm nervous.

Shane: What did you do...

343

Emmett: Oh, he fucked up. Bad.

Wes: Did his actions finally have consequences?

Emmett: Winner winner, chicken dinner.

Wes: We'll be over in an hour.

Oliver: And we'll bring pizza.

One hour and three minutes later, my brothers from other mothers come walking into my house. My back is to them, so I can't see their faces, but judging by their silence, they're probably pretty confused as to what they're walking into.

"What the fuck..."

I turn around to see four blank stares. "What?"

"Did you make a PowerPoint?"

I look to my eight-five-inch television screen then back to them. "I did."

"Can we ask why?"

They all take a seat on the various couches and chairs in my living room. But not before grabbing themselves a drink.

Shane grabs two.

Which, I get it. I'd probably need one too if I walked into a grown-ass man's living room to see a presentation loaded with the title: "Help Me Unfuck Up."

"As you were all clued in on in the text message earlier, the thing all of you predicted months ago has come to a head."

"How did she find out?" Wes asks.

"What makes you say she found out?" I ask.

Wes narrows a look to me.

"She caught Simon and I in her office arguing about it," Emmett says.

344

"What he said," I grumble. "Though that does take away the beginning of the presentation."

"Simon, as a teacher, I want to commend you on taking the time to make this," Oliver says. "But can I ask...why?"

"Great question, number one best friend. As you all know, I have the tendency to act before I think about my actions. Or say things without thinking through them."

"You don't say..." Wes mutters.

"Enough from the peanut gallery." I take the remote and switch it off the title slide. "So I was sitting here and sulking about Charlie, trying to figure out what I can do to get her back. It's why you haven't heard from me in a few days."

"Didn't notice," Shane says sarcastically.

I glower at Shane. "When I get Charlie back, I'm going to look for a new group of friends who will miss me and realize without me saying anything that I'm going through something traumatic."

"No, you won't."

"You're right. Too much work." I turn back to the presentation to see where I left off. "Anyway, I started thinking about what I needed to apologize for, because there are multiple things. And I didn't want to forget any, so I started writing them down. Before I knew it, I was jotting down ways to have her forgive me and all the things I could do for the rest of our lives to make up for it. Before I knew it, I was putting it into presentation form."

"I'm impressed," Oliver says. "But why do you need us?"

"You'll see," I say as I switch slides. "For starters, here are all the things I did that could be, and probably are, things I didn't tell her I did since she came back into my life. Most of them having to do with the diner."

"Holy shit, that's a long list," Wes says as he scooches forward on the couch, I'm guessing to see better.

"I didn't know about the apartment," Shane says.

"Oh, yes. Part of his grand 'make sure she takes the restaurant' plan," Emmett says. "You forgot to put on there that you had it furnished before she arrived."

"Thanks," I say, making a note in my phone to add that.

"You fixed a leaky ceiling? Like with your hands?"

Emmett answers this one too. "No, he paid plumbers a shit-ton of money to fix it in a matter of hours. I had to burn a favor I wanted to hold onto."

"Oh," Wes says. "That makes more sense."

"Why are mushrooms on there? Is that code for something?"

"Not important." I say. "These offenses give you all the scope of all the things I'm apologizing for."

I switch the slide, which features a picture of me hugging Charlie at her opening. "I wanted to share these all with you to show you that everything I did was, yes, in secret and without knowledge, but none were harmful or nefarious. They were all out of love. Just, my brand of love."

"You still lied," Shane said. "And don't give me the bullshit about it was just an omission of truth."

"Wasn't going to," I say. "I know I fucked up. This isn't a get-together for y'all to convince me that I was in the wrong."

"Then why *are* we here?"

"Because I need y'all to help me fix it."

I switch to the next slide, aptly titled "I done fucked up. Help."

"You're an idiot," Shane mutters.

"For once, I'm not going to argue," I say, turning to the next slide. "Here are some of the ideas I have for her to forgive me."

The guys read the list, which features such ideas as rent a plane to fly around town with a banner asking her forgiveness and good old-fashioned begging. That one comes with a lifetime promise for poopy diaper changes, foot rubs, and I'll even open the diner three days a week.

Yup. I'd get up at five in the morning. That's how sorry I am.

"Could you really hire a skywriter?" Oliver asks.

"I know a guy."

"Why isn't just talking to her on there?" Wes asks. "I feel like that should be the winner."

"Because it's not a grand gesture," I say. "Plus, what would I say?"

"That you're an idiot."

"That you fucked up."

"That you want to apologize."

"That you want to propose to her."

We all stare at Oliver for that last one. "Really? That's where your mind went?"

He shrugs. "Old habits."

"I know I need to talk to her," I say. "The problem is that she won't talk to me. So I have to do something big to even get that going."

"How do you know?" Shane asks.

"I've called and texted with no response. It was a familiar feeling. I tried to go to the restaurant each morning, but I'm told she isn't there or just flat-out ignored."

"Okay," Oliver says. "While these ideas are great, they really are, I think you might be going a little too grand."

"Is there such a thing?"

"Simon," Wes says, gesturing for me to sit next to him. "You're new to this. You've never been in a relationship, let alone asked a woman to forgive you."

I start to say something before Shane stops me. "And no. Asking for forgiveness after you called a woman the wrong name doesn't count."

Damn.

"What Wes is trying to say," Oliver says, "is this isn't something you can buy your way out of. Or do something flashy that will distract her from the problem. That's what got you in this mess in the first place."

"Damn..." I say out loud as that nugget of truth sinks in. "You're right."

"So, knowing that, what can you do that shows her that not only are you sorry, but that you truly understand why she's upset?"

I quickly open my mouth but Oliver shakes his head. "No. Think about it. Really think about it."

I follow his directions. He's right. I need to focus on the problem. The real problem.

"Money and the diner," I say confidently. "If I were to pinpoint the biggest issues, it's those."

"What about them?" Wes asks.

"Charlie hates feeling like she's been given a handout. Hell, even the things she knew I did for her she wasn't thrilled with."

"He's right," Emmett said. "I came in and helped her with a leaky sink, and she felt bad. It was literally just tightening the pipe."

"Exactly," I say. "Money has always been a weird thing between us. I never cared how much she did or didn't have, but I know when we first met I was the rich frat boy and she was the college kid who had to work full time just to make it. And I think she still feels like that. Scratch that, I know she does."

"Does she know how hard you work?" Shane asks. "I hate to give you a compliment, but you fucking bust your ass when it comes to your job."

"Thanks," I say, taking in the rare compliment from Shane without a quick retort. "I didn't talk much about work with her or what I did. I didn't want it to slip about the diner."

"Well, she needs to know," Emmett says. "Hell, you closed on a two-million-dollar sale last week. You're damn good at what you do, and I'm proud to work for you. Well, except the lying shit. I'll never do that again."

"And I'll never ask you to." It's right then, an idea comes to me. "But I do know what you can do."

"What's that?"

"Go to the office, get me the lease to the diner."

"Okay, what for?"

"Just go. But then come back. You can join us then."

I turn to my friends with a smile on my face. They aren't smiling. They look terrified. "Join us doing what?" Shane asks.

"We're putting together a nursery."

Chapter 35
Charlie

When I opened the diner, I had hopes that someone would want to use my space for parties or showers.

Who knew the first one would be mine?

Everyone I love is here. Connor brought Lila down so she could be part of this, though she was upset when she found out Jayce wasn't here. She quickly got over it when Magnolia took her under her wing. People from the town whom I've come to love, including my Dice Gal Gang. All of Simon's sisters are here, well, except Quinn. Simon's mom is the master of ceremonies. She, along with Whitley, Betsy, Izzy, and Amelia, planned every detail of this. Mellie coordinated all of the food. They told me all I needed to do was show up.

Which is what I did.

I showed up. I planted a smile on my face. And I'm pretending everything is okay.

Even though it's not.

I keep looking at the door, waiting for Simon to walk in. Because he would. He knows this shower is women only—

Amelia was very clear with him on that fact—but he wouldn't care. He'd come in, likely carrying some extravagant gift or bouquet of flowers, and everyone would "ooh" and "ah" over him. I'd roll my eyes because of his antics, but I'd also secretly love them in the same breath. He'd come over to me, place his hand on my now very large baby belly and give me a soft kiss.

It would be perfect.

I suck in a breath, fighting away the tears. I can't cry. Not today. Not in front of my family and friends and right before we're about to open presents.

"Oh my God, Mellie!" Stella says with half a cupcake in her mouth. "These cupcakes are to die for. Oh my God! There's an actual strawberry in this!"

Mellie smiles at the compliment. "You're too kind."

"No. You don't understand." Stella says as she stuffs the rest of the strawberry cupcake into her mouth. "I have looked all over Nashville, and really, all of Middle Tennessee, for cupcakes for my wedding. And *nothing* has come close to this."

"You haven't tried her cookies and cream cupcakes yet," I say. "I'd do dirty things for one of those."

Stella dabs the corner of her mouth before linking her arms through Mellie's. "Come with me."

"Where are we going?"

"To talk details of how I can hire you to make every cake, cupcake, and cookie for my wedding."

I smile as I watch Simon's youngest sister lead Mellie to an empty table. From the few interactions I've had with Stella, the woman sees what she wants and doesn't take no for an answer. Which means Mellie is about to have the biggest order of her life, and she's not going to be sure how she agreed to it. Stella has this way of getting what she wants with a smile on her face, and not chipping a nail. I don't know how she does it.

"Hey, have you eaten?"

The One I Hate

I turn to see Amelia standing next to me, holding a heaping plate of a little bit of everything that is being served.

"I'm good."

I tried to say that with confidence. Amelia clearly isn't believing me.

"How about we eat anyway." She sits down next to me, handing me a fork. "We have about ten minutes to recover from the games before it's time for presents. Which means you have to be in smiley, happy mode. You need all the protein, carbs, and sugar you can get."

I laugh. "Why did I agree to games again? They exhausted me more than I thought."

"Because we put the two sorority girls Betsy and Whitley in charge of activities. You know if Izzy and I were in charge, it would be food, then presents, then a see-you-later."

I laugh as I take a big bite of the mushroom and cheese omelet. And as quickly as the laugh comes, it dies in my chest.

Because that's where I hurt the most.

Simon and the fucking mushrooms...

"Hey," Amelia says, realizing my swift change in demeanor. "You okay?"

I shake my head, and before I know it, Amelia is taking my arm and leading me back through the kitchen and up to the apartment I've been staying in this week.

"Sit down," she says gently, handing me a tissue. I do my best not to cry—Whitley worked too hard on my makeup for me to cry it away—but a few sneak out.

"I don't know why I'm crying," I say. "I've been good all day."

"You miss him. You're allowed to be sad about that."

Thank goodness all of the women knew what was happening without me needing to tell them. Simon's family doesn't know. Which is how I wanted it. We didn't need anything awkward today.

"I've never been more confused about feelings," I say.

"Have you reached out? Has he?"

"I know he's come by. I've hidden from him." I catch a leaked tear with a tissue. "I know we need to talk. But I'm so confused I don't know what to say. Because I miss him. But I'm mad at him. I don't want to say the wrong thing. And I want to say all the things. I don't want tempers or emotions to get in the way. And then what if we say everything, and we're not on the same page? There are so many what-ifs that I won't know until I talk to him, but at the same time I'd like to know them before we talk. Does that make sense?"

"It does."

"And worst of all, what if he's not ready to talk to me?"

"He's ready."

Amelia and I turn to Izzy, who's standing at the door of the apartment.

"How do you know?"

Izzy walks in and hands me the long, yet narrow, gift-wrapped box. "Because of this."

I look at it, but don't dare start to unwrap it. "What is it?"

Izzy shrugs. "That I don't know. All I know is that Simon showed up at my doorstep this morning—banging on the door and interrupting a very good orgasm by the way—to ask Oliver to wrap this present."

Amelia laughs. "He did not."

"Oh, he did," Izzy says. "He at least brought coffee."

I laugh. "Sounds about right."

"He wouldn't tell us what it was. He just asked me to give this to you. I was going to wait until the end of the shower, you know, in case it was something very Simon-esque that wouldn't be appropriate to open in front of children or his mother, but

The One I Hate

I'm guessing in light of the circumstances of the week, and that the men were over at his house last night until two in the morning, that he's ready to talk."

I have to blink a few times. "Two in the morning?"

"Yeah," Amelia says. "I didn't even hear Shane come in. And before I left for this today, he did mumble that you're too good for Simon and to run. Which in Shane speak means you're in and the guys approve."

"Wow," I say, looking down at the box. I want to open it, but I also don't know what will happen when I do. Will I laugh? Cry? Want to leave my shower immediately? "What do I do?"

"Whatever you want," Amelia says, patting my knee. "We'll go back down and stall. You take all the time you need."

I say thank you to both of them as they leave me in the apartment, holding a box. A long, not normally shaped box. It's light. I know it's not, but the only thing I can think that would fit in here is a magic wand.

It better not be a fucking wand...

"Fuck it," I say, my curiosity getting the best of me. I rip open the paper and take off the lid to find a note laying on top of the tissue paper.

> *Miss Bennett,*
> *I have gotten word from my property manager, Emmett Collins, that you are unhappy with your rental agreement for the property known as Mona's, located at 382 Main Street, Rolling Hills, Tennessee.*
> *If you'd like to discuss your lease going*

forward, I'd be happy to meet with you this afternoon. I've been told you are otherwise engaged this morning. I am free the rest of the day, and all the days after this, at my home office. I believe you have the address.

Hope to see you then.

Best,

Simon Banks

P.S.: I don't know how I made it fifteen years without you because this past week has been absolute hell. I love you and miss you. I hope your shower is the best ever.

Rest in peace, my makeup.

I tear through the tissue paper, but all I see is a rolled piece of paper. I flatten it, only to see that it's not just any piece of paper—it's a bank statement.

A statement for an account that currently has twenty-one thousand dollars in it.

What are you up to, Simon?

Chapter 36
Charlie

I think I set a world record for how fast I opened my baby shower gifts.

I took pictures with every guest in an impressively short amount of time.

And now after what feels like hours later, with Simon's letter, and bank statement, burning a hole in my purse, I'm walking into the home I've missed more than I realized.

"Simon?" I say as I step through the front door. "Hello?"

I look around, slipping off my shoes as I walk down the hall. When I enter the kitchen, I see a sprawling bouquet of flowers on the island, and a card in front of it that just says "Bug."

Happy Baby Shower Day. I love you.

For a man who has made his name for being over the top, it's the simple things that hit me in the heart the hardest when it comes to Simon.

I take in a whiff of the beautiful arrangement of roses before continuing to walk back to his office. The living room hasn't changed—not that I expected it to in three and a half days—but seeing the dark gray furniture in contrast with the light gray walls somehow gives me a sense of calm.

I'm not sure what to expect when I walk into Simon's office. So when he slowly turns around in his expansive executive chair, in a full suit and glasses on, I'm somehow not surprised.

Though I am surprised at one thing.

"Since when do you wear glasses?"

"This is the last of my secrets," he says, making a show of adjusting them. "I use them when I'm reading contracts and going over the small details."

I smile. "Is that what we're doing today?"

"It is." He stands up and comes around the desk, putting his hand on the small of my back as I sit into the chair. "You look beautiful."

"Thank you."

He kisses the top of my head before sitting back down.

"So, Miss Bennett, is it?"

I smile and laugh, realizing this is the bit and apparently I have to go along with it. "Correct. Charlie Bennett."

"Charlie? That's an unusual name."

"It's short for Charlene. Not many people know that. I'm actually quite guarded with my name."

He smiles. "Well, it's beautiful. Should I call you Charlene? Charlie? Perhaps another nickname that you hold near and dear to your heart?"

I swallow my laughter. "Charlie's fine."

"Good. Well, I hate that it's taken me this long to introduce myself. But I'm Simon Banks, head of Magnolia Properties and the landlord of the building that you operate your restaurant, Mona's, from."

He extends his hand, and I meet it. Because why not.

"Very nice to meet you."

"And you."

"May I ask how far along you are?"

I put my hand on my stomach. "Just about twenty-nine weeks."

"Congratulations. I hope the father realizes how lucky he is."

I smile. "I think he does."

Simon sheepishly looks down at the desk before nodding.

I sit back and take him in for a moment. If anyone else were to be watching him right now, they would think this is normal Simon—cocky, confident, and owning the room with his brand of humor and wit.

But I'm not just anyone.

He's nervous. I don't know if I've ever seen the man nervous. His hands are fiddling with a pen. He's rocking back on the chair. His smile isn't as bright as it normally is.

Somehow, that makes me feel at ease. He knows this is serious. He knows this is a moment for us. But he also knows that he had to do it in his way. The Simon way.

And as much as the Simon way sometimes makes me want to pull my hair out, it's what makes him, him.

And I love him.

Cocky smile and all.

"Well then," he says, giving himself a little shake. "I brought you in today because Emmett told me you might not be happy with some conditions of your lease."

"That's correct."

"Well, then, let's take a look," he says. "According to your original agreement, you signed on to pay thirty-five hundred dollars a month, is that correct?"

"Yes, which frankly is a steal for a space like this. And at the time it included the apartment."

"Oh yes, I remember Emmett telling me about that deal," he says with a wink. "We were happy to help you in that area."

"Yes. And if my memory serves me right, Emmett said you were a softie and would be happy to help me."

"Oh, did he now?"

"He did. But I should say thank you. Your generosity was really the only way I was able to accept the lease terms."

"We're glad to help. Here at Magnolia Properties, we always want to be able to work with our tenants to make sure they are able to achieve their dreams. That's actually what we do. We make dreams come true."

"I thought that was Disney?"

"No. That's the most Magical Place on Earth. Very different."

"My apologies."

"I do have a guy, though, that can get you quite a deal on a Disney vacation, if you're ever interested. Maybe take the child there one day?"

I laugh, suddenly having the image of Simon pushing a stroller around the Magic Kingdom wearing Mickey Mouse ears. "Good to know."

"Anyway, back to the arrangement." Simon leans back in his seat, assuming a thoughtful position. "Do you feel that the rent is too high? Do you need to renegotiate?"

I shake my head. "No. That's not the problem. I'm not paying enough."

"Oh really?"

I know this has been playful, which I'm somehow appreciative of because confrontation is never fun, but this is the heart of the matter. The real stuff. He needs to know how I feel, and how it can't go on. I need to stand my ground, no matter how charming he is.

Or how good he looks in that suit and glasses.

"Since I began leasing the space in September, I thought I was paying rent to Magnolia Properties. At first, my checks weren't being cashed."

"Really? That's interesting..."

"I thought so. I brought this up to Emmett, then suddenly they were. It just seems strange."

Simon's cocky smile starts forming. Apparently this acting skit of ours is going exactly how he wants. "Miss Bennett, are you trying to ask me how I was using the money you sent as rent each month?"

I let out a breath. "Yes. I am."

"Do you have the gift?"

"The bank statement?"

He nods. "That's where the money went."

I grab my purse and look at the paper I received earlier.

"You'll see that there's twenty-one-thousand-dollars in the account. Which, if the math is broken down, is the rent you have paid Magnolia Properties these past six months."

"Why is it in a separate account?"

"Because once Baby Bug is born, she will be named the beneficiary of this account."

"She....what?"

He smiles, takes off his glasses and comes around his desk, turning me slightly so he can sit in the other chair across from me. "I would have given this restaurant to you for free, but I know you would have fought me tooth and nail."

"You would have been right."

"And for those first few months, I honestly didn't know what to do with the money. It felt wrong taking money from you. Which I know it shouldn't have, because business is business. I didn't know what to do, so I just didn't cash them."

Simon takes my hands in his, which I don't fight him. In fact, feeling his touch is needed in this moment more than anything. "Then I got the idea to open the account. I know I should have told you about it, but I thought maybe you'd be less mad when you found out knowing that every penny will go toward our daughter."

My jaw drops slightly. "All of it?"

He reaches over and takes my hands in his. "I know money has always been a weird and touchy topic for you, but I need you to know something if we're going to be together. I have money. A lot of it. More than I should probably have. And do you know what I like doing with that money?"

"Buying overpriced baby furniture?"

"Besides that," he says with a laugh. "I like helping the people I love achieve their dreams."

"Is this something you've done before?"

"I have, they just knew about it."

"May I ask who?"

He nods. "Maeve's first interior design client was this house. I gave her the money to buy everything she needed to create the space. Before she knew it, she was designing every bachelor and recently divorced man's house in Middle Tennessee."

"I'm sure that's a lucrative business."

"You have no idea," he says. "Oliver and Izzy's wedding? I took care of your catering bill. For Stella's wedding I've paid for the honeymoon. She'll find that out at her shower. And don't get me started on the amount of shit I've bought Magnolia for her YouTube channel."

"Mag...wait...is that who you named your company after?"

"She might not be blood, but the first time someone calls you uncle, you don't forget it."

Okay, now I'm going to cry. "Simon, why didn't you just tell me? And I know why you didn't tell me you owned it to

362

begin with. You're right, I would've run. Hell, I would've never even come down here to look at the place."

"And then you would have never had your diner. The diner you were meant to have."

"You're right. I probably wouldn't. But after? After we were together? There had to be times you could've told me?"

I see him wrestling with that decision, even now. "There were times. I've sat here for the past three days thinking of every moment I could have. And I wanted to. But I was scared."

"So scared that you risked me finding out like I did?"

"Yeah," he admits. "I went fifteen years thinking you disappeared off the face of the Earth. Every time I thought about telling you, knowing you'd be pissed, all I could think about was my life without you again. Without our baby. Just knowing you as the one who got away again. It scared me so much I was willing to take the risk."

Shit...I never even thought of it from that angle. "Simon... you know I'd never take the baby away. You're her father. No matter what happens between us, now or in the future, this baby will never not know you."

He hangs his head for a second before looking back up to me. "I know. But more than once in my life you've made me a desperate man, Charlie Bennett. And a desperate man doesn't do rational things."

How is that romantic? I don't know how, but it is.

"I'm still mad," I say. "You have to promise me, right now, that there are no other secrets or things you did without my knowledge."

"The glasses were the last of the secrets. And I have a PowerPoint listing all the things I did for your review, in case I forgot any."

"A PowerPoint?"

"Yes. Long story."

I shake my head because I don't know if I want to know. "Promise me, Simon, from now on, you can't go behind my back like that."

"I won't."

"And if you want to help, talk to me so we can figure out a rational way of doing it."

"I'll talk, but not promising rational means."

"I can live with that," I say. "But we need to talk about the money. And Mona's."

We both tense slightly, knowing this is going to be the true battle.

"Will you finally let me just give you the restaurant?"

I shake my head. "Absolutely not."

"Well I'm not letting you pay me rent," he says. "And as I said at the beginning of this meeting, the ball is in your court. I'm here to help make your dreams come true."

I take a breath, hoping that my suggestion will be one he can agree to.

"Would you be open to a rent-to-own contract?"

"Interesting," Simon says as he leans closer to me. "Please tell me more about this brilliant idea."

The weight immediately lifts off my shoulders. "While I love Baby Bug having a nest egg, if I keep contributing to that, she's going to have more money than me before she's two."

"Agreed."

"But I don't want to take that from her either."

"I can invest it wisely, and with that her college will be covered."

"I like that," I say. "But going forward, I'll continue paying my same amount of rent, only now we work on a deal where I eventually buy Mona's. I know you own the whole building, and you can do whatever you want with the apartment and the space next door, but if I were working to buy Mona's, I'd...I'd really like that."

"Yeah?"

I can't help but smile, thinking about actually owning the space. "I never thought I'd be able to own anything, but I always dreamed of it. And if you're about making dreams come true, this is one you could help me with. And we could do it, together."

Simon claps his hands. "Well then, Miss Bennett, I think we have a deal." He takes my hand and pulls me over so I'm now sitting on his lap. "And I don't know how you've done other deals in the past, but I like to seal deals with a kiss instead of a handshake."

"Really? You do that with all your clients?"

He gently brushes his nose over mine. "Only the ones I'm in love with."

Chapter 37
Simon

"Are you going to tell me what is going on?"

"What do you mean?"

I look over to Shane, who is keeping his eyes suspiciously on the road. "You never want to go golfing. Ever."

"That's not true."

"Tell me the latest time we went golfing."

"It was...I don't keep track of that shit."

"You can't keep track of shit that's never happened."

"Just shut up. We'll be there in five minutes and then you can talk all you want."

"Fine," I say, grabbing my phone from my pocket. "I need to check in with Charlie anyway."

"She's fine," Shane groans. "She isn't having the baby today."

"And how do you know that? Are you Dr. Shane now?"

He shakes his head. "Because I wouldn't be that lucky to get out of this shit..."

I ignore Shane's comment to text Bug. She all but kicked me out of the house today when she heard Shane ask me to go golfing. She claimed that she was going to nest today. She had the diner covered and there were some things she wanted to get done with the baby's due date being two weeks away.

I told her to rest. She told me to go golfing and to get the hell out of the house.

> Simon: How are you feeling?

Bug: Pregnant. Uncomfortable. Did I mention pregnant?

> Simon: Do you want me to come home?

Bug: Absolutely not.

> Simon: Why do I feel like you're kicking me out?

Bug: Are you at the course yet?

> Simon: We're about to pull in.

Bug: Well then you're about to find out why you can't come home. Have a fun day Daddy =)

As soon as I look up from my phone, I see nothing but pink and white streamers and balloons waving in the air attached to golf carts.

"What the hell..."

I exit Shane's truck and walk over to the decorated golf carts. Now, my friends and I have a guilty pleasure of decorating for special occasions. Wes's divorce. When Oliver ended up married. Shane and Amelia's first engagement.

And apparently now Baby Bug's expected birth.

"Welcome to your Baby Stag!"

I laugh as Oliver comes over, handing me a box of cigars and a brand-new sleeve of my favorite golf balls. "Baby Stag?"

"You heard us right," Wes says as the rest of the group gathers around. Of course Wes, Oliver, and Shane are here. Emmett is standing in the back next to Amelia's son, Luke, who's next to Connor. My dad's here. Hell, they even invited Stella's fiancé Duncan, who I really don't like, but hey, apparently it's a party. "We know showers are traditionally for women."

"But we also know that you're Simon Banks and that a celebration is definitely needed for the fact that you're going to be become a father," Oliver says.

"So welcome to your Baby Stag party. Eighteen holes of golf followed by Beers, Brews, and Diapers Too at The Joint."

"Guys...wow," I say, speechless. "Thanks, but I'm not sure. Charlie is..."

"A few weeks away from labor?" Shane interrupts. "Yes. We know this, which is why Amelia, a trained and talented—not to mention beautiful—nurse is staying with Charlie all day in case something happens."

"Okay," I say, excited, but also weirdly guilty. "But we shouldn't drink too much. In case I need to get back."

"That's why I'm here," Luke says. "I'm your designated driver for the night. I'm your personal Uber."

I start to open my mouth again, but not before my dad steps forward. "Son. I've taught you a lot of things over the years. Most of them you've done. But there is one important lesson that you need to know now that you're about to become a father."

"What's that?"

"When the mother of your child kicks you out of the house and tells you to go golfing, you get the hell out of the house and go golfing."

I laugh as Oliver hands me a beer. "If you say so."

Everyone grabs a beer except Luke, who is seventeen and

clearly the most responsible one of us today, before my dad makes the rest of his speech. "To Simon. Most days you think everything is about you. Today it is. And for good reason. You are about to be blessed with a little girl who is going to change your life. And we couldn't be more happy for you. Salut!"

"Salut!"

We all take a swig of our beers before loading into the overly decorated golf carts. As we drive to the first tee, I hurry and grab my phone.

> Simon: Thank you. I love you.

> Bug: I love you too. Have a fun day. You deserve it, Daddy.

I smile as Oliver drives the cart down the path. The April sun is beaming down, and the breeze is just enough to make the air not hot. It's the perfect day for golf.

And honestly, it's just a perfect day.

I'm with my boys. And I'm in such a good mood I'll even call Duncan one of my boys even though I think he's a douche and not good enough for Stella.

And when I get home tonight, I'll fall into bed with the love of my life, who's about to have our baby.

Life doesn't get much better.

It's been more than a month since Charlie found out about the diner—and since then, things have been smooth sailing. We redrew the lease to reflect her intent to buy it, with portions of the rent going toward that. The diner is booming, and she has her maternity leave plan in place. Now that she knows about Magnolia Properties, I've been able to go all in on a few projects around Rolling Hills that I was hesitant to start. Between Emmett running my properties and me buying and selling them, we're becoming a well-oiled machine.

The One I Hate

Life is good.

I don't know how it could get much better than this.

"Simon!" Duncan yells from the first tee box. "How about a shot before we get going?"

I let out a low groan. "Why did you invite him?"

"Your dad asked if we could," Oliver says. "And I might be thirty-six years old, but I'm still scared of your father."

I shake my head, grab my driver, and head over to the bar, conveniently next to the first tee. "Sure, but only one."

* * *

"I'M HAVING A BABY!"

Everyone at The Joint cheers and holds up their drinks as I throw back another shot of whiskey.

"Round's on me!"

Porter rolls his eyes as he takes the empty shot glass away. "It's an open bar, asshole. Quit making everyone think you're buying each round."

I slam my hand down. I didn't mean to. It just weighs a lot right now. "An open bar is the least I can do. Did you see how many diapers they got me? There are soooooo many diapers."

"I did," Porter says, and I don't know if it's because I'm drunk, but he seems annoyed with me. "Never did I think I'd have five thousand fucking diapers in my bar."

"Well, you do!" I yell, grabbing another beer. "Because I'm going to be a daddy!"

I stumble away from the bar to head back to the party. This part of the day is a little more rowdy than golf. And a few more people are here. Everyone was invited—no girls allowed, of course—but there was one rule: You had to come with a gift of diapers.

All sizes. Didn't matter how many. But apparently the invitations said: "Simon will be changing diapers for the next few years. Let's help him with that."

The men of Rolling Hills did not disappoint.

"There he is!"

I'm nearly knocked over by Duncan, who I don't know why is still here. Dad left after golf, and I'd assume he'd take his future son-in-law with him.

No such luck.

"Hey, Duncan."

"What's it like?"

"What's what like?"

He throws his arm around me, which for a guy that's barely five-foot-seven, still has a punch. "Pregnancy sex? I heard it was nuts."

I've never liked Duncan. When he first started dating Stella, I called him Duncan the Douche. But I was told by my sisters, mother, father, and Stella herself, that she loves him, so I better get used to him being around.

But right now I want to fucking lay him out.

"Hey, guys. Sorry. I need Simon."

I'm pleasantly surprised when Emmett steps in and drags me away. Literally. I'm not walking great right now.

"Thanks, man," I say. "I hate that guy."

"I met him today, and I get why. He was asking me if there were going to be strippers here. When I told him there weren't he asked if I could hire some."

"Asshole," I say. "Not you. Him. You're not an asshole. You're my friend."

"You're my friend too. And you want to know what friends do?"

"What's that?"

"Shots."

I point to him because that's the best idea I've heard all

night. "You're right!"

"Guys! Picture!"

I drunkenly turn toward the sound of Oliver's voice, who's pointing his phone at us. I don't know what pose Emmett and I make, but I know it has to be reminiscent of photos we took together freshman year at Tennessee. Our chests puffed. Holding a beer like we're fucking cool. Only thing different is my hair is better and I can actually grow facial hair.

And oh, I'm going to be a daddy.

"Hey! Everyone!" I yell as I awkwardly climb to stand on a table. Will it hold me? I think it will. It only wobbles once. "Can I say a few words?"

Someone cuts the music from the jukebox.

"I just want to say thank you to everyone for coming out tonight. Y'all are the fucking best!"

A quick round of applause hits before I motion for them to stop. "I really want to say thanks to my best friends in the whole entire fucking world. Wes, Oliver, and Shane, I fucking love you guys. Thank you for this."

The three of them hold up their beers as the rest cheer. Well, Oliver does it before quickly snapping a picture. He's the photographer of the group for a reason.

"Porter, thanks for letting us have the bar tonight."

"Thanks for paying," he says, which gets a laugh from the crowd.

"Least I can do. Oh! And when you're hungover tomorrow, make sure to go to Mona's for your fix of hangover food. Think of it as helping to support my daughter's college fund. Now everyone enjoy the night! I'm going to be a daddy!"

Another round of applause erupts as I jump off the table and somehow don't break anything.

"Nice speech," Wes says. "You only swore once."

"I know. Pretty proud of myself."

The two of us laugh and collapse into our seats. "I used to say fuck so much I thought that was going to be Magnolia's first word."

I laugh. "What was it?"

"Dada."

That hits me square in the chest. I hadn't even thought about things like first words. Or first steps. Or first anythings.

"Holy shit. In a few weeks I'm going to have a little girl and pretty soon she's going to do those things. Am I ready for her to do those things? Do I need to babyproof the house now? I thought I had time to do that since the first few months she's pretty much unable to move without me or Charlie."

Wes nods. "Can I give you advice?"

"Please, for the love of God, give me advice. And honestly, the fact that you're waiting until now to do it is a little rude."

Wes laughs. "You're going to want be there for all the firsts. Every parent does. The problem is, kids are on their own schedule and do things when they want, not really giving a shit who's around to see it."

"Yeah, I guess."

"I missed a first with every one of my kids. And I beat myself up for it. But then I realized it's not the firsts that are the most important. It's the rest."

"The rest?"

"Yeah. The rest. The birthdays. The dance recitals. The school concerts. The games. Board game nights with pizza on the living room floor. Those are the memories. Those are the ones you're going to want to remember, because those are the ones that you're making together."

Damn. Wes really is wise.

"Can I do this?" I ask. "Am I ready to be a dad?"

Wes puts his hand over mine. "I know we give you shit, and most of the time rightfully so, but if I know one thing about you, it's that you are going to be the best fucking father this little girl could ever ask for. And at the very least, the most prepared for diaper duty."

I laugh as we look over to the mountains of diapers along the wall. "Thanks, man."

"Anytime."

The two of us stand and fall into a bro hug. And just as I'm about to step away, I feel a hand on my shirt pulling me off Wes.

"What the..." Luke is looking at me with a strange expression. "Is it time to go? Just five more minutes..."

"Please, Luke!" Wes whines.

"No. We have to go. Now."

"Why? The bar isn't closing yet."

"Jesus Christ," Luke mutters. "Charlie's in labor. My mom just called me. She's taking her to the hospital."

I know the music is loud, and I'm still pretty drunk, but I think I heard Luke say Charlie's in labor.

Oliver comes stumbling over to me, falling into me but somehow doesn't bring me down. Probably because I'm super strong. "What's going on?"

"Oliver, please explain to Simon that Charlie has tried to call him every minute for the last hour, his phone is dead, and we have to get to the hospital. Now."

"Oh my God!" Oliver yells. "It's time! It's time! The baby's coming!"

I'm still confused. And apparently hearing things. "Guys. Why is everyone saying that the baby's coming?"

I feel a slap across my face I think I'll feel for months.

And Shane standing right in front of me. Where'd he come from?

"Charlie's in labor, asshole. Now get your fucking shit together."

The sting runs through my body, and it takes me another second to...

Holy shit...

I'm going to be a daddy.

Right now.

Chapter 38
Charlie

Well, this is just great.

I've been in labor for ten, no, scratch that, eleven hours.

I've been awake for that entire time, because every time I close my eyes, another contraction hits. You know, just to keep me honest. They are getting closer together now, and I'm becoming very uncomfortable, to say the least.

And then there's Simon. Passed out on the couch in the clothes he was wearing when he got here last night. I'm sure if I walked over to him—you know, if I could walk—I could get drunk from the smell of whiskey coming from him. I should wake him up, but not yet. He needs all the energy he can muster for the fact that he's about to be pushing out a human.

Oh wait. That's me.

"How we doing?"

I look over to see Amelia walking in with a duffel bag in her hands.

"Still pregnant."

She stops in front of Simon, just as he lets out a little snore. "How long has he been out?"

"Since you left," I say. "He told me something about diapers then passed out."

She tries not to laugh. "At least he's here. My ex went MIA when Luke was born. He showed up the next morning like he didn't do anything wrong."

"Wow." I look over to Simon, who looks somehow comfortable on what surely is an uncomfortable couch. I mean, I can't be mad. I told him to go out. I told him to have fun. Who knew I was going to go into labor early? "Oh! Shit, shit, shit!"

Amelia drops the bag and rushes over to me. "You okay?"

"Yeah...contraction...big one..."

Amelia gives me her hand, letting me break a few bones as I let out a primal yell.

"Bug? What? Baby? Here."

I look over to see Simon shoot up from the couch, and since he's still probably drunk, he promptly falls to the floor. I'd normally laugh, but I can't right now. I'm too busy trying to breathe through the longest contraction I've had.

"Simon. Go shower." Amelia's words are firm and take charge. "I brought you clothes in that bag. You fucking stink. And when you get out, I think we're going to start having a baby."

He pops up from the floor. "Really?"

"No. I made everything up. Just go shower."

He nods. "Yes ma'am." He turns to go to the shower, but quickly runs back to me, kissing me on the forehead. "I love you. I'll be right back."

"I love you. Please shower. You just got me drunk."

"Got it."

Simon bolts through the suite to our bathroom, nearly falling again, which I'm now so glad has a shower.

"Is it really time?"

Another contraction hits, and yeah...those two were very close together.

Amelia nods, fixing my pillows. "I think we're getting there. Let me go get the nurse and I'll be right back."

I nod and give her hand a squeeze. "Thank you."

"No need to thank me. You're family. This is what we do."

Amelia leaves the room, and it hits me just as hard as this next contraction.

Family.

For so many years, I thought my family was going to be small and tight. Just me, Connor, and Lila. That's all I needed. That's all I thought I'd ever have.

And somehow, in what feels like a blink of an eye, I have this huge family, and it's all because I fell in love with the guy I used to hate. I have women who not only have accepted me, but are already caring for me and the baby like I'm their blood. Who cleaned my house for me last week because I felt too pregnant to even move. Men who accepted me without question when it came to being with a man they consider their brother. And who put together our nursery and Simon's ridiculous stroller. Even their kids got involved, gifting me with books and stuffed animals from their childhood that they wanted Baby Bug to have.

I thought those were only things blood did for each other. But if there's one thing I've learned since moving to Rolling Hills, is that family isn't always the ones you're born to. Many times it's the ones you choose.

"Okay. I'm here."

Simon comes running out of the bathroom, still putting on his T-shirt. "Did I miss her? Is she here?"

I laugh despite another contraction hitting. "No. She's not

here. You did not miss the birth of our daughter during your five-minute shower."

"Good," he breathes a sigh of relief. "How are you feeling?"

He wrings out a wash cloth on one of the tray tables as I'm starting to sweat. "You know...like I'm about to push a kid out."

"Good. I think that's how you're supposed to feel."

I shoot him a look. The first of what I figure are going to be many today. "I'm going to need you to just stop talking. I know that's hard. But for the sake of our relationship, and me not killing you, and our baby having a father, I'm going to need you to dial back the Simon today."

He nods. "Noted."

Amelia comes back in with my nurse and doctor. "I hear it's time to start having a baby."

Simon and I turn to each other and share a moment that I want to remember for the rest of my life. He brings my hands to his mouth, kissing it softly as I brush his wild hair back off his face.

"Yeah," I say. "Let's have a baby."

* * *

"I need another push, Charlie. You got this."

"No I fucking don't!" I yell, though I do push again. I might break Simon's hand in the process, but I push.

"Three...two...one...and relax."

I fall into Simon's chest, who at some point during labor moved behind me to help me stay up.

"You're doing great, Bug," he says, dabbing my neck and forehead with a wet cloth. "You're so strong."

"Fuck being strong. Fuck being pregnant. Fuck all of this. And speaking of fuck...we're never doing that again."

"Aw man..."

"Okay, Charlie, this is it." Dr. Monty says. "We have a head, and I need one more."

"You got this," Simon whispers, giving me his hand. "Let's meet our daughter."

"This is it!" I yell. "If she doesn't come now, put her back."

"Sounds good," Dr. Monty says. "Ready, now!"

"AHHHHHH!!!"

I don't know how long I push. I don't know what anything is right now. All I know is that one second all I can hear are my screams and in the next I hear the crying of my daughter.

My daughter...

"Here she is." I fall against Simon as my breaths do their best to catch up. "We have ten fingers, ten toes, and a good set of lungs."

I laugh against Simon, who is peppering my cheek and face with kisses.

"Daddy, would you like to cut the cord?"

I look up to Simon, whose face is lighting up with wonder. Excitement. Fear. All rolled into one handsome package.

"Yes. Please."

He carefully maneuvers away from me to go cut the cord. I do my best to watch, but I'm so tired it's hard to keep my eyes open. I do see the nurses take her to go clean her up before she's brought back to me.

"Do we have a name yet?"

Simon and I look at each other, then back to our daughter. She's stopped crying, and I can't stop staring at her. Her little nose. Her little lips. Her eyes are closed, but I just know already she has the most beautiful eyes in the world.

How could she not, with Simon as her daddy?

"Lainey," I say, putting the first of what will be a thousand kisses to her forehead. "Lainey Elizabeth Banks."

Simon and I share a look of love before our stares turn back to our daughter. "We made a baby."

I'm not looking at him, but I'm pretty sure he's crying. "We made a baby. Hey, Lainey. Welcome to the world."

My entire life, I've waited for the other shoe to drop. For the sky to fall.

But not anymore.

Because there isn't a thing that could happen to ruin this moment—this life—I've been blessed with.

And it's all because of the man I used to hate.

Epilogue

Simon

"Are we really doing this?"

I look to Charlie, who's nursing our daughter, giving me the look I know all too well.

The one that screams I'm ridiculous and she doesn't know why she's with me.

"How else are we supposed to introduce our child to our friends and family?"

"Through a social media post. Or having people over in small quantities."

I shake my head. "That's boring as hell."

"I think you meant 'normal.'"

I let out a huff as I kneel down in front of my two favorite girls. "Since when are we normal?"

I kiss Charlie on the forehead before leaning down to kiss Baby Bug. Yes, I know she has a name. But I don't know if I'll ever stop calling her Baby Bug. It's even more fitting than it was before. This girl is going to be the spitting image of her mom. Right now her hair is light. Her eyes are a darker blue. And I can already tell their smiles are going to be identical.

I'm already screwed.

"Can you take her?" Charlie asks as she covers herself up. "Our girl is milk drunk."

"Gladly," I say, grabbing a burp cloth as Charlie gets up. "We got this, Mommy. You go get ready for the big party."

Charlie shakes her head and throws in an eye roll with a smile before heading toward our bedroom. Which gives me a minute to hold my daughter, something that is still mind boggling to me in the week since we brought her home.

"So today's a big day," I tell her as I start to rock. "You're going to meet all your aunties and uncles. And your cousins. And your grandma and grandpa, who have been dying to meet you. So many people who love you. And believe me, they are chomping at the bit to finally hold you."

And that's an understatement. Because Lainey made her entrance into the world a little early, there were a few things to keep an eye on. Nothing serious, but we wanted to play it safe. With that, we asked everyone to hold off on visiting in the hospital, and at home, until we were settled in.

It also gave me an excuse to throw a party.

"I don't know if you know how much you're loved already. See this nursery?" I hold her up like she can see what I'm talking about. "Your aunties and uncles got it all ready for you. Daddy didn't even hire anyone, which you'll know soon enough, is a very big deal."

In my mind, my daughter is laughing. In reality, I think she just pooped.

"Now, you might get confused, because everyone is your aunt or uncle. And you're going to be told that to be an aunt or an uncle, you have to be related to them, but I'm here to tell you that's not true. Your family isn't just by blood. Or marriage. It's the people who love you. Who will have your back whenever you need them. Who will go along with your crazy daddy's

384

ideas and throw you a huge name-reveal party. Also, if your Uncle Shane ever tells bad stories about me, he's a liar. Don't believe him."

Another in-my-mind giggle. Yup. She's pooping.

"And they all love you very much. But do you know who loves you the most in the world? That's me and your mommy. And we can't wait to see you become the best parts of both of us."

I walk over to the changing table. The second I take off her onesie, I'm hit with a smell that's equally foul and impressive.

"I hope you are focused like your mama. Have her determination and drive. I hope you have my willingness to take some risks. Not big ones. At least not yet. But don't be afraid to go for it. You're a Banks. You can do anything you want."

I toss the diaper into the trash and grab a new one, thankful she didn't spring a pee leak between diapers.

"One day you're going to do the math and realize that you came into this world before we got married. When that happens, I want you to ask your mommy why she hated Daddy. She'll get mad at me, and that's okay. I like to push her buttons. Secretly, she loves it too. But no matter when you came to us, you're forever going to be the best thing we've done."

I finish changing her diaper—I'm a fucking ninja at this—when I notice Charlie leaning in the doorway of the nursery.

"How long have you been standing there?"

"Long enough." She smiles and walks toward us, and I swear she's glowing more now than she was when she was pregnant. She has on a long floral dress that softly hugs her curves. Her hair is down and curled, and her red lipstick is making me think things that I can't be thinking. Well, I can. I just can't act on them for another five weeks.

Not that I have an alarm set in my phone or anything.

"Everything I said was true," I say. "She's the best thing we could have ever done."

"I agree," she says as she grabs the outfit we have picked out for Baby Reveal Day. "We made a pretty fucking cute baby."

"Yeah we did."

We tag team getting her dressed—an adorable floral dress that matches Charlie. She'll probably only fit into it once, but that's fine. We accessorize it with a bow that's twice the size of her head. I found a similar floral shirt, because of course my family has to match on such a special occasion.

I pick the baby up, but not before stealing a kiss from Charlie. "You ready, Mama?"

She gently rubs the baby's back and flashes me a smile that I hope never stops knocking me on my ass. "Let's go, Daddy."

* * *

"Is that the music from *The Lion King*?"

"Is Simon about to fucking Simba his kid?"

"Damn right I am!" I yell as Charlie and I slowly walk out to our back yard where all of our friends and family are gathered. The low tone of the music is starting to build and all eyes are on us.

"I can't believe you talked me into this," Charlie mumbles as she walks next to me and the baby.

"Just wait until her first birthday party. I think I want the theme to be One-Derland. Whole Alice and Wonderland theme. It will be epic."

"Let's get through this day first, okay?"

I hear the music building, and I know it's about time. And on cue, just as I practiced all week, I hoist my daughter into the air, a round of applause following from all that have gathered.

"Ladies and gentlemen, boys and girls, children of all ages..."

"Isn't that an old wrestling entrance?" Oliver asks.

"Yes, Oliver. But it works," I reposition the baby back into my hold. "We like to thank you for coming out today and giving Charlie and I some space this week as we got in our groove."

"Yes, thank you," Charlie says. "I know you all wanted to come meet her, so we appreciate your patience."

"And we all know you are anxiously awaiting the name reveal, which will come in a second." I hand Baby Bug to Charlie as I grab a piece of paper from my back pocket. "But first! It's time to announce the winners of the prop bets placed at the New Year's Gender Reveal Bash. The winner of closest to the due date is...Oliver Price!"

A few cheers, and more than a few groans, come out as Oliver runs up and grabs his envelope of winnings. "I had a feeling and ran with it. Thanks, Charlie."

"You're welcome?"

"Next up...the measurements. Our daughter came weighing in at six pounds, ten ounces, giving the win to...Izzy McCall-Price!"

"Hell yeah, wife!" Oliver cheers as Izzy comes up. "I'm calling a sweep!"

"Not so fast, my excited friend. Because the last one of the night was the 'Does Simon cry?' For all of you who said yes, because I did, were placed into a random drawing for the winnings. And that winner is...drum roll please."

A hush comes over the crowd. "Fine, party poopers. The winner is...Magnolia?"

The quiet turns into raucous laughter as my seven-year-old goddaughter struts up to the stage. "Sorry, Uncle Simon. But I knew you'd lose it."

The laughter only gets louder as Magnolia snatches her

money out of my hands. And hope that no one calls us in for underage gambling.

"Enough of the bets. What's the name of my grandbaby!"

"Yes, Mom, it's time." Charlie takes a step closer to me, holding our daughter for everyone to see. "We tossed some ideas around. And while some were great."

"Most I vetoed immediately."

This makes everyone laugh. "Charlie and I came up with a name that not only pays a little homage to our story, but also fits perfectly for Baby Bug."

Charlie and I share a look and nod. It's not like this isn't already official. The birth certificate is signed and the social security card is on the way. "Ladies and gentlemen, I'd like to introduce you to Lainey Elizabeth Banks."

A round of applause hits, though I don't know if any truly know the importance of her name. Emmett would maybe pick up on it, but he couldn't be here today.

"My grandbaby!" my mom squeals as she comes over to us. "May I?"

Charlie nods, gently passing Lainey to her Didi. She's insisting on being called that. "Of course."

Mom coos at her granddaughter as everyone surrounds us, giving us hugs and handshakes.

"Big brother!" Stella squeals as she jumps into my arms for a hug. "She's precious. I can't wait to spoil her."

"I figured you already started," I joke, pointing to her 'In my Auntie Era' T-shirt. "I'm guessing there's something matching for Lainey?"

"Of course," she says with a smile. "It's one of the many presents I brought today."

I laugh and reach out my hand for Duncan. "Hey, man. Thanks for coming."

"Sure..."

The One I Hate

He doesn't look up at me, or return my handshake. His eyes are glued to his phone, and he couldn't give two shits to be here.

God I hate this fucking guy...

I continue saying thanks and visiting with as many people as possible before I see Charlie a few feet away, talking to a few of her regulars. Instead of interrupting I just stand back and watch, in awe of this woman.

I've always lived in the belief that you make your own luck.

I don't know what I did to get Charlie, but I know I'll never be that lucky in my life again. I don't deserve her. I'm probably not worthy. But I swear on everything I have and everything I am I'm going to try every day to be the best damn man for her.

Because she's the best for me.

"I think she's sleepy," Mom says, bringing Lainey back to me.

"I'd assume so. She's been up for an hour, which is a record for her these days."

I take my baby girl, giving her a kiss on her head, before walking over to Charlie. "I'm going to go put her down."

She smiles and waves goodbye to the group. "I'll come with you."

The look in her eyes is her 'don't fight me on this' look, so I don't. We use Lainey as an excuse to bypass a few people as we make our way to the house.

Who knew you could get out of shit because of your kid? This has so many new possibilities...

Charlie slips the headband off Lainey as I change her before putting her into the bassinet. She's out before I even let go, but Charlie and I don't go anywhere. No. I bring her into my arms, holding her as we watch our daughter sleep.

"Can you believe we're here?" I ask.

Charlie shakes her head. "Sometimes it doesn't seem real. Then I remember the labor."

I laugh before kissing a spot on the slope of her neck. "Have I told you today that I love you?"

She turns around and wraps her arms around my neck. "You have. But I don't mind hearing it again."

"I love you."

"Good. Because I love you too."

Our lips meet in a way I can only describe as perfect.

Which is weird to think.

Nothing about us is perfect. Not how we got together. Not how we made this baby. Hell, not even how we make sense.

But all of that imperfect makes us perfect.

And I can't hate anything about that.

Thank you for reading The One I Hate!

I couldn't just leave the book here, because I love these two (and this group) so much. So let's fast forward a few years to see the day Simon and Charlie get married. And where she has a surprise for him he doesn't see coming (again). Click here to get their extended epilogue!

Acknowledgments

I don't know why the end of the series always gets me. But here I am, in my feels, writing this and crying off my makeup because I'm not ready to say goodbye to this series.

But I know it's time.

When I came up with Rolling Hills, I knew I wanted to follow the lives of four guy best friends. I was friends with a group like this. I still am. I've been in their weddings and become an aunt and godmother to their children. My real life Simon is in this group of friends. I knew these guys better than any characters I'd ever written.

What I didn't know about this series was that it was going to heal me in a way I never knew possible. Because what I didn't realize was that I was writing a part of myself into each of these heroines.

And it was the therapy I didn't know I needed.

Betsy's a little lost. Couldn't figure out what she wanted in life. That's me to a T. Hell, I still don't know.

Izzy was hurt bad. She thought she knew love until it ripped her apart. Same. (And yes, I might have used my exes name. Author's privilege).

Amelia was the tomboy. The friend and sister to the guys.

And then there was Charlie, my plus-sized heroine who thought she didn't need love because no one loved her.

Put them together, and you have Chelle.

I'm going to miss this group of friends so much. I found out who I truly am as a writer in Rolling Hills. And while I'm not going too far away from it, nothing will compare to writing these past four books.

So thanks Rolling Hills. I'll never forget you...

Now, to the thank yous that don't make me cry...

First and foremost, my parents. As always, you are my biggest cheerleaders even if you still have no idea what I'm doing. You've allowed me to follow my dreams and my path, and for that I am forever grateful.

To my family and friends: Your support has been amazing. Many of you have no clue how I ended up here, but that doesn't mean the support hasn't been there. I love you all.

Amanda, who would have thought when we met seven years ago that one day we'd be here together? Thank you for keeping my life in order. Thank you for reminding me to drink water. And thank you for being my best friend. I promise I won't fire you this week.

Kelly, you've been with me on this book journey since day one. Not only are you an amazing alpha reader, but you are an amazing friend.

Julia, Georgia, Bella, Mae, and Claire: How did I write a book before I met you ladies? All I know is I don't ever want to write one without y'all again.

Kiezha, thank you for correcting my bad grammar habits and being an amazing editor. Michele, thank you for dotting the Is and crossing the Ts.

Corinne, I'm here because of you. If you wouldn't have given me a chance I wouldn't have started writing. You forever changed my life.

Last but not least: Readers. I love you all. Whether this was your first book by me, or you've been here since Reformation, I'm truly thankful for all of you. There are so many amazing authors you could be reading. I'm humbled that you chose me.

About the Author

Known for her witty sense of humor, Chelle Sloan is a former sports editor who recently completed her Masters in Journalism. She's now putting that to good use—one happily ever after at a time.

An Ohio native, she's fiercely loyal to Cleveland sports, is the owner of way too many — yet not enough — tumblers and will be a New Kids on the Block fan until the day she dies. She does her best writing at Starbucks, or anywhere that's not her house. Oh, and yes, you probably saw her on TikTok.

As for her own happily every after? Maybe one day...

Stay up to date with all things Chelle & join the VIP Squad!

Also by Chelle Sloan

THE NASHVILLE FURY, PRO FOOTBALL SERIES

Off the Record: A secret office romance

Off Track: A surprise pregnancy romance

Off Season: A second chance romance

Off Limits: A sibling's best friend romance

NASHVILLE FURY WORLD

Off the Market at Christmas: A childhood friends-to-lovers romance

LOVE ONLINE SERIES

Thirst Trap: A social media romance

Match Maker: A fake dating romance

Run Run Rudolph: A celebrity, holiday romance

ROLLING HILLS

The One I Want: A single dad/nanny romance

The One I Need: An accidental marriage romance

The One I Love: A friends to lovers romance

The One I Hate: An enemies to lovers romance

GUIDE TO LOVE SERIES

The Runaway Bride's Guide to Love (Coming September 2024)

Made in United States
North Haven, CT
03 June 2024